# HABIT

Book One of The Titan Trilogy

## T. J. BREARTON

Published 2014 by Joffe Books, London

www.joffebooks.com

© T. J. Brearton

ISBN-13: 978-1505204698

# DEDICATION

For Geoff Pierce and Adam Gardam

.

# PROLOGUE

The baby's desperate cries could be heard echoing through the building, coming from one of the many rooms. The detective moved along the dark hallway, his weapon drawn. Sweat trickled down the sides of his face. The killer was somewhere in the place with him, behind one of these doors, around the next turn in the corridor.

*I was born under the black smoke of September.*

His hands shook and his heart slammed against his ribcage. His steps were slow, his legs trembling. He willed that sense of calm to return, that cool head he had worked so hard to cultivate these past days, but the baby's crying tore through his nerves like a thousand cuts. She was close, he knew she was close, but the wailing echoed through the corridor, past the barren rooms.

He renewed his grip on the .38 Special revolver. He inhaled and exhaled through his nostrils. His jaw was clenched shut. He reached a doorway to one of the rooms and made his way towards it close to the corridor wall, constantly throwing glances behind him to see if the killer was there. At the door frame, he held his breath before swinging his arms and his body into the opening, aiming the firearm into the room.

The space was dimly lit, covered in drywall dust. There was plastic on the floor, ladders, scaffolding, and piles of sheetrock. The whole building was under construction. Out the window he could see the lights of the city.

*I was born under the black smoke of September. I was born to you, and your infinite forms.*

The sound of the baby was muffled as he stepped deeper into the room. She wasn't in here. He spun back around, his foot catching some of the plastic on the ground so that it made a crisp noise in the gloom. He winced at the giveaway, and his heart seemed to redouble its beats, pounding in his chest, flushing the blood through the channels of his body. He stepped back out into the hallway, swinging the gun left and then right.

Darkness. No lights, no floodlights. Only the illumination of the city outside the building filtered in, fell against the interior walls of the room, and threw long shadows down the corridor. The corridor banked left further down. He started that way, keeping against the wall, unable to ignore the words of the killer in his mind, incapable of escaping the ubiquitous cries of the child, a noise like an alarm, howling down the halls and through the rooms.

Dear God, would someone come? If only some back-up would arrive, and put an end to this nightmare.

But no one would come, and he could not awake from this terrible dream because he wasn't sleeping. It battened on to him, this terror, refusing to let go. Somewhere in the back of his mind he remembered that today was his birthday. There was no denying that this was real.

He made the turn in the hallway with a sudden move, his finger tight against the trigger, ready to squeeze. The corridor ran some fifty feet to where it ended in a window. Through the glass he again glimpsed the amber and red lights of the city beyond. He held his breath each time he made a turn or cleared a room. He knew he needed to keep breathing, to be steady. To become a machine. To merely track; he was a tracker.

The detective moved a little faster now. At least the corridor along this wing was lit from the window at the far end. He reached the next room, this time on the left. This room had no exterior window. He made his move and navigated in through the doorway and into the blackness. As soon as he was through the door he let go of the gun with one hand and reached to his right against the inside wall, feeling for a switch. There was none. He changed hands and groped along the wall to his left until he found it. He flipped the toggle up. Nothing. Back down and up again. No lights. The power was completely severed. The killer had seen to that, and emergency lights had apparently not yet been installed. The detective's flashlight was long gone.

Still in the murk, but the baby's cries were closer. Weren't they? Like she was just on the other side of the wall. He was close – she was only one more room away, he was sure of it now. He started to back out of the inky darkness and then turned around.

A figure stood just outside the doorway of the room. Scarcely lit by the one window at the end of the hall, the killer was no more than a sketch in the gloom.

*I was born under the black smoke of September*, the detective had been warned. *I was born to you, and your infinite forms, and now I have come for you.*

*To steal your children, to break you under the moon.*

His breathing stopped again, his body grew rigid, his mind blank as he prepared to meet the man standing before him. Everything gone now, his calm found at last, his heartbeat slowing, his posture taking shape, all growing quiet and far away, except for the baby girl. Her pleading cries now infected everything, becoming a siren wail that liquefied the world into pure ether.

# CHAPTER ONE / THURSDAY, 9:02 AM

Brendan Healy wanted a cigarette. It was his birthday in two weeks, and he had vowed to quit smoking when he turned thirty-five. Before getting out of his car and entering the house, he decided to sneak one. He left the car running, lit a Marlboro, and instantly felt nervous.

The house was big, with peeling white paint. In some places the boards were bare, cooked grey from the sun. It was a big three-story farmhouse with black shutters. Off to one side, a large shed gaped open with no doors. Inside was a tractor, a hulking ghost in the murk. Everywhere else was bright and baked brown. It had been a dry summer, and the grass was parched, worn away completely between the two buildings. Sitting further back on the property was a third structure, a barn as tall as a house, its wood the color of charcoal ash.

Brendan dragged on his smoke, and then mashed it out in the ashtray. Someone rapped on his window and he jumped. He pressed the lever and the window rolled down.

"Coming in?"

It was Detective Delaney. Delaney was the senior investigator for Oneida County. He was a bald man with a moustache and a round, puffy face.

"Yeah," said Brendan. His heart started to thump. He fumbled with the button for the automatic window and then turned off the ignition and pulled the keys out. He tossed them onto the passenger's seat and picked up his notebook, with the pen clipped on the front. He took a deep breath, opened the door, and got out.

The heat was instantly oppressive. He could feel it work into his clothes. He wore a pale gold tie, a navy-blue button-down shirt, and a dark-grey blazer. The temperature was already climbing above eighty, and it was only nine in the morning. It was hot for this late in the summer.

Brendan and Delaney just stood there not saying anything. Brendan looked at the house, and Delaney looked at Brendan.

"Okay?" asked Delaney finally.

"Yeah."

"You'll do fine."

Brendan looked at Delaney, his eyes wrapped in crow's feet, squinting in the morning sun. Delaney's kids were all grown up; his wife was a part-time realtor. She liked wearing bright colors. It was rumored that Delaney stepped out on her. He was heavy, Irish, and had been on the job for over thirty years.

The two detectives walked towards the house, crossing the dirt dooryard. A Sheriff's deputy, named Watts, stood just outside the door, which was open.

"Morning," said Delaney.

"Morning," said the deputy.

Brendan glanced at him and offered a thin smile. Then he looked at Delaney. "Any forced entry?"

"None. There are two doors. One in front, one in back. Back door was found locked. Front door was unlocked."

The two detectives entered the house and came upon a foyer with bare, shiplap floors, dark brown. A hall fed into two rooms on the right. On the left was another doorway, and the foot of the stairs.

They climbed the stairs, not touching the wooden bannister. The risers creaked beneath their combined weight. At the top landing they turned right down a hallway and Delaney lagged back so that Brendan took the lead.

The doorway to the master bedroom was just in front of him. His heart continued to hammer in his chest and he willed himself to calm down. There was a flash from the room as the forensic photographer snapped a picture. The CSI unit had already been on the scene for fifteen minutes.

Detective Brendan Healy entered the room.

The sunlight burned in through the windows. The lamps in the room were all off, and the natural light cast a surreal, almost heavenly glow over everything. There was little room to walk. Three CSIs were already present at the core scene, and the room was in disarray, with potential evidentiary material everywhere. There was a bureau against the far wall with two columns of three drawers. The bottom drawer on each side was fully open. Above these, the two other rows of drawers were slightly ajar. The contents of the bottom drawers – clothing – had been mussed and some garments hung over the lip of the drawers. There was a rumpled bath towel on the floor next to the bureau.

There were three windows in the room. Two were on the wall with the long bureau, which sat in between. The third was over the bed.

The bed was queen-sized, not too big; not too small. There was a rumpled white duvet over light-blue sheets. Blood covered much of the linens, with one particular concentration near the rumpled center. Beneath the wad of blankets and blood was the dead woman.

The three CSIs in the room looked at Delaney expectantly. Healy noticed a glance or two alight on him fleetingly, but the senior investigator was who they were waiting to talk to. They were his unit. Brendan recognized the CSI with the camera. His name was Joe Patnode, and he was a crime scene investigator and a forensic scientist whose expertise was in blood pattern identification, trajectory determination, and serology. Patnode was a first responder.

"Morning, Ambrose," said Patnode. Ambrose was Delaney's first name.

Detective Delaney waved a hand in the air. He smiled, his eyes glancing around. "Morning. Are we on the pre-determined path here?"

"You're good," said one of the other CSIs. The two other CSIs were women. Brendan didn't recognize them. They were first-responders, too. Delaney trusted them to secure the crime scene if he wasn't able to be one of the first on-scene himself. He introduced them.

"Alicia, Dominique, this is Brendan Healy."

They said hello. After this brief exchange of pleasantries, Delaney, standing just behind Healy in the doorway, brushed past him. He took two steps into the room and stopped near the foot of the bed. He looked down at it.

From Brendan's perspective, he could only see the arm of the victim sticking out of the large bunch of bloody covers. He smelled perfume in the room, and his eyes landed on several bottles on top of the bureau. One had been tipped over. The bureau had a large mirror affixed to the top. The reflection showed the backside of one of the CSIs, the woman standing between that piece of furniture and the bed. She was blocking what might have been a reflection revealing more of the victim.

Healy didn't scent anything else besides the perfume and faint copper smell of blood. There was no cordite in the air, no lingering odor of gunpowder.

"She was stabbed numerous times," said the CSI standing between the bureau and the bed, the one Delaney had introduced as Dominique. Delaney peered over the bed. They all looked. Dominique shifted her position a little and revealed the face of the dead woman.

Healy blinked and looked away. His heart was beating so hard he thought it might be visible through his suit jacket. His tie must have been thumping. He forced himself to look back at the mirror, at the victim's reflection.

Her eyes were open. Her mouth was slightly agape. She seemed to be looking at the bureau. Looking right at him via the reflection.

For a moment, he thought he was going to have to back out of the room. His legs felt numb. Brendan was afraid that his muscles were going to betray him and he wouldn't be able to stand up. He reached back as casually as he could and gripped the door frame to steady himself. Patnode, with the camera in his hand, looked over. Then he looked away.

Delaney addressed the group of them. "Okay. So?" His two words were a question, inviting their initial assessment.

The CSI named Alicia spoke. "We don't know the extent of the crime scene, but it's likely the whole house, maybe the yard, the other buildings. She called 911 at eight-eighteen this morning, saying that there was an intruder in the house. Said she got out of the shower and heard someone downstairs as she was coming back into the bedroom."

"But she's in bed."

"That's correct. At eight thirty-six, Deputy Bostrom arrived at the scene. He knocked on the front door, got no response, entered the home, called out her name, which the 911 operator had obtained, and still got no response. Deputy Bostrom said he drew his firearm downstairs, and did a cursory check of the first floor. He then proceeded up the stairs. He says he got a 'sense' of something in the bedroom, and turned and came down into the room. That's when he found the victim."

"Maybe he smelled the perfume," said Delaney.

Patnode spoke up. "Her name is Rebecca Heilshorn. She's twenty-eight years old."

"That's quite a name."

"Which?" asked Patnode.

Delaney didn't answer. Brendan thought about the name. Rebecca was typically a Jewish first name. Heilshorn was very likely German. It felt good to think about the name. It was something to focus on. He was starting to feel a little more at ease.

"The bus arrived at eight forty-nine. The paramedics came upstairs and checked the victim's vitals. It was clear to them that the victim was deceased. We arrived – Dominique and I – less than five minutes after the bus. We dismissed them." Alicia glanced at her watch. "Fifteen minutes later, and here we are."

Delaney pointed to the open drawers. "Robbed?"

Alicia nodded, but it was a noncommittal gesture. "Could be. The rest of the house has not been secured. We don't know what – if anything – was taken."

"Okay," said Delaney. "Deputy Bostrom arrived alone and proceeded into the house alone?"

"His back-up arrived just a few minutes after he did. Deputy Lawless. I believe Deputy Lawless was downstairs, too. You didn't see him?"

"And Bostrom came into the house alone anyway," said Delaney. It wasn't a question. Brendan heard a trace of disapproval in the senior investigator's tone, who put his hands on his hips. "Okay. Thank you," Delaney said.

"We've identified no potential hazards, not at least in the immediate vicinity of the core area," Alicia offered.

Delaney nodded. "You called Clark?"

Stanley Clark was the Deputy Coroner.

Alicia nodded. "He's on his way."

"Get Hai Takai here, too."

Brendan knew the name. Takai was an expert in footprint analysis.

Brendan glanced at the mirror again. The face of the victim looked back. Her skin was smooth, her face was pretty though it was spattered with blood. He looked at her slightly open mouth. It was as though she had something to tell him.

# CHAPTER TWO / THURSDAY, 9:13 AM

Brendan felt a hand on his shoulder. The touch made him jump, as if he'd received an electric shock. He turned and saw Delaney standing behind him. Delaney nodded toward the hallway.

"Step into my office."

The hall was dark compared to the bright bedroom. It took a moment for Brendan's eyes to adjust. Delaney's round face loomed before him. The man was over six feet, and looked down at an angle at Brendan, who was five-foot-nine.

"Let's find Lawless, and talk to both him and Bostrom in a safe area."

"Okay."

"We can make the safe area in the grass beyond that dirt patch there, in the front. It's already been trampled with our feet; I don't want to contaminate it further. We want to find out what Bostrom did when he came in, where he looked, what he touched. Our deputies are pretty good, but when the heart is pumping adrenaline on a call, they come in, they don't always think straight. They're thinking about saving a life, maybe their own. They're not thinking about lab tests and evidentiary value for the prosecution. I'm not throwing anybody under the bus, but it happens."

"Yes, sir."

"We need to find out who owns this house. We may need a warrant. You never know who is going to balk about privacy and probable cause, or what defense attorney is gonna cry 'fruit of the poisonous tree'. The victim is ostensibly the only resident, but that doesn't mean she owns the house. She could rent."

Brendan looked away from Delaney and at their surroundings. The hallway was open on one side, blocked with a balustrade that overlooked the foyer, which was a clerestory room in itself. Brendan looked over Delaney's shoulder, down the hallway, his eyes skipping from doorway to doorway. Brendan knew that somewhere in the opposite direction from the bedroom was the shower, where the victim had come from before calling about an intruder, and then apparently getting back in bed. Where had she made the call from? Right here, where they stood, looking over the hallway railing down into where she heard the disturbance? Did she call from her cell phone?

Delaney continued Brendan's thought aloud, "Though why anyone would rent a giant old farmhouse like this is beyond me. The heating cost alone in the winter would be enough to send you to the poor house. Taxes out here are higher than you'd think, too."

"Maybe it's a summer residence," said Brendan.

Delaney's eyes found Brendan's in the dimly lit space. They searched Brendan, appealing for more. "What do you think?"

Brendan took a breath. His pulse had slowed at last, and his heart was beating a good rhythm.

"The bureau," he said. He glanced back towards the bedroom. Through the door he saw Patnode moving around the foot of the bed. The rest of it was obscured from view. Patnode held the camera out in front of him and took another picture.

"Only the bottom drawers were open," Brendan continued. "When you're robbing a place, and you know what you're doing, and you're looking for valuables, you open the bottom drawers first. Then the one above it, and so on, so that they end up all left open. If you go the other way, you've got to close each drawer behind you." Brendan shrugged.

"So we're looking at an inexperienced robber."

"Or maybe not a robbery at all. We won't know until we check the rest of the place."

Delaney nodded. "Like I said, let's go see the deps first while my team documents the scene."

* * *

They spoke with the two deputies in the front yard, beyond the dirt area, as Delaney had instructed. Since they'd been upstairs, two more deputies had arrived. Oneida County was on the big side in terms of geography, and on the small side for population. The Sheriff's Department had six deputies on the payroll. The Sheriff was always lobbying for more.

The other two deputies hung back where the vehicles, including Brendan's, were starting to pile up in the dirt driveway near the shed. There was a line of elm trees running alongside the driveway, which was perhaps an eighth of a mile. Route 12 was in the distance. On the other side of it was a field of corn. The corn had trouble during the growing season, and the gossip was that the crop was bunk. The land on that side with the unhealthy corn was part of a different property – that was Brendan's first guess. No one here grew crops. They may have once, but the place had clearly fallen to disrepair and there were no signs of a working farm. No tillers, no silo, no animals. The only equipment was the tractor in the barn. He needed to get a better look at it, but his gut suggested that it didn't work. There was just no sense of an up-and-running agribusiness here.

"Take me through exactly what you did when you got to the scene," said Delaney to Deputy Bostrom.

The deputy described almost exactly what Alicia, one CSI, had reported upstairs.

"Touch anything?"

"No."

Brendan thought that the deputy resented Delaney's questioning. Delaney seemed affable enough, but there was no doubt he had a tendency to take the tough approach. It was also an unusually high-profile case. Likely only one or two of the older deputies in the department had been involved in a murder case before. They felt out of their element. They were used to domestic violence calls and evictions. Brendan knew the beat.

"Have you ever had to draw your weapon before, officer?" he asked unexpectedly.

Delaney and the deputies looked at him. While they all worked for the Sheriff's Department, they rarely saw one another. And Brendan Healy had only been a detective with Oneida County for two months. He had done road patrol for three years in another department. It was possible there was some resentment because he was new, because he was young, and because he was not a native son.

"Yes. Once."

The deputy then glanced at Delaney. Delaney's eyes lingered on Brendan, who could feel the senior investigator's glare.

A vehicle appeared on the road, and turned down the dirt driveway. It came toward them churning up a cloud of dust. The day grew hotter.

"That's Clark now," said Delaney. "There's going to be people here. Next of kin, reporters, rubberneckers. I want them back. Back by the road; put them in that corn if you can."

"Yes, sir," said Bostrom. He was blond with a good build, probably approaching forty. Deputy Lawless was dark-haired, about the same age, overweight. Delaney looked at him. "Where were you?"

Lawless opened his eyes wider. "I was at the back of the house."

"When we arrived? You were at the back of the house?"

"Covering the back door."

Delaney seemed to accept this. He then turned to Brendan. "Okay. Call the district attorney's office. Let's get that warrant and keep our asses covered, homicide or not. Let's close off this whole site. The house, the outbuildings. Nobody else parks in that driveway. We've already lost any tire tracks. How close is the nearest neighbor? That's the Folwell Farm across the way." Delaney put his hand to his forehead, like a visor, and scanned the horizon. "His house is, what, down there?"

"The Folwell farmhouse is about half a mile south, yes, sir," said Bostrom.

Delaney turned back to Brendan. "You're on eye witnesses. Anybody that saw a vehicle just prior to eight fifteen this morning. Anything unusual. Find out how big this property is, where the boundaries are. Who the neighbors are on this side of the road, that side of the road."

Brendan swallowed. Despite his initial anxiety, he was disappointed that he wasn't going to work the crime scene. "Okay," he said.

"Find out who the house belongs to. Find out everything you can about the girl in there, Heilshorn. If she's married, got a boyfriend, we're going to look at them. We're going to look down their throats and up their asses. It's someone who knows the victim, nine times out of ten."

With that, Delaney turned on his heel and started walking towards the coroner, Clark, who was getting out of his vehicle. Clark had grey hair and wore blue jeans and a white button-down shirt.

Brendan looked at the two deputies. They met his gaze for a moment. Bostrom turned and walked away. Lawless gave a short nod to Brendan. "Good luck," he said, and he followed after the other deputy.

Brendan watched them go. He pulled his cell phone from his pocket, and dialed the district attorney's office. He put the phone to his ear as the call began to connect. He stood looking at the property. They were five miles outside of Remsen, the nearest small village. Upstate, New York was a combination of resort towns, impoverished villages, and long swathes of farm country. The front yard of the grounds was overgrown. The crickets sang in the high grass; the air seemed to buzz with life. On the phone, a ringing began as the call went through.

Suddenly, there was a loud boom. Everybody jumped, including Brendan, whose nerves had just finally settled. A group of birds erupted from the corn field across the street. The cornfield was the source of the noise, which rolled across the land like thunder.

It was a gunshot.

Brendan went into a crouch. All of the other men on the property did the same, and several ran for cover behind the vehicles.

"Jesus Christ!" someone shouted.

The startled birds took to the air in a spiral pattern, rising up into the pale blue sky. Brendan realized something none of them had considered: the killer could still be at the scene.

A voice on the other end of the call broke in. "District Attorney's office. Hello?"

## CHAPTER THREE / THURSDAY, 9:56 AM

In the middle of all the turmoil, a motorcycle came tearing down Route 12.

Brendan saw it from his position crouched behind his vehicle. The police had scattered after the single report of gun fire. Now they were headed toward the cornfield.

Brendan left the cover of the vehicle and started down the driveway toward the road, crouching down as he moved along. He watched as the motorcyclist down-shifted rapidly through the gears, getting the sense that the rider was surprised and distracted by all the activity. As the rider attempted to turn onto the driveway, his front tire caught in the soft dirt and the bike tipped over.

Instantly the rider dropped the handlebars and jumped away. The dirt plumed up in a cloud. Brendan took off in a jog toward the crash. He heard the bike engine still running. And as the cloud dispersed in a hot breeze, he saw that the back tire of the bike was turning, the chain pulling.

After taking a moment to collect himself, the rider hopped back alongside the bike and hit the kill switch. The engine died, and the dust started to settle.

"You all right?" Brendan asked. He slowed his jog to a walk, closing the gap between them. He shifted his gaze to look across the road, where the other officers were talking to someone hidden in the corn. Judging by their body-language, their concerns had eased some.

"Yeah," the rider called back. His voice was muffled by his helmet. "Fine."

"Here, let me help you."

The two of them got their weight under the bike and grunting with the effort, got it standing again. Brendan looked down and saw a knick on the black gas tank, plus a scrape along the chrome exhaust pipe. It was a nice bike. A Harley Davidson Sportster. Fairly expensive.

"Shit," the rider said.

Brendan kept hold as the motorcyclist walked around and pushed down the kick stand with the tip of his boot. With the bike stable, he stepped back and took off his helmet.

"Don't try to start it up right away," Brendan said. "It's probably flooded. The carburetor needs to dry out."

"I know," said the motorcyclist irritably. He tucked his helmet under his arm. He had a bright mop of blond hair and bright blue eyes. He looked around twenty-five.

Once more Brendan shifted focus to the scene along the corn field. Deputy Bostrom and Investigator Delaney stood along the shoulder of the pavement. A moment later, an old man emerged from the corn in a red-checked shirt, torn off at the sleeves. He was holding a rifle or a shotgun – hard to tell at a distance. The three men spoke, and then Delaney turned towards Brendan, and the other deputies spread out over the property. Delaney raised a hand in an "all's well" gesture.

The motorcyclist was looking at them, too.

"That's Mr. Folwell," he said, referring to the old man. "Probably chasing some woodchuck."

The motorcyclist then turned around to look at the house. Brendan stayed close beside him. He was very aware of what the young man's presence here could mean. He wanted to see how it played out before he said or did anything.

The two men watched another deputy who was setting up pole barriers and stretching the nylon belts out which read "Crime Scene Do Not Cross" in between them, cordoning off the front yard all the way to the shed. There were vehicles everywhere. Three Sheriff's Department SUVs, two unmarked sedans, the coroner's car, and an Audi – the car they were presuming belonged to the victim.

Bostrom and Delaney crossed the road back to the crime scene side. Brendan glanced over and saw them coming. They were followed by a third deputy – a heavyset man named Watts. No doubt they had all taken an interest in the newcomer now that the cornfield shooting was settled.

Brendan realized that the entire situation was taking a few moments for the motorcyclist to process. First, there had been the commotion in the front yard and along the edge of the corn field which had diverted his attention. He had lost control of the bike in the soft driveway. Then, Brendan helping him to get the bike upright again. Now the motorcyclist looked like it was all starting to hit home.

Brendan knew what it was like. Your nerves began to disconnect from one another. Like your body, your soul, were fastened together by buttons, the fabric of its being pulled too tight, and the buttons were popping.

The motorcyclist started to take steps back, away from the deputy, the bike, the house.

"Sir, are you, uh, do you know what's happened here?" It was Bostrom calling over, closing in fast, with Delaney at his heels.

Brendan felt like he knew what was going to happen next before it did. He reached out with one of his hands.

In the next instant, the motorcyclist's legs gave out. Brendan gripped the man's leather jacket, but it wasn't enough. The motorcyclist sat down hard in the dirt, his butt and spine hitting the earth like a dropped rock.

Bostrom was there a second later, his hand on his holstered firearm.

"Sir," Bostrom was saying. "Who are you, sir? What are you doing here?"

The deputy then stepped in between Brendan and the motorcyclist, effectively closing Brendan out. He crouched down in front of the man.

The motorcyclist wore a bewildered expression. He turned and looked over to the house. Brendan watched as his eyes wandered up to the second story, the two windows which were the victim's bedroom.

Brendan looked over at Delaney, who stood looking down at the motorcyclist like he was witnessing something unpleasant, or undignified. "I'll call the bus back," Brendan said to the senior investigator. "They can't have left ten minutes ago. He took a spill on his bike here. He could be in shock."

"Who is he?" Delaney demanded.

"I don't know," said Brendan. "He just showed up. Did the coroner call the next of kin?"

"Clark? I don't think so. Not yet. The on-call service isn't here either."

Bostrom was still trying to get the motorcyclist to respond. He clapped his hands in front of the young man's face. The motorcyclist didn't blink. "Sir? Can you hear me?"

Brendan understood the state of shock. He'd known that inability to move, or to speak. Right now, the young man's mouth didn't want to work. His mind didn't know how to form words. He kept looking at the window. He wanted to get in there. He was the victim's boyfriend, maybe. Or, Brendan thought – her sibling. There was some family resemblance.

The motorcyclist pressed his palms into the earth and pushed. He got himself up into a standing position.

Brendan stepped forward, brushing past Bostrom, and hooked a hand under the motorcyclist's armpit. The deputy got the hint and moved around to other side of him and braced him, too.

But the motorcyclist quickly slipped out of their grip and started walking away, walking fast. Now his legs were listening to the commands of his brain, Brendan thought. He wanted to get inside. He *needed* to get inside. To see, to know; he was going to stop at nothing to get in that house, up into that bedroom, to lay his own eyes on the dead girl in there.

"Sir – sir!" Bostrom called after him, walking briskly behind. The deputy reached out and grabbed the motorcyclist's shoulder but he shrugged it off. He started jogging.

The deputy who was putting out the nylon belts, forming the barricade around the front of the house got in front of the man running towards him. Brendan was sure that Deputy Lawless wasn't going to let the kid inside to see the gory mess upstairs. Lawless would protect the core scene.

Lawless spread his arms out and got between the oncoming man in the motorcycle jacket and the doorway to the house. The motorcyclist reached him a second later, not even looking at Lawless, but past him. Lawless threw his arms around the young man, and got him in a gentle, but firm bear hug.

The man started screaming. "Rebecca! Rebecca!"

He kicked and fought, struggling to break Lawless's hold. Lawless was a big man, and the motorcyclist was only a buck-forty, a buck-fifty, tops. Brendan thought the kid looked like some actor, good looking, with hay-straw blond hair. But he was strong, and put up a good fight. Lawless worked hard to wrestle him away from the door. He got himself behind the kid and started dragging. The kid dug in his boot heels – they left tracks in the dirt.

Bostrom reached the fracas before Brendan, and threw himself into the struggle, helping Lawless get the kid under control. Brendan knew the motorcyclist just wanted to see the girl in that room, but the officers had no choice except to restrain him.

The two deputies managed to get him on the ground, face down. Bostrom had a knee on the motorcyclist's back.

"Calm down." Bostrom was out of breath, his face flushed.

Brendan's own face was dripping with sweat. He wiped his forehead with the back of his hand. The day was damn hot.

The kid kicked on the ground. He tried to roll out of the hold. He rocked back and forth, back and forth, looking to throw Bostrom off-balance. He was yelling and grunting, like a wild animal. His breath raised little clouds of dirt. His spit darkened the dry earth.

"Okay," said Brendan in a plaintive voice. "Okay, okay . . ."

Bostrom's head snapped up at the detective. Brendan had heard that Mike Bostrom had a temper.

"What? You want me to let him go? Say the word, Healy, and I'll let him run around like a pinball in your crime scene. Fuck it up even more than I did."

"No," said Brendan. "No, I just . . ." There was nothing to say. He felt momentarily helpless.

"Stop it!" Bostrom yelled down at the kid. "Stop it or you're going to regret it!"

Brendan stood looking down at the kid. He was afraid Bostrom was going to put him in a choke, the way the motorcyclist was fighting. Things were getting out of control.

Brendan dropped down into a crouch, and then bent over so that his head was almost touching the ground. He looked into the motorcyclist's wide, panicked eyes.

"She's dead," he said, loud and firm. "Rebecca is dead. She was stabbed repeatedly, fatally, just one hour ago. Her killer could be still on the property. He could be in the next town, having a coffee. Okay?"

It worked. It took a moment, but Brendan saw that the motorcyclist was growing still. He was listening.

"Now, I don't know who you are, but you obviously know the woman inside. You know Rebecca. You love Rebecca. But I can't let you in there right now."

The motorcyclist started to struggle again. Bostrom cinched his grip tighter, drove his knee in deeper. He glanced up at Brendan, as if challenging him to contradict the deputy's use of force again. Brendan ignored it. While the kid kept fighting, Brendan resumed talking. He used a softer voice.

"You need to keep calm. I need you to help me, okay? I promise you will be able to see Rebecca. In just a few minutes. I promise. But right now, I can't let you in there."

Everything seemed to have grown quieter. The motorcyclist was no longer resisting. Brendan briefly glanced across the big yard and saw that Investigator Delaney and another deputy – Watts – were looking over, watching. He raised a hand, indicating everything was okay. They left the old farmer in the cut-off shirt and headed over anyway.

Brendan returned his attention to what was at hand. There was a still a ways to go to get the overwrought kid under control.

"Now, Deputy Bostrom here is going to slowly take his weight off of you. We're going to help you up. Are you ready?"

Brendan gave it another moment. They waited in the suffocating heat. Brendan wished for a breeze, anything. What a morning. One for the books.

"Okay," came the muffled reply of the face-down kid.

"Okay," said Brendan. He looked at Bostrom again, and gave a nod. Bostrom's face was contorted with frustration, but he wasn't going to hurt anyone. He slowly took his knee off the kid. Brendan helped Bostrom get the motorcyclist to his feet.

The kid's face was covered in dirt. Tears and spittle from his mouth tracked clean rivulets down his face. His black jacket had a huge splotch of yard dirt smeared across the front, his blue jeans were dusted with it too. His hair was a mess, and strands clung to his forehead.

Brendan looked into the kid's eyes. Then he broke eye contact and stepped over to Lawless.

Brendan whispered to him, "What the hell is taking Clark so long up there? Dead is dead, last I checked. Let's get the on-call mortuary service right here, right now. Can you do that for me? Go up there and tell Clark to get moving, please." He added, "Thank you, Deputy."

Deputy Lawless stepped back and gave Brendan an evaluating look. Brendan knew what they'd all been thinking; he was some rookie detective, not from around here. They thought he was a bit of coffee house bullshit, that he probably considered himself hot stuff, a city boy in the country.

Deputy Lawless tossed Brendan a wink. Then he nodded and turned and went in the house to do as Brendan had instructed.

\* \* \*

"What's your name?"

"Kevin."

"Kevin? Okay, Kevin. What's your last name?"

The kid's eyes, bloodshot and ringed with dust, locked on Brendan Healy.

"Heilshorn."

"So you're related to the victim. To Rebecca."

Those same eyes of the kid now welled with tears. "She's my sister," he said. "She's my older sister." The tears spilled, cleaving fresh, clean tracks down his dirty face. His lower lip trembled.

They were sitting back in the grass, halfway between the house and the road. Kevin Heilshorn was on his rear end, facing the house. Brendan had arranged them this way.

Brendan crouched in front of him, but not blocking that view. He observed the kid carefully. He noted where the kid looked: mostly at the house, and occasionally over to the shed.

"So," Brendan proceeded cautiously, "If you didn't get a call from anyone . . ."

"I was on my way here to see Rebecca," Kevin said abruptly. "No. Nobody called me. We had a ten o'clock meeting."

*A meeting*, thought Brendan. It was an interesting way of describing a visit to a family member living out in a country farmhouse.

Brendan glanced around. Delaney had gone back inside. Brendan had assured the senior investigator that he would be able to take care of this newcomer on the scene. It was, he reminded Delaney, what he was here to do. Delaney didn't like talking to people, and never questioned the witnesses. Delaney supposedly was a good cop and excellent investigator, but he was a little bit prima donna, Brendan thought, and seemed to think he was above talking to witnesses or bystanders.

Brendan thought that the unspoken truth was that Delaney had never had any training in proper interview techniques. He was old school, from the era when detectives mostly used intimidation to get information out of people.

"Okay," said Brendan. He decided it was time to get out his notebook. Usually he tried to keep the notebook out of any sort of questioning or interview, because it put a distance between him and the person he was talking to. They might feel reduced to a series of quotes, or he might miss something their body language told him. He didn't need to jot down the word "meeting," but he made a note to check the shed.

He proceeded with a few standard questions. The kid was twenty-five, and the motorcycle was registered in his name. He was close in age to the victim – only two and a half years separating them. His address was Scarsdale, New York.

"Did you drive the bike all the way up? That's a long haul. You couldn't have; not this morning."

"No, not this morning. I stayed in a hotel last night."

"You stayed in a hotel? Where?"

"In Remsen."

Brendan looked off down the road, Route 12. Remsen was five miles south. He looked back at Kevin, whose eyes remained fixed on the house. "You didn't just come straight here? Why stay in a motel?"

Kevin shrugged. Brendan thought he wasn't going to say anymore, when the kid added, "Our meeting wasn't until nine."

"What was your meeting about?"

Kevin closed his eyes. He reached up, and wiped his dirty leather sleeve across his face, smearing tears and dirt. Then he took his fingers and pressed them to the closed lids of his eyes. He sniffled. "It was just a meeting," he said. "We had some stuff to go over."

"Like what?"

He pulled his hands away and his eyes popped open. He gave Brendan a hard look. "Like personal stuff, okay? Private stuff."

"Okay," said Brendan softly. "But when you say 'meeting,' it makes me think business."

"Well, that's how it is. You wouldn't understand, man. I can't . . . fuck." He closed his eyes tight and started to cry.

"I want to understand. Can you help me understand?"

Kevin covered his face in his arms and shook his head.

Brendan was considering whether to let the point go or give it a second and keep pressing, when a vehicle on Route 12 slowed and turned down the driveway, crunching the dirt and small stones. It was a black SUV. The on-call mortuary service.

Kevin lifted his head and opened his eyes. "Is that them?" he said standing up.

Brendan stood up too. They watched as the vehicle parked and a man and woman got out. They opened the back doors and unloaded a stretcher.

Kevin abruptly started walking towards the house. "I'm going to see her now. I'm going to see my sister."

## CHAPTER FOUR / THURSDAY, 10:13 AM

State Troopers had arrived, along with more deputies from the next county, St. Lawrence. They had briefly organized and then spread out, heading off in all directions. Healy saw two troopers cutting a path through the corn, across the road where the farmer had been shooting an interloping rodent. It was almost ten o'clock. Healy doubted they would find anything, but it couldn't be known whether the killer was hiding in the fields, or even on the premises. He could be in that big barn out back, or in that shed with the wide door, tucked away in the dark, waiting them out.

The body of the young woman was brought out the front door. She had been zipped in a black bag. Healy stood next to the young man in the motorcycle jacket, Kevin. The man and woman from the mortuary service gently lifted the stretcher over the threshold and the step, into the dooryard. The black-bagged body wobbled a little.

Kevin Heilshorn reached out, perhaps to touch the body, or to unzip it, and Brendan took hold of his arm gingerly, but firmly. Kevin relented. They walked alongside the gurney as it was trucked over to the SUV hearse.

"Where does she go now?" The young man's voice sounded choked.

"She'll go to the morgue," said Brendan. "She'll be looked after; she'll be fine."

"Are they going to . . . cut her open? Do all that stuff?" His voice broke on the last word, and he sobbed as he walked, swaying a little.

"No. There's no reason for that. She'll be examined. They'll want to take a close look at her wounds. See if she has any . . . other signs that can help us." *A serology check. Blood from her killer. Semen.* Detective Healy didn't say these things.

Stanley Clark, the coroner, came out of the house. As the man and woman loaded the body into the vehicle, Clark approached. Brendan kept an eye on Kevin, but stepped away to have a private word with Clark. Delaney had left the scene a few minutes before, coordinating the area search with the state police and two groups of deputies.

Brendan raised his eyebrows, and Clark gave a brief report. "She has thirteen stab wounds. She has some petechial papules around her mouth and eyes. This could mean she was held down by her throat, and there was some strangulation. Or, it could be some type of pre-existing vasculitis. I won't know until I can perform the autopsy."

Brendan made a clucking sound with his tongue. In a low voice head said, "I just told her brother that wouldn't be necessary."

Clark looked at Brendan impassively. He seemed to regard the detective like some other life-form, one unfamiliar with indigenous customs. "Why would you do that?"

"I was trying to comfort him."

The body was loaded into the hearse and the doors were closed. The man paused to offer condolences to Kevin, who himself looked like someone adrift in a foreign land. Brendan and Clark both looked at the young man, who was out of earshot. Still, they kept their voices low.

Clark asked Healy: "Is he going to call the rest of the family?"

"I'll help him do it." Brendan cut his eyes back to Clark. "What do you think happened in there?"

Clark looked grim. "I think she was forced into the bed. There are also signs of blunt trauma to the head and left shoulder. She was stabbed repeatedly and succumbed. She's dead."

"Thank you."

Clark offered a bird-like nod and swiftly moved away.

Brendan stood for a moment. He had called the District Attorney's office back. He had delegated two deputies to locate the next door neighbors and ferret out any witnesses, a car coming or going, strange noises, screams, anything. It was quiet out here in the country, Brendan thought, you could hear someone crack an egg a mile away when there was no traffic on the road. Route 12 was not a major artery, but nor was it a back road. A fair amount of vehicles had passed since he'd arrived on the scene, many of them slowing to get a look at the activity.

Much of his to-do list would need to be delegated or accomplished back at the station. Finding out who owned the house, if not the victim, establishing a timeline, collating all the information he now had, and consulting with Clark once he had done his examination. He needed to check the victim's phone, and look into all calls from within the past 24 hours, starting this morning and working his way back. Maybe even further back, if need be.

First, though, there were things left to do on the scene. Brendan decided that Kevin Heilshorn shouldn't be left alone for the time being. Kevin could also furnish Brendan with more information — whether his sister had a boyfriend, who her friends were, and above all, who else may have been invited to this "meeting," that Kevin spoke of.

However, one thing immediately didn't wash about the meeting. The victim herself had called 911 and reported an intruder. If she had been expecting her brother, it would stand to reason that hearing a noise downstairs wouldn't have caused her emergency call. She must've seen who'd entered the house, and either didn't recognize him, or didn't want him there.

Brendan's hunch suggested the latter. He couldn't swallow the idea of a robbery, right off the bat. For one thing, the way those drawers were arranged. Still, he needed to ascertain what, if anything, had been stolen.

And there was Bostrom to talk to. Delaney had been brusque with Bostrom, but Brendan wanted to know every detail about the deputy's arrival on scene and his actions step-by-step.

And finally, Brendan needed to venture back upstairs to the core scene, and see where the CSI unit was at, and what else they may have turned up.

Delaney, it seemed, had cut him loose. Brendan felt that sense of unease returning. Not because the senior investigator had basically left him on his own, but for reasons he wasn't quite sure of yet.

He watched the mortuary service do a three-point turn in the driveway, and then head off down the driveway. Clark followed them in his sedan. The two vehicles turned on to Route 12 and headed south, towards Remsen.

Kevin Heilshorn stood in the settling dust. Deputy Bostrom had remained at the house, as per Brendan's instructions. He was off in the sprawling front yard, talking on his cell phone and pacing. Brendan felt that the scuffle with Kevin had unnerved the deputy. That or the fact Brendan had asked him to stay behind and not join the area search.

At last, Brendan looked up at the sky. He didn't think the area search would yield anything significant. The killer, he now felt certain, was long gone.

Brendan twisted his neck and his eyes fell on the bedroom windows where the victim had been found. The killer had made quick work of her. He'd entered the house, which was either open, or maybe he had a key. Rebecca Heilshorn had been getting out of the shower. He imagined her toweling her hair, another towel wrapped around her torso. She'd started down the hallway back to the bedroom where she'd get dressed and ready for this meeting with her brother. Along the way, she hears someone downstairs. The railing along the hallway overlooked the front door. Anyone standing there would be in plain view. So she gets an eyeful, and then runs to the bedroom where she dials 911.

Brendan glanced at Kevin, and then at Bostrom. Bostrom was preoccupied. Kevin was looking around, apparently in a bit of a fugue. Brendan hurried over to the young man.

"I need you to stay here, okay? Can you do that? I need to talk to you some more."

"Okay," said the young man in a dolorous tone.

"Okay," echoed Brendan. "Where will you be?"

"Right here," said Kevin.

Brendan lingered a moment. He needed to run inside. So he left Kevin there. He jogged towards the house again. On his way, he whistled. Bostrom looked over. Brendan pointed two fingers at his eyes and then pointed them back at Kevin Heilshorn. *Watch him.* Bostrom nodded, and lifted a hand in the air. Brendan sprang in through the front door of the house.

* * *

Upstairs, he found the CSI unit still working the room. He nodded at them and then took a look at what he'd come back up to see.

The doors in the house were old farmhouse doors, the kinds that didn't have locks. Brendan examined the door. He put on a pair of latex gloves and then ran his hands up and down the side of the door, and then the face of it. He could feel impressions towards the base. Brendan looked closely and saw what appeared to be a little black smudge. Where it had been kicked.

He then leaned around the door and looked behind it. There was an end table there which looked like it belonged next to the bed, instead of where it had ended up, sitting at an angle. The floors were hard wood. This would make it challenging for the forensics team to lift any hairs or fabric, but they provided clarity for something else. There were whitish scrape marks under the end table.

This was because the end table had been used by the victim to try to block the door, Brendan thought.

He looked up at the man named Patnode, who had been taking pictures of the room earlier. He was now dusting for latent fingerprints.

"Did you get the door?"

Patnode looked around and saw Brendan, who was down on his knees at the entrance to the bedroom. Brendan pointed around to the outside of the door.

"It's been kicked in. Get pictures, and let's see if we can lift this shoe scuff, an imprint in the paint, something."

* * *

The killer had come up the stairs. He had gotten to the top and then strode down the hallway towards the bedroom. He found the door blockaded, and he'd pushed and he'd kicked. It wouldn't have taken much – the end table likely only weighed thirty or forty pounds. After the initial kick, the killer had probably seen that the door gave easily enough. So he'd pushed it the rest of the way.

"And fingerprints."

"Yes," said Patnode. "I was getting to the doorknob next."

"The door was open when you arrived," said Brendan, "but it wasn't when the killer did." All three of the CSI looked at the young detective, and understood.

When the killer reached the girl wrapped in her towels, she was still damp from the shower. Rebecca Heilshorn likely struggled with him at the foot of the bed, and then he pushed her onto it. She scrambled back, trying to get away from him. She had been partially under the covers when they'd found her, and so she'd flailed, she'd probably kicked; she'd worked her way under the duvet.

Then the killer had pounced. He'd climbed on top of her with the murder weapon and pinned her with one hand. What did he want? Just to destroy her? Did he try to get her to do something – agree to something? Many cases like this involved a disgruntled boyfriend, or ex-husband, a rejected lover. When they couldn't get what they wanted, they eradicated the source of their anger or pain. When this woman didn't satisfy what was asked of her, she paid for it with multiple stab wounds, and perhaps strangulation.

Brendan's unease continued to grow. It wasn't the same apprehension of coming across his first murder crime scene as it had been an hour ago – it was shaping up to be this different thing, this different sort of feeling. Like he was missing something vital, standing right next to it, and not seeing it.

He turned and walked out of the room as the CSI began to work the door in earnest.

Brendan ran down the stairs.

He walked briskly into the kitchen, his eyes roving, his head turning back and forth. Within seconds, he found the sheath of knives.

There were ten slots in the sheath. Six slots were filled with a knife. Four others were not.

Still with his gloves on, he started going through drawers. He went through the dishwasher, too (a Maytag, he saw, recently installed) and finally through the dirty dishes in the sink. Each knife he found, he set down on a butcher's block in the center of the room.

The kitchen was old-fashioned and farmhouse-traditional, save for the new dishwasher. The floor was red tile. There was a window over the sink that looked out to the shed with the big dark entrance. To his right was a rudimentary wooden booth built into the wall, bench seats on either side. Then there was a doorway, with no door, to a pantry. This was a small room that took up part of the floor plan of the kitchen, as if added in at some point. Behind him on the other side of the room, more cabinets and a long counter. To his left, an antique hutch with glass doors on top, housing what may have been hand-me-down china. A doorway beside the hutch led to the next room. It was dark, the light not penetrating this far back in a house with southern exposure to its front. Still, the dining room table and chairs were visible. More cabinetry with glass fronts containing dishware, candelabras, and other knickknacks.

He found knife after knife and set them all out, some splattered with food, some still wet from the dishwasher, some dry and dull from a lack of polish, sitting dusty in the drawers. He found mouse turds in one of the drawers.

As he laid the knives out – twelve now – he found himself marveling at how Delaney had left him to this. Finding a murder weapon was priority one. Though since it wasn't a gun, had Delaney deprioritized it? Had he expected – despite the fact that his list of instructions hadn't included searching for a weapon – that Brendan would get to it quickly anyway? Some things about the older detective just didn't make a lot of sense, but Brendan chalked most of it to the quirkiness/arrogance that came with seniority. Still, senior investigators were rarely sloppy. That's why they were still around.

Twelve sharp knives and he could find no more. He found that several of them were similar in appearance. They had the insignia of Royal Norfolk Cutlery etched in their steel blades. A heraldic lion pawed the air next to the name. There were four of these. Four knives and four slots. He slipped the knives in the sheath and stepped back. He heard someone behind him.

It was Delaney.

"How's it going?" The big man darkened the doorway to the kitchen.

"Good," said Brendan. The excitement of the knife hunt was dissipating.

"You get to talk to the Heilshorn kid further?"

"A little, sir."

"What are you doing?"

"Checking to see if the murder weapon could have come from this collection of knives," said Brendan. It was hard not to mask some bit of disappointment he felt.

Delaney walked over at a leisurely pace. He stopped a foot away from Brendan, facing him. Brendan could smell the outside air on the man, and a trace of aftershave. Delaney reached past Brendan and pulled out one of the knives. He wasn't wearing gloves. "They can clear my prints," he said absently. He held the knife, resting the blade on one palm and pinching the handle between the thumb and forefinger of his other hand. He rolled it over. He grunted to himself.

"So you think a missing knife could be our murder weapon?"

Brendan nodded. "Maybe. But this one set is all accounted for."

Delaney raised his considerable eyebrows and looked over the blade of the knife he held up to his face. "You think we'll find a knife with a print on it. Run the print in the database, match it with a felon, and go pick him up."

"Could be."

Delaney nodded, slid the knife back into the sheath and stuck out his lower lip. Then he walked to the sink and turned on the water. He splashed some on his face. "Christ it's hot out there," he said.

He turned and started walking out of the kitchen. "Go finish with the motorcycle rider. I'll have CSI come down and bag that whole assortment of knives. They're moving into the rest of the house. A K9 unit is en route."

Delaney walked out of the room.

Brendan paused, and then pressed his palms to the wooden butcher's block, and leaned forward. He let his head hang. He took a breath.

Then he resumed walking around the kitchen. He stopped and looked at the refrigerator. It was an unusual red color, not quite matching the floor. It was an older model – the handles were chipped, the color dull in places on the face. There were a few magnets on the surface. One was a tiny lobster. One was the flat, thin kind, from a hardware store. There were no notes, no drawings or photos.

Brendan stood looking at the half dozen magnets. A thought occurred to him and he turned and walked away from the fridge. He passed the butcher's block, glancing at the array of knives he'd unearthed. Then he walked into the shadowy dining room adjoining the kitchen.

## CHAPTER FIVE / THURSDAY, 10:35 AM

Brendan wanted to keep close to the K9 unit, but first he wanted to examine the rest of the house himself. He smiled at the two women from the CSI unit, Alicia and Dominique, as he passed them on the stairs.

In the bathroom, he went through the medicine cabinet. He found prescription bottles for Xanax and Klonopin, and a generic menstrual cramp reliever. He left them on the small shelf.

The bathroom appeared undisturbed. The translucent plastic curtain was pushed back, from Rebecca Heilshorn's last shower. The tub was the kind which sat up on feet – the curled paws of some animal, making Brendan think of the heraldic lion on the knife blades. The sink had a rust stain beneath the old fashioned faucet. The rubber drain plug was mildewed. A bar of hand soap sat in a dish. There was a toilet with a chain flush, and a small wicker laundry hamper. Brendan lifted the lid. There were only a few articles of clothing – maybe what the victim had on before her shower. He reached in with his gloved hand and found a pair of yoga pants, a t-shirt which read "Born Lucky – Lucky Jeans," some ankle socks, a pair of underwear, and what may have been the outfit from the day before – jeans, a white blouse with a frilly open collar, and another set of socks and underwear. Either Rebecca had been a very tidy housekeeper who did laundry daily, or she had just arrived at the house.

Brendan made a note in his pad to ask about a housekeeper or caretaker. The house certainly didn't feel lived in. The bedroom and kitchen were the only places with signs of life. The bathroom was well-kempt. There were no stray hairs or soap scum. Nothing, in fact, anywhere in the house seemed to have much dust on it.

He left the bathroom. There was a linen closet on his right, the next door down. The careful arrangement of clean towels and bedding also suggested a very tidy person or help with the housekeeping.

The door at the end of the hallway led to another bedroom. It was nearly twice the size of the bedroom where the victim had been discovered. Bright light shone around the edges of the drawn blinds – fabric blinds that were of a dark, blood-red. The room was much darker than the victim's bedroom. Those blinds, Brendan recalled, had all been up. The room had been bright. The windows, though, the way the sun had burned through them, they had been dirty.

So, a housekeeper then who "didn't do windows." It was laughably clichéd.

There were two dressers – one tall, one wide, like the bureau in the victim's room with the opened drawers. The ones in here were oak, of a set, no doubt. They appeared new. In fact, the bed's mattress was wrapped in plastic.

The ceiling was slanted on either side of the south-facing dormer window. To the right of the dormer, a door led to another bathroom. Brendan walked through the dim room across carpeting which was plush but faded. He clicked the light on in the dark bathroom.

Recently refurbished. A new Jacuzzi, replete with water jets. A new double sink, new cabinetry, light fixtures, the works. It was possible that Rebecca Heilshorn was using the bedroom down the hall while this one, the master bedroom, was being finished. The new mattress, matching bureau set, new bathroom appliances and fixtures – it was a room under construction. Even so, it didn't tell him much. And Kevin was waiting, and the K9 unit would be here any moment.

* * *

He stepped outside into the bright sunlight. He fished his sunglasses out of his inside jacket pocket. Kevin Heilshorn was sitting near where Brendan had left him, picking at the grass between his legs, slumped forward. Deputy Bostrom was nowhere to be seen. Vehicles were everywhere. A dog started barking. The K9 unit had already arrived, and one of the German Shepherds was pulling a cop towards the shed.

Brendan instantly got going. He'd had a feeling about that shed since he'd first arrived. He jumped from the doorway and started trotting over to the K9 cop and the dog. The dog was really pulling on the leash, straining to get to that shed.

"Oh my God," said Brendan. He didn't know why he said it, it just slipped out.

In his peripheral vision he saw Kevin Heilshorn stand and dust off the back of his pants. The K9 unit reached the edge of the shed just as Brendan caught up to them. The two men and the dog went into the gloom, and Brendan removed his sunglasses.

The first thing Brendan noticed was the old John Deere tractor. Its hood was open, engine exposed, looking in surprisingly good shape after all. The bucket was still attached, resting on the dirt floor. On either side of the shed were stacked rows of what looked like cages. The smell of chicken shit was powerful. As his eyes adjusted, Brendan could see the dried white splatters of chicken poop dripping from the cages, and around on the floor.

Chicken feed was turned to mush next to the cages. The dog pulled the K9 cop around to the back of the tractor. Its barks resounded in the dark. There was a sudden intensification of smell – the odor of decay, sour and acute. Brendan braced himself to find another body, perhaps of the killer, who'd come out and slit his own throat after perpetrating the heinous crime inside the house.

But it wasn't a human body that the dog had found. It was a small animal. Maybe a hedgehog, or a woodchuck.

The farmer across the road had been after a woodchuck or some other creature, shooting through the desiccated rows of corn at it.

The stink was even worse back here: chicken excrement, the powerful odor of a rotted animal, and something more. Maggots crawled through the tufts of fur, and flies buzzed and alighted. It looked like a raccoon.

"Ugh." Brendan put the ridge of his hand under his nose.

The K9 cop said nothing, working to restrain the dog from burying his snout in the mess. "What do you think did that?" asked Brendan.

"Have to order the autopsy," said the K9 cop with dry humor. Then, "Dunno. Maybe a coyote. Maybe it just came in here to die."

There appeared to be some blood, but it was hard to tell. Against the back wall of the shed were trash barrels. Two of these had been tipped over. On the ground were piles of what appeared to be household trash; Brendan thought he could see banana peels, plastic food packaging, an empty Cascade detergent box, some kind of noodles, and more. There were also substances which didn't resemble food. Holding his nose, Brendan bent and squinted at what appeared to be a large lump of dark plastic. It looked melted, perhaps some appliance that had somehow been superheated until it severely deformed – there was little light in the back of the shed and so it was hard to tell. Around all of this the ground was littered with the mash of feed, and strands of hay, dirt, small rocks. The cop got his dog turned around, and headed back out into the bright square of sunlight.

Brendan stayed for a moment, looking at the lump of plastic.

\* \* \*

"I need to get the young man a grief counselor," said Brendan to Detective Delaney. "A psychologist. Someone like that. He's having a real hard time. Who do you have around here?"

"Call, uhm, Olivia Jane," said Delaney. He was popping bits of something into his mouth. Sunflower seeds. "She worked with DCH, now she's on her own. She's come down a few times to help with grief counseling, she can help set up temporary housing for victim families, that sort of thing. Works with battered wives a lot."

They stood in the blistering sun. Sweat patches were visible around the armpits of Delaney's grey suit. Brendan glanced down at his own darker apparel, wondering if it too was stained with perspiration. His skin felt prickly, the pores popping open, the tendrils of sweat starting to run from his temples.

"Are we going to put surveillance on the house?"

"Absolutely. What did Clark say?"

Brendan thought back to the coroner. So much had happened in just the past hour. He thought to check his notes, but tried to remember instead. "Looks like one stab wound to the pulmonary artery was the non-survivable injury. The victim likely expired sometime between 8:20 and 8:40 this morning, but we figured that already."

"Anything else?"

"He talked about petechiae." Brendan pointed to his face. "The kinds of blotches that can come from a pinching off of the carotid artery. Typically from strangulation."

"I know what it is." Delaney nodded at Kevin. "Is he going to be alright?"

"He vomited in the grass not long ago. He could need some medical attention. Some mental attention, too. My plan is . . . well."

"What?"

Brendan squinted in the sun at the senior investigator. Then he remembered his sunglasses and put them back on. "I was thinking I could get him out of here. Take him back to Remsen myself. To the motel, maybe to the hospital. Talk to him on the way. Get his statement."

"That's a good idea."

Compliments were rare with Delaney. It took Brendan aback for a moment. Then he added, "I'll have the . . . what was her name? Olivia Jane. She can meet us there."

Delaney spat out a sunflower seed shell. They were at the outlet of the driveway, getting a word in private, away from the house. The whole scene was before them. The dogs were now out back, sniffing around the barn. CSI was working the entire house. The sun had climbed high into gauzy sky.

"I think we want to make sure CSI combs through the shed. There's a dead animal back there, and some interesting refuse."

Delaney raised his eyebrows. "Raccoon?"

"Don't know."

"That's what Folwell was after. Some animal. Shooting at it with his Browning. I'll make sure they go through the trash. Something caught your eye?"

"There's a fireplace inside, yeah? Something may have been burned and then thrown out."

"I want to meet back with you in one hour."

"Okay," said Brendan, and he started to dial Olivia Jane.

## CHAPTER SIX / THURSDAY, 11:08 AM

He was able to convince Kevin Heilshorn to ride into Remsen with him and get a sandwich. In the car, he lit a cigarette. "Mind if I smoke?" Kevin shook his head. Brendan pressed the buttons to roll down both front windows, and then started turning around in the driveway.

"Can I get one?"

"Sure. Take as many as you want. I'm trying to quit."

They turned onto Route 12, headed west. Brendan got the Camry up to speed, and the wind beat in through the opened windows, the antenna shivered on the hood. There was quicksilver baking on the road, and the Camry sluiced through it.

"Hot," Brendan said. "You know, it's late in the summer, too."

"That doesn't matter. It's all getting hotter."

Brendan glanced over. "Global Warming?"

Kevin shrugged. His eyes were ringed red from crying, glassy and small as if shrink-wrapped. He was a good-looking kid, with a strong jaw and straight nose. Brendan's own nose was bent to one side, something he had always been a little bit self-conscious about. That and the smattering of Irish freckles he had around his cheeks and temples. He was grateful he wasn't a redhead. With the rest of his complexion and red hair he would have been Howdy Doody. But Brendan had inherited some of the darker looks of his Italian mother, too. His hair was black. Along with his green eyes, hatchet nose and light complexion, he often thought of his appearance as uncomely, like a ghost's.

Kevin cleared his throat. "I'm not a proponent of anything. It could be CO2 emissions; it could be the Chandler Wobble. Who knows."

"The Chandler Wobble?"

"Haven't you ever heard of the wobble of the earth?"

"I wasn't a Geology major."

"It's like this. Let's say you were to stick a pencil in an orange. Then you put the tip of that pencil on a piece of paper. You spin the orange. A perfect spin, and the pencil just makes a dot on the paper. Now imagine that the orange is *wobbling*, and . . ."

"It makes an ellipse on the paper. What causes the wobble?"

"That's just it. Maybe global warming causes the wobble. Or maybe the wobble causes global warming. It's the chicken or the egg."

The comment made Brendan think of the shed. Particularly of the chicken coop made out of stacks of cages, banded together by some simple one-by-four lumber. "Did your sister keep chickens?"

At first he thought Kevin would answer, but then the young man put his forehead in his hand. His elbow was propped on the passenger door. The wind slamming by sucked at his hair and pulled it out the window. A moment later and he had both of his hands covering his face, leaning forward.

"I'm very sorry for your loss," Brendan said. He realized that while he'd always winced at such generic phrases, there was nothing else to say in moments like this.

"She never should have come up here," said Kevin through his hands. He snuffled back some tears and wiped a hasty hand across his face. He looked out at the scenery rushing by; corn, barns, silos, gnarled oak trees, a long swath of pines in the distance.

"Where did she come up from?" Brendan asked, emphasizing the last word. "On your driver's license, it says you're from Scarsdale. That where she's from, too?"

Kevin cut his eyes over to look at the detective, then turned to look back out the blustery open window. He didn't seem to want to answer the question.

"I'm from Westchester County, too," Brendan offered.

Another sideways glance from the young man. "Oh yeah? Where?"

"Hawthorne."

Brendan had tried not to leap to an instant assumption about where Kevin was from, but Scarsdale meant money. It was the richest city in one of the richest counties in the country. The last he'd checked the statistics, Westchester was second only to Fairfax County for per capita wealth. It was hard not to connect the young woman, who had an entire farm to herself with an Audi parked in the driveway, to a wealthy family supporting her. He tried to proceed tactfully.

"Scarsdale is nice," he said.

"I went to school in White Plains."

"College?"

"High school. We were right along the edge of that district." He paused and added a little defensively, "I didn't go to college."

They were just a couple miles from Remsen. Brendan let off the gas just a little. "No, huh? You seem educated."

"I educated myself."

Brendan could tell this was sensitive territory, and imagined heated conversations Kevin might have had with his parents.

"Are your parents together?"

"That's hard to say."

"But they're not divorced."

"No." Kevin finished his cigarette and pitched the butt out the window.

Brendan took a breath. "Do they own the house where your sister was found today?"

He nodded.

"Well, we need to talk to them right away. The coroner is obligated to call them, and he will, within the next few minutes, I'm sure. Maybe you'd like to call them. Maybe it would be better if they heard it from you."

"No," said Kevin with little hesitation. "It wouldn't."

Brendan considered this. Maybe the kid wasn't prepared to go through it. Family brought out the strongest emotions. Or maybe it would be tough in another way – maybe they would blame him, maybe he was the family whipping boy, who knew?

Or maybe he had something to hide from them.

Brendan, changed tack. "How long has your family owned the place?"

"Uhm, I don't know. Three years? More? I'm sure Bops bought it because he was trying to hide money. Avoid capital gains tax."

"Bops?"

"My father. We call him Bops because . . . Well. Let's just say my parents got into the family game late in life. Both Bops and Ma'am are career-driven people. Bops was in his mid-forties when Rebecca came. He's seventy-one now. Maybe seventy-two; I don't know." Kevin surprised Brendan by cracking a smile. "Man, she was a fucking surprise. Maybe Ma'am's body had rejected the pill by then – she was thirty-five or thirty-eight or something. Ma'am is in publishing. For whatever reason, they started having kids. I'm the last in a line of fucking token children."

Brendan absorbed all of this. The kid clearly expressed bitterness and resentment. It was to be expected, Brendan supposed.

"And how close were you and Rebecca?"

"How do you mean?"

"You talk regularly and stuff? I don't know how it works. I'm an only."

Kevin sighed. He ran a hand across his face again. Brendan glanced and saw the shine of tears. "We were close, I guess, yeah. Not always, but more since . . . we got older. Look, man, I can't, I can't go into this right now." Suddenly he sat up straighter, and his voice grew louder. "Did you get her phone?"

"The CSI unit – that's the Crime Scene Investigation team – they bagged her phone. They'd take any of her personals, like cell phone, computer, wallet, down to the lab. What about the phone?"

Kevin's body seemed to slump again. He returned to looking out the window. There were small, modular homes alongside the road now. They were coming into Remsen. "Nothing," he said.

"Can I ask you something?"

Kevin was quiet.

"Did your sister have any children?"

Kevin abruptly turned his head to the side to cut a look over at Brendan. His jaw was set, his lips pursed. "No," he said.

Brendan felt like the kid was lying.

After that, they lapsed into silence.

* * *

At the diner, Brendan ordered a BLT and a coffee. Kevin said he wasn't hungry.

"I know it's probably not appealing," Brendan said. "But you should eat something."

Kevin conceded to an order of eggs and toast. He had an orange juice brought over with Brendan's coffee. He sipped the juice, and grimaced. "Bitter," he said. He pushed it away.

"Kevin, I'm having someone meet us here."

The young man raised his eyebrows. He made solid eye contact most of the time, Brendan thought, but always looked away first, as he did now, scanning the other patrons in the diner. It was fairly busy for a Thursday morning. A group of four older men sat at a nearby table. One was wearing a trucker's cap which read "American Legion" on it. They wore flannel and suspenders and their shirt pockets bulged.

Brendan and Kevin sat in one of the booths by the window. There were five booths in a row. In the next booth over, behind Kevin, Brendan observed a young woman with a baby. The child was crying as it was fed mashed potatoes.

"Who's meeting us?"

"She's a grief counselor," said Brendan.

Kevin didn't look pleased. He pushed the silverware around on his paper placemat. He glanced up at the far door as if he were considering leaving.

"You've been through an incredible shock," said Brendan. "I can't begin to imagine the loss. But, Kevin, these first 48 hours are crucial. If we're going to find your sister's killer, I'm going to need your help. But I don't want to neglect your own personal needs; what you're going through. It's a tough situation."

Kevin looked back at Brendan. His blue eyes seemed to darken. "Tough? Sorry, but you don't know anything about tough right now." He gripped the table in front of him. "I don't like this. I don't like counselors, all that." Indeed, the young man seemed to be getting agitated. His eyes, glassy and red, darted around the room.

"Why is that?"

Those eyes pinned Brendan, even darker now, as if drawn into harder material, like pits. "You like to be under the microscope?"

Brendan sipped his coffee. He thought of the nervousness he'd felt this morning, coming upon his first official crime scene up here in God's country. It still came around, sometimes, his doubt in himself. But for some reason his gut told him that this wasn't the reason why Kevin was apprehensive. Again, it felt more like the young man had something to hide. "Nobody really likes being . . . looked into. But I think what you learn is how to be gracious."

"Gracious," Kevin scoffed, spitting the word.

"Are you a user?"

"Excuse me?"

Brendan kept his voice low. "I mean do you use drugs. Did Rebecca use drugs? Illegal or prescription?"

"See? This is what I'm talking about. Do *you* use drugs, detective?"

Brendan had expected the young man to be combative. It was better that he got riled than panicky, and ran out.

"I used to," said Brendan.

"So? What about you? Let's talk about you. See how you like people prying into your life."

"It's not fun; you're right."

"What is a guy from Westchester doing up here in Podunk central working as a detective?"

Brendan took a deep breath, and exhaled. He moved his cup of coffee in front of him and took it with both hands. He spoke in a clear voice, not too soft, not too loud.

"I was born and raised in Hawthorne to a middle class family. I got a scholarship to a school where I studied the biology of the brain. Particularly, I studied how we formed habits, did things routinely. Everything from muscle memory, to the basal ganglia. I didn't graduate top of my class, or anywhere near it. I barely made it through. Then I came close to receiving my PhD in neurobiology when I was your age, but fell short."

"Why?"

"I don't know how I made it through, even that far, because I was drinking the whole time. I had met a girl at school, and we were married in two years. We had a child the year I was finishing. Then, I lost it all."

He paused there, and gauged Kevin's reaction. The young man seemed incredulous. "You almost got a PhD in neurobiology? What the fuck are you doing as a cop? That can't pay much."

"Neither does neurobiology. It's a myth that a doctorate automatically translates into a high income. I wasn't going to be a brain surgeon. I did research. It all depends on who you go to work for as a researcher, or if you stay in academia and go after grants. At the time, with the economy, let's say the prospects were grim. But that's not why I became a cop."

"Then why?" Kevin seemed genuinely more relaxed with the focus off him for now. And some of the combative energy seemed to have temporarily subsided. You could often reveal more about a person of interest by talking about things other than themselves. Sometimes the indirect approach worked best. Back in Westchester, a policeman named Argon had taught Brendan that.

"I became a cop because of everything I lost. My wife, my child, my life. I sobered up, thanks to the help of someone who came into my life just when I needed it most. That man was a cop. It took me time to get myself together, but during part of my recovery, I went to the police academy. I figured lots of push-ups and sit-ups would be a good thing."

Brendan shrugged, and sat back, letting go of the coffee cup.

Kevin's face was open now. He regarded Brendan plainly from across the table. His fight or flight impulse seemed to have subsided. A moment later, a woman appeared. Both men glanced up, thinking their food had arrived.

Instead of the waitress, they saw a pretty brunette in jeans and a white blouse, a small bag over her shoulder.

She smiled at them. "Good morning. I'm Olivia. Can I join you?"

Kevin looked across the table at Brendan. His eyes were bloodshot.

"I don't want to talk to this woman."

Brendan was opening his mouth to speak when the grief counselor responded. She addressed Brendan directly at first.

"Good morning, Detective. I'd like to start by being clear about something; about who my client is. My client is this man, Kevin. It is not the Sheriff's Department."

Now her eyes drifted over to Kevin, who was looking down at his hands. "What you and I discuss is entirely confidential. My job is to help you through this process. If you feel like you are in a good condition to help the police officers after we speak, then that is for you to determine. But, you may not. And that's okay, too."

Kevin lifted his head up and met her gaze.

## CHAPTER SEVEN / THURSDAY, 12:12 PM

Brendan left Kevin with the grief counselor and headed back to the scene. It had been about forty-five minutes, and he needed to debrief with Delaney. The CSI unit would probably be close to finishing up the first round. One or two of them would take all the evidence collected so far to the lab. The others would stay behind. It might take the entire day to process the scene. Brendan wouldn't have to wait for it all to be collected – he would want to get going right away on some priority items like the cell phone. He also wanted to talk to the owners, who he'd found out from Kevin were the victim's parents, right away.

He and Olivia had agreed to meet at her in-home office that afternoon at four. She had very quickly volunteered to bring Kevin Heilshorn back to the house, back to his motorcycle.

Brendan didn't pretend to know her methods, but he felt intuitively that besides being polite and helpful, the therapist may have seen value in returning to the scene of the tragedy with the young man whom it affected so deeply. Perhaps more effective "work" could be done if they were in the presence of what had caused such tremendous grief, rather than away somewhere else, where it could be dulled or sanitized. Either way, Brendan was grateful for her offer. He had consulted with her at the door, on his way out the diner, and had stressed to her that he needed to keep Kevin Heilshorn close at hand. She understood.

The next few minutes unfolded like a kind of dream. Several news vans had arrived on the scene. Eager reporters were held back by the barrier the deputies had placed in front of the driveway. Bollards had been placed along the front edge of the property where it abutted Route 12 by State Troopers.

Two trooper vehicles sat in the road, their lights flashing. The sun crawled even higher, and baked the already scorched grass and corn. Small bugs zipped about in the air. Bees droned past. The voices of reporters drifted over from where they talked with deputies and State Troopers.

Brendan walked from his car, which he'd parked along the shoulder of Route 12, and over towards the house. Delaney stood in the center of the giant front yard, holding a cell phone to his ear. Two men in white Hazmat suits were coming out of the shed with large bags. He also saw a new face, over by the victim's Audi, talking to one of the CSIs. He knew by reputation it was Howard Skene, the Senior Prosecutor for Oneida County.

Delaney snapped his phone shut. He too looked across the dry grass at Skene, and said to Brendan, "You're just in time. Let's go tell him how much we *don't* have to go on."

Skene walked over. He had a peculiar gait, as though his pleated pants didn't fit quite right around his crotch. Delaney would say he had a stick up his ass. Skene didn't shake hands either, but parked both of his palms on his hips. Brendan could see the heat of the day getting to the prosecutor, too. His upper lip was beaded with perspiration, and his dark hair was damp around his ears and forehead.

"Morning," said Brendan.

Brendan and Skene had never met in person, and Delaney made introductions. Skene nodded. He wore black sunglasses, but Brendan could sense the prosecutor's eyes examining him. After a moment, Skene said, "So?"

Delaney took a barely perceptible step to the side and looked at Brendan, indicating that he had the floor.

"Well, sir," Brendan began doubtfully. He tried to sort the information in his head in order to proceed articulately. "The victim is 28 year-old Rebecca Heilshorn. What we know right now is that the house and the property are owned by her parents, also named Heilshorn."

"Is she married? Kept her name?"

"There was no wedding ring on her finger, but I have yet to get with CSI and establish a real inventory of the contents of the home. Right now the house doesn't seem very lived-in. The kitchen and the bedroom and upstairs bath are the only places that show real signs of habitation. There's thick dust over everything else. Some plastic on the furniture in the living room. However, the master bedroom upstairs looks like it recently underwent a renovation, as if someone were planning a more regular occupancy of the home."

Skene was expressionless. He said, "That's a very nice description, Detective." He turned to Delaney. "Any leads?"

"A brother of the victim showed up not long after we got here," said Delaney. "He wrecked his bike, he was hyperactive. He had to be subdued by one of our deputies."

"That's interesting," said Skene, raising his eyebrows. He then turned and glanced towards the group of reporters, held at bay by the driveway gates.

"He's grief-stricken. In shock," Brendan interjected. "He laid down the bike because he hit the soft dirt of the driveway. That could suggest that he's never been here before, except he told me the name of the neighbor, Folwell. He knew who he was."

Skene's head swiveled slowly back to look at Brendan.

Brendan continued, "As he approached, police were on either side of the road. The Folwell farmer had been shooting at a pest in the corn. There were people everywhere. The brother was distracted and confused. In any case, it would be outlandish to return to the scene of a crime less than an hour after perpetrating it."

"Unless that's his defense," said the prosecutor flatly.

Brendan skipped past it. "We have her cell phone and a laptop found in the bedroom. We're going to go through that. I'll contact the parents next. My hope is that I can get them to come and ID the body. If they are unreachable, we can have the brother Kevin do it, to keep things moving. The coroner determined the victim expired due to an injury to her pulmonary artery – a stab wound, one of several. She was naked in the bed."

"So I heard. Raped?"

"We'll know more when we get the results of the PERK," Brendan said.

"Which will be when?"

Brendan glanced at Delaney, who seemed to be enjoying himself. His face was hidden in part by his own sunglasses and his mustache, but Brendan got a sense the senior investigator was taking pleasure in the interaction between Brendan and Skene.

"As soon as Clark's investigators and his forensic staff perform the autopsy. The forensic pathologist will verify Clark's original cause of death, perhaps elaborate upon it or invalidate it. But if there was rape, it will show up in the PERK."

"Again, how long?"

Brendan was taken aback. Skene had been with the prosecutor's office for a decade or more. He knew the routine. He knew that with a homicide autopsy, there was limited access, the surgeries performed in a special room, everything photographed and documented down to the last detail. "It could take all the rest of today, maybe until tomorrow," said Brendan. He realized as soon as he answered the prosecutor why the man had asked a question about something he more than likely knew the answer to.

"That's not good enough," Skene said.

The prosecutor didn't want to be the one breathing down the Deputy Coroner's neck. He wanted Brendan to be the one to keep the pressure on.

"I understand," Brendan said quietly.

"I hope you do. Look, I'm not trying to be an asshole here. I know you're new to Oneida. But this is the first homicide we've had in two years. People are going to be terrified. If there is a killer on the loose – I don't have to tell you we need to act quickly. And here you are already defending the kid who shows up, wrecks his bike, and gets in a fight with our deputies at the scene of the crime. That's fine. But if there's a rape, let's get the serology report sooner rather than later. Let's get prints from the house, more serology from the sheets, and let's get the bastard responsible for this. Do you even know if he's the victim's kin? Did you check his ID? Did anyone?"

Skene looked from Brendan to Delaney. Delaney nodded towards the road. "I was dealing with Elmer Fudd over there," he said.

"Jesus Christ," said Skene. He reached down and adjusted the waist of his pants. Then he looked back at Brendan.

"I checked his ID. Kevin Heilshorn, from Scarsdale."

"Okay. Tell me what else you have."

"In the shed," said Brendan. "There appeared to be a burnt device in the trash."

"A 'burnt device'? What does that mean?"

"Burned. Cooked. Incinerated. A computer, maybe. Someone torched their laptop. The one upstairs could be a dummy."

"Why would you think that?"

"A hunch. I also . . ."

"A hunch. Who are you, Kojak? Check it anyway."

"Jesus Christ," said Brendan. He turned and started walking away. His head was blazing hot from the sun beating down on his dark hair. His suit was itchy. The breakfast he'd horked down at the diner wasn't sitting right in his stomach. Suddenly, he stopped, and bent forward, putting his hands on his knees. There he swayed. He thought he was going to vomit, just like Kevin Heilshorn had.

He closed his eyes. He could hear Delaney and Skene mumbling behind him. Skene sounded agitated, incredulous. Delaney was placating. A moment later, Delaney walked over and put a hand on Brendan's shoulder.

"You alright?"

"Of course, sir."

"Don't let him get to you," Delaney whispered. "He's a fucking prick. It's an election year. Now come on. Stand up. It's almost over."

Brendan slowly got to his feet. He felt lightheaded, but the sensation was starting to subside. He looked at the house. With sweat in his eyes, it took on the look of a looming funhouse, pitching and yawing. He wiped the moisture away with the back of his suit sleeve. A second later, he took off the jacket and tossed it in the grass.

When he looked back at Skene and Delaney, Delaney's mouth was open, his hands out in front of him, ready to minister the make-up between the prosecutor and rookie detective. Brendan said, "I have something else to show you."

Skene's flat face showed a tremor of response to this. He came over, with his weird, shit-pants walk. Delaney, a little dumbfounded, followed. As they approached, Delaney's expression tried to convey, *What aren't you telling me?*

Brendan unsnapped the sleeves of his shirt. He rolled up the cuffs to his elbows. He looked at both men, their eyes concealed behind their sunglasses. Then he turned and started towards the house.

\* \* \*

Inside, the kitchen was gloomy and refreshingly cool.

Skene goggled at everything, his eyes darting around like a kid looking for Christmas presents. Delaney wore a mildly puzzled, mildly amused expression. Both men had removed their sunglasses and perched them atop their heads – Delaney with a few wispy hairs left, Skene with thick salt-and-pepper curls.

"What are we looking at?"

For a moment, Brendan saw Delaney's eyes drop to the pile of knives on the butcher's block. Brendan shot Delaney a look that conveyed: *It's not the knives.* They walked further into the room, passing the appliances, including the new dishwasher, the sink, the counter space, the spice rack and two hanging bunches of dried herbs, and through into another room.

Brendan flipped the light switch.

The large oval, antique dining table had a leaf added to its center. Eight chairs were around it. As Brendan had told Skene outside, the furniture was thick with dust. Silken cobwebs were festooned around the corners of the room. There were no placemats or adornments to the table except for two cast iron candelabras, giving the whole set-up a rather macabre feel. Flanking the table were two banks of cabinetry, all white, with small wood knobs on the drawers. Fine dinnerware was stored in the top glass cabinets.

In between the rows of drawers and upper glass-front cabinets, was an open shelf. Other candles and candle holders sat there, as well as a basket of faded cloth napkins. Everything was covered in dust. Including the dozen or more framed photographs.

"This is how I've come to suspect that Rebecca and Kevin are, in fact, brother and sister," said Brendan. He pointed to a photo, a studio portrait of the victim, perhaps only eighteen, and a fifteen or sixteen-year-old Kevin. The young Rebecca was posed behind the young Kevin. Her smile looked genuine, his perhaps a little manufactured. Skene began to drift through the room, lit by the overhead chandelier. While the faces in the frames, too, were covered with a film of dust, there was no mistaking them. Here was Kevin and Rebecca again, even younger, with two older people.

"Bops and Ma'am," said Brendan.

Delaney glanced across the table at him. The senior investigator was on the other side, where more photos decorated the other shelf. "The parents," he inferred.

Brendan nodded. He returned his attention to the last photo in the display on his side of the room. There were others – Bops standing next to a guide boat; a mountain vista with the four of them posing in tourist's garb; a prom picture (Rebecca was a beautiful girl); and a young man in a black and white photo – likely Bops in his prime – standing shirtless next to the open hood of a cherry muscle car. But the last one had been what Brendan had been unable to get out of his mind all day. "This one here is of particular interest," he said. "And one over where Detective Delaney is standing that would seem to correspond to it."

He pointed to the picture, in an ornate gold frame, of Rebecca Heilshorn. Here she looked almost the same age as the girl who had stared at Brendan in the reflection of the mirror this morning, her eyes haunted, her mouth open. Here, she was the portrait of happiness, and why not? She held a beautiful bouncing baby girl on her lap.

The child, only a few months old, had a bow on her nearly bald head.

Skene looked at the image for a moment. Something may have struck him, but he dismissed it, Brendan thought.

"So she has a child," said Skene. "Or it's her niece. Or a friend's kid. What does it mean? How does it help us?"

Brendan turned to Delaney. He nodded at a frame propped on the shelf on the senior investigator's side of the table. Delaney got the message. Typically cavalier, Delaney picked up the frame with his bare hands, studied it for a second, then faced it forward and held it out over the table for Skene, who leaned in to see.

This picture showed Rebecca and the child again. The child appeared to be about the same age.

"As you can see, the victim has company in this photograph," said Brendan.

A man was standing next to Rebecca, just behind her. He was in his late thirties, dark-haired, dark-eyed, handsome, smiling. It appeared, in all ways, to be a quaint family photo.

"With any luck," said Brendan, "we have his size-eleven boot print from where he kicked in the door upstairs. As soon as the pathologist finishes the investigation of the body, we could have his blood and semen, too."

Skene remained fixed on the picture. He only glanced at Brendan briefly.

"I don't believe in luck," he said.

## CHAPTER EIGHT / THURSDAY, 3:12 PM

Donald Kettering was cordial and cooperative on the telephone. He invited Brendan to come and see him at his hardware store in Boonville, a village ten miles north of Remsen. He left the offices of the Sheriff's Department in Oriskany, got in the Camry and drove with the AC on. Oriskany was south of Rome, and the drive up to Boonville took an hour. Brendan took a route that went up 26 and entered Boonville from the west. Along the way he found himself thinking of the past.

Kettering looked the same as he did in the photo. Clean-cut, with a kempt appearance. He wore a fresh pair of Carhartt work pants and a button down white chambray work-shirt with an incongruous geometrically-patterned tie. His smile revealed Chiclet white teeth, and his grip was firm and dry as he shook Brendan's hands on the steps outside of "Kettering's," his eponymous hardware and appliance store on Erwin Street. There was no wedding ring on his finger.

Boonville was bigger than Remsen, with a population of almost five thousand. Erwin Street was busy with traffic and people out running errands. The sun was just past its zenith overhead, and the pavement and sidewalk radiated heat. Kettering invited Brendan into the store, where it was cooler and darker.

"We're actually not so much a summer town, really," Kettering said as he led Brendan further into the store. There was white tile underfoot, scuffed but squeaky clean. Brendan noticed that the front door was left open, even though the air conditioning inside was blasting. Kettering either had money to burn or wasn't thrifty. "But we're more of a winter place," he said. "'The Snow Capital of the East.'" He turned as he walked, slowing his pace, and frowned. "But you probably know all that, I'm sorry. This is your county. You probably know every nook and cranny. I just start rattling on when a new face shows up. It's the salesman in me." He smiled, showing his white teeth again.

He was in considerably good spirits for a man who'd been told, thirty minutes ago, that someone he was close to was dead. Then again, he had a business to run, and keeping up appearances was probably second nature to him. Brendan wondered if he would take a day, shut down. Then again, the detective didn't know the extent of the man's relationship with the deceased woman. He had decided to save his questions until they were in person.

"I don't mind," Brendan said about Kettering's exposition. Brendan had a chance to glance down one or two aisles – racks of nuts, bolts, and washers, cans of house paint stacked ceiling-high, a wall of uncut keys, and a duplication machine – before Kettering said, "My office is right back here."

He led Brendan around a long white counter where a young male employee with a rash of acne looked back at Brendan with a mixture of awe and fear. The youth's eyes seemed to probe Brendan's person for where his firearm might be tucked away. Brendan offered a reassuring smile.

They went through an open door and into a decent-sized space. It was at the back of the building, and two windows overlooked a parking area outside.

"Please take a seat."

Brendan sat in one of two chairs across from what looked like a school-teacher's desk, a double pedestal model. Kettering sat down and his chair squeaked. Behind him was a peg board filled with bulletins, flyers, newspaper clippings, and pictures. There were filing cabinets, a small couch beneath one of the windows, and an exercise bike.

"Thank you," said Brendan as he got comfortable. He added, "I really don't mind hearing about the town. I try not to hide the fact that I'm new here. A big snowmobile destination?"

Kettering lit up even brighter. "Oh, absolutely. That's when things get really booming in Boonville. The Oneida County Fair, the Woodsman Field Days, really great events, without a doubt, but the Snow Festivals are one of a kind. We're the only village in Upstate New York to really do winter right, if you ask me. Up Saranac Lake they have a nice Winter Carnival, too, historic and all that. These Snow Festivals we got though . . . boy."

Brendan watched Kettering's enthusiasm dwindle as he settled into the business at hand. "So, how can I help you? I mean, this is . . . a terrible tragedy. Terrible." His facial features rearranged into a properly downcast expression.

Brendan put a small tape recorder on the desk. "Is this okay with you? Otherwise you can go and give your official statement at the office. But then you have to take a trip and repeat yourself."

Kettering only glanced at the recorder. "That's fine."

"How long have you known Rebecca Heilshorn?"

He leaned back and his chair squawked again. His eyes rolled up to the ceiling, and he rubbed at his closely-shaven chin. "Oh jeeze, now. Let me think. We met in . . . oh I think it was three years ago?"

"How did you meet?"

"Right here," he said with notable pride. "Right in my store. She was getting some hardware for the house. She came back two more times, and I asked her out for a cup of coffee."

"And then you were together? I'm sorry to ask such a personal question."

"No, no, I understand."

Kettering leaned forward now, resting his elbows on the desk, his eyes still darting around. "I understand. We, uh, well, we dated a little while, if you could call it that. We'd go for walks, I'd meet her at the house – the whole thing was kind of under the pretense that I could help her fix it up. But it never came to that, really. She was always coming and going from the area. Hard girl to pin down." He offered a laugh and a wink. "So, I don't know, for about two years we saw each other on and off."

"What was she doing up here?"

"Well, first she was meeting with the realtors, and those types. Then, you know, closing. All of that stuff takes so much time. She was coming back and forth, back and forth."

"To buy the house?"

Kettering raised his eyebrows. "Oh, right. Sorry, yes, I wasn't sure what, you know, what of the particulars you already had."

"Assume I know nothing."

A look from Kettering. "They bought the old Bloomingdale farm."

"The place south of here, about eight miles."

"That's right. Everyone calls it the Bloomingdale farm. There's been a lot of development in this area over recent years, but that farm, that's been there . . . jeeze, since the area was settled. Early 1800s, maybe. It's been redone, you know, this patched up, that. I think the original barn caved in and a new one was erected in the 70s. But it was originally built by Arnold Bloomingdale."

"Why was Rebecca interested in it, do you think?"

Again, Kettering seemed to pause for some silent evaluation. It was only a second or two, but Brendan couldn't help but record it in his mind. "I couldn't honestly tell you. I've met them, you know. Alex and Greta. I think the kids call them Bops and Ma'am. Very nice people." His eyes seemed to narrow a bit. "Very wealthy. Different sort of people than everyday folks like you and me. Know what I mean?"

"Money can change you, sure. Or, you're born with it. So she was brokering a deal for her parents? Not buying the house herself?"

"It was their money, if that's what you mean, yes."

"But she came here for hardware, you said. Before she bought the place she was making repairs?"

Kettering blinked, seeming momentarily derailed. "No, ah, she was staying in a little rental right here in Boonville. Sometimes she stayed at motels, she told me, but then she rented this little place. If I recall, there was a leak, and she wanted to fix it herself. She was very self-reliant."

Brendan made a mental note to look into this rental situation later. "Does she have any siblings?"

Another pause. "Her brother, Kevin."

"No others?"

"Not that I know of, sir. Why?"

"Well, I've met Kevin, actually. He made a comment about how he was 'the last in a line of token children.'"

Kettering sat back again, giving this consideration. "I see. Well, again. Different strokes. You know, some of these wealthy types, they don't have children always out of love. It may be, what's the word?"

"Perfunctory."

"That's it. To have an heir, to pass on the family business."

"And what is their business?"

"That I couldn't quite tell you," said Kettering. "It's all Greek to me once it gets up into the mega millions. After that, it just seems that money makes money. I think he's in medicine, though."

"Alexander Heilshorn."

"Yuh."

"So it might be new money. Some sort of patent, or investment. Maybe a company that has done very well."

Kettering scowled with thought. "Rebecca said something once about her father having his finger on the pulse when it came to biotechnology. A technocrat, she may have said. But, even though we were fond of each other, there was this air of . . . what do I want to say? They were just private about it. I didn't ask."

"And you never married Rebecca."

Kettering came to a full stop this time. He stopped moving, his face stopped emoting. He seemed to look across the desk at Brendan like he was an auditor. "No," he said.

"Can I ask why?"

"You can, but I don't know that I can tell you that, either. It wasn't for lack of trying, I can tell you that."

"So you proposed."

"Not in so many words, but yes. We talked about marriage. I brought it up. She's . . . Rebecca is several years younger than me. I'll be fifty in December. So, there's that." He seemed to grow uncomfortable.

Brendan decided to push a little further. "Was she afraid her parents wouldn't approve?"

It took him a moment, and Kettering found the words. "Rebecca was very independent. I know that's, ah, maybe incongruous with how it looks, her buying a place with her parents' money and living there, but she didn't do anything she didn't want to. And she did do the things she wanted to do. You see what I'm saying?"

"Yes. You're being very helpful, Mr. Kettering, and I appreciate it."

He seemed to soften a little, to revert back to the glad-handing salesman. "Feel free to call me Donald."

"Thanks, Donald. Just a few more things I'd like to ask and then I'll get out of your hair."

"It's no trouble." A cloud seemed to pass over him. "Jesus, this is just terrible. How did she die?"

Brendan was careful. He had told Kettering on the phone that Rebecca Heilshorn's death was unnatural, but had left it there. "She was viciously assaulted and murdered," he said now.

Donald Kettering put a hand over his mouth. Through his fingers he said, "As in . . . beat up? Shot?"

"I'm sorry I can't say just how. But to call it foul play would be an understatement."

"Terrible. Oh my God." Kettering took his hand away and looked out the window over the couch.

"It is. And I'm sorry for your loss. When did you last see Rebecca?"

His gaze lingered on the parking lot outside. His voice was distant. "Oh, well, has to have been a year." Now his eyes came back and focused on Brendan. "Yes, about a year."

"No phone calls during that time? Emails, anything?"

He shrugged his shoulders. "No. When Rebecca broke something off, she broke it off."

"So, if I may, you dated for about two years. But then you became . . . more serious?"

He nodded. His face seemed to contort with a painful memory and he looked down at his desk. Brendan leaned forward a little. "What is it?"

Kettering shook his head. He seemed to snap out of something. "It's just. I just can't believe this."

"Did you live together?"

"No. She wanted her space."

"But you were exclusive."

His eyes came up. They had a haunted look. "I hope so, Detective."

"And this went on for how long?"

"Just about a year."

"How about friends? Did the two of you go out to dinner, double-date? Who did Rebecca know in the area?"

"Nada. Zip," said Kettering. "We never did anything, despite my trying. We went to the mall once to buy some things for the house. I mean, we would go to dinner every once in a while if I pried her, but she was always looking around like she didn't want to be seen. She never talked about any friends."

"Really? Not even an acquaintance? Someone that knew her at the local bakery, let's say? Anything. You see, the details are critical to this investigation. Where she may have been the night before the tragedy is very important. Who she might have been with. I hate to ask this again, but you're sure you were exclusive? She didn't see other people?"

"No. She was. Ah, I don't want to sound cruel here. She was frigid."

"You two never . . ."

"Oh we did. We did. But, you know."

"I understand. And there's no one, not a single name you can think of, someone she may have talked to, even just once or twice?"

Kettering looked like he was probing his memory. His grimaced and said, "There was a vegetable stand we stopped at a couple of times. She thought the woman who worked there was nice. A little blue hair." He held up his hands. "That's it."

Brendan nodded. "Okay. If you think of anyone, anyone or anything else at all, you'll please call me, alright?"

"Alright."

"Okay," said Brendan. "Almost finished."

Kettering said nothing. The armor of his convivial nature, it appeared, had been penetrated.

"What about Rebecca's child?"

Light came back into the man's eyes again. Brendan saw a few things Donald Kettering seemed to countenance at once: protectiveness, love, pain, and vulnerability.

Like a parent, thought Brendan.

"Leah," said Kettering, pronouncing it *lay-uh*.

"Leah? That's the girl's name? Is she yours, Donald?"

A tear slipped out of the corner of the man's eye, which he wiped away with a knuckle. "No," he said. "She's not."

Brendan's voice was soft. The room was very quiet. "So she was Rebecca's child with another man. When did you first meet her?"

"Not until Rebecca finally moved in. She brought Leah up only a few times. Once was . . . I guess two years ago. I convinced her to go to the mall with me in Rome. They have a, uh, you know, a studio there." He frowned. "I know it's old hat, getting pictures done in a mall – everyone just snaps cell phone pictures today. But I wanted to. It was our anniversary."

"I understand," said Brendan. "That was a nice idea." He shifted a little in his seat.

Kettering looked positively broken. He hunched forward, staring down at his desk.

"Did you ever meet Leah's father?"

Kettering's head came up, and something flashed in his dark eyes. "No," he said. "And she never wanted to talk about him. Rebecca just . . ." Now he pushed back from the desk, the chair pealing out another rusty squawk, and turned his head to the side and put a hand to his mouth. He was a man showing frustration; it was an outlet, perhaps, from grief. Like putting on a happy face might be.

"She was just . . . she just did as she pleased, like I said. If she didn't want to do it, she didn't do it. Didn't want to get married, didn't want to move in. Leah mostly stayed away from the area. And I would say, 'Just come up here full time. I have enough money, you don't need anything. We can make a home for Leah. We can make a life.'" He reached out his hands then, as if seeking to embrace that phantom life, and then dropped them on his lap and blew air out of his lips. "But I guess little Boonville, little hick-ville, wasn't it for her. I don't know what was *it* for that girl. It wasn't me, I know that. It wasn't this. But she was after . . . something."

He turned, finally, and looked at Brendan, and his mien evoked a kind of man-to-man attitude now. "I don't even live in Boonville. I have a beautiful place in Alder Creek. Right on Kayuta Lake. Just beautiful. Perfect place for a kid to grow up. Just . . . you know."

"I know," said Brendan consolingly. "Can you give me the name of Leah's father?"

"Eddie," Donald said. "That's all I know."

"Thank you. Last question, Donald. Can someone, maybe one of your employees, place you here between seven and nine this morning?"

Kettering stopped and inhaled through his nostrils. He folded his hands together for a moment, and seemed to be getting a hold of himself. "Of course. You can talk to Jason Pert, right out at the counter. He comes in at eight, after I open the shop at seven-thirty. Or Community Bank, just down the street, where I was right at nine. Or, if you need something earlier, I stopped at a little place in Forestport for coffee and a breakfast sandwich at seven this morning."

Brendan was nodding. "Thank you. That's more than enough. I'll just have a word with Mr. Pert on the way out and that will be it."

Brendan picked up the recorder, shut it off, and stood. Kettering stood, too. They shook hands again across the desk. "I can show myself out," Brendan said. "Thank you so much for your time. You've been immensely helpful."

Kettering, for once, didn't seem to have anything to say. He just nodded.

## CHAPTER NINE / THURSDAY, 4:08 PM

He was a few minutes late arriving at Olivia Jane's house, just outside of Barneveld. She lived in a Cape Cod-style house with a columned, wrap-around porch. The home was on Trenton Falls Road and sat across from a river that burbled softly in the afternoon. Brendan stepped out of the air conditioned Camry, the atmosphere was hazy and humid, the heat cloying, like a thick blanket. With any luck it would start to burn off in the next hour. The radio claimed the temperature had hit 95 in Utica.

He had parked in the driveway behind her pea-green Aztec, and now walked up the short path to the front door. She must have heard his approach, because the door swung open before he reached the bottom of the steps to the porch.

"Hi," she said. She had traded in her blue jeans for a pair of brown shorts, and her white blouse for a red tank top. Her brown hair was tied back showing her forehead dewy with perspiration. A smudge of dirt was on her jawline. "Come on in. I'm just pulling some more vegetables."

Brendan smiled and walked into the house, which was cooler than the outside, but not by much. The place was roomy. An open area just inside the doors turned right into a dining area and kitchen, left into a living room with two couches facing each other and a baby grand piano in the far corner. Straight ahead were mahogany stairs that went up to the second floor.

Olivia walked past the small dining table and through the kitchen and into a back mudroom, Brendan close behind. "Come outside if you wouldn't mind," she said, and headed out a back door and into a vibrant garden.

There was a wheelbarrow in one of the paths between the raised beds of vegetables and wildflowers. In the wheelbarrow was a crop of carrots, and what looked like rutabaga, beets, squash, beans, and more. "Wow," said Brendan.

"I love the harvest," she said. "I've just got this last row and then I can clean up and we can talk. But we can talk too, now, absolutely. I'll just be . . . let me just tend to this last bit."

"Of course," Brendan smiled, and added, "I don't feel so bad for being late."

She was already on her knees and leaning forward into a row of green sprigs of something. She lifted her head and turned to look at him. "Are you late? What time is it?"

He took out his cell phone. "4:10."

She turned back to what she was doing. "Wow. It never ceases to amaze me how I just get lost out here."

"I'll bet. What have you got?"

She looked at him again, unsure what he meant.

"For a yield, I mean. What did you grow?"

"Oh. Everything and anything that will grow. Cucumber, peas, celery, beets, carrots, you name it. There's some potatoes in that barrel there on the end. And herbs. Cilantro, Oregano, Basil, Dill, Mint. It's tough to grow mint."

"It is?"

"It looks like clematis. It just blends in. Chives are easy. Chives grow if you stomp on them and call them bad names. They just keep growing."

"Resilient."

He put his hands in his pockets, and suddenly felt strangely self-conscious. He found himself looking down at his appearance. He was wearing jean-like khaki pants and monk strap shoes, black. He had changed his shirt at the office before going to Boonville – it had been soaked with sweat – and opted for another button down, white. He felt oddly overdressed, like he ought to be in jeans and a t-shirt. He wondered how Olivia Jane kept her hours. Here it was mid-week and she was gardening at four p.m. Likely she made her own schedule.

"So," he said, "How does it work? With your . . . field? You're out on your own, so to speak?"

She nodded, her head half-buried in the greenery. "I got my licensure a few years ago after working with the county. I started my own private practice. Thing is, grief very often doesn't want to come to you. You have to go to it."

"Denial," he said softly.

She retreated from the garden bed and glanced at him approvingly. "Exactly. The first step in the process of absorbing a tragedy or a loss doesn't exactly get them out and about and ready to talk feelings."

Her attention returned to the vegetables. She started pulling several out, clumping them together. Bright orange carrots. "So I continue to work with Oneida, but it's not at the clinic. They call me when someone has . . . well, you know."

"Right. So, how was he?"

"Well," she said, grunting and getting to her feet, "that's a good question." She turned and dropped the bunch of carrots in the wheel barrow. Then she dusted off her hands. "Let me go wash up. You drink iced coffee?"

"Sure."

"Okay. Thanks for letting me finish that up. I hate leaving things undone."

"Me too," he said. He followed her back into the house.

* * *

She sat him at the dining room table. The white curtains blew in the breeze coming in from the casement windows, which were swung open about half the way. She washed up and spent only a minute making the iced coffee – there was already coffee brewed in a pot on the stove, and she poured this over ice cubes, and added milk and sugar, per his approval. Then she sat down across from him.

"Kevin is experiencing the acute loss of his sister, of that there is no question," she said, affecting an instantaneously professional demeanor. "He also is a very troubled young guy."

"In what way?"

She shrugged. "In every way. He resents his family, he is shiftless, without a job or what he feels is a calling. He doesn't want his family's money but he needs to live, so he feels bad about taking an allowance. He has no spiritual ballast that he can describe. He's basically atheist, which there isn't anything wrong with, but in his case, he's searching for something."

"Where was he this morning? At the motel?"

She raised an eyebrow. "That's where your job begins and mine ends, Mr. Healy. I didn't inquire as to his whereabouts. I tried to help him deal with the pain and loss of his departed older sister. My job is to help people try to find the coping mechanisms in their own lives to help them face the immense challenges that come with the loss of a loved one. It's not easy. Most people, they do what they know how to do. They drink, they retreat into themselves, they engage in some sort of compulsive behavior, anything to keep distracted, to keep the pain and grief away. I'm not all rah rah, siss boom bah, bring on the pain; that's not the point. You don't try to cultivate grief where there is none, or make yourself suffer if you are not. Sure, there's healing in a good cry, but some people just don't cry. Kevin, he's not a stoic. I think his father is, but he's not. He's more sensitive. But he has no way to cope that I could see, or he could share with me."

"He seemed okay when I was with him," Brendan said. He raised a hand from his coffee to indicate he wasn't being argumentative. "I mean, he was certainly distraught. Which is why I wanted him to see . . . someone. But he seemed to be dealing."

He made a mental note that Olivia had mentioned the father, Alex, as if she knew something about him.

"Sure, Kevin was dealing. I deal. You deal. We all deal. We're more afraid of social impropriety than we are of actual, physical pain. That's been shown in studies. It's true. We'll choose a broken arm over a public humiliation any old day of the week. That's a lead-pipe cinch as my grandmother would say. We're conditioned from a young age to have manners, be polite, speak in turn, and so on, until it becomes like a part of our DNA, like an instinct, like adrenaline. It's actually quite easy to act like nothing is wrong."

"A huge habit," he offered.

"That's right. Unless someone is oppositional-defiant, or has an anti-social personality, or these types of things, they tend to be very afraid of bad social graces."

"And you don't think he has any of these . . . things you said?"

"I don't know, Mr. Healy. I just met him. I couldn't diagnose that. Besides, that's not my area. I work with grieving people. People who have just been in crisis. Their personalities, or any disorders certainly have bearing on how they cope with that grief, but I tend to consult with other therapists about that, wherever possible. Psychiatrists sometimes, too."

"But you said he was volatile."

"I said he was troubled. And that's not to mince words. Is there something troubling you in particular?" Her eyes were kind but direct and no-nonsense.

"It's just that he lied to me."

"About?"

"He said his sister, the victim, had no children. But, as it turns out, she does."

He could have been mistaken, but he thought he saw something pass over Olivia's features. A memory, perhaps, or something she chose to keep internalized.

Her mouth opened. "He needs a grief counselor, and I'd . . ."

As she spoke, Brendan heard the approach of a motorcycle on the road along the river. It made the noise of some giant, angry wasp. Olivia must have sensed Brendan's distractedness, because she abruptly stopped talking. But she heard the bike, too, which now sounded like it was slowing. She opened her mouth again, perhaps to comment on the traffic outside her home, when the window exploded behind Brendan's head.

The first thought that flashed through his mind was that the bike had driven right up to the house and launched into it. This dissonant, unrealistic notion was followed less than a second later by the idea that a rock or some other heavy object had been thrown. Neither of these scenarios smacked of the truth, but they passed lightning-fast through Brendan's mind before more gunshots slapped the air.

* * *

The window exploded again, and Brendan launched himself from the table and hit the floor. He started crawling on his hands and knees around to the other side of the table as splinters of glass rained down around him. Olivia was half out of her seat by the time he reached her. Her arms were thrown up over her head and she was bent to one side. Brendan reached up and grabbed her by the elbow and yanked her down to the floor with him.

He had counted seven shots in all. His ears were ringing. The floor was covered in shining glass shards that glinted in the sunlight. Olivia was taking deep, startled breaths. She was trying to get up; some instinct was telling her to stand upright and look, perhaps to see who was firing, or assess the damage, or run away. Brendan held her fast. "Stay down," he whispered.

There was one more shot. A bullet punched into the exterior of the house, missing the window this time. The shooter was just far enough away that the velocity of the bullet and the time for the sound to travel were about the same. The impact and the explosion of gunpowder had created a simultaneous boom. Then, silence. Brendan waited to hear the motorcycle take off again, and roar away down the road. His ears still rang with the resonance of all the shattering glass. He didn't hear the motorcycle engine rev up to speed again. Instead, he thought he heard someone approaching on foot.

The shooter had gotten off the bike and was walking up to the house. Even through the ringing in his ears, Brendan thought he could make out the sound of a fresh clip of ammunition being slammed home. The shooter was coming, and he had just reloaded.

"Jesus Christ," breathed Brendan. He scrambled to get to his feet, keeping bent at the waist. He bent and reached for Olivia, who was on her side, drawn up into a fetal position, her arms wrapped protectively around her head. He pulled her arm, and she looked up with wide eyes. She seemed to understand what was happening, based on his expression. She rolled over onto her front and with his help got to her feet, as well.

"Come on." He took her hand in his. Together, bent in this running-from-the-helicopter fashion, they headed towards the back of the house. As they entered the kitchen, Brendan glanced behind them. There on the front porch, the shooter stepped into view. He was just a shape in the doorway, a dark human form behind the white linen curtain that hung in the front door window. A second later, the door flew open.

Brendan faced forward again. He pulled on Olivia and they ran through the kitchen and into the mudroom area, and then into the rear of the house, where the back door led to the garden. The shooter opened fire. As Brendan and Olivia exited out the back, the kitchen was exploding. Ceramic dishes and jars of things were smashed to bits by the rounds pumped into the space. At the last second, just before Brendan and Olivia leapt down the three steps onto the ground in back of the house, one bullet penetrated the wood of the door casing, while another slapped a groove in the air just next to Brendan's ear. The shooter had come into the kitchen and gotten a straight line of sight.

They almost lost their balance when the two of them hit the grass. Brendan managed to keep his feet underneath him, and still had a good grip on Olivia, though she was mostly making it on her own. He considered letting go of her now that they were outside; they would make smaller targets on their own. Further, he couldn't get to his weapon, strapped to a holster next to the left side of his torso, unless he had his hands free. But he held on to her, anyway.

He looked around. Beyond the half dozen garden beds was a small shed. It had a sharp angled roof and a single door in front. At the peak of the roof it was probably only six feet, and the steep pitch would make it very cramped in there. Not a good place to get stuck in. Surrounding it were higher grasses, some giant sunflowers, and cattails. He threw a glance to his right: Olivia's single car garage was there. To the left, more high grass and then trees. There were no visible neighbors. He opted to get them around to the other side of the garage. If they could keep the shooter following them, Brendan thought maybe they could buy a few precious seconds, then make like hell for his car and get away.

He turned in that direction, pushing Olivia gently but firmly. She glanced up at him and then to where he was looking and again seemed to understand his intention. Just as they started in that direction, the shooter materialized in the doorway overlooking the garden. It might have taken him a second to see them through the boscages of high grasses and flowers, or he may have just been watching which way they were going before opening fire again.

There were three shots. As they ran, Olivia jerked to the side, as if hit. The two of them stumbled again and for a second Brendan was sure they were about to tangle up and fall to the ground in a heap, making themselves fatally vulnerable to the gunman. But she kept her balance, and the two of them made it to the garage and ran behind it.

\* \* \*

As soon as they had cover, Brendan let go of Olivia and pressed her against the wall to stop her from moving and to look her over.

"Are you okay?"

He saw no blood. She nodded, wide-eyed, her mouth open, and she then looked down at her feet. *Ankle*, the gesture seemed to say. She might have twisted it. As they were having this exchange, Brendan had pulled his pistol – a .38 special – from its holster and had opened the wheel and checked it. Back in Westchester, old Argon had sworn by the .38, claimed it was the most reliable handgun, and had taught Brendan how to handle it adroitly, even under great pressure. He slapped the wheel in place and cocked the hammer.

He had just enough time to say to Olivia, "I'm going to fire on him, then we're going to make it to my . . ." when a fresh round bored into the corner of the garage, dislodging a small chunk of cement.

Brendan gauged the height of the shot and calibrated his next move. He dropped down and stepped out from the cover of the garage and took aim. The shooter was right in the middle of the garden, standing near the barrel of potatoes and almost in the bed of recently harvested carrots. His gun was aimed in Brendan's direction.

It was Kevin Heilshorn.

Brendan fired. Kevin fired back a split second later, but his shot went wide. Brendan had hit him. The round from the .38 seemed to tag the young man along one side of his neck or jaw. Brendan had shot from a low angle, and had compensated by aiming upwards, but his angle had been a little steeper than he would have liked; he'd intended in hitting Kevin in the ribs or stomach. A man-stopper wound, but less chance of fatality. The bullet contacted higher than Brendan would have hoped.

He couldn't risk lingering even for an instant, however, and so ducked back behind the cover of the garage. He reached for Olivia to grab her up again, but his hand only found air. He snapped his head around to look and saw that she was already gone. He followed her most likely path around the back of the garage, where he had wanted to go anyway. As he rounded the next corner he saw her, pressing along through the tall grass that abutted the building, running her hand along the concrete wall. He quickly caught up to her. By the time they were at the front of the garage they were together, and Brendan was able to reach out and clutch a handful of her tank top to keep her from going any further. He had no choice but to yank on her to stop her momentum and get in front, so he could clear the way.

The garage door was open. To the right was the house. There was a small space – just a few feet – between the buildings. For the moment, they remained concealed from the shooter's view. But as soon as they left the shelter of the garage, they would be instantly visible through that gap.

Brendan was calm. His heart beat good tympani in his chest and his nerves hummed. He didn't know where this steeliness came from and didn't question it. He simply pitched himself forward, leaving Olivia behind for the moment, his .38 thrust out in front of him, gripped with both hands. As he moved forward, he swiveled right at his waist. The space between the garage and the back corner of the house grew in size, and the view of the garden opened up. Kevin was there, having anticipated Brendan's trajectory. The young man was holding his neck with one hand, and aiming his firearm with the other. He fired. A bullet droned past Brendan's head, missing him by inches. Brendan returned fire. Two shots, in rapid succession – *bang bang.* He was in motion, so he knew his accuracy would suffer. But the rounds hit home. It was hard to see where – only that Kevin Heilshorn crumpled to the ground.

Olivia was just behind Brendan. She stopped and turned to look, and she cried out.

"Back!" Brendan growled. He shouldered up to her and pushed with the side of his body against her, so that she would get back in front of garage and out of the line of fire. He kept both his hands on his .38. Once she was safely out of Kevin's view, Brendan started moving in.

The young man had fallen mostly out of sight, hidden by green thickets of something like squash or cucumber. Brendan could only see Kevin's feet, and one of his hands. It was the hand that had been holding his neck, and it was streaked with blood.

Slowly, carefully, Brendan passed through the opening between the house and garage and into the garden area. Kevin was prone just a few yards away. The lowering sun glimmered through the neighboring trees, while the house threw a large rectangular darkness over the greenery. The stalks of grass and copses of vegetables still in the sun painted shadow-webs over the ground. The afternoon held the heat from the earlier day, but a cool breeze moved in from the trees surrounding the place, and some leaves detached and drifted into the garden area, twirling to the ground to rest.

Kevin Heilshorn was on his back. Brendan spied the gun – a Glock pistol, by the look of it – a few inches from his open hand. The young man was staring up at the sky. He had fallen into one of the raised garden beds, and his hips were out-thrust since he had landed across the wooden gusset of the bed. There was blood everywhere. On the vegetables, on the grass, on Kevin's clothes and skin. A tear just below his jaw, where the round had nicked his carotid artery, was oozing dark fluid. Brendan could smell the metallic odor of blood amid the flowery scents of the garden.

Kevin was breathing. Brendan stood over him with the .38 aimed down. Cautiously, with an even, smooth movement, he bent and reached for the Glock pistol. He pinched it by the handle-grip and lifted it up and tossed it to the side, just beyond the bed. Then Brendan stood back up.

Kevin Heilshorn's eyes rolled down to look at Brendan Healy. His breaths were shallow and rapid. His artery pumped out the blood into the garden bed where it was sucked into the dark, rich soil.

*Why?* Brendan wanted to ask. He suddenly felt nauseous, his calm broken at last. He felt hurt too, as if there were something terribly wrong with this scene, and more than just the obvious gore and violence of it. Looking down at this twenty-five-year-old man, with his surfer blond hair, his good looks, his grief and torment, Brendan felt like he was looking at a victim, not a killer.

Still, the young man had just driven up to the house of the psychologist, Olivia Jane, and started blasting away. He had attacked a woman and a police detective in broad daylight, with a kind of machine-like determination. He had put Brendan in a situation where the detective had no choice but to protect himself and the woman, and take deadly action.

*Why?*

The question lingered. Brendan sensed Olivia very gingerly approaching from behind him. He took his free hand and reached down to his belt and plucked his cell phone from its holder. He brought it in front of his face and dialed 911. He pressed the phone to his ear.

During all this, Kevin Heilshorn continued to watch the detective. His eyes were alert, seeming to take everything in. His body, however, remained motionless. Brendan had shot the young man in the neck, in the arm, and in the chest.

Brendan felt detached, as if operating his muscles now from somewhere remote. He heard himself talking to the 911 operator. He gave her his name and badge number with practiced ease. He described his location, and the nature of his call. There was an officer-involved shooting. A man had been hit three times and was suffering from massive wounds. An ambulance was needed on the double. A woman had been involved and needed medical to check her out, too.

The sound of his voice was strange, as if the vocal chords belonged to someone else. He hung up and put his phone back in its holder. Brendan felt that calm continuing to slip away. His nerves no longer fired in perfect sync. He began to feel dissonant and out of touch. Warm waves of nausea filled his stomach with sourness, and there was a distant firing of pain in his gut.

"An ambulance is coming," he said to Kevin Heilshorn. But Kevin Heilshorn was dead. His eyes now looked at nothing but the picture of the last thing he had ever seen, frozen forever in his idle mind.

Brendan dropped to his knees, turned to the side, and retched into a clump of fragrant herbs.

## CHAPTER TEN / THURSDAY, 7:43 PM

"It doesn't make sense."

"It makes perfect sense. This guy is your killer. And you want to hear why?"

Brendan sat back and inhaled slowly through his nostrils. He was on the couch in Delaney's office. Through the glass wall between Delaney's office, the hallway, and senior Deputy – a woman named Benedetto, he could see Olivia Jane. He watched her lips moving as she gave her statement to the officer.

Brendan's head pounded. The Sheriff's Department offices seemed more cramped and garish than he remembered. He longed to be outside and away somewhere, but he knew he needed to stay. He needed to remain in the right headspace, figure this thing out. Delaney seemed like he already had closed the case. He didn't wait for Brendan to respond and ask why the senior investigator had it right.

"Because I got the PERK kit back from the deputy coroner," he said. Delaney was standing next to his desk. He picked up a large file and tossed it casually into Brendan's lap. "And there's some sick shit in there."

Brendan looked down at the file. He pulled his hand away from his neck where he had been gently massaging the same spot where Kevin Heilshorn had been gushing blood. For some reason he didn't want to turn back the cover of that file. He didn't want to see what was inside. But, he had to.

Delaney rambled on. If ever there was a movie with a surprise ending, Brendan thought, Delaney would ruin it for everyone if he got half the chance. The large, balding detective said, almost excitedly: "He was balling the sister. We found evidence of, you know, promiscuity in the victim's PERK kit. Something about the vaginal lining. She's had many sexual partners. There's a good chance one will turn out to be the brother."

"You're kidding," said Brendan. Of course, there was nothing funny about it. He started to feel sick to his stomach again. He stood up, letting the file fall from his lap onto the couch, spilling some of its contents. He reached and leaned and grabbed Delaney's trash can and then slid it back across the floor to him. Delaney watched all of this like a man watching an injured bird flit around on the ground flapping one wing. He scrunched up his face. Then the kinder Delaney re-emerged.

"You okay?"

Brendan leaned over the trash can. "Yeah," he said. His voice echoed.

"You'll have to talk to the IACP right away, you know. I can help you with all of that. That's the tough part, talking to those guys, filling all that stuff out. But, it's got to be done. You, uh, you ever . . .?"

"No." He had never shot anyone in the line of duty before.

"You did an amazing job. Seriously. From what I've put together, just outstanding. The Sheriff is going to be here in a minute to talk to you."

"I don't think he did it," said Brendan.

"Think?" Delaney now reverted back to the bit of a hardcase he could often be. Brendan imagined that he also kept it as tight as possible with Senior Prosecutor Skene, and Brendan had heard a rumor that the ADA, a woman named Selena Joanette, was riding his flagpole.

"There's nothing to think," said Delaney. "The kid was at the scene of the crime. He fought with deputies. And I guarantee you that his fluids will match up with the serology report." Delaney wagged a finger at Brendan. "You said yourself he described some vague 'meeting' with the victim. You know how these weird, superrich families can be. For all we know, he and the sister were regularly involved in sexual congress."

"We don't even have the evidence yet to prove that they're even blood related," said Brendan softly. The feeling of nausea passed for the moment, and he leaned back away from the trash can.

"All the more reason, then, to suspect. He could be an adopted brother, for all we know. But, we'll clear all that up within a couple of hours. I just don't understand how you can argue this kid's culpability when he shows up and opens fire on you. I've been an investigator for thirty-one years. In that time I've learned two things. One, with a homicide, it's family or close friends ninety percent of the time. Two, there are no coincidences."

"How is she?"

For a moment, Delaney acted like he didn't know who Brendan was referring to. Then he turned to look through the glass walls behind him at Olivia, talking somberly with Deputy Benedetto. "She's fine. A couple of scrapes. Some bruising on her arm."

"I mean, mentally."

Delaney shrugged. He stopped leaning on the cabinet and stood up. "I don't know. She'd know better how she was doing than I would. Look. You've got your evening cut out for you. Give your statement, don't leave out a detail. I can be there if you need me. I'll help you through.

In the meantime, I'll get the blood and toxicology report from the kid. I'm telling you, we're going to match it up with the victim's PERK, and it's going to be case opened and closed in one fucking day. Some perverted family thing."

Brendan sighed. He didn't have the energy to argue. And some of what Delaney was saying sounded convincing. It was tough to lobby for the innocence of Kevin Heilshorn given all the circumstantial evidence. None of it was enough to mount an ironclad case, not without the hard forensics, but Delaney seemed more than confident. He and Skene would be on the same page; a posthumous conviction was impossible anyway. They would be unable to pursue criminal prosecution against Heilshorn because a dead man couldn't defend himself.

Though pinning it on him would let them drop the case.

Brendan closed his eyes. The world was dark for a moment, and then Kevin Heilshorn's face swam into view. Brendan saw him staring up at the sky. He saw the blood spatter, showering the flowers and plants and vegetables. Then time moved backwards. In his mind, Kevin was standing in the garden, one hand on his neck, the other pointing the gun. Brendan pulled the trigger. Bang. Bang.

His eyes fluttered open. He got to his feet. Delaney watched him closely.

"I've got to get out of here for a minute," said Brendan. "Get some fresh air."

"Sure," said Delaney.

Brendan left the room.

## CHAPTER ELEVEN / THURSDAY, 8:18 PM

It was now twelve hours, give or take a few minutes, since Rebecca Heilshorn had been stabbed to death in her own bed. Or at least, the bed in a house owned by her family. Brendan realized that other than her previous relationship with smiling-Don Kettering and that the house was not in her name, he knew very little about the victim. Not a good spot to be in after an entire twelve hours. Granted, it had been a very eventful day, but now he had to deal with Internal Affairs and sit and explain the events at Olivia Jane's house. A necessary part of police procedure, but a hassle, and counterproductive to his needs.

Brendan lit a Marlboro and looked at the dreary street in Oriskany. The sun was setting and the shadow of the Sheriff's Department draped itself across the pavement. Brendan stepped off the curb and walked out into the street where the low sun burst from between two buildings, spangling him in light. He closed his eyes and dragged on his cigarette. He mused, just for a moment, how cigarettes were less of a concern to him later in the day than they were when he smoked in the morning.

He wished he had time to speak with Olivia, but IA was waiting for him upstairs. The sooner he got to them, the sooner it would be over. The Sheriff would be there, too.

Brendan tossed away his cigarette and returned into the three-story, grey building.

\* \* \*

On the third floor, Brendan spoke with Internal Affairs, one man and one woman, for over an hour. Sheriff Taber sat with his arms folded. He was the man who had hired Brendan, and watched the proceedings carefully. Not two months on the job and Healy was already involved in a shooting. It seemed unavoidable, and not the young detective's fault, but then again, did the Sheriff have a cowboy on his hands? Taber was trim and fit, not exactly the picture of the rotund, bumbling Sheriff stereotype. He was a health-nut, coming to work in the morning with cereal bars instead of donuts. He worked out at the gym in the building three days a week. He was young for someone holding an elected position. Perhaps since he was 48, Taber's relative youth had helped Brendan Healy get the job, since there wasn't much more than ten years between them.

"And then what happened?"

The Q&A went on and on. The windows turned black as the sun set and night filled in. The fluorescent lights buzzed overhead. Brendan could feel another headache coming on. He answered every question as plainly and articulately as he could. He left out no detail, but offered no speculation, unless it was solicited by IA. They didn't seem to care much for his professional opinion on the whys and wherefores of the events surrounding the shooting of Kevin Heilshorn. They simply wanted to record the details, and evaluate the state of mind of the detective.

At last the man and woman closed their red binders and stood up. They smiled and shook hands with Brendan, and then left him and the Sheriff alone.

Taber headed to his desk. He had been sitting on a side couch and now he moved across the room with athletic power. Brendan wondered if Olivia Jane was still in the building. He doubted it. Then again, IA could be asking her a few questions, too. More likely though, they would get her statement from Deputy Benedetto and see if it gelled with Brendan's own account of the gruesome afternoon.

The Sheriff took his chair and looked across the desk at Brendan.

"You did good." Taber leaned forward, his chair squeaking, as if he was going to say more, when a figure appeared in the door to his office. It was just the dark shape of a man, obscured by the smoky glass. There was a tentative tap-tap.

"Come in," said Taber, and sat back.

Delaney entered. He was holding a manila envelope.

"How did it go?" He looked at the Sheriff while asking the question. The Sheriff held out his hand, gesturing that Brendan ought to answer.

"Fine," said Brendan.

Delaney took the seat next to him. All three men looked at the envelope. Delaney seemed to let the moment linger, and then reached in and pulled out a book.

"From the house," he said. "It's already been processed for latent prints, everything."

He handed it to Brendan. It was a copy of *The Screwtape Letters*, by C.S. Lewis. Brendan held the book, turned it over, turned it back. It was a well-worn copy. He opened the cover and flipped through the first few pages. As he did, a small piece of paper dropped out.

"Prints came back as the victim's, and then a million others. It's a book, after all. But the note is interesting."

Brendan read the note aloud. " 'Danice, May you be lifted up by the Lord. I love you, -K.' "

"Oh boy," said Taber.

Delaney looked at the Sheriff with what Brendan thought was a certain smugness. "Read the passage."

Brendan looked at the page the slip of paper had bookmarked. A section was underlined in pencil. He lifted it closer to his face and read.

" *'The truth is, that wherever a man lies with a woman, there, whether they like it or not, a transcendental relation is set upon them which must be eternally enjoyed or eternally endured.'* "

The Sheriff furrowed his brow and wrinkled his nose, as if he had tasted something unpleasant and unfamiliar. "What does it mean?"

Brendan answered him. "It means that whenever you have sex with someone you are linked to them for all time."

"It means," said Delaney next, "That the victim, and her lover-boy brother Kevin, were doing the horizontal mambo, and then Kevin grew a conscience. Got religion, whatever."

"How do we know it's Kevin?" asked Brendan.

Delaney reached across the space between them and tapped the note Brendan was pressing to the book with his thumb. Delaney's yellowed, clam-shell fingernail tapped the letter "K."

"Right there, Colombo. 'K' for Kevin."

"But it's addressed to 'Danice'."

"Yes. I can see that. 'Danice' in quotes. A nickname. A little pet name they used for her. Maybe it was so they could correspond about their escapades in secret. Or maybe it was the name of some teddy bear she had as a girl, who she used to have go down on her. Who cares?"

"Maybe 'K' is a nickname too. It doesn't tell us anything."

"Delaney," interjected Taber. He spoke in a sober, fatherly tone. "Let's please show respect for the departed."

"And plus," said Brendan, still arguing with Delaney, "it doesn't make sense as a motive. If Kevin had found God and was looking to break things off, why kill Rebecca?"

Delaney withdrew his hand, sat back, and shrugged. "He had opportunity. Okay? We've established that Kevin was in town, he checked into the Econolodge last night. This morning, he shows up within an hour of the body being discovered."

"Why would he come back?" asked the Sheriff. Brendan found he liked Taber more all the time.

Delaney shrugged again. He reached into his inner breast pocket – he was still wearing the suit from that morning, likely stained with sweat – and pulled out a Ziploc bag filled with sunflower seeds. "Maybe he forgot something. Maybe he wanted to get caught. The way he acted with the deputies, you know. Suicide by cop, that sort of thing."

He popped a seed into his mouth and started making little chewing motions. "Motive? You know, I think this is one for the shrinks. For Olivia Jane, maybe. Once you get into the territory of incest and all of that . . . forget it. I'm lost."

Brendan felt annoyed. "But we still don't have the report. We don't know they're blood related. We . . ."

Delaney's head whipped around to look at Brendan. "Yes we do. While you were sitting in here, I was on the phone to the lab. Deputy Coroner Clark has matched their blood types. They are both B negative. That's the second rarest form of blood type. Plus, well, he said they bear a strong familial resemblance. So, there's that."

"What about DNA?"

Delaney narrowed his eyes. "Clark is fast, but nobody is that fast. Especially in a homicide. Come on, now. Typing won't be determined until at least tomorrow, midday maybe. Don't tell me this is your first rodeo."

Brendan ignored the barb. Delaney knew exactly how much experience he had, and what Brendan's background was – Brendan had already been put on the spot earlier that day by Skene. Delaney was acting this way for the Sheriff's benefit. Fine. It was late and he was exhausted and he decided to play a little hard ball.

"I understand all about the process, just as I reminded Skene today. First there is the cleaning and decontamination of the work site. Documentation begins as soon as the evidence enters the work site, via the chain of custody. Clark has two bodies now, so that makes for extra quality control measures. The initial phase of body fluid screening can be tedious and time-consuming. I did assume, though, that your CSI unit on scene used the alternative light source to screen for any fluids?"

Delaney spat out a seed casing into his hand, and looked at Brendan the way a hawk might regard a shrew. "They didn't bring their ALS equipment, no. They're not used to this kind of high-profile case. Clark showed up early, so there was no time."

"I know," said Brendan coolly. "And I know *you* know that if there isn't any biological material, there isn't anything to test for DNA. But even if there wasn't any semen or saliva for the rape kit swabs, there are other probative materials, like the bloodstains. My guess is that this is where Clark established the blood types. The PERK has indicated the victim has had a few partners – but I've heard nothing that says the victim was definitely raped this morning. And my guess is that you haven't, either."

Delaney chewed. His face was now a mask to conceal his emotions. The Sheriff's head ticked back and forth between the two of them, as if watching a tennis match. "Go on," Delaney said.

"Well, that body fluid screening usually only takes two or three hours. But let's put a pin in that for now and come back to it. Isolating the DNA from the bloodstains would be next. The DNA differential extraction can take up to eight hours. Then there's the quantitation using, if the lab is up to snuff, a real-time PCR technique. This takes minutes to hours, depending on the number of samples running on the instrument. So then the copied and tagged DNA is run through the 310 Genetic Analyzer. The whole thing can take two days of round-the-clock work by the forensic analysts. So no, Delaney, this is not my first rodeo."

Finished with his spiel, Brendan felt hot around his neck and ears. He wanted another cigarette. Instead, he looked down at the book in his hand, and at the handwritten note. He read the message again to himself, and then the passage, as Delaney and the Sheriff sat in a suspended awkward silence.

Finally, Taber broke the ice. "So, when will you know if it was a rape?"

Delaney opened his mouth, but Brendan cut in. "We would know by now. But it's not conclusive yet." He heard Delaney's mouth shut with a clack of teeth.

"You don't think it's rape," said Taber.

"I don't think anything," said Brendan. "The fact is, all we know is that a girl – maybe a girl who slept around – was murdered, and then her brother went Rambo and tried to kill me, or Olivia Jane, or us both. This neither makes him more a suspect or less so, in my opinion. This makes him a very tragic young man. But I haven't even had the time yet to look at the victim. Who she was, or anything about her other than some hearsay. And if she was promiscuous, that only widens our search. The fact is, Sheriff Taber, this book, and this note, with their riddles, exemplifies where we're at right now."

"Which is?"

Brendan jerked his head toward Delaney. "Despite what he says, we're in the dark."

Brendan plucked the manila envelope from Taber's desk, where Delaney had set it down. He carefully slid the book and note back into it, and folded the flap down. Then he stood up.

"If you'll excuse me, gentlemen, I need to go home. Just for an hour. Just to take a breath. Then I'll be back to work on this."

The Sheriff nodded. Brendan didn't look at Delaney. It seemed that in one day, the senior investigator had gone from mentor to antagonist. Brendan knew the hour and the stresses of the day had finally gotten to him, and he was likely taking things too personally. There was no evading his emotions now, though, he needed to leave. He slipped out of the Sheriff's office, and headed out of the building.

\* \* \*

Outside, the night held some of the day's heat, but the air was cooling. In the parking lot at the back of the building, he saw Olivia Jane getting into her car, and it stopped him in his tracks. His heart did a double-beat.

He started walking towards her again. She looked up and saw him approaching.

Brendan imagined a scenario in his head:

She says, *What a frigging day. You want to get a drink?*

He says, *I don't drink. But I'll get a coffee with you.*

She agrees and off they go.

But as he drew closer to her, Olivia Jane offered the detective a wan smile, and then dropped out of sight as she settled into her car. She looked like she had been crying. Her door shut and the engine started up and he stopped.

She backed out of the space, the car jerked into forward gear, and she pulled away.

He caught one last glimpse of her. She was focused straight ahead, and didn't turn to look at him.

She drove off, and Brendan stood in the dark parking lot, the manila envelope in his hands.

## CHAPTER TWELVE / THURSDAY, 10:55 PM

Brendan lived in the small community of Stanwix. The Sheriff's Department in Oriskany was smack in between the small cities of Rome and Utica. Stanwix was close to Rome, about three miles from his office in Oriskany. He rented a two bedroom house on Toni Hill Road. It was a small colonial-style home, with a red door, and a whitewashed fence in front. Not the ideal trappings, but he'd taken it on the fly.

The job offer to work as an investigator for Oneida County had come out of the sheer blue. Seamus Argon, a lifelong beat cop in Hawthorne, had told Brendan about it one morning on road patrol.

Brendan had been doubtful. "Investigator? I've got three years as a cop in Hawthorne. I went to school for neurobiology, for Chrissakes, Argon. How am I going to make detective? I'd need at least two or three years in the civil office, or a stint on patrol before they even considered me."

But Argon was insistent. He had just heard about the opening for an investigator in Oneida, specifically someone who was skilled at going door to door. "You're good with people," said Argon.

"I am?"

Argon was in his mid-fifties. When it all came out, he knew the Sheriff, and could pull strings. Brendan thought about it for two days – that was all the time Argon said he would have.

"You trying to get rid of me?"

Argon was a large man with a flat Irish-cop face (though the fact that he was Scottish was something the hardened cop liked to remind Brendan about) and a no-nonsense attitude. He claimed to possess a bullshit detector to rival a Geiger counter. One tremor of BS, and his sensitive instrument picked it up readily. "You hate it here," said Argon.

"How do I hate it here?"

But Argon only raised his eyebrows, and both men knew he was right. Not that loving where you lived was a prerequisite for any job. In this case, there was more to it. Brendan was haunted. He looked at his own hangdog face in the mirror every morning and knew it. Argon had become his best friend, even his mentor, but the sight of the man constantly reminded Brendan of the day his entire life had changed. The day he had privately come to think of as The Reckoning.

"Domestic disturbances and speed traps are where I belong, not you," Argon had said at last.

They'd been sitting in the cruiser on Elmwood Ave. Brendan remembered the day with startling clarity. It had been the tail end of winter, and icy rain had spacked against the windshield. Argon, who never liked to turn the heat up in the car, had been sitting in the driver's seat with a steaming cup of coffee, his skin ruddy in the cold, his thick red mustache twitching as he spoke.

"You've watched every aspect of the investigations we've been around. Your head is in the detective work, my friend. Plus, all your background peering into microscopes and all that fuckin' shit. Now this position, though, this is primarily for questioning the witnesses, getting statements. The big shit up there is an old codger named Delaney. It's the Sheriff's county, but Delaney thinks it's his. He's a nice enough guy, unless you get in the way of his agenda. He likes his pussy, too, pardon my fran-swaz, so he's gotten himself into trouble once or twice and is on thin ice with the department. He's got the hots for the ADA, maybe the staff shrink, whatever wears a skirt and stands upright. If IA ever comes around, you'll see Delaney lick his palms and slick his hair back. The deps and the local PDs are gonna go door to door, too, just like we've done. But they had some case up there not long ago with major blowback because of how some dumb cop like us blew it getting an accurate statement from a witness, and it ended up a ragged case for the DA, who let this guy walk. Guy ended up killing someone a few weeks later. So you've got Delaney with something to prove, and the Senior Prosecutor, I think he's called Skene, with a wild hair up his ass, too. You'll be on the outside up there, but keep your head down and do the job. The Sheriff will have your back, and that's all that matters."

"You act like I've already taken the job."

Argon had turned to look at Brendan in the passenger seat. His dark green eyes had flicked back and forth, seeing through to Brendan's core. "You have," he said.

Still, Brendan had taken the 48 hours Argon said he had to decide. Somewhere around the fortieth hour, with an early spring snowfall coming down outside his apartment, he had started to pack his things.

It had been three months. Brendan looked around now at the two-bedroom house he lived in. Most of his belongings were still in the mover's boxes. There were three boxes marked "family," and these were piled closest to the back wall of the dining area, sitting beneath the white lacy curtains that had come with the place.

Brendan set his bag down inside the front door and walked into the kitchen. The room was off the dining area, a small galley kitchen, with white flooring, mirrored counter spaces, a sink and dishwasher on one side, cabinetry and refrigerator on the other. He opened the fridge and peered in. He found the grape juice and pulled it out. He took a glass down from one of the cabinets and filled it with ice from the refrigerator's ice machine. The machine labored and clunked and finally spat out four wedges of ice in a rush. He poured the grape juice, put the bottle back in the fridge and returned to the entrance hall where he picked up his bag. With the ice tinkling in his glass and holding the bag by its leather strap he walked into the back of the house where his darkened living room was.

The living room consisted of one small sofa, a coffee table, and end-table and a lamp. There was no stereo, no flat screen TV. On the coffee table was his laptop computer.

He set the bag down on the coffee table next to the laptop and the drink on the end-table. He unzipped the bag and started to unpack its contents. After a moment, he had everything laid out in front of him. He opened the laptop and booted it up. Then he placed a call to the Sheriff's Department, to Deputy Benedetto, and requested that a patroller make regular passes in front of Olivia Jane's house throughout the night. He knew that surveillance was already on the Heilshorn property, and that the Department would be spread thin. But Benedetto agreed without much protest.

After he hung up, Brendan took a sip of the grape juice, loosened his collar, and went to work.

* * *

Gentry Folwell, who lived across the street from the Heilshorn place, had been questioned by Delaney after the old farmer had gone on a shooting spree in pursuit of a woodchuck. The Heilshorn place was isolated, so there were no other neighbors to question. Brendan looked at the copy of Folwell's statement.

The old-timer had neither seen nor heard any suspicious activity across from his home that morning. He was an early-riser, he said, getting out of bed when the cock crowed, doing his stretches. That was how he stayed fit to run the farm. There were annotations that Folwell went on about his suspicion of global warming as the reason why his corn had failed. He was afraid of the farm going bankrupt.

He had noticed the Audi in the driveway the day before. He was asked if that was the first time he'd seen the vehicle, but he couldn't recall precisely. In other words, there was the possibility that Rebecca Heilshorn had only arrived at the house the previous day. Brendan jotted a note down in his black book that said "Timeline." He made this the first entry. Tomorrow, he would construct a bigger version of the timeline on large sheets of paper at the office. Most detectives today used computers to build the timeline – there were several software programs – but Brendan felt he wanted to hand-write and lay everything out. It was a practice he'd begun back in the lab at Langone.

The comments Folwell made about his farm potentially folding prompted Brendan to look into the records of the Heilshorn place. He consulted the notes from Donald Kettering, the hardware store owner and ex-boyfriend of the deceased girl. Kettering had called the place the Bloomingdale Farm. Brendan found tax records for it online, and a history of its turnover on a site called Zillow. The records went back to 1962, when the farm was sold for $82,000. This particular site didn't list who the seller or buyer was, but Brendan already felt sure that the initial sale was by Bloomingdale.

Brendan whistled through his teeth when he thought of buying that place for a $82,000. The tax maps showed it to be over 15 acres. The house was three stories with four bedrooms. There were two outbuildings, the tractor shed and a small kennel, and then there was the barn – the barn had appeared recently resurrected or rebuilt completely. Brendan checked the Kettering notes again. Kettering said it had been torn down and rebuilt.

The property sold again in 1988 for a much heftier sum. It had almost tripled in value, according to Zillow, and had been purchased for nearly $200,000. There was no other record of sale until three years ago, when the building was sold and bought once more, this time for a cool million.

The Heilshorns.

Brendan sat back and ran a hand across his face. He took another sip of grape juice. He shut his eyes and rubbed them with his fingertips. Then he continued.

Next, his mind jumped to suspects. He prepared to make a list of them. The tip of his pen hovered over the paper. Kettering had acted a little strangely, and might even have motive as an unrequited lover. But his alibi was strong.

Still the pen hung in the air.

Kevin Heilshorn had been emotionally distraught, but understandably so. In cases where someone close to the victim was the culprit, that person usually employed a different method to conceal guilt – they acted cool as a cucumber. What often aroused suspicion of a husband or boyfriend as the murderer was when they acted almost glib in their willingness to cooperate. Their lack of emotional outburst, lack of defensiveness, especially when accused of the crime, betrayed the dark truth. Kevin, on the other hand, had behaved like a grief-stricken brother who had expected to see his sister that morning and had been horribly and unexpectedly denied. Still, there was the glaring caveat of his actions later that day. Brendan could see him standing in the garden. He could feel his own finger pressing against the cool metal of the trigger, ready to squeeze. Bang. Bang.

He didn't believe Kevin Heilshorn had killed his sister.

He turned his mind to the possibility of a break-in, of burglary, or, at least, a stranger. In certain cases he'd researched, victims of a violent crime suffered because of the misfortune of being in the wrong place. The aggressor held the grievance against someone else, or sought to steal something no longer there. Was it possible that Rebecca Heilshorn was just in the wrong place at the wrong time?

Brendan thought again of the arrangement of the dresser drawers and how only the bottom drawers had been open. An inexperienced thief may have started with the top drawer and had to close each drawer to get to the next one while working down the column of three, but professional thieves weren't likely to hit places out in the middle of nowhere, especially old rundown farms. It seemed more likely that the perp was in the house in search of something specific and had killed Rebecca in the process either to keep her quiet, or for some other reason.

Brendan would continue to investigate prior ownership of the property to see if anything turned up that would hint at some discord between anyone and a previous owner, or anything to suggest something of value on the property. But, it wasn't a priority right now.

He still hadn't listed a single suspect.

The biological father of Rebecca's daughter was next on his mind. He knew nothing about the man except his first name. Eddie.

Was it Eddie whose boot print was on the door to Rebecca Heilshorn's bedroom? Had a disgruntled ex come back seeking revenge for emotional pain, for a daughter that had been kept from him?

Brendan needed to find Eddie and talk to him. The way to locate him might be through a signed paternity statement. He needed to find out the hospital where Leah was born. He needed to find everything about the little girl.

Just as much, or even more, he needed to thoroughly research the victim. Where had she gone to school? Who were her friends? What was she doing in an old farmhouse owned by her parents, miles from where she came from?

It was interesting, the parallel between him and the victim. Brendan sat back from the computer and his notes, massaging the bridge of his nose. Both he and Rebecca were from Westchester. Both found themselves smack in the middle of New York State, the leatherstocking region of flat land, a few rolling hills, and hundreds of miles of green.

He wondered if Rebecca had a past similar to his, too. Something driving her. Something she was running from. Had he run? Had Argon offered him, not the start of a new life, but an escape hatch from the pain of his old one?

Lastly, Brendan opened up the manila folder and pulled out the worn copy of *The Screwtape Letters*. He pinched the note between his thumb and forefinger and pulled it out. What was the significance of the passage? He read it again. He looked at the note. Who was Danice? Was it her nickname? Was 'K' actually Kevin?

Brendan's thoughts circled back around to the young, angry brother. Kevin had lied about Rebecca having a child. Why? Maybe he was trying to protect her from someone like Eddie? If so, then why had Kevin come after Brendan and Olivia like a psychopath on a killing spree?

And why in the hell was Brendan convinced of the young man's innocence? Maybe he felt some sort of strange kinship with Kevin Heilshorn.

With these ideas tumbling through his mind, still sitting up on the couch, his shirt unbuttoned, the ice cubes snapping in his glass of grape juice as they melted, Brendan laid back on the couch.

It wasn't until he was flat out that he realized how exhausted he was. It had been one hell of a day. And as he dropped into an inevitable unconsciousness, his day finally came to an end.

## CHAPTER THIRTEEN / FRIDAY, 7:03 AM

His cell phone was ringing. At first, Brendan was disoriented. He thought he was back in his house on Elmwood where he'd lived with his wife and daughter for two years. He could see their faces.

He picked up the phone and answered. "Hello?"

"Detective Healy?"

"Yes."

"This is George Mace at the lab. I work with Stan Clark. Did I wake you?"

"No." Brendan's eyes felt puffy, and he could barely see.

"Okay. Ah, I thought you'd like to know right away. The laptop recovered from the trash at the victim's house. Well, it's crispy. There was no data we could get from the hard drive, which is melted to almost nothing. But we got something else."

"Yes?"

"We were able to raise a serial number from the drive casing, which is metal. We got most of the numbers of the SN. Partial on the last two. So you'll have a couple of possible permutations. I mean, twenty possible combinations. But, it's something. Like to have what we got?"

"Yes," said Brendan. He sat up straight and fumbled for his pen. He wrote down the string of letters and numbers that the analyst gave him.

* * *

Brendan had a quick shower and a cup of black coffee, before heading to the offices in Oriskany. The day promised to be cooler than the previous one, according to the weather report on NPR's "All before Eight" program. It was only supposed to reach the upper seventies. The sky overhead was the color of brushed steel, and the large cumulus clouds floated along with bright cottony nimbuses from the rising sun.

As he drove, Brendan made his mental to-do list. He still hadn't spoken with Deputy Bostrom. The day had been so hectic he hadn't even gotten a statement from the first person to arrive at the scene of the crime. He needed to check back in with the lab later, of course; prints not belonging to the victim had been found throughout the house and the core scene of the victim's bedroom. They would be run through the AFIS system to see if they matched anything on record, but Brendan's job was to provide suspects who might match the prints. The lab would check Kevin Heilshorn, of course, but there was no probable cause to check the prints of Donald Kettering. He had already admitted to having been in the house anyway, and his alibi was strong. Unless a felon matched the prints, they'd get nowhere with them.

The boot print on the door was the same story. The size and make of the shoe could be determined from the lifted print, with any luck, but matching that to the bottom of a real person's shoe was a long way off. He only had the first name of Rebecca's ex, Eddie, the supposed father of Leah. A cursory online search, pairing her full name with his first name, had yielded no salient results. He would have to look into it more thoroughly.

As he turned onto Rome-Oriskany Road, Brendan thought that there might be an even more pressing issue. Kevin Heilshorn had agreed to be the one to contact the parents. Kevin's personal identification had been enough to qualify him as a viable next-of-kin to identify the victim. As far as Brendan knew, the Coroner hadn't placed a call to Rebecca's parents. Perhaps now that he also had Kevin's body on the slab, and his relation verified posthumously, Clark would have placed a call, but Brendan couldn't be sure. It was possible that no one had yet contacted the parents of now two dead children. As far as he knew, their only two children. It might fall on him to break the news.

He lit a cigarette as he pushed the Camry up to sixty-five miles per hour. The first cigarette of the day always felt like a mistake, like a relapse. He understood habit to be a very primal situation in the brain. All habits could be broken down into a simple equation: cue, routine, reward. Right now, his nerve cell receptors were being rewarded by the release of dopamine. What was curious, even after years of neurobiological study, was that Brendan could feel the physical satisfaction of the nicotine as its molecular components triggered the neurochemicals in his brain, yet he also felt the guilt.

Nothing he'd seen in six years of study was able to account for what human beings call a conscience.

## CHAPTER FOURTEEN / FRIDAY, 8:11 AM

Brendan saw News Channel 6 was camped out in front of the Sheriff's Department, and parked in the lot behind the building. A white van was there with the Syracuse News insignia on the side. A sliding side door rolled open, and a reporter and cameraman hopped out.

"Shit," he said inside his car. He banged out the door and walked briskly to the rear entrance of the Department, the reporter and his cameraman chasing him as he went.

"Investigator. Investigator, please have a word with us."

Brendan's mind raced. He hated this sort of attention. This was what they meant when they called a case "high profile." A dead girl in a well-known farmhouse in the region. Not only dead, but stabbed repeatedly. Grisly, unexpected, sensational.

He had two options. He could dart inside and see himself on TV later running from a news crew, or he could stop and face them. His heart thumped in his chest. His skin grew hot despite the cool morning. He turned to them before he reached the door.

"Investigator." The reporter was a young man, a little breathless. His brown hair was perfectly coiffed, and his face looked like it had just been painted. "What can you tell us about the young woman murdered in Remsen?"

Brendan felt all his nerves firing. The camera light beamed upon him. The reporter stuck a microphone in Brendan's face.

"We're working on it."

The microphone flipped back to point at the reporter's mouth. "Any leads?" The microphone switched back.

"We're developing and following up leads as swiftly as we can." His voice sounded like someone else was saying the words coming out of his mouth. He was reminded of standing over Kevin Heilshorn's bleeding, dead body. Brendan's skin rippled with gooseflesh.

"And what can you tell us about yesterday's police shooting? Is it true that the victim is actually the brother of the deceased Remsen girl? Is he a suspect in the murder investigation?"

Brendan smiled grimly. "If you'll excuse me, I have to get to work. We will be giving the press an official statement later."

He quickly made his way inside, leaving the reporter calling after him.

\* \* \*

Delaney was not yet in the building. Brendan kept his head low as he walked along the corridor of the third-floor of the Department, and slipped into his office quietly, shutting the door behind him.

He sat at his desk, opened his bag, and got out the case-file. He took a few moments to slow his pulse, to get himself under control. He stared at the binder and then, after a minute, he slid it aside. He reached into his shirt pocket and pulled out his small notebook and flipped through it until he came to Olivia Jane's number. He picked up the phone on his desk and dialed.

The voice on the other end sounded wary. "Hello?"

"Ms. Jane? I'm sorry to call so early. This is Investigator Healy."

"I know who it is." She didn't sound upset, only tired; a little feisty.

He sat back in his chair, fiddling with the phone cord. He'd called her on impulse, and now he wasn't sure what to say. He opened his mouth to speak, but she beat him to it.

"I'm sorry about last night," she said. "That was . . . I just needed to get out of there."

"I understand, I understand." He leaned forward again and put his elbows on the desk. "How are you?"

"I didn't sleep. I locked all the doors and checked them three or four times during the night."

Brendan searched for the right words, something comforting, but his mind drew a blank. She continued, "There was a cop outside for most of the night. At first it scared the hell out of me – I saw the headlights sweep over the front window. God, it's still a mess in here."

"We'll get that cleaned up," he said right away, remembering the windows in the dining room exploding as the gunman, Heilshorn, opened fire on the house. The memory was surreal, like it had been no more than a dream. Or a nightmare.

He sat back again, his knees bouncing as his feet jittered on the floor. "Have you eaten anything?"

"I just keep seeing it," she was saying. "The way all that glass went flying. I have bullet holes in my wall."

"I know. I know. We'll get it cleaned up, I promise. Listen, are you going to be able to sleep today?"

"I have clients today."

"In your home?"

"Yes."

He realized he hadn't been in Olivia's home long enough to see her office. But he knew she was licensed for private practice and saw her patients from a home office, as well as making house calls and assisting with crime scenes. "You'll have to cancel them, Ms. Jane."

"Olivia. I can't cancel them. These people . . . there's a woman that . . . I can't just cancel on my patients at such short notice."

"I understand your reluctance. You don't want your personal circumstances to affect your professional life."

"It's not that, Investigator. I don't give two barbarians at the gate about that." She stopped herself, and he could hear her rustling against the phone, like she had started pacing around. He found himself grinning, just a little, at her comment. He thought it was a euphemism for not giving a shit. "I just can't *leave* them. Okay, a couple of them, its maybe not such a big deal. But I have two patients in particular that really need their sessions right now."

"Ms. Jane. Olivia."

"Yes?"

"Far be it for me to tell you how to do your job. You sound like a very dedicated therapist. I understand your need to not let down your patients."

"You keep saying you understand."

She was clearly tired and a bit off the rails. Brendan could scarcely imagine the woman he'd met the day before being irritable or insulting in any way. The situation was clearly ungluing her.

"Olivia, you've just been involved in a very serious incident. And you're now part of a criminal investigation that involves a murder, and two dead people. The man that attacked us yesterday, well, we don't know if he was after me, or you, or us both, or what."

"Did you send the police out last night? To check on me?"

"I made a call, yes. Listen . . ." He sighed unintentionally, and then took a deep breath. She was silent this time, waiting. "I'm not saying you *can't* see your patients today. I do need to speak to you, and you are intertwined in this case now, no matter whether it interferes with your life, or not. I'm sorry for that. But what's more important here is whether or not you are in a condition to even be of the best help you can be to your patients today. Don't you think?"

He winced a little, bracing himself for a backlash. He hadn't intended to insinuate a lack of professional capability on her part.

He heard her take a breath, too. The exhalation made for a digital ruffle of air on her end of the conversation. "You're right," she said in a quiet voice. "There's no way I can compartmentalize this one. I mean, Jesus."

Brendan remained silent now, and let her continue to think it through. After a few moments, he said, "You need to eat something. I'm going to come by to pick you up at ten. We'll get some food in us, and we'll talk it through, okay?"

She was silent, perhaps hesitant.

"I need to have your official evaluation of Kevin Heilshorn." He realized what a crazy thing that was to say and added, "Before."

"My evaluation? I'm not a psychiatrist working for the DA, Investigator Healy."

"Brendan."

"My job is to *counsel*, to listen and respond to the needs of someone involved in a tragedy."

"I'm sorry, I misspoke. I mean to say, I'd like to hear your opinion about how you found Kevin Heilshorn to be yesterday morning, when you had your time with him."

"That's still the same thing. You want to know whether or not I found him to be acting guilty. Did he seem to be experiencing grief, or guilt concealed as grief. Or, did he appear unemotional. Remorseless. So you can put it in your report and call on me when you need a witness for the prosecution. I told you, I don't do that. I don't know how long you've been doing this, but this isn't how you get a professional witness on the stand. First of all, I'm not her. Second of all, this isn't the way. Coercing someone out for a meal so you can use them to ratchet up your investigation."

The conversation fell so abruptly silent that Brendan thought she'd hung up. He pulled the phone away from his ear for a second, and then put it back.

"Did you hang up?"

There was one last moment of silence. Then she said, "I don't hang up on people. I'm thirty years old. But I am going to go now, Mr. Healy. Good luck."

And then she did hang up.

Brendan slowly set the handset back in the cradle. He stared at the black phone with its multiple lines and telltales for a moment. "That could have gone better," he said to it.

* * *

Sheriff Taber came into Brendan's office a few minutes later. Brendan read the fifty-year-old's face: It looked like he had news he was conflicted about revealing.

"Morning," said Taber.

"Morning, Sheriff."

"Get any sleep?"

"I'm not sure you'd call it sleep. I was unconscious for a few hours."

Taber grinned, but his eyes belied this other agenda.

Brendan sat back and folded his hands. He took a breath. "What is it, Sheriff?"

Taber, as ever, came right to the point. "I'm wondering if you need time. After yesterday."

Brendan felt as though he'd been punched in the solar plexus. He'd expected this question, but it still drove the air from his body. His first case for Oneida County and he was involved in a shooting. Now all eyes were on him. His competence would be in question, no matter everyone's support and best intentions.

"I'm fine, sir. I'd like to continue."

"Good," said the Sheriff. "I'd like to keep you on." His expression reflected that other purpose again, and he said, "We're adding an investigator from the State Trooper's Squad to the case. His name is Rudy Colinas."

Brendan looked into the Sheriff's eyes. "Okay."

"This is a big investigation. As you know, it's not unusual for the State to assist us, especially since we're still lacking another department investigator."

"I understand. Can I just ask you one thing?"

"Of course." The Sheriff was still standing with the door closed behind him. He looked hopeful.

"Does this have anything to do with the shooting yesterday afternoon?"

The Sheriff sighed. "Yes and no."

"That's honest."

The Sheriff shot him a look, perhaps probing for insolence. Finding none, he continued. "Delaney is working the evidence. That's his bag. He's got a laptop, a cell phone, a vehicle, fingerprints, boot print, tracks on the property – in fact, a whole property to continue combing. He's working with the Deputy Coroner on the bodies, as you know. Your job is statements from any witnesses, neighbors, anyone who passed by the house during the timeline for yesterday morning. And suspects. It's a tall order, and you need help."

"Because I tend to shoot my suspects."

The Sheriff looked at Brendan, again trying to gauge the younger man. Brendan had to wonder at the words coming out of his own mouth. "I'm sorry," he said right away. "I just . . ." *I just got off the phone with a woman who handed me back my best intentions,* he thought.

The Sheriff waved a hand in dismissal. He then looked around Brendan's small office like he was searching for something. "I want to have a conference with you and Delaney and Colinas this afternoon at one o'clock. In the meantime, bring him up to speed, and work your suspects.

What's the word so far on the father of the victim's little girl?"

"I'm working on it next."

The Sheriff nodded. "And the parents?"

"Do I need to call them?"

The Sheriff narrowed his eyes. The notion of the detective who had killed their son calling the parents of the deceased was almost absurd. "The Coroner has called them. There's no way you're allowed to communicate with the Heilshorns at this time. But we need to know everything about them."

Brendan understood. With few suspects and an unknown motive, everyone needed to be looked at for potential culpability. The conflict of interest for him to do the investigation on this situation was enormous. "Then Detective Colinas will work them while I find out more about Eddie."

"Eddie?"

"Possibly the biological father of the little girl. All I have right now is his first name."

The Sheriff lingered for a moment. Then he nodded again, and opened the door behind him. "I'm going to send in Detective Colinas."

"Okay."

The men held each other's gaze for a second, and then the Sheriff left.

* * *

Rudy Colinas had an olive complexion and eyes so dark they appeared as all-pupil. His tight, curly hair was carved into a brick. He was well-built, in his forties, and spoke with a slight lisp, as if his tongue pressed against his front teeth for a fraction of a second longer on his Ts. He wore a well-fitting suit, dark grey, and no tie. He had a binder with him and a pen clipped to his shirt pocket, which he slipped out and clicked.

They made cursory introductions and Rudy Colinas sat in the one chair across from Brendan as he took him through the case. Most of it Rudy was familiar with, nodding here or there, but he remained absolutely silent the entire time, and jotted down occasional notes. When they were finished, Brendan's stomach was growling. He looked at the clock on his phone and saw that it was almost ten in the morning.

It was absurd to think of devoting precious time now to the therapist, Olivia Jane. Brendan needed to do what was prudent and procedural – to work his suspects, as the Sheriff had reiterated. Eddie, the Heilshorns, the dead brother. Kevin Heilshorn's death would become its own case. Brendan felt a knot of dread when he considered this prospect – yesterday's meeting with IA was only the beginning in what was often a protracted matter: the investigation of a police shooting. There would be more meetings, and there was always the possibility of a lawsuit. Brendan found the words came with difficulty as he tried to explain the situation to Colinas. It felt like he had marbles in his mouth.

"Tough situation," said Colinas. It wasn't clear whether he was referring to the shooting of Kevin Heilshorn, or the conflict with Brendan, as the shooter, continuing an investigation which involved Kevin's parents. Maybe both.

Colinas gazed off into the air in the small office space. "I had to draw my weapon on someone once. My heart was beating so hard. I didn't know . . . you know, if it came down to it . . ." He trailed off, and then his eyes came back to Brendan. "So, where do we go from here, boss? I'm on the parents, got it. I'll be extremely gentle with them. But suppose I don't get through, or it takes a while, what next? You want me looking into the victim?"

"Absolutely," said Brendan. He was already liking Colinas. "Everything about her. Where she went to grade school up to where she shopped for groceries last week.

Of course I'll help you. I've got to see about something else first."

"What about this Eddie? You want me to look into that, too, right?"

"I'm hoping they dovetail," said Brendan, getting up and collecting his bag. He slipped the manila envelope, containing *The Screwtape Letters, into it*. "Finding out the history of Rebecca will hopefully run right into the chapter where Eddie was in her life. Hell, check Facebook. See what her timeline has to offer."

"On it."

Brendan stuck out his hand. "I'll be back in an hour. Oh. I have one other thing." Brendan pulled the piece of paper out of his notes which had the serial number on it for the melted laptop. He handed it to Colinas. "See if you can find who this laptop computer was registered to, who purchased it, anything."

The men exchanged phone numbers, shook hands, and Brendan hurried out the door, thinking about the best way to evade the reporters if they were still downstairs.

# CHAPTER FIFTEEN / FRIDAY, 10:12 AM

He pulled up to Olivia Jane's house and found Deputy
Bostrom parked out front. Brendan opened the driver's
side door to the Camry, dropped and squashed his
cigarette butt along the shoulder of the road, and got out.
He noticed instantly how crammed Olivia's short driveway
had become. There was a dark blue Chevy Caprice, with a
long antenna, parked in behind her green Aztec. It was a
State Detective Squad undercover vehicle. Probably just
like the one Rudy Colinas drove. Behind it was a Land
Rover.

Bostrom's Sheriff's Department car was parked at the
edge of the driveway, near the shoulder of the road. He
was sitting in the vehicle as Brendan approached. As he
neared the house, the garage came into better view, and
the space between, through which the garden was visible.
He could see the gold of police tape fluttering in the wind.

"This is insane," he muttered.

Bostrom rolled down his window, seeing Brendan
approach. The two men greeted one another, and Brendan
looked at the house.

"Two State Dicks in there," said Bostrom.

"When did they get here?"

"Bout seven-thirty this morning. Maybe a little before. I came on at seven."

Brendan nodded. He looked over at the Land Rover, which was close enough to spit on.

"The woman's lawyer," remarked Bostrom, looking at the vehicle. His front bumper almost made contact with it.

"And when did he or she arrive?"

"She. Maybe ten minutes after the dicks."

*That could explain Olivia's behavior on the phone*, thought Brendan. Last night his own department had responded to the scene when he'd called 911 and given his badge number after shooting Kevin Heilshorn. Now that he was back here, the scene replayed itself yet again. He could see right where the young man had been standing. Brendan began to feel light-headed.

Bostrom was looking at Brendan's hands. Brendan looked down and saw that they were shaking. He was holding the manila envelope, and it was quivering against his leg.

"You alright?" Bostrom's question was genuine. The two men may have had some tension the day before, but there was no hint of pleasure in Bostrom's face as he asked the detective how he was doing.

"I don't know," answered Brendan honestly.

"Rough night," said the deputy.

It was all anyone seemed to know how to say. *Rough night. Tough situation.* He felt like they were the kinds of euphemisms people offered to someone with a terminal sickness. Brendan wondered how much longer he had on the case. The Sheriff was in his corner, but that might be it; Taber wanted a conference later. Ostensibly, it was to go over case notes and put together a more official progress report. But Brendan knew what the ulterior might be; further questioning of his ability to continue with the investigation, given the extreme developments of late.

Brendan started up towards Olivia's house without another word to Bostrom. The deputy leaned out of the car and asked, cryptically, "You sure?" Maybe what he wanted to ask was, *Are you nuts, heading in there?*

Brendan didn't know how dialed-in Bostrom was to the situation with Olivia Jane, but perhaps he was intuitive enough to understand that, given the circumstances, it was an odd choice to go house-calling when the State Detective Squad was running this side of things, and the woman had her goddamn lawyer present.

The lawyer was a curious addition to the equation, Brendan thought. Likely, though, it had far less to do with any possibility of culpability on the part of Olivia Jane, but more to do with her need to protect her confidentiality, and guide her role as it pertained to both investigations.

He looked at her quaint Cape Cod-style house, with its elegant porch and lathed posts and railing spindles. The windows which had been shot out were crisscrossed with masking tape.

Brendan stopped. He tapped the manila envelope gently against his leg. His shaking was subsiding, his heart rate resuming a normal tempo. The day was shining, and bright bulbs of clouds sailed overhead.

Halfway up the path, Brendan decided to turn around.

He started back towards the driveway, and could see some sort of relief in Bostrom's face, who was watching. Then Bostrom's eyes flicked over Brendan's shoulder as he looked up at the house.

"Investigator Healy?"

He looked back and saw Olivia Jane. She stood on the porch at the top of the three stairs down to the walkway. He took a few steps back in her direction, and then stopped again when he saw she had ventured no further herself.

He tried on a smile. "Wanted to see if you would go get that breakfast with me, after all."

She gave him a look, trying to size him up. He saw her eyes fall to the envelope he was carrying, and so he lifted it up. "Something I really need to get your opinion on. But it can wait. Sorry to bother you." He smiled again and gave her a short nod, almost a bow. Then he started to leave once more.

"I can meet with you tomorrow," she said.

He paused. He looked at her across the short distance, twenty feet or so, between them. She was wearing grey slacks and a white dress shirt, the short collar open and revealing her neck and collar bones; and a grey vest, buttoned. Her hair was pulled up, her face open, and tired. She looked exhausted and pretty at the same time.

"That would be great," Brendan said.

"Around noon?"

"Yes," he said.

"Okay." She left the porch without lingering and went back inside.

Brendan stood on the walkway for a moment after the door closed and then resumed walking back to his car. Bostrom was gaping. "Did you just score a *date*, Detective Healy? Gonna roast the broomstick or what?"

Brendan ignored the remark, but felt the corner of his mouth curl up a little. He passed Bostrom in his vehicle and got back into the Camry.

* * *

Brendan ate by himself at a diner near the department, which was often populated by policemen and construction workers. At ten-thirty, hardly anyone was around. He spread his notes out on the table and ordered a coffee, an omelet with ham and cheese, toast, bacon, and hash browns. He doubted he would finish it all, but he'd felt ravenous when he ordered.

He worked his case notes for a while and ate. Then he took out his phone, found Colinas's phone number, and called him up.

"Rudy Colinas," said the State Detective.

"Colinas. Healy."

"You get hit by those reporters on your way out?"

Brendan had managed to slip by them this time. "No. Why?"

"There's more of them. From Syracuse, Albany, and word is, on the way from New York. I guess Heilshorn, the dad, he's a big time doctor in the city. Someone in his office overheard something, maybe Heilshorn talking to the coroner, some nurse, who knows, and the press knows and is on their way. He's a pretty big deal, I guess. He apparently saved some woman's blue-baby by injecting it with oxygen, or something. You believe that? It lived for thirty minutes without taking a breath."

"So who's making a statement?"

"Skene. Your Oneida Senior Prosecutor. He's on his way, he says, press conference in about an hour. I guarantee you he's waiting for New York press to show up."

Brendan put his head in his free hand and massaged his temples. He imagined the headline: Cop Shoots Son of Wealthy Doctor While Investigating Daughter's Murder. This was getting worse by the second. He wasn't going to be able to carry on an efficient investigation this way, and Delaney would know it. It was Delaney's call, anyway. They were short on detectives, yes, but they were already adding in people from the State, and they could pull on city investigators too, from Utica and Rome.

While he was thinking these depressing thoughts, he heard Colinas rustling about on the other end. Colinas said "What?" then, "Yeah, okay."

"What's going on?"

Colinas came back over with a clearer voice. "Delaney and Taber want to meet with you. Where are you?"

"I'm at the diner."

"He's at the diner," Colinas said, once more with his mouth not quite to the phone. Back again: "Okay, yeah.

Stay there. They'll be right over." He added, "Hey, good luck."

Then, just when Brendan was about to hang up the call, Colinas blurted something. "Oh! I found out about the serial number." There was genuine excitement in the State Detective's voice.

"Tell me."

"You're going to love it. The laptop that got melted to shit is registered to user 'Eddie Stemp.' "

"You're kidding."

"I'm not. Think that's our Eddie?"

"Either that or it's one hell of a coincidence. And from what those older, bitter cops all tell you, there's no such thing."

"Ha. Right. So, not bad. Two birds, one stone."

"Thanks, Colinas."

"You bet."

Brendan hung up.

* * *

Delaney was red-faced when he came into the diner. Apparently he'd hustled his ass. Taber, younger and in better shape, didn't look so out of breath.

They sat down across from Brendan. The waitress appeared.

"Just coffee," said Taber. Delaney asked to see a menu. They waited while Delaney traced his finger along the menu, a long laminated sheet with pictures and descriptions on both sides. He flipped it over, examined it, and then flipped it back again. Finally, he looked at Brendan's plate, which was mostly cleared, and said, "Whatever he had."

The waitress left. Brendan looked at his two superiors expectantly, but he was already bracing himself for the inevitable. They would deliver the news that he was off the case and on administrative leave, he'd plead why he needed to continue, they would explain the particulars to him, and that it was non-negotiable anyway. They would blame bureaucracy, and talk to him about his mental health.

"Heilshorn called shortly after you left," Taber said.

"You spoke to him?"

"I did." Taber gave Delaney a look. The two men were almost comical, both of them considerably large individuals, crammed into one side of the booth next to each other. "He's not pleased."

"Oh?" Brendan figured he might as well pay the check and leave.

"He's not," Taber went on. "He wants to bring in his own investigators."

Brendan opened his mouth to say something, he wasn't sure what. Maybe, *Okay, you can find me at home if you need me, staring at a dark wall.* The thought of drinking passed through his mind, like a reflex, and he even thought he could taste the whiskey on his tongue. It filled him with a kind of nauseating warmth, and an excitement, like the idea of getting suddenly rich.

"It's liable to turn into a fucking circus," said Delaney before Brendan had the chance to speak.

"But we're not going to let it," said Taber.

Brendan regarded the two men. "How does he think he can bring in his own investigators? P.I.s, you mean?"

Taber was nodding. "Yes. He has a private investigator. Jerry Brown. Maybe more than him. Not only do we have to, by law, allow them to adjunct the investigation, but Heilshorn is putting in calls to determine which detectives will work the case up here."

"That's insane. Who does he think he is?"

"He's a very wealthy man," said Taber.

"Oh Jesus. Why does it always have to be, 'He's a very wealthy man'?"

Both Taber and Delaney looked at Brendan like they didn't quite understand the reference. Brendan asked, "Don't you guys ever go to the movies? It's always some rich family. It's never a movie about a poor family."

Taber blinked. "I went to see the *Expendables II*. My son took me. Arnold Schwarzenegger, Sylvester Stallone, all those guys."

Brendan suddenly laughed. Taber was so matter-of-fact, Brendan had to wonder if there was a figurative bone in the Sheriff's earnest body.

"I'm surprised your son knows who those guys are," Delaney interjected. "How old is Tom? Eighteen?"

Taber was nodding. "Eighteen. Freshman at UAlbany. Oh, he knows who they are, I guess."

They quickly returned their attention from this little digression back to Brendan. At the same time, Taber's coffee came. "Thank you," he said absently, and leaned into the table. "We said, 'We're not taking Healy off the case.'"

" 'Fuck this guy,' we said," Delaney chimed in.

Brendan gaped at his two superior officers.

"You did what you had to do, you held your own in the line of duty," said Delaney. "Who knows what was going through this Kevin-kid's head. You saw how he was – grief stricken and mentally unstable. We know you did what any good cop would have done. And we told Heilshorn that, with all due respect, he was just too upset to see it. That we needed to keep you on the case because you've been a part of it, every moment since it began."

"For the last thirty hours," Taber added. He sipped his coffee.

It took Brendan a moment, but then he waited for the penny to drop.

Taber set down his coffee. "But we had to make a deal with him. For the sake of the girl, this poor girl, we had to make a deal that would do the best for the investigation. Plus, it is completely routine to have you take an administrative leave, or a temporary duty assignment. In this situation, we think it's best for you and all involved if you just take a few days. IACP will be following up with you next week, and Police Psychological Services are very thorough."

Brendan felt the hairs on the back of his neck start to prick up, as if by electricity. His eyes flicked back and forth between the two men across from him, both of whom now wore hangdog expressions. "You made a deal with him? What deal?"

Taber glanced at Delaney, as if suggesting he answer. Delaney did. "That if you're off the case, he'll let us pursue things the way we know best, and won't interfere. We didn't have to tell you any of this, you know. The Sheriff could have just invoked a mandatory psych leave."

Taber cut his eyes at Delaney with an expression that said, *Enough now.* Then he turned to Brendan. "Otherwise, he's going to make things hell for us. He's a grieving father with a lot of money and power. It's the last thing we need up our ass while we're trying to figure this all out."

Both of them fell silent. They seemed to feel their explanation and presentation was sufficient, and now they waited for the diplomatic response from Brendan.

Brendan's mind was whirring. He saw Kevin Heilshorn lying in the garden, drenched in his own blood. He saw Olivia Jane as she had been standing on the porch just moments ago. And he saw Rebecca Heilshorn: her reflection staring back at him as he first set foot on the crime scene, a time which already felt like long ago.

Brendan opened his mouth, and closed it. He picked up the napkin in front of him and wiped his lips with it. He started gathering up his notes, and stuffing them back into the binder. Delaney and Taber watched this like they were witnessing something embarrassing, or ugly. Both men kept glancing away. When he was finished, Brendan pushed the binder towards Delaney.

"There you go," he said.

Delaney made a conciliatory face but said nothing. Finally, the Sheriff spoke up.

"I want you to take the rest of the day," he said, "And then the weekend. On Monday, hopefully this thing will have all blown over."

"Shit," said Delaney. "With any luck, we'll have it all wrapped by then anyway."

"You can start fresh at the top of the week. I've got other things for you to look into anyway." Sheriff Taber smiled and tried to look helpful.

Brendan reached down to the booth bench and grabbed the manila envelope. He set it on top of his binder. Neither Taber nor Delaney seemed to pay it any mind.

"Eddie Stemp is your next person of interest," he told them.

Both men reacted; Delaney tilted his head, Taber's eyes widened a little.

"He's the owner of the laptop which I found burned in the garage. Like I said before, Delaney, the laptop you have could be something, could also be a dummy. We couldn't get anything but the serial number from the damaged computer, but Eddie Stemp is the man it was registered to. It's also possible he is the father of Rebecca's daughter, Leah – that's in Donald Kettering's statement."

Brendan slid out of the booth as the waitress came over with Delaney's meal. She put it down in front of him, along with a set of utensils wrapped in a white napkin.

"Can I at least keep my gun?" Brendan looked at Taber.

Taber nodded. Brendan looked at the two of them still sitting there, both of them avoiding eye contact with him. Then he turned and left.

# CHAPTER SIXTEEN / FRIDAY, 11:16 AM

"Motherfuckers," Brendan said inside his Toyota Camry. He remained motionless for a moment, the car idling, then dropped it into gear and pulled away from the diner.

His first real case, and it was being pried from his hands by relatives of the victim. He felt frayed, as if someone had come and forced him to shut down construction on a new house he was building, leaving him in empty rooms with bare studs and the wind blowing through.

He drove home, holding onto his anger and resentment. His thoughts were a mess veiled behind a red curtain. By the time he pulled into the driveway of his modest rented house, his ire had only increased.

Then he looked at the stout little Colonial he'd been calling home for the past three months, and was reminded of something.

In a crime like this, there was nothing more critical than determining what a victim was doing in the hours leading up to the incident. So far, there had been nothing to go on. The neighbor, Folwell, reported seeing the vehicle the day before the murder, but couldn't recall if it had been there the day before that. He had made a general observation that the car sometimes appeared, and sometimes was not there, and mostly he paid no attention. He'd never met his neighbor across the road.

Donald Kettering had claimed that he and Rebecca Heilshorn had been anything but a sociable couple. She preferred quiet evenings at home. So much so that Brendan got the impression that if Kettering were to really insist that they went out, she would threaten to break it off with him. He was sure such a scenario had taken place, maybe more than once. It was a strong hunch.

They'd gone to dinner a few times, he'd said, and once to the mall on what he dubbed "their anniversary" (though Brendan doubted Rebecca had acknowledged as much). What was she doing with a man like Kettering anyway? Passing the time? Brendan supposed everyone had needs. It had been two years since he had felt the warmth of another person, and there were times he'd felt inclined to just make something happen. People needed people. Maybe Rebecca was lonely, even in her self-imposed isolation.

Yet, her test results indicated that she was likely to have had numerous sexual partners. If she was so liberal with herself otherwise, why had she been so reluctant with Kettering? Maybe she'd had a bad experience; been abused by Stemp or someone else. Or maybe Kettering just hadn't been her cup of tea. Someone from her sexual past, Brendan thought, had murdered her.

For all any of the investigators knew, Rebecca had driven up from Westchester – or somewhere else for that matter – the day before. She had spent the night alone, and in the morning, she'd seen the killer come to the door, had placed the call to 911, and the rest was history.

The case required more information about Rebecca Heilshorn's life outside of the region. Who was she elsewhere? Surely she had friends, even enemies, in other parts of the world. Chances were she was liquid, and highly mobile. But, it was beyond Brendan's grasp now. Wasn't it?

What jogged this thinking, though, was looking at the house he was renting. Kettering had talked about Rebecca coming in for some home-improvement hardware. He said it was how they met. But Rebecca had yet to go to closing on the Bloomingdale farm, according to Kettering. In the interim, she'd been staying in a rental property; perhaps she'd grown tired of hotels. Kettering had described a house just outside of Boonville.

For some reason, Brendan's mind fixed there now. Maybe because it was the only thread connecting Rebecca to a life here prior to the murder.

Still, it was from over two years ago. Even if the owner of the property remembered Rebecca, it might not have any bearing on what had happened to her. Then again, it might. Just like Rebecca needed Kettering's body next to her on some cold nights, she likely needed a friend, too. Someone to talk to.

Brendan sighed. He'd lost his appetite halfway through the conversation with Taber and Delaney. *You could barely call it a conversation*, he thought. *They shotgunned me.*

He couldn't blame them, though, much as he might want to. Especially Delaney, giving Brendan that dead mackerel look. Son of a bitch.

The anger bubbled back up, and Brendan was suddenly afraid he didn't know what to do. He had a weekend ahead of him where questions would dance endlessly in his head. It would drive him nuts, sitting around.

The image of a bottle flashed in his mind. He could feel the sting of alcohol touching his lips, and the prickly warmth of it slide down his throat and balloon in his stomach, full of comfort and numbing love.

He turned to his cell phone then and flipped through his contacts. He lit a cigarette and dialed the one man he thought could help him.

But the old cop, Seamus Argon, didn't answer his phone.

## CHAPTER SEVENTEEN / SATURDAY, 8:14 AM

The night had featured staccato moments of fitful sleep. At one point Brendan woke up and was sure he felt a hand on his head, cool to the touch. It wasn't the memory of his wife, however. The hand touching him was quite large. It had been the solitary comforting moment in an otherwise tormented night. His dreams were a macabre highlights reel of the past 48 hours, the reflection of Rebecca Heilshorn in the dresser mirror, her eyes wide and haunted; Kevin, her brother, dying in the garden, his dark blood smattered along the fronds of summer squash. His wife and daughter were strangely absent from the surreal episodes, when they were usually the stars of the show. He couldn't remember the last time he had spent a night without their restless souls in his mind.

In the morning he made coffee. He'd bought a can of Folgers months before, when he'd first moved in, and had only used it once or twice, since he was usually out the door bright and early and bought his coffee on the road. The brewed coffee this morning tasted like dishwater, and so he added more grinds and tried again. The next batch was no better, only tasting bitter and burnt.

He headed out for coffee in his sweatpants and a t-shirt which read: *METAL HEART*. The day was cloudy and grim, the temperature somewhere in the mid-sixties. As he drove he considered his situation. He felt a bit surreal, like a character in a movie. Along with most everyone else, he'd seen the stories where cops got thrown off the case by their superiors. And there was often some rich guy, like Alexander Heilshorn, who either thwarted the detective on the case, causing general havoc throughout the investigation, or became a benefactor of sorts. But, while the stories might repeat themselves, they drew from real life. Reality was stranger than fiction, anyway. One could consider the Lindberg case, the recent Main Line case or even the wild Patty Hearst scenario which had her posing with an AK-47, to verify the absurd nature of the human crime drama. There were too many bizarre cases in the world to count.

On his way through the Dunkin Donuts drive through, Brendan had an idea. After getting his coffee and egg white sandwich (it flopped in his grip like rubber matting), he drove to Rome to find a bookstore.

He'd given over the copy of *The Screwtape Letters* to Delaney. It was mandatory to turn over any evidence if you were taken off a case.

He could practically recite the highlighted passage from memory; he'd looked at it so many times. But he wanted to read the whole book.

He knew of one bookstore in Rome, called Pack Rats. Within ten minutes, he was standing in his sweatpants and t-shirt examining the section of the store on Philosophy and Spirituality. Not finding the C.S. Lewis book, he asked the teenager working the counter. The teenage girl said they didn't carry that particular book, but she would be happy to order it and have it here in five to eight business days.

Brendan said no thank you and asked for directions to the next bookstore.

"Uhm, there's Galaxy Comics."

"I don't think they'll have it," Brendan replied.

She looked around as if to see who was watching, and then she lowered her voice, "You can probably order it on Kindle."

He whispered back, "I don't have a Kindle. Isn't there, like, a Borders around here?"

She blinked at him and then stood up straighter, and elevated her voice to normal speaking level. "Borders closed years ago. Like, the whole thing. The chain, or whatever."

"Oh. Right. I remember that. Well, look, short of going out and buying a Kindle . . ."

"You can download Kindle for your PC, too."

Brendan smiled. "You're a salesperson for the wrong business." He winked and started walking away.

"Okay," she said, sounding challenged. "You can, like, try the Bookstore Resur."

He stopped and looked back. "What's that?"

"The, uhm, Bookstore of the Resurrection Life Church."

* * *

As directed, he drove down Turin Street past Fort Stanwix Park and made the left onto Floyd Avenue. The bookstore was in the same building as the Resurrection Life Church. It was a single story structure set back in a sizeable parking lot. There was a cathedral ceiling and large windows over the main entrance. The bookstore was off to the left side. Brendan parked the Camry and went inside.

He found a man of about his own age organizing a stack of books near the back of the room. On the shelves were many Bibles, and books by Christian writers like St. Thomas Aquinas, Lee Strobel, Tim Lahaye, and Rick Warren.

"Oh, C.S. Lewis," said the man tending the books. "Absolutely." He stood up and walked over to one of the sets of shelves and waved his hand in front of them in a show of display. "We don't carry the *Narnia* books, but we have *Mere Christianity*, *The Great Divorce*, and here, the one you asked about, *The Screwtape Letters*. This one is my favorite."

He pulled the book, one of a dozen or so copies, from the shelf and looked at it admiringly for a moment before handing it to Brendan. In that time, Brendan regarded the man. He was slender and angular, with prominent cheekbones, and wide-set eyes. His hair was black, and his eyes were startlingly blue. He was dressed in loose-fitting black clothes.

"Anything else you might be looking for?"

"No, this is fine, thank you."

The man paused, looking at Brendan, as though trying to read him. Brendan realized how he must appear. His hair was unkempt, his clothing disheveled. He hadn't even showered. His breath undoubtedly reeked of coffee and cigarettes. The man blinked at him.

"Are you a member of the Church?"

"No. How much for the book?"

"There's a twenty percent discount for members."

"I see. No, thanks; I'm not a member."

The clerk offered a tepid smile and then seemed to decide something. He started walking towards the front of the store, and Brendan followed. There was a counter and a computer there, and the clerk rang up the purchase. "I joined just a few years ago," he said as he looked at the screen. He took the book and used a scanner on the UPC symbol and then slipped it into a brown paper bag. "Best decision I ever made. That's eleven ninety-eight with tax."

Brendan reached into his sweatpants pocket and dug out his wallet. He found a ten dollar bill, but no more cash. He opted for his debit card and swiped it through the console at the counter.

"Are you a fan of C.S. Lewis?"

"No." Brendan realized he was being a bit standoffish, and corrected himself. "Well, becoming so. I recently took an interest."

The man seemed genuinely pleased as they finished their transaction. "Well good for you. It's best to stay productive, and busy. You know what they say – Nero fiddled while Rome burned."

Brendan forced himself to return the man's smile, nodded, and left the store.

* * *

Back in the Camry, he sat in the parking lot and took the book out of the paper bag. He started flipping through the pages, seeking the spot where the note to "Danice" had referenced a specific passage which had been underlined in pencil. After a few moments, he found it. His memory proved good; he already knew it word for word.

"'*The truth is that wherever a man lies with a woman, there, whether they like it or not, a transcendental relation is set between them which must be eternally enjoyed or eternally endured.*'"

He set the book on his lap, holding the page open. He thought about this, as he had been thinking about if off and on for the past day. The sentence seemed to be saying that sex was not to be taken lightly, that much was obvious. There were not-so-subtle implications that where the sexual congress was not the right choice, it would have to be eternally "endured," as in a hellish way. Every sexual partner a person had would be linked to them eternally. So you needed to be prudent in your decision to take partners, if not downright chaste. The data suggested that Rebecca Heilshorn had not been very chaste. And obviously, only having sex with your husband or wife was the ideal. Clearly a religious idea.

But, it also didn't have to be a religious idea. Brendan looked at the book again and thought about a more secular application, so to speak. What if this passage had been referenced by a scorned lover? What if that was who had given the book to Rebecca? Someone she had been with once and then rejected. This could be a way for that rebuffed lover to say, "Once you've been with me, you'll always have to be with me." You'll always have to endure me. It was a classic situation of, "If I can't have you, no one can," only with this subtle variation.

That reinforced the idea of possible suspects in the ex-lover stable. This, though, was nothing ground-breaking. Most crimes of this nature were crimes of passion, more often than not perpetrated by past or present lovers, family, or friends, like Delaney had said. In this case, there was Donald Kettering. He certainly fit the profile of a rejected lover. He'd gone from cracking jokes and being a man proud of his business and community to veritably morose when talking about Rebecca, a woman he found, "hard to pin down." If anyone had a reason to feel unloved, unappreciated, it was him. Brendan wished he'd asked the man about the book. Maybe that was the key. Maybe a return visit to ask Kettering what he knew about *The Screwtape Letters* could unpack a few things from the man's closet.

Was he really going to do that though? Brendan lit a cigarette and rolled down the window. Was he really going to go running around and performing an investigation when he'd been removed from the case? In real life, hotshot renegade cops didn't go off against their superior's orders and magically solve the crime. Instead, they got suspended, or fired. They could even be brought up on obstruction charges.

Still, what if, just as a civilian, he should happen to stop by the hardware store for some home improvement materials? He was renting the house in Stanwix, but that didn't mean he hadn't gotten the go-ahead from the owner to paint the bedroom. He could just swing by, pick up some paint, ask Donald for some advice on water-based brands, and maybe casually bring up the book he'd been reading, *The Screwtape Letters*. While he was in Boonville he could drop by the place Rebecca had rented a couple years prior and inquire about its availability.

Brendan suddenly laughed out loud, and clamped a hand over his mouth. Smoke issued from his nostrils. He got himself under control and shook his head slowly. It was all ridiculous. Even if he did find something out in either case, in Kettering's reaction to the book, or by visiting the rental property, how would he explain it to Sheriff Taber or Delaney? They would never buy that he was making idle chit-chat with the ex-lover of the deceased about a book that was involved in the investigation of her murder, or that he was thinking of moving to a house in Boonville, ten miles further away from his job.

His smile faded and he grew serious again and looked at the book. He riffled the pages. He decided to think about it in another way.

Besides an unrequited lover, who or what else might have prompted the book to come into Rebecca's possession, and why? What else was there? The sentence was cautionary. It was a presentation of a moral or, spiritual truth. Sex was not just carnality – it was infused with the spiritual life of a person. It affected the soul, the part of the being that was eternal. It was a warning against frivolous copulation.

In what ways did a person think of sex as frivolous? Well, certainly casual sex, an attitude arriving in the sixties and having never left, was a large part of modern society. They called it now a "hook-up culture," and it was said that women especially had come to see casual sex as part of their independence. Modern women, outperforming men in many areas of education and myriad job sectors didn't want to suddenly get bogged down in a marriage, and kids. So they kept it casual with their sexual counterparts. They were now just as noncommittal as men, according to certain studies and articles.

So the C.S. Lewis reference could be a response to that. Rebecca could have been keeping her relationships at a distance and having sex when and where she wanted to. It made sense when you considered Donald Kettering. But what didn't add up was him describing her as frigid. Of course, a man describing a woman as frigid when she didn't want to have sex with him meant very little. That was a Factual Attribution Error which men were famous for making. A woman who rejected them once, was a bitch; who refused sex, was a cold fish; who cheated on them, was a slut. It was unfair any which way.

Brendan mashed the cigarette out in the ashtray. This last idea hung in his mind.

If the book wasn't sent by a scorned lover, or a religious zealot, who did that leave? More importantly, what reasons, other than discouraging casual sex, might someone have for passing the text to Rebecca?

Brendan turned the key in the ignition and dropped the Camry into drive. He turned out of the parking lot and back onto Floyd Ave, heading northeast.

If she was promiscuous, that was one thing. But so far there were no known relationships, at least in the area, besides Kettering and mystery man Eddie, the alleged father of Rebecca's little girl.

Kettering had described her as "tough to pin down," but faithful, for all he knew. And Brendan believed Kettering. It had been an important question, one that Brendan had carefully slid into their conversation, whether or not Kettering and Rebecca had been "exclusive."

"I hope so," Kettering had answered, and Brendan had felt something resonate. There was a sense of truth to that. It hadn't sounded even remotely threatening, like "She better have been," but really, a display of true male vulnerability. All a guy could do, in the end, was believe his woman would be faithful, and hope that she was.

If she was promiscuous in the general sense, then she was clandestine about it. Maybe she hooked up with absolute anonymity – that was still possible. Brendan knew very little about her life outside of the region. But it was only in the context of the region that Kettering had known her. It was certainly possible, even likely, that someone from her life outside the area had portaged in and done the deed, but Brendan just had a hard time wrapping his mind around Rebecca Heilshorn inviting some random person to her hideaway home in farm country, when she seemed to fiercely guard her privacy in other ways. Or was he missing the obvious? Had she just been cheating on Kettering, and that was it? Leading a double life of some kind?

It was someone specific who'd sent her the book. That was the feeling. Someone with real cause, and not just a previous sexual partner who wanted more from her.

The medical examiners had so far been unable to show conclusively that she had been raped. Rape wasn't always so violent that it left marks, or anything for serology. Coercive sex was always possible, with an aggressor who covered his tracks well. But what was known definitively was that the victim had been stabbed multiple times in a savage fashion. The killer had been more than disgruntled; the killer had been absolutely enraged. Sadistic and brutal. It didn't fit together, the idea of a "mild" almost invisible rape, and then a violent killing. It was almost as if there were two different aggressors at work.

Brendan drove past the residences on Floyd Avenue. They were Colonial, Victorian, Federalist. Mostly white or yellow with black shutters. Large pick-up trucks and minivans in the short driveways. A few people were out, wearing light coats. A mother pushed a stroller, and two young boys rode on their bikes. A person would never know that murder existed in a world this quiet and simple.

The air that blew in through the open window smelled of leaves and impending rain. Indeed, the clouds had knitted together overhead, and were ready to open.

The questioned gnawed at him. The reason for someone giving Rebecca this book was elusive. And how did he even know it had been given to her? The note said

"Danice" after all. Didn't that make it even more likely that *she* had been planning to give the book to someone, and just hadn't gotten the chance?

He hoped and trusted that Delaney and Colinas were running the name Danice right now, and looking to match it with Rebecca.

"Eternally endured," Brendan said softly as he drove.

What else would cause someone to have multiple sexual partners? Casual sex certainly wasn't the worst possibility. Two consenting adults with mutual respect could, theoretically, "enjoy" their congress eternally. Sure, it would be better to spend eternity with that person you loved most, but it was possible to enjoy multiple partners, too.

So who wouldn't enjoy their partners?

"Prostitutes," he said to the empty interior of the Camry.

Prostitutes. Certainly a woman who had sex with innumerable partners over the years, likely deriving little to no enjoyment out of any of them, would be a candidate for suffering them eternally.

It would be hell, when you thought about it. All those men, all those experiences, repeated for eternity.

And, Brendan supposed, porn fell into the category, too. Porn was another form of prostitution. Most people didn't think of it that way, but the people involved in porn got paid to have sex. That was the prostitution of their *corpus*, if you asked Brendan.

And, to C.S. Lewis's thinking, the prostitution of their soul, too, for which there was no redemption.

As he headed back to Stanwix, still debating on whether or not it could work to drop in on Kettering, Brendan imagined the killer standing in the doorway of Rebecca Heilshorn's home on the morning of Thursday the fourteenth.

Who was he? Kettering, in a fury driven by romantic rejection? This mystery man Eddie, come for retribution for his lack of custody over the daughter he shared with Rebecca? Kevin, her brother, who had been, as Delaney suggested, into some kinky incestuous relationship with his sister (which corresponded to Kettering's description of her icy, isolated nature), upset she had broken it off? Or come back to break it off himself? Had he then turned the gun on Olivia Jane because he had told her about it in a moment of grief? Was he terrified of having the information about a sordid relationship with his sister come out in public?

The killer, standing there, alarms Rebecca, who calls 911. Then the killer goes and gets a knife from the kitchen while Rebecca flees to her bedroom and shuts the door. Or maybe the killer already had the knife, and Rebecca had seen it, and her alarm prompted her to place the emergency call before seeking refuge in the bedroom.

The killer climbs the stairs, the knife glints in the early sun blooming in the windows of the clerestory room. He savagely kicks in the door. He tells her to get on the bed, now. He gets on top of her, but does not necessarily rape her. Instead, maybe, they have a brief and tense exchange. He asks her something, or he blames her, or he pleads with her, or he just starts slashing at her.

When it's over, he goes through her drawers. Either it's a slipshod attempt at making it look like a robbery, or there's something he wants. Something he's trying to find.

"Ah," said Brendan.

If it was the killer who had given Rebecca the book, wouldn't he have taken it back then? Why leave anything for the police that could be linked to him?

It seemed more and more likely that Rebecca had been the one to give the book to someone. That, or some third party calling her "Danice," had given it to her. The former scenario sounded more probable, but Brendan still gave due consideration to the latter.

The killer then leaves the house. Does he burn the laptop and throw it in the shed? No, not enough time, and nothing was hot or freshly burned. The stuff had to have been burned in the fireplace the night before. Someone should ask the neighbor, Folwell, about any odd smells coming from the Heilshorn house that evening before the murder. Like burning plastic.

Rebecca was likely the one to have done it. But why? What was she hiding? And from whom?

The killer, likely. Anticipating his arrival, perhaps. But then why call 911 right away?

Brendan sighed. He was almost home. He had to get his mind cleared – it was all jumbling up again, with overlapping puzzle pieces and gaps where none seemed to go. He had to wash up and get dressed; he had a meeting with Olivia in two hours, and he had things to do first. Time to get moving.

And while he showered and put his clothes on, that image lingered – the silhouette of the man in the doorway. Rebecca's killer, leaving, slipping away. He disappears as the sun rises, and the heat burns the dry land. The police scour the big, rambling house and ask their questions.

Who was he?

## CHAPTER EIGHTEEN / SATURDAY, 12:15 PM

Olivia Jane had insisted that her suggestion for a noon meeting didn't mean a lunch date, but Brendan was able to persuade her anyway. "You need to eat; keep your strength up."

She finally conceded, but he knew it wasn't because she agreed with his reasoning. She didn't want to meet at her own house, and she wasn't about to go to his house, so a neutral location made sense.

They met at the Rome Savoy. At noon on a Saturday in the summer, the place was busy. The décor was friendly and familial. Framed photographs adorned the wood-paneled walls. The images showed large families, black-and-white weddings, and regal men wearing double-breasted suits. College sports team pennants hung from the crown molding.

It took Brendan a moment to realize that he was bothered by the place. It reminded him too much of a bad time. A time he wished, and would wish forever, could be taken back. The Reckoning.

He forced himself out of the sour feeling and made small talk with Olivia about the weather. They ordered their food and drinks. Brendan sipped on a coke while Olivia opened a bottle of water and poured it over ice.

"I've been removed from the case," he told her.

Olivia's eyes widened a little. "Why?"

He looked at her levelly and said nothing. He let her put it together.

After a moment, she asked, "Is that unusual?"

He shrugged.

"So what are you going to do?"

"Take the weekend, show up for work on Monday, get reassigned to something else."

"How do you feel about it?"

"I feel great about it."

She smirked and raised her eyebrows.

"Yeah, it sucks. They've brought in State Police Detectives."

"Now, I know that's not unusual."

"They were at your house."

"They were at my house, yes."

"And your lawyer, too."

"Are you driving at something, Detective?"

"What did they say to you?"

She surprised him by laughing. She had a pleasant laugh, and her teeth flashed briefly before she pressed her lips together. "Does this usually work for you? You know I can't talk to you about yesterday."

"You can't? Why not?"

She cocked her head. "Are you trying to exasperate me? We haven't even gotten our food yet."

"What *can* you talk about?"

She looked at her water for a moment, and took it with both hands. "I can talk to you about Thursday. As a friend. About what happened. About how you feel about it."

"I feel great about it."

"Now that's just bad taste. Have you ever had to shoot anyone before in the line of duty?"

"No."

"Do you remember what we were talking about the other day? Before . . . everything happened? About absorbing a tragedy?"

He shifted in his seat. "I think so. You were saying that it's not normally the first stage of grief to want to sit down and *talk about it*." He hung his fingers in the air to indicate quotation marks around "talk about it."

"Right," she said.

"But you're asking me to do just that."

"I'm wondering whether or not it was a tragedy in your eyes."

He scowled. "Of course it was. What else would it be?"

"Getting the bad guy."

"Why would I think Kevin Heilshorn was the bad guy?

She scowled at him. "I don't know . . . because he tried to end our lives? Boy, you like to be contrary. Let's talk about *that*."

He leaned forward. "Wait. That has to come from somewhere. Your meeting with the State Detectives yesterday. They're looking to hang the murder on him, too?"

Her gaze became evasive. "I wouldn't say that, exactly."

He was growing a little flustered, but kept his cool. "Please, Ms. Jane. Olivia. What do you think? You spent an hour with him. Do you think he did it?"

"I can't say."

"Off the record, come on. Why do you think he came after us?"

"Us? Maybe he came after you."

"You don't think he resented you for talking to him? Like you say, about how people aren't ready for that. Did it set him off?"

"Are you insinuating that my brief encounter with the aggrieved brother of a dead girl prompted him to come back and try to kill me? Or you?"

He leaned back. "No."

"It sounds like it. Where are you from?"

"Where am I from?"

"Yes. Where were you born? Where did you grow up?"

"I was born in New York City. St. Luke's-Roosevelt. We moved to Westchester when I was a kid. New Rochelle, then Hawthorne."

"With both of your parents?"

"With my mother."

"Your father stayed in the city?"

"He was a doctor. He couldn't do a commute."

"Was a doctor? No longer a doctor?"

"He passed away."

"I'm sorry. So you were raised by your mother. Where is she now?"

"Buried next to him."

Olivia blinked. She took a drink of her water. "I'm sorry for that, too. They were buried together?"

"They never divorced, just separated. Neither one of them found anyone else."

She looked across the table at him. Her brown eyes were soft. "What about you?"

He drank his coke. "What about me, what?"

"Ever find someone? Ever been married?"

He took a breath and looked around the restaurant. People chatted and ate and rattled their silverware. A little boy dropped his napkin on the floor, got off his chair, retrieved the napkin, and then started to crawl around underneath the table.

"Yes," said Brendan.

"Yes what? You were married?"

"I was."

Olivia watched him closely. She let up on the line of questioning. A few moments passed, and they both observed the rest of the restaurant. Then their food came.

Once the plates were in front of them, the conversation livened up again, kindled by some idle chatter. Then Olivia got back to business.

"Why did you want to see me?"

Brendan felt a little stubborn. He responded with his own question. "Why did you agree to be seen?"

Olivia looked up from her plate, with a frown. Brendan pulled something from his valise. He set the brown paper bag down on the table and reached inside of it. At the same time, Olivia sat up and pulled away from the table, as if the bag contained something dangerous. "I told you," she began. "I'm not able to help you with this case."

Brendan pulled the paperback book out. "I'm not on the case anymore. This is a book I picked up at a bookstore around the corner. Have you ever read it?"

She looked dubious, gauging him, but then she lowered her eyes and read the title aloud, "*The Screwtape Letters.*" Something registered in her gaze. She nodded. "I think so. Years ago."

"What did you think of it?"

"I don't really remember." She picked it up and then read the subtitle. "*Letters from a Senior Devil to a Junior Devil.*" Her eyes flicked up to him. "Sounds like inter-office politics in hell. Why do you have this?"

"It's a copy of the book found at the scene of Rebecca Heilshorn's murder."

She dropped it like it was suddenly contagious. "You're outrageous. This is unprofessional. Are you trying to get me to leave? I can go, you know." Her voice remained calm, but her eyes danced with electricity.

"It's not unprofessional. You and I are two people sitting down, discussing a book."

"Is this how they do things in Hawthorne?"

"I wasn't a detective in Hawthorne. I was a cop."

"You're telling me that if your boss knew we were here together that he wouldn't suspend you immediately? Or fire you? I shouldn't be here; I'm putting your job and mine on the line."

She started to make moves like she was about to leave. He reached across the table and gently took her hand.

"Look." Brendan kept his voice very low, but emphatic. "A girl was murdered. We know very little about her. She's not from the area. Seems to have no friends. Comes from a wealthy family. Her brother shows up and finds out she was killed. Now, I don't think, and neither do you, that his grief threw him into a homicidal rage. Nor do I think he was the one who killed her. I don't know why, I only spent about as much time with him as you did, but it just doesn't sit. Unless he was absolutely crazy, and returned to the scene of the crime less than an hour after killing her. And you don't think he was that crazy, or egomaniacal. I know you don't. Was he antisocial? Bipolar? You don't think so, and neither do I. But his father put pressure on the department to take me off the case. Not because I was doing a poor job, but because of what happened with Kevin. It's understandable, but listen. I believe the killer is still out there."

Olivia looked at his hand. She sighed. "Then let your co-workers handle it. Leave it to Delaney. I'm sorry, I just can't be involved." She pulled her hand away, but she remained seated. Brendan was nonplussed by her mention of Delaney.

Neither of them had touched their food for a while, and now their waiter seemed to take notice. He materialized next to their table.

"Everything okay here, folks?"

"Fine," said Brendan. He offered a smile. The waiter eyed their plates, and then returned the smile and left.

Olivia was looking at Brendan.

"You weren't a detective in Hawthorne. You were a cop, you said."

"Yes."

"So you've been a detective for . . .?"

"Three months."

She shook her head, as if to say, *This isn't how it is done.* "Why did you become a policeman in Hawthorne?"

"I do think Kevin was involved somehow. I think he knew something. The question is, what?"

"Did you always want to become a cop?"

"Just help me. Please."

She dropped her hands onto the table in frustration, rattling the silverware against the ceramic dishes. "Just what do you think it is I can do? Detective, this book could mean nothing. Nothing at all. You're off a case which has no leads, and you're probably grasping at straws. Want to know why?"

"Why?"

"Because of what happened two days ago. You have your own grief to deal with, Mr. Healy, and you're trying to cope with it by rushing to solve a case you're no longer lawfully allowed to. You think that by finding this killer you say is out there that you'll be able to release yourself from these feelings."

"Oh, don't try to therapize me," he said, feeling a stab of anger. "You were there, too. You were shot at, too."

"I'm not trying to therapize you. You and I both *know* I can't therapize you. What I can do – what I'm trying to do – is be a friend to you. But you're not making it easy because you keep acting like such a jackass."

She fell silent, and then began gathering up her things.

"Maybe you're right. Maybe I've got skin in the game. We both do."

She glanced at him briefly, but kept on readying herself to leave. She took money from her wallet and set it down on the table.

He watched her.

"I asked Kevin Heilshorn if he was willing to sign a release so I could potentially share any pertinent information with the police. But he wouldn't sign anything. And unless he told me he was the killer, or was going to hurt himself or hurt someone else, our relationship was confidential. I hoped to help him through his tragedy. But he remained volatile." She stood up. Her eyes seemed to charge him with being "volatile" himself. "If you ever feel like you want to talk to me about this – as a friend – stop your obsession and give me a call."

"Please take your money back. It's on me."

"I'd feel better if I left it."

"Okay."

She lingered for a moment. "Take care of yourself."

"You too." He didn't know what else to say. He watched her walk out of the restaurant.

\* \* \*

Brendan spent the afternoon on the computer and phone. He found the house Rebecca Heilshorn had rented and dialed the property manager. A woman answered. He asked if it were available for rent. It wasn't, and he then inquired about a former tenant.

"Rebecca Heilshorn. This would be about two years ago," she said.

"What about her?"

"I'm an old friend and I'm just trying to track her down. Do you remember her? Did you rent to her?"

"No."

"You're sure. You don't want to check your records or anything?"

"Sir, I've been recently contacted by the State Police about this same person. I'll tell you what I told them, I have no records of a person by that name renting the house. We've represented the owner for six years."

"Who is the owner?"

"I'm sorry, you say you're a friend? Why do you want to know who owns the house the woman you're friends with never rented?"

"I'm really just in a bind trying to find her. I'm getting married and we were old college friends. It would mean so much to me if I could track her down."

"Well, I'm sorry I can't help you."

"Maybe you could just try one more thing? Just check and see if the home was rented to anyone at that time by the name of Danice."

An exhalation over the phone. "Alright. Hold on please." She came back only a few seconds later. "No, I'm sorry. No one named Danice. Now, I really can't continue with this, sir. What did you say your name was?"

"Seamus Argon," Brendan lied. "If you could please just . . . I'm really desperate here. I need to get in touch with her. Please, the name of the owner?"

There was another sigh, and then a pause. "Reginald Forrester," she said.

The name didn't ring any bells for Brendan. He made a note to have Colinas run it. "Ok. Thank you so much. I'm sorry to be a trouble." Brendan hung up.

Following up with Donald Kettering didn't work, either. An assistant in the hardware store informed Brendan that Kettering was away for a couple of days. Out of town for the weekend on trade show business. Brendan thanked him and got off the line.

He turned his attention to his laptop. He sipped on an iced tea and lit a cigarette. He wasn't supposed to smoke in the house he was renting, and so far had taken his cigarettes outside. This afternoon he didn't care. He used a plastic cup with some water in it for an ashtray and pecked at the keys of his Compaq.

He tried several searches. He cross-referenced Danice with *The Screwtape Letters*, C.S. Lewis, and the names of Rebecca Heilshorn, Kevin, and the whole Heilshorn family. Nothing cogent appeared. When he entered Heilshorn alone, it drew some slightly more interesting results.

There was a Laura Heilshorn who was a faculty member in the bioengineering department at MIT. He read parts of her biography out loud in the empty living room. Her interests were described as including regenerative medicine, engineered proteins with novel assembly properties, microfluidics, and stem cell differentiation. Practical applications included spinal cord injuries, Parkinson's disease, and strokes, in which she performed tissue engineering and designed cellular transportation scaffolds.

There were other Heilshorns as well, an artist among them. He scrolled down on one page and his breath caught. There was a hit on neuroscience in correlation with a Heilshorn. "Decorrelated Neuronal Firing in Cortical Microcircuits." But the correlation was insignificant – the Heilshorn in the same hit was not the neuroscientist, but a man named Hung-foo. Besides, the only reason it had struck him, he realized, was because of his own field of study back in his academic days.

He cross-referenced Laura with Alexander Heilshorn. There was nothing to indicate any relationship between them, either familial or professional. He'd thought maybe that medicine ran in the family. It was still possible that they were related, but he wondered how much it would matter anyway.

Here he was, at nearly five in the afternoon, no longer on a case, trying to make something out of phantoms.

Maybe Olivia was right. Maybe he was grasping at straws.

At five o'clock, he checked the local news online, and watched the live stream. After a few other breaking stories, a feature discussed the Heilshorn murder. He winced as he saw a replay of himself talking to the reporter behind the Sheriff's Department building. It was only a brief clip – likely they had run the whole thing the evening before, he had carefully avoided watching it – and then Senior Prosecutor Skene was standing in front of the microphones on the steps at the front of the building.

Brendan watched Skene repeat the usual rhetoric: We have strong leads. We're working every angle and adding value to the case all the time. We'll have it solved soon.

Refer to the hotline if you have anything you think might be helpful. Be sure to vote in the upcoming elections.

The story ended and the news turned to national stories on wildfires and tornados. Brendan closed the window on the screen and sat back in the couch.

It would make sense to let it all go. Not only could he lose his job, but he could end up interfering, and be brought up on charges. As it was, he still had the whole situation with the Kevin Heilshorn shooting to look forward to. It would take up much of next week, for sure. There would be an immense amount of paperwork, and more meetings with Internal Affairs.

He sighed and looked at the book sitting next to the laptop. On the cover of this edition of *The Screwtape Letters,* was a cartoonish trident, pointing toward the sky, with flames snaking around the handle.

He studied the image for a while. He picked up the book and turned it over and over in his hands.

Something occurred to him and he set the book down. He opened the internet browser again and tried one last search.

He looked for "Danice" and added the key words "Sex, Sexual partners, Promiscuity, and Eternity."

He took a sip of his iced tea, and clicked the button to engage the search.

When he saw the results page, he tried to set the iced tea down on the coffee table and nearly missed. The drink slopped in the glass.

Brendan put a hand over his mouth.

"Holy shit," he said.

# CHAPTER NINETEEN / SATURDAY, 5:22 PM

Sheriff Taber was diplomatic on the phone, but he couldn't entirely conceal his excitement.

"I can't tell you how sensitive this is going to be. How sensitive it already is," Taber explained.

"I understand."

Brendan had taken to pacing around his house. Some automatic bean-counting part of his brain estimated he'd done at least twenty laps already, from the living room to the bedroom, to the kitchen and back again. His laptop sat open on the coffee table. The website he'd found was still up. He found it hard to look at.

"We have to be very careful about how we present this information," said Taber, thinking out loud. "Especially, how it was come across. Even if we say that you just happened to be surfing, and came across it completely coincidentally, it just . . ."

"I know. It's a stretch. You can give it to anyone else. Say that Delaney found it."

The Sheriff was silent for a moment, and then cleared his throat. "You know Delaney won't go for that. Not with this type of . . . thing. He has . . . he has his own issues which may conflict."

"Then say it was an anonymous tip. Someone saw the photo in the papers and then called it in. They wanted to remain anonymous for obvious reasons."

"That may just work."

The regional papers had run the story on Friday, front page. The New York Times had covered it that morning. The same picture of Rebecca Heilshorn had accompanied each article. Brendan had all of them stacked on his kitchen table.

It was no doubt an old image of Rebecca. She was sitting on a bench in front of a college campus. One paper claimed the source "Courtesy of Cornell University." In truth, the reporters had dug up information on Rebecca's history quicker than the investigation had. She had done undergraduate work at Cornell in Psychology. None of the articles mentioned where she had done any graduate studies, or if she had obtained a Masters or PhD.

"Heilshorn is arriving tomorrow."

"I see."

"He's going to be more controlling than ever with this new information."

"Mmhmm. How is it going with the Eddie Stemp lead?"

"You'll have to talk to Colinas. He's on it."

"What's Delaney doing?"

The Sheriff was silent for a moment. Brendan worried he might be pushing the Sheriff too much. But Taber came through. "He's doing what he does. He's gone through all her phone records, done a thorough examination of the laptop we found – not the disintegrated one, the other one – and so on. I guess you had Colinas look into the social media stuff?"

"Yeah."

"She has no Facebook, nothing."

"So where did the papers get the info about her undergrad at Cornell?"

"Hell if I know. But I'm friendly with Mark Overton at the Sun. It's not uncommon for papers to get to some of the more clerical stuff first. I hate to say it, but they have better contacts, and our databases sometimes can't compete with a simple pair of drinking buddies. Overton is friendly with the Dean at Syracuse. I guess there's a simple way you can tap into student registries and that's how he found her at Cornell. She didn't graduate, though."

"She didn't?"

"No. Dropped out junior year. For all we know, the photo the press ran of her was at the end of her short collegiate career."

"Makes sense."

"What does?"

Brendan glanced at the laptop again, then looked away. "She got into something else."

"Ah," said the Sheriff.

"You mind if I call Colinas about Stemp? Just . . . professional curiosity."

The Sheriff sighed. "Fine. But keep it on the . . . whatever my son says. The DL."

"Will do."

"Healy."

"Yes, Sheriff."

"Well done. Not a word about this."

"Not a word."

The Sheriff grunted, and then hung up.

Brendan put his phone back in his pocket. He wanted to call Colinas right away, but his mind was distracted. He kept looking at the laptop. Drawn to it, as if magnetized.

He walked slowly over to the couch and sat back down. He steeled himself and started moving the cursor around.

The site displayed thumbnails of multiple videos. There were pages and pages of these videos. The one featuring "Danice" was near the top. He had already watched it, but he clicked on it and watched it again.

After only a few seconds, he shut it off.

There was no doubt that the girl in the video was Rebecca Heilshorn. He'd already sent the Sheriff the link – and only the Sheriff – and Taber had corroborated that the girl did, indeed, bear an unmistakable resemblance. They would have to verify it, but it was her. Brendan knew it was her, and he felt that the Sheriff did, too.

Brendan saw her corpse staring back at him, reflected in the mirror on her bedroom bureau. Trying to tell him something. Was it this?

He felt a bit nauseous then. It was a very strange thing, a very uncomfortable thing, watching a murdered girl alive again. In this case, in a pornographic video.

He closed the window to the site, a porn smorgasbord called "Red Light." He sat back on the couch, thinking for a minute.

It made sense. Whoever had sent her the copy of the book was clearly giving her a message: This kind of behavior was wrong. It was not spiritually tenable. This kind of behavior would result in an eternity of suffering.

It was a sobering thought.

Brendan found his mind lingering on the master bedroom in the Bloomingdale house. Renovations: the king-sized bed, the large bathroom with new fixtures, the furniture; dressers with empty drawers. Had Rebecca just been moving into a bigger room, stretching out a little? Or had someone been planning on moving in with her, making a cozy home of it? Had she turned a corner?

The first internet search had revealed a video with a significant date. It was three years old. Brendan had then used the search engine within the Red Light site to find other Danice videos, and found two more. Their dates were not far apart, the most recent posted two and a half years ago. Right before she met Donald Kettering.

It didn't mean there wasn't more pornography featuring Rebecca Heilshorn online. She could have used yet another alias at any time. And it didn't mean that online videos were the extent of her involvement in the business. Conversely, the videos indicated something of a career. They were not amateur productions. A cursory examination of any porn videos could determine their degree of professionalism. The videos had been arranged into sections, with a "home video" cache among them. (Others tended to be categorized by fetish, by female body types, ethnicity, and so on.)

The sick feeling in Brendan's stomach persisted.

He got up from the couch, went into the kitchen and drank a glass of water. He lingered at the sink, standing with his hands on the edge of the counter and his head down.

He closed his eyes for a while, but this was no good. Images of the dead girl mingled with these fresh visions of the porn video and made for a terrible slideshow in his head.

He needed to get out. He needed to call Colinas right away.

## CHAPTER TWENTY / SATURDAY, 6:47 PM

From his car, headed away from Rome and Stanwix and into the countryside, he called State Police Detective Rudy Colinas. Colinas didn't answer, so Brendan left a message. He chose his words carefully, mentioning Taber's approval of the inquiry. He urged Colinas to call him back at his earliest convenience. Not long after he'd hung up, his phone rang. He hadn't yet put her name into his contacts, but Brendan thought he recognized the number.

"Olivia," he said when he answered.

"You never told me you had a degree in neurobiology," she said.

"Tough as it makes me seem, I try not to use it on chicks."

"Very funny."

She paused, and ruffled against the phone on her end. "I'm sorry about today."

"You're pretty hot-headed for a grief counselor."

"Watch it."

He found a wide spot along the shoulder where he could pull off the road. "I shouldn't be putting you in the position I keep putting you in. I'm sorry."

"You're just driven."

"Thank you for not saying what you really think — 'obsessed.' "

There was a pause. "Where are you?"

Brendan actually had to look around. He had just been driving, not really paying attention. A few landmarks and he realized at once where he'd gotten himself to.

"Uhm, not far from you, actually."

"Oh really," she said. He thought he could hear a smile in her voice. "Checking up on me?"

"There still a County car outside your place?"

"No. I think they've given up worrying about me."

"I haven't."

There was a moment of awkward silence. Brendan closed his eyes, wondering, as usual, if he'd gone too far. Why was he so pushy?

"We didn't eat much of our food," she said. "Did you take it home with you?"

"Yep. In fact, got it right here on my lap."

"Do you?"

"No."

She laughed. "Can you come by, then? I'll make you something."

"Okay."

* * *

Something had changed. The house, only two days later, seemed to have rid itself of the specter of what had happened. It smelled, anyway, like detergent and antiseptic. The two damaged front windows had been replaced.

"Who did that?" Brendan jerked a thumb at the new glass.

"Local contractor."

"That was fast."

"I've been here longer than you. I know people."

They were standing just inside the entrance. The lights were dim in the living room, off to the left. Pillows had been fluffed. The white half-curtains enclosing the many, classic, four-paned windows had been freshly ruffled.

"You've been cleaning."

"I have. Yes, I have." She clapped her hands together. "Drink? It's late enough, right?"

He smiled. "I don't drink."

There was the briefest moment of awkwardness, something which usually came with this revelation, but it was gone in a second. Olivia was genial. "You *do* too, drink. I saw you drink a coke today."

"If you have a coke or something like it, that would be fine."

"Good. I'll have one too. It will keep me up all night, but who cares. I'd be up anyway."

"Fix yourself whatever you were thinking of. Don't drink New Jersey chemicals for my sake."

She looked at him with curiosity. Before he had a chance to explain his glib attempt at humor, his phone buzzed in his pocket.

"Excuse me."

He let himself out onto the porch. The sun was still up, but buried behind a low bank of clouds close to the horizon. The world was cast in a cold steel, and the temperature was lower than the previous two days.

"Hello?"

"Healy? Colinas. Got your message."

"Thanks for getting back to me. Any word on Eddie Stemp?"

"Oh, plenty."

Brendan felt his heart rate pick up a little. He walked to the edge of the porch and gripped one of the posts framing the steps down. "Tell me."

"Well, he's a real dyed-in-the-wool homesteader, I can tell you that. Got a big place in Barneveld."

"Barneveld? Jesus, that's where I am now. Just outside."

"Then you're close. I was there earlier today."

"You spoke to him?"

"Oh yeah. Pleasant guy. Real religious-type. Fundamentalist, ya know? Down to brass tacks, nothing rank and file. Think he said he goes to church three days a week."

"Which church?"

"Ah . . ." Brendan heard Colinas flip some pages in his notebook. "The Resurrection Life Church."

"You're fucking kidding me." Now Brendan's heart was racing.

"You know it?"

"I was just there today."

Silence from Colinas. Brendan closed his eyes for a second. "I mean, I went to the bookstore. I was looking for something; they have a bookstore there."

"Right," said Colinas. He didn't sound convinced, but he let it alone.

"So you talked to Eddie Stemp?"

"Yep. Stemp and his wife, and their two little kids. Nice family, real polite. They were all there. Real Little House on the Prairie stuff. They had it all – pigs, chickens, the whole Old MacDonald's Farm."

"And what did he say about Rebecca?"

Colinas seemed to hesitate. Brendan didn't know if it was because he was wondering how much he was permitted to tell an investigator off-the-case – Taber's blessing or not – or if it was because he wasn't used to referring to the deceased girl so familiarly.

"He was devastated. Really had some issues with it. Read about it in the Friday paper and was just heartbroken."

"Was he?"

"Well, you know. Seemed genuine to me. He talked a little bit about his time with her. They were married for only a real short time. Six months. And this was a few years ago. About five years. He's almost ten years older than her. Anyway, back then he says he was a real asshole. His words. A real asshole. An alcoholic and all of that."

Brendan felt something twist inside of him. He swallowed and tried to listen as intently as possible. He sensed Olivia in the house behind him, near the windows, looking out. A cool breeze blew in over the front yard and ruffled the tall rows of sunflowers.

"Said he always regretted how things ended between them, but, that was life. He was making . . . um, what did he say . . . ah, 'reparations,' or something."

"With her? Did he try and contact her?"

"He said he'd meant to, but he hadn't gotten the chance yet."

Brendan tried to unscramble the thoughts which were coalescing in his mind. "Five years ago, but he lives up here. Doesn't make any sense. She only just started coming here two years ago. Just bought the house. Doesn't know anybody. Did he say where they lived when they were married, or why he was here now?"

"He was evasive about most of it. He said she was out of college by then. She had dropped out. Was drifting about. That's it."

"Dropped out of Cornell."

"That's right."

Brendan licked his lips. "Colinas, I want you to take this guy very seriously. He's her ex-husband. The book found in Rebecca's . . . in the victim's home, is the same book they carry at the store his church owns."

"I've looked into the book. It's not exactly *Girl with the Dragon Tattoo,* but it's sold something like a million or more copies. That book is probably lots of places."

"All the same . . ."

"Healy, listen. His alibi is positively fucking unsqueezable. I said he goes to church, right? Three days a week. He was at church Thursday morning. With his whole family. With an entire congregation who saw him there."

Brendan was silent.

"So . . . I dunno. I hear you on the ex-husband thing, but. You know, this guy seems pretty ship-shape. He was emotional, yet cooperative. Nothing to hide. Loving wife and family. Relationship with the victim pretty much ancient history. . ."

"But they live a *few miles* away from one another."

"I hear you, I hear you. It's small world, though. You said yourself you happen to be not far from his place now. I mean, look. I got to go. I'm happy to talk to you more, but I've got to debrief with Delaney now."

"Okay." Brendan took a breath. "Thanks, Colinas."

"Yup."

"Hey . . ."

"Yeah?"

"I need to ask you one last favor."

He heard Colinas sigh.

"Just this one last thing," said Brendan.

"Go ahead, man."

"I turned in all my casework. Can you get me a transcript of the 911 call? I just want to look at it one more time."

Colinas paused. Brendan imagined the State Detective was wondering why he was interested in the call, in the light of this new information about Eddie Stemp. That was good. Brendan wanted Colinas thinking along those lines.

"You can email it to me."

"Yeah, okay."

"Thanks."

Brendan ended the call and put his phone in his pocket. He turned and walked back inside. Olivia was sitting on one of the living room couches. It was an open-plan room, with plenty of space and furniture to fill it. There was a closed door along the back wall. Maybe leading to an office.

Brendan felt like Olivia had quickly slipped over and sat down when she'd seen him coming. She affected an innocent face. "Everything okay?"

He remained standing. "Two major revelations in one day. And I'm not even on the case."

She waited, perhaps having grown just a little tense.

"I think we may have found our guy. I mean, *they* may have found the guy. It will take a little work, but I have a feeling."

"That's great news."

"Yeah. It's just . . ."

He stopped himself and walked over and sat down on the loveseat adjacent to the couch. A glass of coke with ice was on the coffee table. He took a sip. The sweet, smoky, rusty taste of it was very good.

"Anyway," he said.

"Anyway," she echoed. "You're a neurobiologist? Tell me about it."

And he smiled a little and got comfortable and tried to make himself sociable.

\* \* \*

About fifteen minutes later, they took their drinks to the porch, and he lit a cigarette. Olivia watched him smoke it.

"You ever try CHANTIX?"

"No." He exhaled a puff of smoke, blowing it away from her direction.

"You've made your mind up about it, I see."

He chuckled. "Yeah."

"Why?"

He shrugged. "All that I did in six years of school, all that was to eventually study habits."

"And you did? You worked in your field?"

He nodded. "I went to school at NYU's Neuroscience Institute and was earning my PhD while finishing up school working at the Langone Medical Center. But I only worked there for one year."

167

"What did you do?"

"Like I said. I studied habits."

"How?"

"Mice. Sometimes students."

"I've never met anyone who actually did studies with mice before."

"I preferred human beings."

"What sort of studies?"

"Langone really has a strong emphasis on wellness. Not just treating a disease, but increasing overall wellness. Wellness is largely determined by genetics. But it's obviously affected by habits, too. The thing is, genetic precursors have a lot to do with why a person starts down the path of this or that habit."

"So it's all genetics? I don't buy that."

He took a drag and looked at her. "You're a 'nurture over nature' person."

"I'm a therapist. Absolutely."

"Well, you're not alone. All the recent advances in neuroscience show plasticity to the brain that wasn't previously considered. In fact, that was my area. Trying to 'nurture' positive habits, life-changing habits, even in the face of strong genetic contradiction."

"Like what?"

"Oh, like lots of things. Like taking a person born with an exorbitant amount of fat cells, who is inclined to sedentary behavior, and getting that person more oriented for routine exercise, like someone naturally more athletic might be."

"And?"

"It's tough. Habits are underrated. Habits take root in one of the most ancient areas of the brain. This is why we could use mice effectively, because the basal ganglia of the brain are at work in both mice and humans. Habits are rudimentary. No species is immune."

He was finished with his cigarette. He field-stripped it by rolling out the ember and letting it fall to the wood floor and then squashing it with his shoe.

"You can throw that out inside. Come on in. It's getting cool out again."

"It is," he agreed. The sun had been dropping and with it, the temperature. It would be dark in half an hour or less. They returned inside.

She pointed him to the trash can in the kitchen, and he dropped in the cigarette filter.

"Why were you only there for a year?"

He'd been waiting for the question and wondered why he had even told her about his short stay at Langone anyway. Of course it would provoke an inquiry.

"Personal reasons," he said.

"I see." She looked around the kitchen. "Am I making dinner, or are you taking me out?"

\* \* \*

It was dusk as they drove towards Utica, where they had decided on a restaurant.

"So if you're a nurture person, I've got a question."

"Oh boy."

He smiled. "What would make someone go into porn?"

He braced himself for her reaction. She would ask him why in the hell he'd brought up a subject like that at this time, on what might in fact be their first date.

But she didn't. "Oh that's definitely nurture."

"You think?"

"Come on. You're the neurobiologist. You're the detective. You ever found anything to suggest someone got into porn because of genetics?"

"Well, sure. Their looks, for one. Body type. But also their neuropsychological make-up. Kids on the playground, four and five-year-olds, some of them are extroverts, some are quiet and shy. They can become adults who are exhibitionists, free-spirited types, or they can hide their lamp under a bushel basket."

She scowled at him in the dark. "Did you skip over developmental psychology, doctor? And by the way, why don't you call yourself doctor?"

"I never finished. I said I was earning my degree. I left first."

"Huh. Well, I'll call you doctor anyway. And developmental psych is a sophomore class. Kids have been majorly sculpted by the time they are the four and five year-olds you describe hopping around the playground, some of them flashers, some of them agoraphobics."

This elicited a laugh despite some fresh stomach pains Brendan felt building. He was having a nice time, but he couldn't get Rebecca out of his head. The image of her in the bedroom, the recent video discovery, any of it. And all of this playing the searchlight over the wreckage of his past; it was hard to deal with.

"Well, now, you know certain kids are born a certain way. Given the same exact set of parents, let's say, doing the same exact things; some kids are apt to be criers, some are more passive. Some babies are colicky, some sleep through the night, right away."

"All nurture. All environment."

"No way."

"I have a feeling this is an argument we're probably going to have our whole lives."

He glanced at her for a second and then put his eyes back to the road. He could feel the little bit of awkwardness that followed her comment. He was sure she felt it, too. It suddenly reminded him of being sixteen years old, and holding a girl around her waist at the dance, having trouble making eye contact.

His stomach started to calm down. The atmosphere in the car lightened. She clicked on the radio and went up and down through the band until she found the station she was looking for. "You like classic rock?"

"Sure. It's both, anyway."

"What's both?"

"It's nature and nurture. There's no distinction. Genetics are the template, then environmental factors begin their influence even in the womb. The babies who were in utero during the Hunger winter in the Netherlands in the 1940s. Many of them developed weight conditions and diabetes later in life because their bodies had learned to hoard any fats and sugars they got. Epigenetics switch on the genes for this or that right from the start – we're changing from the moment we're first formed."

She raised her eyebrows. "You're obsessed."

He smiled. "I just don't want us to waste time having that argument the rest of our lives."

They drove the rest of the way to the restaurant, listening to the music in silence.

\* \* \*

Dinner was more relaxing. Olivia didn't ask Brendan any more questions about his past. He worked to keep his mind off of the case. He asked her about her own background. She was from the west suburbs of Syracuse and had gone to school at Bishop-Ludden. She had done her undergraduate work at Hobart and William Smith, and then obtained her masters in Psychology elsewhere – she didn't say. Instead, she explained how she had to pass several tests; the Examination for Professional Practice in Psychology and a Licensed Professional Counselor exam before she was able to practice on her own.

She had three brothers, and she was the youngest. "My mom was so thrilled when I came along," she told him, without a trace of ego. "I got a lot of extra attention, so I'm probably a bit of a spoiled brat. But I had three older brothers who were constantly fighting and eating and stinking up the house. I think my mom wanted to protect me from that a little bit." And she smiled, flashing her teeth for just a moment, in a way he was becoming familiar with.

The evening ended with a quiet drive back to her house. Both of them seemed lost in thought. He opened the door for her. The gesture provoked a painful memory which he quickly pushed away. She thanked him and kissed him on the cheek. As he pulled out of the driveway, he saw her standing on the porch, and she waved.

It was on.

Yet the feeling growing in him was no longer the awkward teenage high he may have felt for a moment, earlier in the night. Instead, it worried him. It worried him because of what secrets it meant he might have to reveal, and it worried him because of the ongoing investigation with the Heilshorn girl.

Olivia was involved in the case, whether she wanted to be or not. She was definitely a tough woman, able to hold her own, he thought, but she had also been protected her whole life. Protected by three older brothers; protected by her mother, by her own admission.

Until this case was solved, and the killer found, Olivia was involved. She'd already been put in harm's way once. He worried that as long as he continued to keep in contact with her, she was likely to be in harm's way again. So the two impulses clashed within him; the urge to protect her, and the sense that he needed to create a distance.

This conflict roused his sleeping stomach ache, which returned with vigor. He took three *Rolaids* and tried to sleep. When he finally fell into unconsciousness, his dreams were plagued by lurid sex and violence. Olivia was in them, often taking the place of Rebecca, performing lascivious acts. He was both aroused and revolted, and the conflict within him continued to grow.

## CHAPTER TWENTY-ONE / SUNDAY, 7:06 AM

He sat drinking coffee and watching the news online. He searched for fresh reports on the case. Nearly every station reiterated the same facts with some repackaging. Skene was there, standing at the microphones, giving his vague, politician's statement to the press. Bottom line: There were several persons of interest, but no real suspects.

Until Brendan had shared the information about the porn video, no doubt Delaney and the State Detectives had been steering the investigation deeper into Rebecca Heilshorn's past. They would've been looking into her day job, if she had one, and her co-workers. They would have peered into her college records and tracked down old roommates. The same things Brendan would've been assigned to, were he still on the case.

The crucial forty-eight hour time period following the murder had come and gone. During that time, the investigation had yielded only a few results, most of which had turned into blind alleys. Previous relationships, with airtight alibis. A laptop which had been utterly destroyed. Brendan wondered what the phone records had turned up.

Likely a few calls to family, a couple of banks, maybe, and who knew.

Brendan opened his email and found the 911 transcript that Colinas had sent over.

The sight of the little paper clip in his email window, indicating an attachment, filled him with dread. Delaney had already been over the transcript, and if there had been anything significant, it would have already been added to the case. But Brendan had yet to read it.

He was saved when his phone rang. He glanced at the caller ID. It was Taber.

"Good morning, Sheriff."

"Detective Healy. Sorry to call so early."

"Not a problem. What can I do for you?"

"Okay," said Taber. He cleared his throat. It sounded like he had only recently gotten out of bed himself. "Here's how we're going to play this."

Brendan waited. He felt a little trill of electricity run up his back.

"Delaney and I have consulted. We need you back on the case, but we're going to play it very close to the chest, do you understand?"

"Yes, sir."

"Nobody will know you're still actively investigating. In fact, I've got something else which will be your cover for a few days, should anyone nose around about what you're working on."

"Will IA know?"

"IA is not interested. They're going to follow up with you on the shooting, as I'm sure you've been looking forward to."

"Very much, sir."

Taber either missed or bypassed the sarcasm. "Delaney will meet with you at eight at your house. Can you meet at eight?"

Brendan looked down at himself. He was in his underwear and a t-shirt. He glanced at the time. "Yes, sir."

"Good. He has something to go over with you."

"What do you want me to do?"

Taber paused again. "This thing with the videos. We, ah, we have to keep it ultra-quiet. I don't want the press even getting the faintest scent. I certainly don't want the Heilshorn family to know. Not in this way."

"But, sir. They may already know about it. They may be the best people to talk to about it."

"Which is why Delaney is going to handle them for now. He'll be feeding you anything he gets from them which may be relevant at your end."

"But . . . is Delaney the best man for that job? He can be . . ." Brendan stopped himself. He could sense the Sheriff growing impatient. Taber knew Delaney's limitations; he didn't need to be told by the rookie Investigator what they were. If the Sheriff was playing things this way, it meant he had considered all the variables.

"I'm happy to do it, sir."

"You and I will consult privately every day at five o'clock until this thing is resolved. Good luck."

"Thank you."

\* \* \*

By the time Delaney arrived, Brendan had showered and dressed but was too nervous to eat. He felt like he had the morning that he'd arrived at the murder scene. His head was buzzing with questions. What-ifs.

Delaney came inside Brendan's house and took in the décor, or lack thereof. It occurred to Brendan that Delaney had never visited before. "Moving out?" Delaney looked at some boxes at the far end of the living room.

"No. In. Just not much of an un-packer."

Delaney had a folder with him and set it down on the kitchen table. Both men took a seat. Throughout their conversation, he made little eye contact with Brendan.

Brendan wondered if Delaney resented the Sheriff's decision to bring Brendan back in.

Shit happened.

Delaney opened the folder and pulled out Rebecca Heilshorn's phone records. There were several numbers highlighted.

"We've made sense of all the rest of these." He pointed to each number as he explained its significance. "Heilshorn's financial advisor, number one. Heilshorn's financial advisor, number two. Community Bank. Heilshorn house in Scarsdale. This is a moving service. This is a car rental. This is a day spa in Utica. This is a local contractor. We think maybe she had some work done, handyman stuff, on the house. We're looking into it."

Now he moved to the highlighted ones. "These numbers we believe have to do with the new situation. With the, ah, video. That line of work."

Brendan distantly observed that the subject of pornography, something two men might ordinarily discuss with pleasure, felt taboo. Delaney seemed a bit uncomfortable. Brendan remembered Delaney had a daughter, about the same age as the deceased. Maybe that had something to do with it. Or maybe that he was rumored to have slept with the Assistant District Attorney; that in thirty-one years he may have climbed the fence more than once.

Delaney's eyes briefly cut over to Brendan. "Have you studied the 911 transcript?"

"Colinas just sent it to me."

"I know." Delaney said no more, but the words felt accusatory. "Well, check it over. You've got the name, Danice, you've got the videos, you've got the 911 transcript, you've got these numbers. My guess is that laptop would have given us a lot, and that's why it was destroyed. We looked at everything, twice, on the laptop recovered at the scene. There wasn't any trace of these types of videos in the event history in the browser, and not a scrap of . . . pornography . . . on the hard drive. The other one was likely burned because it would have been rife with the stuff. She wanted to get rid of it."

"Or someone else wanted to get rid of it."

Delaney raised his eyebrows with skepticism.

Brendan explained. "It's a mistake to think that Rebecca was contrite. It could have been someone else trying to get her to stop. Hence the book, with that passage, a warning. And the laptop could have been destroyed, you know, sanctimoniously."

Delaney said nothing for a moment, only stared down at the phone records, his palms out flat on the small kitchen table. "This your table?" The question was a non sequitur.

"Came with the house."

"Place came furnished?"

"Some furniture, yeah. I needed a bed, couch, stuff like that."

Delaney glanced around. "So what in the hell is yours?"

"Ah, the computer. Some books."

Now Delaney made direct eye contact for a moment. His eyes were smoky grey, small, shot with red. His mustache twitched. "You really just bombed up here from downstate, huh? Came in like a bat out of hell."

"I got a tip on a job."

"Yeah, oh, I know all about it. Seamus Argon. Him and the Sheriff."

Brendan cocked his head. His nervousness had abated, and now his defenses were rearing. "Is there something you want to say to me, Ambrose?"

It was hard to get a bead on Ambrose Delaney. One minute he seemed like the consummate kindly mentor. The next he acted like a jealous older brother, one prone to teasing or bullying. Brendan remembered that people were often more than the singular attributes we associated them with. If someone offered a kind word, we said they were a *nice person*. If they cut you off in traffic, they were a *total asshole.* It was that Factual Attribution Error at work again. But people were always more complex.

One could consider Rebecca Heilshorn as a case-in-point.

"I've been trying to figure you out," said Delaney.

"I've been trying to figure you out, too," said Brendan.

The mustache twitched again. Delaney looked away, and then stood up with a grunt. "Good luck."

He showed himself out.

Brendan flipped through the pages of the 911 transcript. He took a deep breath.

\* \* \*

911 Dispatcher: *911 Emergency Response.*

Caller: *Hello, my name is Rebecca Heilshorn. I live at 2488 State Route 12 in Remsen. There's someone in my house.* [0:11]

911 Dispatcher: *There's someone in your house? Is there an intruder in your house?*

Caller: *Yes.*

911 Dispatcher: *Do you recognize the intruder?*

Caller: *He's downstairs.* (There are scratching/rustling noises on the caller's end) [0:19]

911 Dispatcher: *Ma'am? Where are you now? Ma'am?*

Caller: *I'm in the bedroom.*

911 Dispatcher: *Okay. Is it safe to stay in the bedroom? Can you stay in the bedroom?*

Caller*: I don't know. Yes, I can stay in here. There's no lock on the door. He's downstairs; he's in the kitchen.* [0:39]

911 Dispatcher: *Ma'am, I want you to just stay in your bedroom. Does he know you're in the house?*

Caller: (Barely audible) *Yes, he knows I'm in the house.*

911 Dispatcher: *Okay. Just stay there. Just stay in the bedroom. The police are on their way. You said 2488 State Route 12, is that correct?*

Caller: *Oh God.* (There is a noise like something dropping, or a door slamming) [0:53]

911 Dispatcher: *Ma'am? Can you verify the address as 2488 Route 12?*

Caller: *He's coming up the stairs.*

911 Dispatcher: *Can you put something in front of the door? To barricade it?*

Caller: *Yeah.* (Sounds of rustling, then sound of something scraping or sliding) [01:18]

911 Dispatcher: *Did it work? Ma'am? Are you there? Stay on the line, Rebecca. Stay on the line with me.*

Caller: (Barely audible) *He's right there. He's right there on the other side of the door.* [01:36]

911 Dispatcher: *Stay on the line. You don't have to talk. The police are on their way. Just hang in there, Rebecca.*

(Sound of crashing. Caller screams. The call is disrupted) [01:52]

\* \* \*

Brendan set down the transcript. He felt chilled, nauseous. He had read over the call at least five times now. The whole thing had transpired in less than two minutes. It didn't reveal much more than what the crime scene indicated. The only thing that continued to grab his attention was the way in which Rebecca Heilshorn had started the call. He'd seen various 911 transcripts over the years. Only infrequently did the caller begin with such a cordial, informational demeanor.

Rebecca Heilshorn had said "Hello, my name is," at the beginning of the call. Perhaps this was nothing more than the way she had been raised – to be polite under any circumstances. He hadn't listened to the actual voices yet – Delaney had – though the transcriber's annotations helped to convey some of the "feel" of the call.

Rebecca had clearly indicated that the killer was in the kitchen.

Brendan had checked a set of knives and found them all accounted for, but that didn't mean the murder weapon wasn't taken from a drawer, the sink, anywhere. The

Sheriff's Department and the State Troopers were all over the house and surrounding area searching for a knife, hoping to find one with prints. So far, nothing had turned up. Delaney, in a fashion uncharacteristic of a lead investigator, had acted almost nonchalant about finding the weapon. He'd even seemed sarcastic, insinuating that Brendan was naïve for thinking that they would find it.

Maybe Delaney had good reason. Maybe finding a knife in Oneida County, with its long tracts of farmland and country in between the small cities, was like trying to find a needle in a haystack. The killer could have taken it with him. Knives were easier to transport from place to place than guns. Especially when they were just ordinary household knives.

But that was an assumption. Yes, the killer had gone into the kitchen. But he could have been doing something else. Maybe he had his own knife all along. He could have done any number of things while he was down there.

Brendan looked at the time signatures during the call. Rebecca had said *He's downstairs* at about twenty seconds into the call. She then said *Kitchen* twenty seconds later. *He's coming up the stairs* happened at about a minute. That gave the killer at least forty seconds downstairs, maybe all of that time in the kitchen.

What took forty seconds?

Brendan got up from the laptop. He walked into his own kitchen and took out his phone. He activated the stopwatch function and began to time himself. He acted as though his own kitchen were unfamiliar. He started going through each drawer, each cabinet, until he grabbed a knife from the drawer next to the sink. He stopped the timer on his phone.

Eighteen seconds.

Granted, his kitchen was smaller, and granted, he was familiar with the layout of it even if he'd tried to pretend otherwise, eighteen seconds was not a long time.

That left more than twenty seconds that the killer could have been doing something.

Plus, there was that obvious sheath of knives. Even in an unfamiliar kitchen, it wouldn't have taken the killer a full forty seconds to spot the knives on the counter and pull one out.

Had he been toying with Rebecca? Taking his time to torture her a little?

That seemed unlikely. If she had seen him when he came in downstairs, he had seen her, too. The upstairs hallway crossed over the large foyer with the open story. From that hall balcony you could see the front door, plain as day, and vice versa. He must've known she would call 911. Who didn't have a phone?

A killer concerned with being identified, for one, wouldn't have lingered.

Brendan walked back to the computer and looked at the transcript again.

911 Dispatcher: *Do you recognize the intruder?*
Caller: *He's downstairs.*

Rebecca hadn't answered the question, exactly. Either she hadn't heard it, or she had been under too much stress to answer, or she had outright avoided it. Those possibilities ranged from most likely to least likely, in that order. Why would a victim want to protect her aggressor?

Maybe she had been under duress – certainly she had been addled, nervous, maybe panicked. Still, if she recognized the intruder, she'd want to offer that, even if she hadn't heard the question.

There was no forced entry to the main door. Yet Brendan didn't think, from what he'd been coming to learn about Rebecca Heilshorn, city girl, anti-social around the area, that she was the type to leave her front door unlocked overnight, alone in the country.

Maybe the killer had a key. Or, maybe she had been expecting someone.

So she either didn't know the killer, or didn't want to say that she did on the call.

Ugh. It seemed to go round and round.

And still, the fact of his being in the kitchen for forty seconds – or at least downstairs for that long – was disconcerting. And after the lapse of forty seconds, the transcriber had noted a sound like something hitting the floor, or a door slamming.

Brendan had an idea. He called up Delaney.

"You solve the case?"

There was that dripping sarcasm again.

"I need to get into the evidence room."

"For?"

"The picture frames."

"We left those."

"Were they dusted for prints?"

"Of course they were, Healy. The whole house was dusted. We got very little for prints. Some might be Donald Kettering's. One set we think may be the guy who did some handy work last month. We're looking to clear him this afternoon. Otherwise, we have an assortment we may never match. What else you got?"

"The killer could have worn gloves. But I want those frames for another reason."

It sounded like Delaney was eating something. Perhaps more sunflower seeds. Brendan wondered how a man grew so large eating seeds. Likely it was a cross-addiction.

"Your work is pretty cut and dried," Delaney said.

"Looking at the frames is part of my work."

"Picture frames related to erotic videos?"

"I'm going to the house."

"Fine. Don't let anyone see you or we're all fucking screwed. Do you understand?"

Brendan winced. Delaney's sudden vehemence was surprising, even for a man whose temperament was as capricious as the senior investigator's.

"I do. I won't."

He hung up, feeling a bitter taste in his mouth.

There was no reason to link some picture frames in the house to the porn video. It was just a hunch. Brendan put on his gun and jacket, grabbed up his badge, and headed out.

# CHAPTER TWENTY-TWO / SUNDAY, 9:22 AM

The Bloomingdale house was quiet. There was a deputy parked near the sugar maple tree at the end of the driveway. Brendan pulled alongside him.

"Morning," said Deputy Lawless.

"Morning." Brendan could see a scratch along the side of Lawless' face, a reminder of the struggle he'd had with Kevin Heilshorn. He suddenly felt awash in the surreal misgivings of déjà vu.

"Taking another look around?"

"Yeah. Just routine."

Lawless nodded as if to say he knew all about routine. He tipped his hat and Brendan rolled off in the Camry towards the house.

He approached slowly, taking it in. A sense of anxiety came over him, similar to what he'd experienced when he'd first arrived Thursday morning. That felt like a long time ago now. The anxiety quickly passed. He thought about having a cigarette and sitting for a minute, but he decided against it. He got out and walked towards the house.

He pushed past the caution tape over the front door and slipped into the gloom. The day was overcast and the house had none of the regal light filling it as it had on Thursday. There were no bright spots or shadows, just an even pall of dusty gray.

He glanced up the stairs, towards where Rebecca Heilshorn had looked down and spied her killer. He turned right, as he believed the killer had, and headed into the kitchen.

Past the kitchen, he entered into the dining room. The framed pictures were there, as Delaney had indicated. Brendan stopped in front of the one depicting the happy family – Rebecca, Donald Kettering, and baby girl, Leah. The child was maybe eighteen-months-old in the image.

Brendan picked it up and studied Rebecca's expression. When he had first seen it, he thought she had been the model of happiness. Now he saw that she had put on a convincing face, for sure. She was pretty, not in a pin-up way, but in a girl-next-door sense. Her eyes betrayed her conflict. Brendan stared into them, as he had at her eyes in the reflection. These eyes told him a story, too. *I'm not happy. Something is wrong.* She wore a manufactured smile. He tried to reconcile the woman he was looking at with the woman in the videos. The process made him uncomfortable.

He started to set the picture back down and then stopped. He hadn't come all this way just to convince himself of something he already knew, that Rebecca had been unhappy, or to freak himself out and leave.

He flipped the picture over and undid the small latch pinning the back into the frame. He took this away and removed the cardboard backing, revealing the photo paper beneath.

There was a date in the upper right corner, laser-printed.

Then, towards the bottom, a hand-written sentence. Brendan read the words, and a cold hand settled around his heart and squeezed.

*I was born under the black smoke of September.*

He committed the message to memory. He put the frame back together and then left the room. He suddenly needed to be out of the house and in the fresh air.

\* \* \*

Outside, he called Colinas. Colinas was nearby, and Brendan convinced him to come meet him.

Brendan found a spot not far from the Bloomingdale house, where there was a small gas station. He got a coffee and bagel from inside. He showed a picture he carried of Rebecca Heilshorn to the clerk.

"Yeah," said the clerk, "like I told the cops the other day, I seen her a few times. Came in for milk, eggs, got gas." He shrugged.

Brendan went back outside and waited for Colinas. The state detective showed up five minutes later, turning into the gas station at a good clip, churning up the dirt along the edge of the lot so that it boiled beneath his car.

The men stood talking next to their vehicles.

"I need to know about Leah, the daughter. I never had a chance to get into it."

Colinas looked suspicious. "The Sheriff is okay with this?"

"What do you care?" Brendan snapped. He didn't mean to be curt, but he was getting sick of being treated like the new kid in school.

Colinas gave a face like, *Your funeral, buddy.*

"Let's not get into impeding the investigation because of some rich control freak."

"I hear you. Uhm, what I know about the daughter. Hang on."

Colinas ducked into his black Caprice. The car was the same as the one parked in front of Olivia Jane's house on

Friday. Brendan wondered how many state police were currently active on the case, with its different components. He felt out of the loop, and he didn't like it. But he understood that the Sheriff wanted him compartmentalized from the rest. Still, he needed all the information he could get.

Colinas reemerged with a folder. He licked his thumb and flipped through the pages. Brendan sipped his coffee. The day was cool and still. Autumn was a kind of silent promise.

"I need to know when she was born. What month, in particular?"

"Okay . . . here. Uhm, she was born in May."

"How old is she now? Three or four?"

"Yeah. She's three."

"Say where?"

"Yup. St. Luke's-Roosevelt."

"No shit."

Colinas raised his eyebrows and looked at Brendan. "No shit?"

"That's where I was born. It's in the city. In New York."

"Huh. Small world."

"Been a lot of that lately."

"Oh yeah? Like what?" Colinas folded his arms and leaned back against the Caprice, clamping the folder closed in one hand.

"Like . . . well, okay, the family has someone with the same surname, maybe a relative, maybe not, who has a background similar to mine."

"Which is?"

"A branch of biology."

"You went to school for biology?"

Brendan nodded. He eyed the folder. "What's her custody history?"

Colinas stood motionless for a moment, then reopened the folder. "Uhm, mother had custody all the way through.

Grandparents have custody now. Well, it's in the works. There's something called 'Grandparent's Rights.' But the child is with them already."

"Nothing about Eddie Stemp?"

"No. There's no record of paternity."

"But when you went to see him, did the subject of the child come up?"

"No."

"You didn't bring it up?"

"No. It wasn't relevant. There's no proof he's the father."

"Hmm. Kettering is the one who first pointed to Eddie as the father. I think it's very relevant. We have very few leads here. You know that. This man was her ex-husband. They divorced before that child was born."

Brendan watched Colinas consider the timeline, as he had. If Stemp and Rebecca had been together for about six months, some five years before, and the child was three and a half, there was a chance she had been conceived by Stemp and Rebecca, but it was slim.

"Maybe there's someone else," Colinas said. "Maybe she cheated on Stemp. That's why there's no record of paternity. She didn't want one."

Brendan thought of the videos. *Dear God*. He felt nauseous again. The coffee he was drinking was suddenly too bitter. He lit a cigarette and felt Colinas watching him.

"Tell me what you're thinking," said Colinas.

Brendan took a long drag and let it out slowly. "Rebecca is pregnant when she proxies the buy on the Bloomingdale house for her parents, who are footing the bill. Bank records show it's their mortgage. Maybe it's Stemp's baby she's pregnant with, but our timelines suggests likely not. There's some reason that she settles here, though. And I don't think it's arbitrary. It's key.

"While closing on the place she rents a house outside of Boonville. The woman I spoke to, who is the property manager, doesn't remember her, but it could have been because I didn't stress that she was pregnant. I didn't have a chance to really put together the timeline before I got shucked off the case.

"So she's freshly divorced, maybe still in the last stages of it, and she's going to have a baby – She goes to Kettering's hardware store – according to his statement, that's how they met – and then they start dating, sort of, but she doesn't really want to commit.

"Kettering, meanwhile, sees 'instant family.' Or something, something really makes him want her in particular. He's smitten by her and really tried to work her over, but she's not into it. She comes and goes, he says, and he can't really control her."

Brendan took a breath and asked, "How old are his kids?"

Colinas blinked. He seemed to have been transfixed by Brendan's narration. "Whose? Ketterings? I didn't think he . . ."

"Stemp's."

"Ah, they were two and four."

"Interesting. Stemp has a kid who's four, too, as if he wasted no time during the divorce."

"Maybe she cheated, maybe he cheated."

"Maybe. But I don't think it's cheating on her part. In a way, but . . . not when it's work."

"Work?" Colinas gaped at Brendan.

Brendan realized his mouth had gotten away with him. He considered telling Colinas anyway. This was ridiculous, compartmentalizing the case like this. There needed to be total disclosure of information all round. Anyway, how else was he supposed to follow the porn lead? Chat rooms? Watch more videos? A man could take only so much – after the initial rush of hormones, repeat viewings revealed something grotesque in its mechanical, often violent, nature.

Colinas was really staring at him. "What's going on, Healy? First you're off the case, then you're back on the case, but it's all hush-hush. Delaney tells me that only me and him and the Sheriff know. I'm to give you whatever you need, but not to ask any questions. What the fuck is going on?"

Brendan pitched his cigarette away. He clamped a hand on Colinas' shoulder.

"Come with me."

# CHAPTER TWENTY-THREE / SUNDAY, 10:43 AM

They caravanned briefly, Colinas following Brendan's Camry. After a couple of turns, Brendan pulled off at a fruit and vegetable stand.

The men got out and Brendan headed over and picked up a shiny red apple. He headed inside, Colinas scowling after him, scratching his head.

There was an older woman inside, sweeping. She smiled when she saw the men. Her hair was white, with a faint blue tint.

"First of the season," she said about the apple, and got behind the counter. "Is that all? 25 cents."

Brendan fished for a quarter. He realized he didn't have one. Colinas saw this and stepped forward. "I got it," he said brusquely. Then he smiled at the older woman. The two of them, Brendan and Colinas, were suddenly seminary school boys, charming the friendly woman.

"Ma'am," said Brendan. "Can I ask you a question?"

"Of course."

He took a picture out of his pocket. "Do you recognize this woman?"

"Oh yes. Very nice young lady. Makes regular visits in the fall."

Brendan glanced at Colinas. Clearly the woman didn't know about Rebecca's murder, despite the major media surrounding it.

The woman's brow creased with worry. "Is everything alright?"

"Do you remember this woman as being pregnant?"

She nodded. "Sure. We talked about what natural foods are best for a baby. I fed all mine pureed summer squash. That's the best."

The men smiled in the presence of such nurturing. Then Brendan grew serious again. "Did she ever have a man with her?"

The woman thought, and then she frowned. "More than one."

Brendan described Kettering's appearance.

"Yes, him."

Then Brendan looked at Colinas, who got the hint. He stepped forward and gave a description of Eddie Stemp.

"That sounds right," she said. "Him, too."

Brendan turned to face Colinas. He couldn't quite conceal his expression, and Colinas read him, loud and clear. "Okay," he said softly. "So Stemp wasn't telling me the whole truth about his relationship with her. We'll have another look at him."

"Thank you ma'am," said Brendan. He smiled and took a bite of the apple. "Delicious."

The detectives started walking away. The woman was still frowning.

"And there was one other fellow, too," she said.

* * *

Brendan and Colinas stood back at their vehicles. Colinas glanced at his watch. Then he looked at Brendan, and his gaze was level and direct.

"Ok. I'm at the end of my patience. Tell me what's going on. What have you got?"

Brendan leaned back against his Camry and considered. He had a piece of apple stuck between two teeth and he picked at it with his fingernail. He could feel Colinas's frustration mounting. This wasn't exactly a ploy, but he knew he was hooking Colinas, getting him really interested, and he needed to. He needed Colinas – he couldn't do this alone, no matter what the Department said.

"First let me ask you," said Brendan. "What do you know about the case on the Kevin Heilshorn shooting? My shooting? I know your squad got involved."

"Yeah, they're involved, they're investigating, business as usual. So what? The Sheriff acts like you're in protective custody. He says IA is handling things about you and will share the info on an as-needed basis."

Brendan considered this. He really felt like the Sheriff was in his corner.

"Okay. Thanks for that. Here's what I've got. I think you need to press Delaney to take a hard look at this handyman, or whatever he is. A third guy – you heard what that woman just said. Older guy, greying around the edges. We've got no forced entry to the house. Think the victim left the door wide open, a city girl with a troubled past, alone in a big old country house in the middle of nowhere? I still lock my car and house, though most people I know around here don't, except for the old, paranoid types."

He looked hard at Colinas.

"I'm completely certain that Rebecca knew her killer. But she omitted identifying him when she called 911. That's major. Why did she do it? I figure there are three possible reasons. Either she was too frayed in the moment, or she didn't think he was going to hurt her, or because she was trying to protect him."

"Trying to *protect* him?"

"And I rank those from least likely to most likely."

"Why would she call 911 and not report the name of the person she was afraid was going to hurt or kill her? If anything I'm more inclined to your second theory, that she didn't think he would hurt her."

Brendan shook his head. "Maybe, but I don't think so. Why did she call and not name him? Maybe she thought he would talk a while and the police would get there in time. Or maybe she knew that he was going to hurt her, but the reason to protect him was so important that she didn't say his name."

"Why? I'm still not seeing the reasoning to protect someone you think is going to hurt you."

Brendan glanced at the vegetable market, the rows of shining apples and pears. He thought of the woman inside saying she fed summer squash to her children. *That's the best.*

"What is the one thing a woman is willing to protect above all else?"

Colinas blinked. He didn't have the answer.

"Obviously you don't have a family."

"I'm engaged."

Brendan thought of his own wife and daughter. The feeling of them was familiar, and old, and had lost some of the acuteness of its pain. It was blunt now, like something rusty. Still painful, but mostly just messy, just dull.

"Her child," he told Colinas.

"She protected the man who killed her because she was protecting her child? How's that work?"

Brendan shrugged. He was reminded of Kevin Heilshorn lying about his sister having a child. "That's what I'm going to figure out."

Colinas frowned. The wind picked up and tousled the men's hair. Grains of windblown sand clicked against the vehicles. "That's what you're going to figure out?" He sighed and looked around. "That's a lot of circumstantial stuff, Detective Healy. Lot of speculation."

"And finally," Brendan pressed on, "these are our suspects, as I see them. Kettering, Stemp, Kevin Heilshorn, and this handyman – who's possibly an older guy. Do you have a name? Has Delaney checked him out?"

"That's my next item. I'm late to meet him."

"Who is he?"

Colinas's looked at Brendan with hard, dark eyes. "Healy, I like you. But what this has to do with porn videos is beyond me. You're out there, man. You need to play the hole you're on."

"That's a golf analogy? That's terrible."

"You don't play golf."

"No."

"Well, I may not have kids, but I play golf."

"Okay . . ."

"Look, man. If I tell you who the handyman is, I don't want you to go off all half-cocked. He's not even really a man. So, it's not our gray-haired guy, or whatever. He's a young guy."

Brendan blinked. "Okay. Tell me."

"He works for Donald Kettering."

\* \* \*

Brendan showed up in Boonville half an hour later.

The clerk with the acne was not behind the counter, but instead a middle-aged woman stood at the register. She wore a flannel shirt and had broad shoulders and short hair. She looked like she could get mean if she needed to, Brendan thought.

He flashed her his badge, looking around. "Mr. Kettering back yet?"

"Back?"

"I called earlier. You said he was returning from his trip. A trade show? Hardware convention?"

"Yes. The National Hardware Show."

"So he's back?"

"Can I ask what this is about?"

Brendan regarded the woman who outweighed him by thirty pounds. "Ma'am, these are simple questions. Is he back? Is he here?"

She turned accusatory. "There's just been a lot of you coming around lately. I wonder if this isn't some sort of police harassment."

Brendan tilted his head, and glanced at the ceiling for an instant, as if he was thinking. "Nope, it's not." He started away from the counter and deeper into the store. "I'll just show myself back, if Mr. Kettering is here."

She said nothing.

Brendan found the door Kettering had led him through three days before. He could feel the woman's eyes boring into him. He rapped his knuckles on the door, the way Argon used to, following a domestic disturbance call. *Everyone knows the cop's knock*, Argon liked to say.

The door gave with the knock, indicating it was unlatched, and Brendan pushed it open the rest of the way.

Kettering was there, leaning over a box. There were several boxes around. He offered a very quick smile. His eyes were dancing with anger.

"Hello, Detective." Kettering stood upright.

Brendan looked at the boxes. He still had boxes of his own piled in a corner of his house. The ones marked "family."

Kettering explained, "New products from the convention. Most are free samples. What can I do for you?"

Brendan stood inside the door. He didn't ask to sit, nor did Kettering offer. The air of conviviality Kettering had possessed on the first visit was gone. Kettering looked tired.

"You lied to me, a little bit," said Brendan. He knew it was dicey to lead off with an accusation, but on the other hand, if Kettering sensed where Brendan was going early on, he might insist on a lawyer, and take a turn down that road. If incensed, he might give up more.

"Excuse me? I did what?" He pointed, "I've cooperated with every policeman who's come through that door. And counting you, there have been three. Maybe you all ought to communicate with each other, instead of coming in here one at a time to ask me the same questions. That's what's called a duplication of efforts."

"Cops are like that," Brendan said. "They duplicate all over the place. It's interesting you bring up the idea. Maybe this is a question you haven't been asked: Did you have a key to Rebecca Heilshorn's house, or did you ever make a copy for her and keep one for yourself?"

Kettering looked positively furious now. His color had risen and his cheeks were flushed. He was a big man, and balding. His face was starting to look like an anti-aircraft balloon wearing a wig.

"I had a key, yes, briefly. She had me come by a few times when she was out of town. I was helping her to remodel the master bedroom."

"You helped her add some appliances, too. Yes? Like a Maytag dishwasher."

"So? It was a gift. Don't you ever give gifts?"

Brendan nodded. "Ever give the gift of her key to someone else? Your employee, Jason Pert. Did he do work for her as well?"

"Only once or twice," said Kettering. His eyes flicked past Brendan, presumably to the door. *He wants to run.*

"Which? Once? Twice."

"Two times, Detective," Kettering nearly bellowed. "Two times he went and did some work in my stead."

"Any reason why she would have called him? Rebecca? From her cell phone? Because we have a call placed to his number. That was why one of the other investigators came by. The call was traced to your Mr. Pert. Your employee. The young man with the . . ." Brendan passed a hand over his face to indicate acne.

"No. I have no idea why she would have called him. You'll have to ask him."

"Where is he?"

"I don't know. He no longer works for me."

"Oh, come on." Brendan scowled at Kettering. It was too obvious.

Again Kettering glanced over Brendan's shoulder. Brendan turned. The woman in the flannel shirt was looming just outside the open door. She craned her neck to get a better view into the room. "Everything okay, Mr. Kettering?"

Brendan slammed the door shut.

Kettering flew into a rage. "Who do you people think you are?"

"My partners are talking to your employee. Why I came here was for another reason. You never mentioned to me she was pregnant when you met her," said Brendan. It was almost a growl.

"Get out of here."

"Fine. I can arrest you and we can talk at the Department."

"What do you want from me?" Now Kettering was yelling. He was standing over the same box. White Styrofoam peanuts had spilled around it. Suddenly he kicked through them, like an angry teenager. "I've done everything. I've been cooperative and patient. What the fuck more do you want?"

"I want you to tell me about Rebecca's career in pornography," said Brendan, in a measured, ice cold tone.

Kettering stopped all of his antics at once. The color drained from his face. "Aww, Jesus," he said and put his head in his hand.

# CHAPTER TWENTY-FOUR / SUNDAY 12:18 PM

Kettering was brought in for questioning. He rode in Brendan's Camry, silent the whole way. It had been a tense, awkward drive. A half an hour later they were in Oriskany, and Kettering was in a room with Colinas and Delaney. A Sheriff's Department detail had been dispatched to bring in the employee, Jason Pert, aged nineteen.

Brendan knew he had taken a risk. It was a bit outside the circumspection of his end of the investigation. Delaney was appeased, however, when Brendan suggested that the senior investigator do the questioning himself, along with Colinas. The Sheriff was in agreement.

Brendan and Taber stood looking through the one-way glass, listening to the recorded conversation, which was piped into the viewing room through a pair of speakers.

"This is the last time you can be in here," said Sheriff Taber. He meant the department offices. "Heilshorn is coming tomorrow."

"I understand," said Brendan. The truth was, he didn't like it. He knew certain situations required a kind of tact at odds with standard procedure and that, in the end, everyone's interest was in bringing Rebecca's killer to justice, but it meant some controlling, rich, father of the victim wanted him off the case.

"What do you know about Rebecca Heilshorn's involvement in pornography?" Delaney was asking the questions. He stood with one leg up on a chair. Colinas was against the far wall. Kettering sat at the table. There was a video camera mounted in the corner, and a parabolic microphone in front of Kettering. Senior Prosecutor Skene was going to arrive any minute. He wouldn't like that the questions had begun without him, but he could always watch the tape. Kettering had agreed to meet without a lawyer, claiming he had nothing to hide, but only on the stipulation that he be kept no longer than three p.m., when he had to leave for an appointment.

Brendan kept his eyes on Kettering while he answered.

"I don't know much. I mean, I don't know how she got involved, or why she did it."

"Was she actively . . . pursuing that career when you met her?"

"I didn't know if she was or not, I . . . no. She wasn't. Well, she was active. But she wanted out."

Kettering was nervous. Brendan was trying to get a fix on why. So far he was their front runner in the list of persons of interest. He was close to being a suspect. But Brendan had a hard time hanging the brutal crime on Kettering. He thought maybe the man was nervous for other reasons.

Delaney continued, "And she was pregnant when you met her."

"Yes."

"Why didn't you share this with the investigator who questioned you?"

Kettering took a moment to answer. Delaney seemed to grow impatient. Finally, Kettering said, "Because I didn't want to come across as some . . . I don't know. I saw her and just . . . I really liked her. I thought I could help her."

"Help her get out of porn?"

"No. I mean, yes and no. She just needed someone. She didn't really know anyone around here. She had this big house she was buying. She was pregnant, and she wouldn't talk about the father."

"Mr. Kettering, are you the father of Rebecca Heilshorn's daughter?"

"No. Absolutely not."

Watching through the glass, the Sheriff leaned over to Brendan and whispered, "We could poly him."

Brendan nodded. He already thought Kettering was telling the truth. Then again, he'd thought Kettering was being up front when they had first met.

"You're in a picture with Rebecca and Leah, when the baby was about twelve or eighteen months old."

"Yes. Are you kidding? That doesn't prove I'm anyone's father."

"But you wanted to be, is the point."

Brendan felt his body temperature cooling, his heart speeding up a little. He suddenly wanted a cigarette, but there was no way he was leaving the room. He had told Delaney about the writing on the back of the framed picture. Delaney seemed like he was working it into the interrogation. Brendan felt a twinge of jealousy, but quickly dismissed it as juvenile and egotistical.

"I had an idea that I could be good to them. That I could help them."

"Young woman, pretty, single mom of a cute baby girl, seems vulnerable. You thought, 'instant family.'"

Brendan felt invaded. The exact phrase had been in his thoughts. Again, he tried to rise above any petty rivalry with Delaney. Delaney was, after all, the senior investigator, and Brendan was lucky to still be a part of the case, at all.

Not that Kevin Heilshorn was his fault.

Suddenly he saw the young man again, on his back in Olivia Jane's garden. The dark blood on the bright green leaves. Flecks of it on Kevin's face, his wide, open face, dead eyes looking up to heaven.

Kettering was growing agitated. "No, I didn't think 'instant family.' I thought I could help them. I loved her. I loved both of them."

"Have you made any attempts to get in touch with the daughter?"

"Absolutely not."

"The family? Have you ever contacted the victim's parents?"

"No."

"How about her brother?"

Kettering hesitated for only a second. "Why would I contact her brother?"

"You haven't answered the question."

"No. I never contacted her brother."

Brendan felt like Kettering had just uttered his first lie. He leaned toward the Sheriff. "Yeah, definitely a poly."

Taber nodded. At the same time, the door opened behind them and Skene slipped in, quiet as a cat.

"Mr. Kettering, did you write something on the back of the family picture you're in with Rebecca and Leah?"

"I was told this was going to be about me providing some helpful information about Rebecca. Okay? I'm sorry I didn't bring it up before. I should have. That's all I've been trying to do is help. I wanted to help her. Take her to the Winter Festival, bring the baby, bounce the baby on my knee. Okay? Fuck me for trying to do the right thing."

"Mr. Kettering, it's all right. Please, calm down."

"And now you're interrogating me as if I'm a suspect. I think maybe unless you are going to arrest me, I should go. I could have your badge."

Brendan heard Skene swear under his breath. Brendan felt himself smirk. Skene was like the father who comes into the room right as the nudity or violence happens in the movie the teenager is watching on the TV.

Delaney did his best to smooth things over. "Okay, you're right, I'm sorry."

Colinas stepped away from the wall. "Mr. Kettering, we're just trying to establish any connections between the evidence we have, and the life of the victim. You're coming here today is very helpful. We know you just want to help, and that you wanted to help the victim, too. Do you think that someone would have written on the back of that photograph for a reason?"

"What does it say?"

Colinas glanced at Delaney, who nodded. "It says, 'I was born under the black smoke of September.' Crazy, right? Makes no sense to us. You ever heard of anything like that, Mr. Kettering?"

Everyone watched Kettering closely. "Never," he seemed to say without guile.

Colinas seemed to get comfortable with the reins. "Think someone was jealous of you? Of what you had with Rebecca and the girl?"

"Of what we had? I had nothing but their fumes. I only saw the girl a dozen or so times; I've already told Detective Healy that. Mostly I chased after Rebecca. Okay? It's a little humiliating."

"Humiliating?" Colinas made a face. "Oh man, that's all I know. Every woman in my life I chased over the river and through the woods. My wife only agreed to marry me after I'd run a marathon to win her over. I understand. But, see, to other people, it could have appeared effortless. You know? You're sitting there, in a restaurant or something, and in comes this beautiful little family. That's what you see. Handsome, successful hardware-store-owner Donald Kettering and this younger, beautiful woman with her precious daughter, all sitting down to some spaghetti. And what bliss they must be in. See? We don't think about what might be beneath the surface. We like to feel bad about ourselves, so we make out other people to be happier."

Everyone was quiet after Colinas's little speech. In the viewing room, Skene grumbled something about State Detectives.

"No," Kettering said at last. "I can't think of anyone who might have been jealous."

Brendan was never so sure of a balder lie. What was Kettering hiding? Who was he protecting?

Delaney piped up, his arms folded, foot still up on the chair. "What about Jason Pert?"

Kettering seemed to instantly grow upset again. "Look, I told you. Jason dropped a few things off once at the house. I was helping her remodel the master bedroom. I mean, it was brief. I was only working on it for two weeks. We broke up shortly after."

"How did you break up? What were the circumstances?"

Brendan watched Kettering closely. The man's face had grown long, his eyes drawn into his head, ringed with fatigue. "How does anyone break up? It's not a lot of fun."

"I understand, I understand. Can you tell me again, though, how you knew she was in pornography? Did she tell you? Was that why you broke up?"

"She wasn't *in* pornography, okay? She did some videos. She never said why. She would never talk about it. We *broke up* because I proposed to her three times. On the third, I decided to give up. Okay? I believe in the sanctity of marriage. I did a lot of talking to the members of my church, and I searched my soul. In the end, I couldn't keep chasing, couldn't keep living that way."

"Which church do you go to?"

"The Resurrection Life Church."

Brendan felt a shiver of excitement. He pressed his lips together and kept listening.

"Ok, Mr. Kettering. Thing is, you're saying a couple of things here. And I can dig it; women are complicated. You say that you chased Rebecca around trying to make her happy, but that she also needed you to help her get away from something – though she kept it a secret from you. So, what I'm especially unclear about is one thing. If she never talked about it, how did you know about the videos?"

Kettering looked positively deflated now. His big, lunky frame seemed to try to shrink itself. It was hard, even, just to look at how uncomfortable he was. He didn't answer. He didn't have to: Kettering knew about the videos because he had watched them. And then one day, like a gift from the gods, the young woman shows up in the flesh.

"And was that why you didn't say anything about this before?"

Kettering's lower lip started to tremble. The men watched as the large, balding, small business owner began to cry.

"I didn't want . . . I loved her. How could you tell people about something like that? About the woman you loved? I didn't want people to know that about her. It wasn't who she really was . . ." He trailed off, sobbing.

Skene turned to Brendan and Sheriff Taber. The prosecutor was grinning like a hyena. "He saw her when he watched one of the videos himself. Then he recognized her when she showed up in Boonville, when she came into his hardware store."

Taber nodded. He totally bought it. Brendan thought it was partly true. Skene turned and glared through the one-way glass, scenting blood. Then the prosecutor asked, "When do we bring in the kid? The employee?"

"Right now," said Taber.

* * *

Jason Pert, just a kid, had little to offer. His story matched Kettering's. As for the phone call, he said that Rebecca had called him in the weeks prior to her disappearance to ask him a question about the plumbing in the master bathroom. It was a little odd, because she and Mr. Kettering hadn't been seeing each other for a long time, Pert said. But she said she just wanted to finish the master bathroom – she'd wanted to know if it was okay to hook up a "diaper sprayer" to the line coming into the toilet tank. Pert had told her he didn't really know too much about plumbing, and that he no longer worked for Kettering. He was preparing for college in the fall and needed the few remaining weeks of summer to get things in order. He was going to UAlbany to enroll in business classes.

Delaney and Colinas grilled Pert about the nature of the phone call. How Rebecca had sounded, anything else she may have said. Pert said it was very brief, and that she sounded "normal." They then asked him about the key. He said he had left the key in a drawer at the hardware store, where it had been usually kept. At that point Taber stepped out of the room to contact a deputy and have an officer stop into the hardware store and verify that the key was there.

Twenty minutes later, word came back that it was. It didn't prove anything, Skene observed, except that the kid was telling the truth about that one thing. Skene was hunting for another suspect to pin the murder on.

Pert agreed to be fingerprinted and have a sample of his blood taken and his shoe size determined. Kettering reluctantly agreed to the same tests. Then, since neither man was being charged, they were released. The whole thing had taken almost five hours.

After the interrogations were over, Brendan turned his attention to something else. He sat in his office and focused on obtaining as much medical information as he could on Rebecca. This was something else he would have done if he hadn't been booted from the case and then brought back on in this clandestine fashion. Who was her doctor? Who delivered her baby, Leah? Did she have any conditions? He made several phone calls to area hospitals, and then hospitals in Westchester, and finally to the place of his own birth, St. Luke's-Roosevelt. Lawrence Hospital, in Westchester, had a record of Rebecca's birth, but nothing after that, and no information about her baby, Leah.

He supposed he would have some luck with that last question by talking to the deputy coroner. He called and found out that Heilshorn didn't have any ostensible health conditions or sexually transmitted diseases. There were signs of a possible abortion, a birth, and certainly many sexual partners. The girl was being prepared for the arrival of her parents, and her subsequent identification by them. They would no doubt be pressing for arrangements for her funeral, and Clark, the coroner, was reluctant to give her up. With the investigation ongoing, she needed to stay in the morgue.

Brendan wondered about Rebecca's phone call to the kid, Pert. If the teenager was to be believed, Rebecca had asked about a diaper sprayer. There was no biological indication that she was pregnant again, and three was a bit old for a child to still be in diapers, but that didn't mean it wasn't possible. Maybe little Leah was a late-bloomer.

Colinas knocked on the door, which was open.

"Come in."

The State Detective, with the light brown skin, took a seat across from Brendan, where he had first sat two days before when he'd been inducted into the case.

"That was interesting," said Colinas.

"It was."

"Too bad we didn't get anywhere."

"We didn't? There's still all of the forensic data. Something may pop up."

"You think that nineteen year-old kid did her in? Working for Kettering? He was desperate, jealous, and he has her taken care of? 'If I can't have her, nobody can have her?'"

Brendan leaned back in his chair. He had a pen in his hand and tapped it against his lip. Then he stuck it in his mouth. Maybe he could fool himself into believing it was a cigarette. "I don't know."

"I've got a theory," said Colinas, sitting up straighter.

"Let's hear it."

"Kettering sees the girl in the porn video. He does his thing, you know, rubs one out, and then a few months later, holy shit, she's standing there in his store."

"That's Skene's inclination, too. But there's a caveat; she doesn't have the house yet."

"Hmm. There is that." Colinas furrowed his brow. "So Kettering's description of how they met is bullshit?"

"I think so. I bet he saw her on the street. From afar. Something. And he worked his way into her life. Eventually he convinced her to have him help her make improvements on the house, and all of that."

"But that still doesn't make him our killer."

"No, it doesn't," Brendan agreed, and sighed. "Just a guy caught in a very embarrassing situation."

"Well, bear with me. She's preggo at first, so she's sort of out of the game. But, then, a couple months go by, the kid is born, and maybe she gets back into it. Kettering doesn't like it now. Or, maybe he does. Maybe he wants to make his own videos . . ." Colinas trailed off. His inspiration faded. "Fuck. I don't know. It feels like a dead end."

Brendan smiled. "That's your theory?"

Colinas looked wounded.

"Here's something interesting. You remember what Kettering said about the church he goes to? Resurrection Life Church. Same as the one Eddie Stemp goes to."

Colinas was nodding. "That's right. That's right."

"How many of these churches are there in the area?"

"I'll find out. Probably not many. May even only be the one."

"Well, if it's only the one, then we ought to have that second look at Stemp sooner than later."

Colinas shot Brendan a look. Brendan amended, "Maybe *you* should have that look at Stemp again."

Colinas started to get up. "What are you gonna do? What else is there with the porn thing?"

"Where did you get to with Rebecca's Cornell records? Her roommates?"

"Uhm, we tracked down one, thanks to the Sheriff's connection through Mark Overton."

"Did you talk to her?"

Colinas turned to face Brendan directly, but he seemed to evade direct eye contact. Brendan frowned. "What is it?"

"Look, this whole thing, you know? Normally the State Police would take Rebecca's homicide, but your Sheriff's Department was first on scene, and I guess Delaney really made some noise to get it."

"Colinas, what are you talking about?"

"I mean, so, we're here to help, you know? But the thing with Kevin, that's separate."

"I know that. I don't understand what …"

"I talked to my Detective Sergeant. This stuff, one case spills into the other. We've got to be careful. I knew this would come up when I found out about the roommate, so I asked. I can tell you – I'm compelled to tell you – but you're not going to like it."

"Spit it out, Rudy, Jesus. What did the roommate say?"

"I asked her the usual stuff. How Rebecca was as a student, a roommate, if she was heavy into partying, that sort of thing. It was pretty brief."

"What did you get?"

"You know, not much. Rebecca was quiet, kept to herself, studious. No reason or explanation for dropping out so close to the end."

"Did they stay in touch?"

"Uhm, the roommate was sort of vague. Said they bonded a little over some shopping and shared classes, but that was about it."

"Well," said Brendan, "I'll have a few more questions for her, given what we've found since then."

"Totally," said Colinas.

"Can you give me her name, number, address?"

"This is the part you're not going to like. Gimme a minute."

Brendan felt the hairs rising along the nape of his neck. He watched Colinas leave and waited until he came back a minute later with a file. He dropped it on Brendan's desk.

"There you go."

Brendan opened it up and read the information on the first page.

It read: Olivia Jane, 6223 Route 365, Barneveld, NY.

"What the hell is this?"

Brendan stood looking at the file. His lips suddenly felt numb.

Colinas sighed. "That's her roommate, sophomore year. Roommate was a senior. They shared a little house together."

"Why didn't you tell me this before? Why did she say anything? My God." Brendan rubbed his jaw. His whole body felt raw, scrubbed with gooseflesh.

"Like I said, it's two separate cases cross-pollinating. I don't know why she didn't offer this earlier. We asked, of course, but she had a lawyer there, and the lawyer was worm-tonguing in her ear the whole time. So, you know, like I said, we asked her the standard questions. She said it was a long time ago. Rebecca was quiet, pretty normal, decent grades..." Colinas shrugged. At last he met Brendan's gaze. "I'm sorry."

"Yeah, right."

"What do you mean by that?"

Brendan jabbed the file with a finger. He felt betrayed, livid. "Colinas, this is the woman who served as our grief counselor for Kevin Heilshorn. She went to school with his sister, Rebecca? For chrissakes, Delaney was the one who referred her. This is a mess."

Colinas looked hurt. "I'm trying to help you out, buddy, best as I can. Yeah, it's a jurisdictional clusterfuck, and this shit with the family, roommates, it gets messy. And when I met with Olivia Jane and her lawyer, another State Detective was with me. We couldn't push her on the issue about not coming forward sooner, because that's your case. The case we were working with Olivia Jane? The shooting of Kevin Heilshorn. And you're the shooter in that case. So you can see the position I'm in."

Brendan quickly grabbed up his stuff and left the office.

## CHAPTER TWENTY-FIVE / SUNDAY, 5:48 PM

He tried to drive at a reasonable speed, but couldn't. He flew along the highway. He blew through traffic lights. Within minutes he was at Olivia Jane's house. Her car was not in the driveway. He parked and went to the porch. The front door was locked. He walked around to the back of the house, trying to get his nerves under control. He didn't let himself look at the garden, to where Kevin Heilshorn had fallen, gunned down by Brendan's own hand.

*Kevin knew her, after all*, he thought.

Olivia would be in a lot of trouble. She had withheld vital information. If she had been roommates with the victim, Rebecca, she would very likely have known about Rebecca's brother. It wasn't clear why she wouldn't have disclosed that information, but Brendan felt sure it had been a conscious act, nothing she had simply "failed to mention."

It seemed like a virus. First Kettering and now Olivia who weren't showing all of their cards. He wondered if it was something Investigators encountered a lot. He felt a twinge of embarrassment, but he couldn't say why. Had he missed something due to his inexperience? Had he screwed up the very thing he was hired to do – to use his "good instincts" questioning persons of interest, getting information from them?

He found the back door unlocked and let himself into the house. It was quiet and cool inside and smelled of cleaning products.

He did a cursory check of the main part of the house, going through the kitchen, dining room and living room, not quite sure what he was looking for, just trying to calm down. He found some framed pictures on a bookcase. She liked to travel. Here was a picture of a younger Olivia standing alone on the Brooklyn Bridge with the World Trade Center in the background. Here was Olivia in an athletic outfit on top of some mountain or other, her arm around a woman who looked a bit like her. Her sister maybe. Brendan recalled some of their dinner conversation, but despite some basics, he realized he still didn't know much about Olivia's background.

He supposed she didn't know much about his, either.

In another picture, she was dressed up, sitting at a table at some function or banquet, smiling along with four other people also dressed handsomely. There was one smaller frame, only three-by-five, showing Olivia holding a small baby in her arms, possibly a niece or a nephew. Then there were several photos elsewhere in the living room with pictures of people he didn't recognize.

At the back of the living room was the door to her office. He went to it and found it locked. He left it for now. He backtracked to the rear entrance where the stairs led up. He ascended to a short hallway which fed into a bathroom and two bedrooms. One of the bedrooms was a den, with a small settee by a window which overlooked the garden and the roof of her office below. The office was maybe an add-on to the original house, he thought, given this view of the design. There were more books here and some pictures on the wall. Most were scenic views. There was only one with people, and again he didn't recognize the faces.

He left the den and walked back down the hallway, and turned into the bathroom. One thing he remembered from Argon was that you found out the most about people from their bathrooms and their bedrooms. The living rooms were where people kept up appearances. The kitchens were usually just functional, the dining areas formal. In bathrooms you had the medicine cabinet, the products and appliances. Were they terribly vain and high maintenance, or was there just a toothbrush in a cup? Were they home a lot, or very little? Were the towels clean and packed away in a closet, or damp and on the floor? Olivia was somewhere in between. The bathroom was used regularly and she had a hair-straightening iron and the requisite conditioners and lotions. He felt a little bit guilty going through her stuff, but reminded himself that she had withheld critical information. Still, the right thing to do would have been to go into the Sheriff's office and meet with Taber and Delaney about it, and go from there. Maybe get a warrant.

But on what grounds? Because she had told one investigator, but not another, that she had once been a roommate of the deceased? No judge would go for that. No, it was better this way. Maybe emotionally-driven – he had to concede that to his own analysis of the situation – but better.

There was nothing overtly incriminating in the medicine cabinet. Just Aspirin, vitamins, and plenty of lotion.

He found one bottle which seemed out of place. It was children's Tylenol. For infants.

He considered it, turning it around in his hands. Maybe she was averse to strong medicine. Many people took baby aspirin, for instance. Or, maybe she had another reason.

He put everything back the way it was and left the bathroom and was heading to the bedroom, when he heard a car pull up in the driveway.

* * *

He expected her to be irate. To be indignant about his presence in her home. Even to threaten to call his superiors. It seemed like something she would do, from what he'd come to know of her.

Instead, however, she met him in the living room as she came in the front door, and her eyes only widened for a second. She took off her shoulder bag and set it down on the dining room table. Her gaze fell away from him, and she started towards the kitchen.

He watched as she got down a drinking glass, poured in some ice cubes from the ice machine in the fridge, and then filled the glass with water from the tap. She took a long drink, and then looked at him again.

"Hello, Detective Healy."

He said nothing. She left the kitchen and returned to the dining room table where she set down her water and removed the light jacket she was wearing. Then she bent and took her shoes off and stuck them by the front door, only a few feet from the window which Kevin Heilshorn's bullets had smashed through, nearly killing them both.

Brendan could feel his anger rising again.

He stood there in the space between the kitchen, dining area, and living room and watched as she crossed in front of him, sipping her water, and sat on the couch.

"Come on and sit down. I'm guessing this isn't a social call."

He strode over towards her but didn't sit. He could feel himself fuming.

"What the fuck is the matter with you?"

She blinked at him. She didn't affect surprise or offense at his language. Her expression only conveyed curiosity, perhaps even concern. It infuriated him.

"I guess you're here because you found out I knew Rebecca Heilshorn."

"Yes," he said. He clenched his teeth. "That's why I'm here."

"You seem very angry."

He cocked his head. "Oh yeah?"

"Yes."

"And why do you think I would be very angry? Huh? Would it have something to do with the fact that you have kept this information from me?"

"Detective . . . Brendan, please sit."

"I don't want to sit."

"I think it would help you be . . . less angry."

"I don't want to be less angry."

"Ah," she said. She took another sip of her water and then set the glass on the coffee table. She folded her hands on her lap and crossed her legs. She was wearing jeans and a hooded sweatshirt. She hadn't come inside with any shopping bags.

"Where have you been?"

"That's really none of your business."

That was it. He couldn't take it any longer. He thought of Donald Kettering's bright red face. He supposed his face was as red now, but he couldn't help it. He yelled at her. "Yes it *is* my fucking business, Olivia. Yes it is. So is knowing that you were roommates at Cornell with the victim in a major homicide case. That you knew the man who tried to shoot and kill me. The man who I had to fucking shoot *dead*."

He was taking huge breaths now. He clenched his fist. He wanted to smash something. A preposterous thought occurred to him, a memory of childhood, of watching an old TV show. *Hulk smash.* It almost made him start laughing. But if he started laughing, he might not stop.

"Brendan, please. Slow your breathing. In five minutes you won't be so distressed."

"I won't?"

He remained standing. His muscles were tensed. His stomach throbbed. He felt ready to kill. Not Olivia, but something, someone.

He saw the victim's eyes looking back at him in the bedroom mirror.

"No, I promise you. But, fine, stay standing. Whatever makes you . . . Whatever you want."

She uncrossed her legs and leaned forward, elbows on knees. She seemed to be waiting for him to get himself under control.

It took a moment, but he could feel his pulse rate slowing, and he breathed more shallowly and gradually.

"I want you to consider the following with a clear head. Can you do that? I'm not going to try to convince you of anything. I am just going to give you the facts. Okay?"

He waited.

"Okay. I have known Investigator Delaney for several years. I told you I know more people around here than you. I met him when I began offering services in grief counseling. Frankly, he used to hit on me. But, we're past all that. So, he called on me when this all happened. You then brought Kevin to me. I attempted to do my job, which was to help him with the extremely fresh, extremely recent tragedy."

"Did you know him?"

"I'd never met Kevin before Thursday."

He opened his mouth to ask her another question, but she cut him off.

"Please just hear me out. I'll answer your questions as best as I can as soon as I'm finished. And yes, I can see by your face that you're irritated with the fact that I'm not able to tell you everything you want to hear, as soon as you want to hear it, but that is the nature of things. You'll see why."

She took a breath. "Rebecca and I were roommates for one year. That you now know. Let's just stay with that fact for a moment. You're upset because I didn't tell you. After you and I met, when you dropped off Kevin with me, we arranged to discuss that meeting. You wanted to know whether or not I thought he was guilty. But that's not my field. I could only tell you about his state of mind, and he was indeed grief-stricken and addled. When we met here, that afternoon, I planned to share with you that I had known the victim, that I went to school with Rebecca. But we were interrupted."

"That's one way to put it."

"Yes, that is one way to put it. As you know, that interruption led to a whole new chain of events. You and I were separated at the Department. I gave my statement, and then I left."

"You got in your car and drove away from me."

"I was instructed not to discuss anything with you, since you had done the shooting. I was told that if I did, I could be interfering with the internal investigation which necessarily follows an incident like the one with you and Kevin. The next day I was approached by the State Detectives. Colinas sought to question me about my relationship with Rebecca, which he had learned about from college records. At the same time, Detective Ritnowar was working the case on you and the shooting. Naturally, I called my lawyer before speaking with them. Not that I have anything to hide. But the matter seemed to grow quickly complicated, and I needed to be careful about anything I said. And then I was informed that you had been removed from the case. At that point, I mean, there was nothing I could say to you."

"Why? Why all of this . . . slinking around? I don't understand."

"For one, Brendan, it's because confidentiality extends beyond death."

She fell silent, allowing this to sink in. It took him only a moment.

"Rebecca was your *patient?*"

"My client. Yes."

He felt the anger returning. "And you didn't feel compelled to share that either?"

"Emotionally, yes, I did. But professionally, in fact, I am not compelled. My patients are confidential, and their sessions with me confidential, and remain so, even after death."

"Jesus Christ," said Brendan. He at last broke out of his vigilant stance and started pacing back and forth. He ran a hand over his face. "And have you been served a warrant?"

"Right now the State Detectives are seeking a warrant to review records of any medical history involving Rebecca, as she was under my care. But Rebecca was never institutionalized, never sent to any hospital. So, they won't find much. My personal session notes are another story."

"This just makes no sense to me. This is a *murder investigation*, Olivia. What if your notes are able to reveal the identity of the killer? What if one look at them cracks this whole thing wide open?"

She said nothing. She watched him pace.

"It makes no sense," he repeated. "I can understand that while a person is living they want things to be kept confidential. But she's dead. She would want to have her killer found, don't you think?"

Again, Olivia said nothing, and Brendan found himself remembering something he had told Colinas.

*She protected her killer to protect her child.*

A second later he thought: *I was born under the black smoke of September.*

"Jesus," he said again.

"You get very angry like this, Brendan, is that true?"

"What? What the hell are you asking me?"

"You didn't just arbitrarily choose to leave behind your career in neurobiology and become a cop. That's a substantial socioeconomic shift, and a very different kind of field. You didn't just wake up one morning and decide take a pay cut, did you?"

"What are you asking me? What are you doing?" His lips felt numb again. He wanted a cigarette.

"Anger, like everything else, is habitual. You know that. People who are quick to temper are that way because the circuitry keeps going that way, isn't that it? You've been working on keeping it all under control though. Maybe you thought that by being a policeman you would be safe. It would be the safest place for you. Surrounded by the law, by duty. But the thing was, you couldn't keep staying in the same place, the same city, the same house. So you took the job up here."

He felt sick. Goddamn it.

"Olivia . . ." He felt weak in the knees. Brendan found himself sitting on the edge of the loveseat adjacent to the couch.

"I'm very sorry," she said, "that I haven't been able to give you what you want. I am not trying to impede your investigation, or hurt you in any way. I am certainly not trying to be in the way of resolving this horrible crime. But this is my job. This is my life. I must honor the agreement I have with Rebecca, even after her death. Through the proper channels, all will be revealed. But you have to go through those channels, Brendan. This is the way it works."

She moved closer to him, resituating herself on the love seat.

"In the meantime, I want to help you."

He lifted his head and looked at her. The sense of defeat he was feeling was starting to give way once more to ire.

"I want you to talk to me about what happened to your wife and child. About what happened to *you*, Brendan. Not as a therapist, but as a friend. And I think it can help you with this case. I do. I may not be able to just hand you over my sessions with Rebecca. But I can talk with you."

She moved a little closer. "And trust me, I want to tell you. I want to tell you everything, because I care about Rebecca, and I care about you, too."

Her hand touched his leg and he abruptly stood up. He looked at her office door, the one that was locked.

"We'll get the warrant and subpoena your session notes. This bureaucratic bullshit has held up things long enough."

"It's not up to you, Brendan."

He glared at her.

"This is my case."

"My understanding is that Rebecca's father is coming tomorrow, and you are to make yourself scarce. You told me that yourself. And you have this investigation of your own to deal with, about the shooting. That's what you need to focus on, Brendan. Let the rest of this work itself out."

"With Rebecca's killer out there? Walking around? Breathing air? I'm not taking a time-out to do a little soul searching."

He started towards the front door. He grasped the knob and then looked back around at her.

"What's with the children's Tylenol? Expecting company? Jesus, for all I know, Alex Heilshorn is going to come over and have a tea party with you. Little Leah will run around, and say hi to Auntie Olivia."

"That's ridiculous," she said but suddenly looked less composed.

"That's about how much I can trust you, or anything you say."

He banged out the door and into the late day.

\* \* \*

As he drove, his fury gradually waned. Dusk was creeping across the land. The Camry moved swiftly from farm country back into the ordered, residential streets outside of Rome.

He formulated a timeline in his mind, with questions arising at every marker.

Rebecca and Olivia meet at Cornell as undergrads. They rent a house together. Around the same time, Rebecca gets involved with some other people, people who lead her into the business of making those videos. Or did they come later?

Did she already know these people? Were there even any people, or did she just up and decide to make erotic films one day?

She drops out of school. She might have returned to Westchester for a while, but Brendan doubted it. He wasn't quite sure why, but he imagined her father frowning on her return home. Or, more so, her reluctance to return there herself. So, where does she go?

Wherever it is, she meets Eddie Stemp. The two are married. They possibly conceive a child together – that's Leah, now going on four years old.

But six months years later, they divorce, before she's even carried the baby to term. Stemp is a local man affiliated with a church in Rome. So, for that matter, is Kettering. Did she meet Stemp in the area? Or did she meet him elsewhere and the two moved here? If so, why would she stay in the area after the divorce? So Stemp could visit his daughter? It was altruistic, and unlikely, Brendan thought.

He made a turn into a busy street. Something occurred to him: Maybe Stemp had something he could hold over her. Maybe he blackmailed her to stay.

Still, Brendan felt hung up on *why* this area in the first place. But maybe that was because he felt *his* living here was random. He asked himself "why this place?" almost every day. Not that there was anything wrong with the area. There was a certain rugged charm in between the more central leatherstocking region and the Syracuse metropolitan area. There was a mélange of architectural styles, from Colonial to Federal, Victorian, and Georgian.

There was a good deal of poverty, but the people had grit. Historically the region had suffered a great deal.

Early stockaded villages had been settled by Dutch fur-traders. Merchant villages were often viciously attacked by marauding parties of French-Canadians and Indians. From Schenectady to Rome, villages were often built with defensive barriers of timbers driven side by side into the earth.

Aggressors burnt villages to the ground. Inhabitants were killed, others were taken as prisoners, but the burgeoning region could not be stopped. Two years later, the Stockade was once again flourishing as a fur-trading outpost and a place of industry and commerce. The Dutch settlers endured, along with English and Scots, building robust, unyielding homes, the ones Brendan admired.

He liked the idea of something fortified, something unyielding.

He returned his mind to the timeline, but discovered that he had already come to the end of the lighted path. Rebecca used her parent's money to buy a house. Her motivation for resettling in the area remained unclear. He did wonder, though, if it had to do with Olivia.

Maybe Rebecca had relocated to the region because her former roommate was now a practicing psychotherapist. Maybe Olivia represented to Rebecca a time in her life before things had turned ugly. Or, maybe she had been drawn, like Brendan was, by the power which lurked beneath the crumbling façades, the kind of desperate strength of a place with cities named after kingdoms, villages which refused to be conquered and spawned tough cities.

Yet, *Nero fiddled while Rome burned.*

He suddenly turned around, leaving the city limits behind. He headed towards Eddie Stemp's farm.

# CHAPTER TWENTY-SIX / SUNDAY, 7:12 PM

Brendan was greeted by a man with a rifle. Stemp was cold and unemotional at first, not the warm and caring Christian that Brendan had anticipated. He handled the weapon like a military man.

After he defused the situation and got Stemp to put away the Winchester 30.30, the men got to talking. Stemp insisted they stay outside.

The sun was setting, drawing a lavender twilight around them as it sank. With it, Brendan felt that time was running out. For him, for Rebecca, for catching her killer.

Brendan was as forthcoming with Stemp as he could be. The man had intense eyes that exuded both intelligence and a strange, cultish edge. To put a finer point on it, he looked drugged, as though he'd drunk some of the Kool-Aid.

"You're dealing with the life of a very troubled woman," said Stemp.

The two men sat at a picnic table near the barn. There was a clothes line and a small flower garden. The farmhouse was warmly lit, in the near distance. The night was cool but not uncomfortably. The insects, however, were coming out. Mosquitos whined in Brendan's ears, and he swatted at the air. Stemp didn't seem to notice the bugs. He sat with his hands folded, the rifle on the bench beside him. He wore a flannel shirt and tan Carhartt overalls.

"Tell me about her," said Brendan.

"Well, I'll tell you what I told the other detective. Cortez, or what have you."

"Colinas."

"Colinas, right. I told him about the laptop, too, by the way. I bought that when Rebecca and I were together. I have no idea why she threw it out, or burned it, or whatever he said she did. But most likely it was where she had kept certain . . . information about her other life."

"Okay. Thank you."

"So, I pray for Rebecca every day. I pray for her soul. We said a special prayer for her in church this morning."

"I'm sure she . . . I'm sure that's appreciated by her family."

Stemp nodded as if he heard this all the time.

Brendan looked around, taking in the night. It was a nice spread and back from the main road. Things were quiet, with only the crickets singing and mosquitos whining.

"Well, you know, like I said, troubled girl," Stemp said.

"Like what? What were her troubles?"

"Well, it's not for me to judge. That's for the Lord. But I can recognize the symptoms of a sickened soul."

"Could you please share them with me? I'd be grateful to hear your thoughts."

"Like lewd and lascivious behavior, that's what. Now, like I say, I'm not one who can talk. I had my share of a dark night."

"A dark night?"

Stemp made eye contact. "A dark night of the soul. Everyone has them. Some are longer than others. Some dark nights . . . they get complicated. There are forces which can get in there and . . . just make things a whole heck of a lot worse."

"Forces?"

"Demons."

"Ah."

"My mother would say that once visited by demons, and then purged of them, a person would have to replace the void with something else. Something holy. If not, the demons were invited to return, and they would return sevenfold."

For some reason, Brendan found himself thinking about Delaney, and his sunflower seed habit. He knew cross-addiction wasn't entirely what Eddie Stemp was referring to, but maybe it was, just a little bit.

Stemp looked at Brendan flatly. "Do you have access points?"

"Sorry?"

"Spiritual access points. Ways for unclean spirits to enter you. My guess is that you do."

Brendan rubbed at his jaw and looked away. He needed a moment; he didn't want to offend Stemp. Demons, and demonology, as far as he was concerned, were nonsense. Life was conducted through chemicals, not angels and demons. When Brendan didn't answer, Stemp moved on.

"My dark night and Rebecca's dark night coincided. Sometimes that's how it goes with people. You meet when you are in crisis, and you can't do anything to help each other. You're attracted to the darkness in each other. At the same time, maybe you want to believe that the other can heal you. There's some people who think we're just searching for our mothers and fathers in our chosen partners, and that we expect our partners to meet the need that our parents didn't, or couldn't."

"I'm familiar with the idea. Do you know Olivia Jane?"

Stemp frowned. "No. Don't think so."

"Was Rebecca seeing a therapist when you were together?"

"I have no idea. It wouldn't have done her any good anyway. Therapy and pills can't treat the soul."

"Was she involved in pornography when you were together?"

Stemp made eye contact again. His expression turned grave. "I've made my peace with that. I tried to get Rebecca to atone for her own sake."

An alarm flashed in the back of Brendan's mind. Especially at the reference to atonement. And he realized that Stemp wouldn't likely have said any of this to Colinas, because Colinas hadn't known about the videos. Inadvertently, Brendan's eyes dropped to the rifle sitting beside Stemp.

"What else? Can you tell me more? How did you try to get her to atone?"

"To pray. To join the church. Look, I was no good for her when we were together, I know that. So does the Lord, which is why it was pleasing to Him that I had the marriage properly annulled. But He made a deal with me."

"The Lord?"

"Yes. He granted me my forgiveness and annulled the marriage, he gave me the wonderful gifts of my wife, Trudy, and our two children, and in return, he asked me a favor."

"To turn Rebecca towards the faith?"

Stemp raised his eyebrows. "Yes. And to have her come to understand her dark night for what it was. To show her that the light existed, and she could find it, as I had."

"So you visited her frequently in the time before her death?"

Now Eddie Stemp looked forlorn. "No. Things were complicated with our first birth, Trudy and me. The Lord gave us a child very quickly, but it came at a price. Our first baby has CF – that's cystic fibrosis – and I wasn't able to get away much. I was needed here. And by the time she was older and things were smoothing out, the farm here was in full swing, our second baby was arriving, and I was a leader in my church."

"Did the Lord let you out of the deal?"

Stemp searched Brendan's face, perhaps looking for guile. Brendan was only speaking to the man in his own language.

"We amended the deal, you could say."

"How so?"

Eddie shifted on the picnic table bench. It seemed to Brendan that they had reached a juncture. It was a place that almost every interview came to, where the person being questioned stepped out of their comfort zone. It was a critical moment. The dusk had fully enveloped them now. The evening sky had turned indigo, with a solid deck of low clouds and only an umber scattering of sunlight. Brendan urged Eddie forward. "Please, how did you amend it?"

Possible answers to the question tumbled through Brendan's own mind.

*The Lord told me to save her brother, Kevin, instead.*
*The Lord told me to kill her.*
*The Lord told me I was born under the black smoke of September.*

"First, you need to know something else. I'm not some man who is hopped up on his own self-importance. Not because I found the Lord, or my church. I know you're sitting there in judgment of me, and that's okay. I would have been, too, years ago. I'm not some dumb country bumpkin. I lived a lot of life before I came into the fold. And I made some terrible decisions. One of those involved aborting my own child."

Brendan leaned back, absorbing this. He thought for a moment, and reached into his pocket and took out his cigarettes. Stemp watched as Brendan lit one. Brendan offered.

"No, thank you. I quit those like I quit a lot of bad habits."

Brendan exhaled smoke. "Rebecca had an abortion?"

"*We* had an abortion. I don't care what they say; the father is just as complicit."

"Okay."

" 'We had an abortion.' That's a euphemism. Meant to sound like something procedural, almost cosmetic. 'We killed our child.' That's the correct phrasing. I don't care what you believe, what faith you have or don't have, the minute that cell divides in the womb, that is a human being. Left uninterrupted, unmolested, it will become a one year-old baby, a twelve year-old girl, a seventy-year-old grandmother."

Brendan nodded. In no way was he going to engage this man in a debate on abortion, which was the biggest quagmire of all topics, in his experience.

"But she got pregnant again very quickly, didn't she? Or . . .?"

Stemp seemed to search Brendan deeply, as if evaluating whether or not the man could be trusted. He then made a decision.

"Leah is not my child."

Brendan swallowed and found his throat was dry. "So you and Rebecca didn't get pregnant again."

"No. We had the abortion, but then we tried to marry – but the death of our child haunted us, and it did what it tends to do – it pulled us apart. And, rightfully so. It was the Lord. The Lord pulled us apart in His wisdom."

"Do you know who the father is?"

"No."

"You mentioned that the symptoms of Rebecca's spiritual distress were her lewd and lascivious behavior. I take this to mean you knew about Rebecca's involvement in making erotic videos."

"That wasn't all of it."

"No?"

Stemp shook his head, somberly.

"Can you tell me what else?"

"It all goes together. Not for everyone, I'm sure; it's not all the same for everyone. But Rebecca started out seeking something . . . I don't know. She was in Albany for a while. She was someone . . . one of those girls who escorted the rich businessmen, the government officials, in secret. The Elliot Spitzers."

This was a vital piece of the chain. Rebecca had started not in videos, but in a higher-end escort service, if he was to believe Stemp.

"How do you know this?"

"I wasn't always a farmer. You're not the only man around here whose past is very different from his present. Look around you. Why else would we be tucked away up here? I wasn't born here."

"What do you think you know about me?"

Stemp shook his head, dismissively. "Now, don't get all detective, Detective. It's just a call. You have an accent, like Putnam, Rockland, maybe Westchester County. The way you dress. Walk. I don't know."

Brendan decided to let it go. "What did you do? In your previous life?"

"I served in Desert Storm. Later I worked as a bodyguard. That's as far as I'll care to go along that line. My personal history is immaterial."

"Can I ask you one thing?"

"Maybe." Stemp glanced at the house, as if growing impatient.

"You said that your deal with the Lord was amended. You were no longer meant to cure her of her ways, because you just didn't have the time. You had your own family to deal with."

"I wouldn't say 'cure her of her ways,' but . . ."

"Sorry, best choice of words I could come up with." Brendan stubbed the cigarette out on the table without thinking about it. Stemp looked at the burn mark and frowned. "So if you didn't have the time for that," Brendan continued, "What did you have the time for?"

Stemp sighed. "I put in some calls. I used some of the information I had gotten from Rebecca, some names, and I decided that the best thing I could do was help to try and prevent something like this from happening to anyone else. But I was out of my league."

"You mean you called . . . who? Officials? Police? People you used to work with? Did you call her father?"

Stemp stood. He picked up his rifle. "I'm sorry, Detective, this really is where I have to get off. My family is waiting for me to come to supper, and I have nothing more I can add. None of what I did made any difference. That's something I have to live with. Like a lot of things."

"Please, I need to know. Her killer is still out there, and you still have a chance to help Rebecca. If you could just give me something. Anything. Anyone. Just a name. Who did you call?"

Stemp sighed again. "Maybe I made a call to her father. And maybe he made an anonymous phone call to the State Attorney's Office. It was all I was able to do in that regard. In the end, that wasn't the real amendment, anyway."

"What was?"

"To pray. Now, thank you, and have a good night."

Brendan stood, too. He called to Stemp as the man turned away.

"Eddie."

Stemp stopped and slowly turned back. Both men were in the dark now. Standing a few yards away, Stemp was just a sketch, his rifle hanging at his side.

"Is the child in danger? Is Leah in danger?"

"We're all in danger, Detective. Not from one another, but from God's righteousness. What we do to one another is ineffectual. The Lord works in mysterious ways, but the sinners are punished. Always."

"Did you give *The Screwtape Letters* to Rebecca? With a highlighted passage? Addressed to the name she used in pornography?"

Stemp was motionless. His voice carried over. "Yes."

"Why did you sign the note, 'K'?"

Stemp sighed. "My first name is Kim. I am Kim Edward Stemp. We used to joke about it. Only she ever called me Kim. We had some good times, Detective. But she was always looking for something else. Always had one foot out the door."

It sounded like something Donald Kettering would say.

"Do you know Donald Kettering?"

In the gloaming, it was hard to make out Stemp's features, but Brendan thought the man's brow lifted. "Of course. He's a member of our congregation."

"Did Rebecca ever go with you to church?"

"Only once or twice. Now please, Detective . . ."

"Did you write a phrase on the back of a picture in her house, *I was born under the black smoke of September*?"

"No. I did no such thing. But whoever wrote that . . . well . . ."

"Do you know what it means?"

"Not exactly."

"Not exactly?"

"It makes me think of something. I'm not sure what. Maybe September is, you know, 9/11. Detective, I have to go. Please, I've been very patient. Good night."

Stemp turned away again. His outline shrank as he moved through the night towards his country home. Brendan could see a figure in the window and assumed it was Stemp's wife, awaiting his return.

He left the picnic table and slid into the Camry and switched on the engine. After a moment, he realized the bell for his seatbelt was chiming. He had just been sitting there, his head buzzing with all of this new information. For one thing, he needed to get the photograph with the sentence on it to a handwriting expert. But tomorrow,

Heilshorn was arriving and Brendan would have to deal with the investigation around the shooting. All of this going on, and he was going to have to fade even further into the background.

He drove away from the Stemp farm into the darkness, unsure of where to turn.

\* \* \*

Back on the road, Brendan's thoughts churned.

Who wrote the phrase on the back of the photograph? He leaned heavily toward the idea that the author and killer were one and the same.

On the other hand, it always could have been Rebecca herself.

He realized how little he still knew about her, the woman central to this entire investigation. He had learned some information, but felt like her personality was a mystery. For all he knew, she had untreated mental health issues such as bipolar disorder or schizophrenia.

He wondered about Stemp's interpretation, that it had something to do with 9/11. That felt like an entirely new can of worms, though. A thought occurred to him: he needed to go back to the house, yet again, and examine the rest of the photographs. To see if there was writing on any others.

He pulled over and did a hasty three-point-turn. A vehicle blared its horn at him and drove past. He ignored it and headed to the Bloomingdale farm.

# CHAPTER TWENTY-SEVEN / SUNDAY, 10:23 PM

He pulled in to the quiet farm. The big house lurked in the dark. He stepped out of the Camry. Overhead, the moon was just a sliver, occasionally disappearing completely behind the clouds.

The clouds looked like smoke.

He slipped into the house and went to the dining room, off the back of the kitchen. He used a flashlight instead of turning on the lights, and he put on his gloves.

He went through the framed pictures one at a time. His heartbeat accelerated as he did. His breathing quickened.

He found four photos with cryptic phrases written on the back.

He didn't need a handwriting expert to confirm that they were written by the same person. He could see that with his own eyes. In fact, he wondered if he even needed an expert to compare the phrases to the victim's own penmanship.

His blood chilled by what he was reading, he set the photographs down momentarily and darted into the unlit kitchen.

Everyone had a "junk drawer." A catch-all drawer with old birthday candles and forgotten candy, wine openers and little notes with phone numbers. The drawer had already been gone through by CSI, and most of it had been bagged, but Brendan figured they were likely to have left something behind.

He found the drawer and searched through it with his flashlight. There wasn't much, and there were no notes, no pieces of paper of any kind.

He turned to the rest of the kitchen. He looked at the fridge. Nothing stuck to it, not a single magnet. He then moved towards the pantry, which was a closet-sized room next to the kitchen table in its little breakfast nook.

He found what he was looking for. There was a notepad with a pen on a string. A little gimmick for grocery lists. There were two words written on the top page. *Parsley* and *Sage*. He flipped to the pages after it, but there was nothing. Just those two words were enough, however. While the phrases on the backs of the photographs had been written in bold, architectural style, these here were penned in a kind of juvenile cursive.

Nevertheless, he ripped off the top sheet and returned to the back dining room. He held the small piece of paper next to the photos. No way were they written by the same person, unless the person had split personalities.

It was a possibility, but a remote one. So was the chance that someone else had written the names of the herbs, someone other than Rebecca, and that the difference didn't clear her at all.

These unlikely scenarios notwithstanding, Brendan felt a rush of excitement. He was even more sure that the sentences on the backs of the photos were written by the killer.

They were haunting. In the cool, drafty farmhouse, he shuddered as he read them. He placed them in a logical sequence and looked them over once more, together. After the original phrase, a kind of darkly poetic message formed.

> *I was born under the black smoke of September*
> *I was born to you, and your infinite forms, and now I have come for you.*
> *To steal your children, to break you under the moon.*
> *There I once was cradled in that autumn wind, a human as unsympathetic as the winter which follows, with its starving creatures, coming in low through the howling cold.*

It wasn't Edgar Allen Poe, by any stretch, but the poetic prose indicated a couple of things. One, that someone who had access to Rebecca's home – or had broken in, granted – had premeditated doing her harm, or at least conjectured about it. Two, that the author, the killer, had some degree of education, tainted as it might be by a skewed version of the world.

In the mind of this killer, the world was a cold, haunted place. He seemed to place himself in a superior position. "Born to you, and your infinite forms." It was kind of pompous.

It was also potentially filial. But Rebecca had no children older than Leah. She would've had her daughter at 24 or 25 years old, and while having children younger than that was certainly possible, to have one who was capable of writing this kind of message on the backs of pictures, would have made Rebecca sixteen or younger when she gave birth.

Brendan hesitated. Well, that wasn't completely unheard of either. Was this message written by another child of Rebecca's? Someone she'd had at a very tender age who was now twelve, thirteen, even fourteen years old?

He would need to check hospital records again. Problem was, it was like finding a needle in a haystack. So far he hadn't even been able to turn up where Rebecca had given birth to her daughter, three and a half years ago. He had begun to suspect she hadn't had the child in a hospital at all, but perhaps had had a home birth.

He would need the little girl's social security number, her birth certificate, but those might be out of reach. She was the ward of Rebecca's parents, and the chance of them turning anything over like that was slim to none, controlling and protective as Alexander Heilshorn seemed to be.

Brendan sighed and ran a hand across his mouth. He winced, tasting the rubber of the gloves he'd forgotten he was wearing.

It was all so speculative. He was on the outside now. Pushed out of the investigation by the victim's own father. He felt so close to something, and yet he didn't have the proof, the inarguable evidence to connect the dots in his mind.

The killer wrote these words. He was sure of it, but he couldn't prove it, and it didn't tell him much about the killer's identity except for possibilities, interpretation: maybe he had an inflated sense of self, maybe he was Rebecca's child, maybe he was fucking crazy. Maybe, maybe, maybe.

He would have to turn in the pictures. For one, the handwriting could still be matched to anything else forensics had taken from the house, or anything still left in the house, which may have similar writing on it, and may serve up the author. A long shot, but totally necessary.

The third man that the woman from the vegetable market had seen with Rebecca had hair greying around the temples. He was older than the others, the woman had said. Colinas had later gone back to the elderly woman and shown her pictures: from Kevin to his father, and a slew of others, but she had been unable to identify any of them.

Who was this man? Did he like to write on the backs of photographs?

There was nothing else to go on.

He put the photos together on the table and headed back out to his car. He thought he had an evidence envelope in a box in his trunk.

He left the house and walked through the dirt dooryard. Headlights suddenly blinded him.

Brendan stopped immediately and raised a hand to shield his eyes. Whoever had just flipped on the lights had their brights on, and the lights were fairly high from the ground. They were just sitting there in the driveway, as if they'd been waiting for him. Chances were, whichever deputy was watching the house was going to chew Brendan out for being there. Not because they would know he was off the case, necessarily, but because protocol was to notify the deputy on surveillance, and because whoever it was, Brendan had apparently slipped by them.

He resumed walking, a little smile on his face, and started down the dirt driveway toward them. The vehicle sat with its stunning lights. A second later, the engine came to life.

Brendan slowed and shielded his eyes again, but didn't stop.

The vehicle dropped into gear – Brendan could hear the transmission. It took a second for him to register what was happening. There was no reason for him to suspect anything. When the vehicle lurched forward, its tires spinning in the dirt, Brendan was shocked.

It came at him full bore. He had the chance to involuntarily utter one phrase – "Oh my God" – before he started to run out of the driveway.

He ran away, taking to the large front yard. He realized only after he had gone this way that the vehicle, with its bright lights shining high from the ground, was a big truck or SUV. It turned and followed him into the yard with no problem. The engine growled as it clunked off the dirt and into the grass, and then it gained speed.

Brendan turned and sprinted towards the house. His only chance was to get inside.

The vehicle was right on top of him, closing in too fast. He wouldn't make the front door in time. At the last second, he leapt to the right, and the vehicle roared past him – almost. It caught his left side and spun him like a top.

Two revolutions in mid-air, his body twisted like a rag doll, and Brendan came down on his back. Thoomp. The air burst out of him – every last cubic centimeter.

He could hear the vehicle come to a stop and the gear shift into reverse as he struggled to take a breath. No air was getting into his lungs. The vehicle started to back up – it was only a few feet from the front door, and then it turned to the left, prepared to circle around and come at him again.

Finally he sucked in a huge whooping breath of air. He scrambled to his feet, completely unaware of his injuries at first. Then his left leg and hip were white hot with pain, and he almost passed out. He had to put all of his weight on his right foot. His lower back was a mass of agony as he turned and started limping toward his Camry.

The vehicle was a big truck. The crescent moon, visible now in the sky, painted the truck blood red. There were roll bars on top. It grumbled and thrummed and came around in a wide circle, going a ways out into the yard before it was able to aim at Brendan again.

As he ran, hopped, towards the Camry, his lower body a symphony of pain, he realized that the truck was bound to get him again. By the time he got to the Camry, opened the door, got in, started it up, and pulled away, the truck would be upon him.

He turned then, changing his trajectory to the shed, on the other side of his vehicle.

The truck finished its wide arc and started coming.

Brendan ran as fast as he could. His hip threatened to give way completely on the left side, spilling him helplessly to the ground. He gritted his teeth. He could feel bones crunching each time he brought weight down on his left leg. The truck bore down on him, its engine as loud as thunder.

He bypassed the Camry, bracing himself temporarily on the hood as he slipped past. A few more feet and he would be inside the shed.

He realized that the maniac in the huge pick-up could just plow into the fragile building. It was mere board and batten, nothing that could stand up to a steel beast ramming it at full power. Still, he slipped into the darkness of the shed.

It was only dark for a moment, and then the truck lights illuminated it like the sun.

The lights fell on the tractor, shining off its metal hide, and Brendan, making a snap decision, started to climb up to its seat.

The truck slammed into the shed. Boards burst into a million shards and splinters, instantly reminding Brendan of Kevin Heilshorn shooting out the window.

The entire structure screamed and groaned and listed hard to the left, away from the blow of the truck. Wood squealed against metal as the truck started to back up. It had approached at an angle, and so had taken a huge bite out of one side of the open entrance to the shed. The next time, Brendan knew, the truck would come straight on, and straight in.

He reached the leather bucket seat in the tractor. He looked around for the key.

It was all just coming to him in the moment. There was no plan. All he knew was that as rundown as the old farm was, he was grateful that this John Deere tractor was in good condition. He wondered if he had Donald Kettering to thank.

These were the only coherent thoughts Brendan had for a while. He was distantly aware of his incredible luck that the last person to have driven the tractor had left the keys in the ignition. Outside, the truck withdrew, dimming the light Brendan could see by, but there was time to grab the keys and turn.

Nothing happened.

Brendan remembered about diesel engines. You had to prime them. There was a toggle on the dashboard that he flipped up. An orange telltale lit up above the toggle after a few seconds. Then he tried the key again.

The engine grumbled to life.

He was a city boy, and had never ridden a tractor. But he knew where the gas was. When that truck appeared again, he would slam down on the pedal and ram that motherfucker.

* * *

The truck stopped. Its headlights flooded the shed with blinding light. Brendan's foot hovered over the gas pedal. A second later, he pulled out his gun.

The lights made it nearly impossible to see anything other than the shape of the truck. The tractor rumbled beneath him, and the truck's engine idled. The air throbbed with the combined machinery; Brendan felt it vibrating his bones.

There was a *thunk* and Brendan cocked his weapon. Had the driver just got out? A second later, this suspicion was confirmed when a figure stepped in front of the bright lights.

Brendan aimed his gun at the silhouette with both hands. He hadn't expected this. He was now a sitting duck. If the driver had a weapon too, there would be no contest. Brendan was nearly blind looking into the flood of bright lights, but he would be perfectly illuminated and an easy target for the driver.

"Stop right there, don't move!' He had to shout over the noise of the engines. "Don't move, or I'll mow you down. Who are you? What are you doing here?"

His arms were shaking. His entire left side was pulsing with pain; it felt like electric shocks running up and down his leg, like teeth biting into his hip. It hurt just to sit on the tractor seat.

The figure was motionless. It was hard to make out the shape, but it looked like the driver was standing with his arms at his sides. Tough to know if he was carrying a weapon or not.

"I'll ask you again – who are you, and what are you doing here?"

For another agonizing moment, the vehicles rumbled and the driver said nothing. Brendan couldn't make out any information, not a license plate on the truck, or its true color. The driver was a silhouette. There may have been some slightly visible human features – some skin tone, the edges of clothing, but nothing definite. In the middle of it all, the fear, the anger, and the pain, Brendan felt a gnawing guilt: He had allowed himself to be trapped like this. He had been backed into a corner, and now he was feeble. Helpless.

He thrust out his gun.

"Answer me!"

The driver spoke. He raised his voice as well, but he didn't sound like he was shouting. He didn't sound strained at all.

"Did you visit Eddie Stemp tonight?"

Brendan's mind raced. His whole body shook. "I asked you who you were. Answer me and I'll answer you."

The driver took a step forward. Brendan squeezed the trigger. One more ounce of pressure, and he would be in his second officer-involved shooting of the week. He would take this man down.

"You know who I am," said the driver.

Brendan froze. The man standing there at the entrance of the shed was the killer.

"Stop right there," Brendan said. "Don't come any closer." His voice sounded like it was coming from far away.

The driver repeated his question. "Did you visit Eddie Stemp tonight?"

Brendan licked his lips. They felt numb. He took a stab at something. "I think you already know the answer to that."

"What did he tell you?"

"Nothing."

He was aware that the power was in the hands of the killer. This man had him pinned. He had every advantage.

Bile rose in Brendan's throat. He thought he was going to throw up. Yet all he had to do was pull the trigger. The killer's silhouette was thinned by the immensely bright lights. It was still a good enough target.

"He told you about things?"

"'Things?' No. He didn't tell me about things.'" Brendan's heart slammed against his rib cage. He thought his pulse must be visible. With every beat his body must be pulsing in and out.

He saw a flash of his wife and daughter. They were both sitting in the car. His wife wasn't looking at him. His daughter was in her car seat in the back, looking at a toy. It was the last time he had seen them.

Then his daughter looked up and smiled.

Brendan fired his gun.

* * *

He knew that if he fired and missed, any chance of a second shot would be minimal. The killer would either draw and return fire, or simply duck out of the lights. Outside of the sun-like blast of headlights, the world was pitch black. Brendan could keep firing, but he would be wasting time getting to cover if he did.

His shot missed.

When the killer disappeared from sight, Brendan dropped his gun and tramped down on the tractor's accelerator. The tractor lurched forward, nearly bucking him off.

The thing was, it did not move very fast, even though he had put the pedal to the floor. Its engine roared, but it closed the gap between it and the truck far too slowly.

The killer had gotten back into the cab of his pick-up, and thrown the vehicle into reverse. The truck backed away from the oncoming tractor just as the two machines were about to collide.

Brendan drove the tractor on, clearing the shed. Once outside, he could see a little better. The front of the large pick-up swung away, and Brendan caught a glimpse of the killer behind the wheel, caught in the lights of the tractor. The face was just a blur, a flash of salt and pepper hair, there one second, gone the next, and Brendan expected the truck to lurch forward.

It didn't. The window came down. Something poked out of the truck that was no handgun, it was bigger. It was the muzzle of an automatic weapon.

The tractor was still moving forward when Brendan leapt from the seat. He hit the ground hard and rolled away, fresh and terrible pain tearing through his leg and hip. When he landed, bright pain encircled his ankle like barbed wire. He rolled in the dirt driveway. He was vividly aware that he no longer had his revolver.

Bullets first sang off the metal of the tractor and then punched into the earth inches from where Brendan lay. The tractor kept advancing, however, and it forced the killer to drive on in his pick-up.

Brendan scrambled to his feet. He thought only briefly about taking shelter in the shed once again. Bad idea. It was just a runway for the truck. He glanced at the house to his left. While the pick-up was traveling away from the front door of the house, the tractor was already slowing and the truck would have a clear line to drop into reverse and come after Brendan as he made for shelter inside the house.

He remembered the barn out in the back. He started hobbling towards the side of the house. It was narrow here between the shed, the trees, and the house; it wouldn't be easy going for the big pick-up. Brendan ran as best as he could, but his legs weren't cooperating. His left hip still felt terribly *crunchy*, as if bone fragments or cartilage grist had been knocked loose in there and were grinding together. His right ankle was a screaming throb of pain from his jump from the tractor. He could barely put weight on it. He took a few awkward, lunging steps and toppled back to the ground.

He desperately turned his head to look behind him. In the front yard, the truck was turning around. Narrow passage or not, it was going to come for him again.

Brendan screamed. He hadn't expected to; it just came out of him. A wild, guttural yell from somewhere down in the pit of him. It was an animal scream, wretched and primal. In the midst of it he closed his eyes. And then he did something he hadn't done for years.

He prayed.

He did not pray for long. He opened his eyes and started to pick himself up again. At the same time, he saw something new. At the head of the driveway, another set of headlights turned in from Route 12.

Brendan started dragging himself towards the side of the house. The truck completed its turn and was aiming back towards him, but it had stopped. Brendan continued to yell as he pulled himself along. His words were garbled and made little sense. "Help me. Stop him. The killer."

There was a flash of light coming from the new headlights. A wave of nauseating terror swept through Brendan as he thought: *accomplice*. It wasn't the first time he had considered that maybe more than one person was responsible for Rebecca's death. Now here was someone else firing at him. He heard the shot a split second after the flash of light. Nothing had impacted anywhere near him. There were more flashes, more *pop pop* of gunfire in the night. The newcomer was shooting at the truck; Brendan heard the distinct sound of bullets biting into steel. Not an accomplice after all – help had arrived.

The pick-up truck was facing the wrong way to return fire. Its passenger side was facing this new vehicle. The truck started to back up. It gained speed and then swung around in reverse to face the other direction.

The flashfire gunfight continued, a barrage of bullets coming from the new vehicle. Now the pick-up was in position to return fire.

There was the menacing noise of a submachine gun. The weapon had a suppressor on it, so that it seemed to drum the air – *Budududud*. The recently arrived vehicle was raked with the shots.

Brendan, in the meantime, had reached the house. He pressed himself against the exterior. He smelled onion grass growing along the foundation. He tasted blood in his mouth and wondered distantly if he'd bitten his tongue when he'd jumped from the tractor. He realized he was going to go into shock, if he wasn't there already. A second later, he passed out.

## CHAPTER TWENTY-EIGHT / MONDAY, 2:33 AM

Brendan awoke from nightmares in which he relived the terrible ordeal at the Bloomingdale farm again and again. Only in his dreams, it wasn't an indistinct killer at the wheel of the truck. Instead, his wife and daughter were in the cab, and he rammed the tractor into them over and over again.

As he came to and got his bearings, he was aware of how dry his mouth was. Next, he realized he was hooked up to some tubes. An IV. His vision came into focus and he looked around. He was in a hospital bed. Machines whirred and beeped nearby. A curtain cordoned off his area.

He lifted his head in order to look down at himself and take inventory. He tried to lift his legs beneath the covering blankets. Something was restricting his movement; a brace of some kind around his thigh and hip. After only a short time, he dropped his head back to the pillow, exhausted. The attempts to move about aroused a dull pain that began to spread up from his hip. He gritted his teeth and moaned as it reached a startling climax. He was afraid he was going to pass out again. What had happened to him down there?

He tried to recall everything as best as he could. The blood red pick-up truck swam into his mind's eye. The killer silhouetted by the dazzling headlights. He searched his memory for what had happened next. The arrival of someone else, possibly one of the deputies supposed to be keeping surveillance on the farm. He remembered crawling away, dragging himself to the side of the house. And now he had formed a complete picture of the recent events.

He closed his eyes as the pain in his hip slowly abated. As it waned, sleep overtook him again.

* * *

An hour later, and he was awakened by the Sheriff. For a moment, Brendan thought he was back in his rented house, sleeping on the couch. He wondered how the Sheriff had gotten in. Usually, Brendan locked his doors. He tried to ask Taber this, but found his mouth was dryer than ever.

"Water," he croaked.

Taber looked around, and then disappeared out of the curtained area.

A minute later he returned with a cup full of ice.

"The nurse said you can have these ice chips. No water right now." He passed Brendan the cup and looked him over. "I'm sorry," he said. Brendan didn't think the Sheriff was just apologizing for the lack of water.

Brendan greedily dumped as many ice chips as possible into his mouth. He felt some of them fall onto his neck and chest. He sucked on the jagged bunch of them. Nothing had ever been as satisfying. When they had melted to thin slivers, he crunched away the remaining bits and then tipped the cup back for more. In the second round, he emptied the cup.

Taber waited patiently. Brendan's eyelids fluttered as he experienced the momentary bliss of the ice chips. He swallowed and looked at Taber.

The Sheriff affected a lopsided grin. "Given an ability to forecast these recent events, I wonder if you would have still taken the job up here."

"Sure," said Brendan.

"I . . . How are you feeling?"

"Okay. Pain in my hip. Ankle."

Taber nodded. "They've got you on a little morphine. But I'll go easy on you and won't take this out of your vacation days."

Brendan smiled feebly. Taber ran a hand through his hair. He seemed uncomfortable. Maybe it was being in the hospital. Brendan didn't particularly like them much, either.

He tried to sit up a little. "Did you get the guy?"

Taber shook his head, no.

"I have a description of the vehicle. Couldn't get a plate number. The lights, it . . ."

Taber patted the air with his hands. *Calm down.* "It's okay. Deputy Bostrom got a good look at the vehicle just before it hightailed out of there. Red pick-up. We're thinking a Ford, Heavy Duty, maybe a recent model. It's on the wire."

"Bostrom didn't give chase?"

"He called it in the second he could. By then it had already left the scene. Bostrom checked you out instead."

"God dammit." Brendan tried to get comfortable. Everything hurt.

"Look, he did the right thing. A high speed chase in the middle of the night wouldn't have helped anyone. Not you, nobody. You're lucky Bostrom acted fast. You were bleeding pretty badly."

Brendan considered this new information. He remembered tasting blood in his mouth. That was nothing though, just a split lip or a bitten tongue. Then he thought about the pain in his hip. Maybe it wasn't a break or fracture, but a laceration?

"Bleeding from where?"

Taber looked at Brendan's body, hidden under the covers. "They said you had internal damage. Didn't say from what. They'll talk to you about it."

"I can't be on morphine," Brendan said. Taber either didn't hear him or didn't understand, and cocked his head quizzically, leaning forward.

"I'm a recovering addict," said Brendan. "Painkillers are no good."

Taber leaned back, frowning. "Well, from what they tell me, Healy, you need the meds." He blinked. "You'll be alright." Clearly he was someone who didn't understand addiction. Brendan was used to that.

He wondered if he had any choice anyway. He had no idea what the full extent of the damage was, or the pain, if it was already being ameliorated by drugs.

He sighed, and looked up at the ceiling. "This is a total fucking mess," he said.

Taber looked tired. "Did you get a look at the guy at all?"

"About six feet, Caucasian. 180 pounds. Black, greying hair." Brendan shrugged. "That's it."

"That's okay, Healy. That's something."

"It was him. I had him, and I let him go."

"We don't know who that was."

"Who else would it be?"

"What were you doing there, anyway?"

"I found more messages."

"More messages?"

"Things, phrases, written on the backs of the photos. The dining room." Brendan's mind was wooly. It was a challenge just to form coherent sentences.

Taber was nodding, but his expression was dubious. "You think they're linked to the porn videos?" He lowered his voice on the last two words.

"All linked. The whole thing is right there. Right in front of us."

"Then who is this new guy?" Taber raised his eyebrows. It was a challenge. So far during the investigation, Taber had seemed right there with Brendan. He could feel it. Maybe it had to do with being vetted by Argon; Brendan didn't know. When Delaney was around the Sheriff had often acted skeptical and deferred to the senior investigator, but one-on-one Brenan felt like Taber really listened. It felt like Brendan was at last beginning to lose the man's faith in him.

Brendan shook his head. "That's the last piece. I don't know. But he's a hired man."

"Why do you say that?"

"Sub-machine gun, Sheriff. I know there are rednecks around these parts – there are rednecks everywhere. But typically disgruntled ex-boyfriends or ex-husbands who got religion don't go out and get a machine gun to seek revenge. This guy, last night, he works for someone. An organization."

"Our killer used a knife, Healy."

"Doesn't matter." Brendan licked his lips. He wanted more ice chips. "I talked to Stemp last night, too. He told me. Something."

"What? You talked to Stemp?"

"He said Rebecca started out as an escort. I think that's why she left school, to work for a service in Albany. Government types with fetishes."

Taber looked nervous. "And you believe Stemp? I thought he was just a religious nut."

"That's maybe what Delaney told you. But Stemp is an educated man. Used to work in some capacity. For the . . . brass. I don't know politics. I was a goddam science major . . ."

Brendan's mind started to drift. He could feel sleep pulling at him. He saw a vision of his wife. They had met in school. She was standing in her cap and gown. She looked worried.

"So Rebecca drops out of school to be a high-class pro? Why? She had all the money she could need."

"Maybe. Maybe she did, maybe she didn't. Maybe that's why her father is so keen on controlling this case. Influencing it, whatever. Maybe he doesn't want it to come out."

"What to come out?"

"That he cut her off. Who knows? Feels responsible for what she did. What she became."

His mind was playing nasty tricks on Brendan. Now he saw Rebecca in one of her porn videos. She was grinding away, but she was looking at him, looking at him the way her lifeless eyes had stared back from the bureau mirror in the bedroom. And then his wife was there too in this phantom video. His wife became Rebecca.

"Dammit," he muttered. "Stop."

Taber looked around. His tired face was expressing more concern by the second. "Let me go get you a nurse. That's enough for now. We can finish debriefing when you're better."

"Where's Delaney?"

"At the scene."

"Tell him to go fuck himself."

The Sheriff offered a surprised laugh. Then he started to leave.

"Wait."

Taber stopped as he parted the curtain and turned.

"Did you know about Olivia?"

The Sheriff took a step closer. He wrinkled his eyes in question.

"That she was Rebecca's therapist. Did you know?"

"I had no idea."

"Did Delaney?"

"I can't say. But if he did, he would have introduced it."

"Is there any reason he wouldn't have? Any reason he would keep it to himself?"

"I don't think so. I hope not. Why?"

Brendan said nothing else. His eyes were glazing over. The last thing he saw was the Sheriff stepping away, and he heard him calling for a nurse. By the time one arrived, Brendan had slipped into unconsciousness again.

# CHAPTER TWENTY-NINE / MONDAY, 8:52 AM

"Well hello there," said a voice.

Brendan opened his eyes and saw the doctor.

"How are you feeling?"

"Like I got hit by a truck."

The doctor smiled. "Sounds about right. Well, you have a hip fracture. A hairline crack in the upper quarter of your femur. How is your pain?"

"My groin hurts."

"That's common. You've asked to be taken off the morphine."

"Yes."

The doctor frowned. He was perhaps forty, and prematurely balding. He wore glasses. "I really don't recommend it. Your injuries are bound to create . . . a lot of discomfort."

Brendan opened his mouth to say something, and then thought better of it. He changed what he was going to say. "What about the bleeding?"

The frown deepened into an almost paternal look of concern. "Are you aware of your peptic ulcers?"

"Ulcers?"

"You have a tear in the mucosa of your esophagus, and in the antrum, located in your stomach. Do you take aspirin or Motrin?"

"No."

"Good. I have to ask you – do you have a history of stress, or drug and alcohol addiction?"

Brendan was silent.

"Mr. Healy?"

"I'm a recovering alcoholic. Stress comes with the job. I'm a detective."

"I understand. Do you get frequent stomach aches or pains?" The doctor folded his hands in front him and looked down for a moment.

"Yeah, I get pains. Ulcers – that's why I had blood in my mouth?"

The doctor looked up. "I believe so. You suffered quite an ordeal, from what I've been told. The shock to your system has really exacerbated your ulcers. It's important that you keep your stress levels way down while you recover."

"How long is it going to take? For my hip?"

"That depends on you."

Brendan fought the urge to roll his eyes. He shifted his position in the bed, and felt the pain flare up around his thigh and groin. He tried not to let the doctor see, but it was futile.

"Just ballpark it, Doc."

"I'm going to recommend that you're on leave from your job for at least two months. Maybe longer. And that's just for your hip. Ulcers take a long time to repair. The mucosa is sensitive in the lining of your esophageal tract and in the antrum. You don't want it to spread to your duodenum."

Brendan sighed. He noticed that the curtain had been pushed back. There was another bed in the room, empty. He could see through the doorway out into the hallway.

"Have I had any other visitors, besides the Sheriff?"

"No. Not that I'm aware of."

"Okay." Brendan lay back. He looked up at the ceiling. "Keep the morphine coming," he said. "I don't care."

* * *

He was taken home two days later by Deputy Lawless. Lawless passed on information from the Sheriff that the IACP investigation had been suspended pending Brendan's full recovery. Taber didn't want to add stress to Brendan's life of any kind.

Brendan laughed.

The deputy took the wheelchair and set it up in Brendan's driveway and helped Brendan into it.

"Anything happening with the Heilshorn case?"

"I don't know."

"Or you're not supposed to say."

Lawless was silent. Then, "How are your injuries?"

"I have what they said was an intertrochanteric fracture."

"Ouch."

"Actually, it's better than what they first thought. The X-Ray sort of got it wrong, but the MRI was more definitive. The type of fracture I got is in a place with good blood supply. I'll be playing basketball again in no time."

"You play?"

"It was a joke."

"Oh."

Brendan gave Lawless the key and the deputy opened the front door and then pushed Brendan inside.

Once in the house, Lawless seemed awkward. "Anything else I can do for you, Detective?"

"Actually, there is."

Brendan rolled himself into the bedroom, having some difficulty fitting in through the narrow doors in the little house. He was able to reach under the bed and get the cash box he kept. He gave Lawless some money and a short list of things to get at the store.

Lawless considered the list, and for a moment Brendan though the deputy would refuse the request. But he didn't. He was back half an hour later with the booze.

## CHAPTER THIRTY / MONDAY, 7:33 PM

Night seemed to be coming quicker these days. Halfway through September, and it was already dark outside by seven o'clock. It seemed earlier than in years past. Brendan wondered if something was happening with daylight saving time that no one had told him about. Or with the earth, the cosmos; time was speeding up. He poured himself another drink of vodka and thought about it.

He booted up his laptop. He had already watched Danice's videos several times each. They at once repulsed and aroused him. There was a whole glut of revolting videos on the Red Light website. He spent time, too much time, trying to get his mind around it. The pro videos he could more or less understand. The women involved still might be damaged in some way, but for the most part, they seemed in control. They were making bank. They oohed and aahed demonstratively and threw their hair back.

The amateur videos were a mixture of voyeurism and sheer perversion. Sometimes there was a video of a couple, having some fun with exhibitionism. In other cases, the women were clearly not enjoying themselves.

These were, in a word, horrific. What brought these women here? Were they under duress? Was it a desperate cry for attention? An urgent need for money? Or were they coerced?

One of the Danice videos was an "interview." Brendan watched the beginning, the bit before the sex, a dozen times or more. She came into an office and sat on a couch. There were two cameras, one stationary and one handheld. Her hair was long and flowing, and she wore glasses in this video, as if she were applying for a secretarial position.

The interviewer asks her what her qualifications are. She's great at collating, she says, and making copies. He asks her if she's good at giving head. Yes, she says, she's good at that too. Then he asks her about her physical qualifications. Would she please give a visual demonstration of what she would bring to the company. And she stands and begins to take off her clothes. The interviewer moves in with the handheld camera. He begins getting extreme close-ups of her attributes. This part Brendan only watched twice. When the interviewer comes around the desk and is visible in the stationary shot, his head and face are blotted out with a masking effect.

Danice's other videos took place in a totally different context, the first of which was dated two years later. Brendan wondered if the first video actually served an ulterior purpose. If he was to believe Eddie Stemp and the story of the high-end escort service, then the "interview," as playful as it was objectifying and demeaning, could have been part of an online catalog. But Brendan thought any "casting" video was more likely a sick ruse used to get young women to perform sex acts on the spot. Finally, Brendan wanted to learn more about how the videos were distributed, but there were nothing but dead ends.

Two videos had tags down below, advertising the websites which offered them. One was tagged "Adult Royale dot com;" a video in which Danice strutted around a fancy home wearing high heels before she was approached by a muscular young man. The other was the mock interview video, and the tag read "XList," with a heraldic lion unfurling a long tongue as its emblem. Brendan had decided to visit that website first, and had scoured it for contact information. There wasn't much more than a hard copy order form. He hadn't looked it over thoroughly enough, however, and now at home, perpetually on the couch, he had more time to do so.

He found that there was an email address for problems with orders or shipment. He took a long pull of the Stoli vodka, emptying the glass. He then spent the next ten minutes concocting a fake email account. He named himself John Porter and set up a Gmail address in which his username was johnporter645.

He decided to just act as though he wasn't aware of how to select and order a video, though the site certainly made it easy enough for any moron.

> Dear XList,
> I am trying to find a video featuring Danice. I can't seem to locate one. Sorry, but I am not great with computers. Could you please help me?
> Thanks, John Porter

He hit send and then flopped back on the couch. He realized that he needed to keep looking for these types of sites which sold any of the other videos, either in DVD shipment or as downloads, but for the moment, he couldn't stomach it. All of the sites featured ads in the margins with looped graphics of people engaged in various acts. They covered the gamut of human perversion, but tended towards the absurd, the grotesque. There was animated porn, he had discovered, and every kind of fetish, known to him and not. He was tired of looking at it.

He exited out of the sites and poured himself another glass of vodka.

## CHAPTER THIRTY-ONE / TUESDAY, 9:44 PM

"Nothing," said Delaney.

"Nothing? And Heilshorn has his own private investigators?"

"Just like he said. You doing alright? You don't sound too good."

"I don't know why. I slept most of yesterday."

Brendan looked outside. It was indeed dark again. There was a light rain falling.

"I can't believe we're gonna lose this," said Brendan.

"Lose it? We're not going to lose anything. It hasn't even been a week. These things can take time. They can take years."

Brendan grunted. He was on his fourth vodka of the evening. He had eaten a peanut butter and jelly sandwich earlier that day. He couldn't remember if he'd eaten anything else.

"Did you know Olivia Jane was Rebecca Heilshorn's therapist?"

He heard Delaney breathing for a second. "You know, I really don't appreciate you asking the Sheriff that. Those relationships are kept strictly confidential."

"So I've been told. Have you been able to obtain her session notes?"

"Jesus, Healy. No. Don't you understand? Time. These things take time."

"Rebecca doesn't have time."

"Rebecca's dead."

"Exactly," said Brendan. "Exactly. Time means nothing to her now."

"Are you . . . Healy, are you drunk?"

"Far from it, my friend. You know, you can be a real hardcase, Delaney. A real asshole. But I like you. I don't think you did anything wrong."

"Fuck you, Healy."

Brendan started to laugh.

"I'm doing you a favor even talking to you," Delaney said gruffly. "Next time you want to know anything, you call the Sheriff. But remember, this is no longer your case. Not the house, not the people, not the porn. Out of your territory now."

Brendan lolled on the couch. "Did you, ah, oil your broomstick with Olivia Jane?" He closed his eyes.

Delaney responded, sounding farther away, "Hey, Healy. Do me a favor. Look around. See anything?"

"No."

"Exactly. That's your territory right now."

Delaney hung up.

Brendan looked at his phone and frowned when he saw the "Call Ended 6:03 mins" flashing. He threw the phone across the room where it knocked hard against the wall. He propped himself up and reached for the milk jug next to the couch. The wheelchair was so tough to get in and out of, and using the crutches made it impossible to piss standing up. Sitting was too painful, even with the meds. And the vodka made him have to whiz frequently. He just peed next to the couch.

## CHAPTER THIRTY-TWO / THURSDAY, 10:14 AM

He realized the pee jugs were full. He also realized his house was disgusting.

Brendan's head pounded. Lawless had brought him five bottles of vodka and a case of Miller High Life. He was halfway through the fourth bottle of vodka and so decided to switch to beer. He would need to come down a little in order to be able to go out and get more vodka. This time he would get a case of it.

He needed to stay drunk enough that the depression didn't crush him, but sober enough to be able to drive. Plus, he had returned to the videos. For the three that showed the male involved clearly, he had written out a physical description of each. His handwriting was messy chicken-scratch. He needed to transcribe it into a proper document. He figured a little housework would help put him in the mood.

He started to get off the couch and realized things were worse than he'd first feared. The pain in his groin had been muted by the painkillers, but so, it seemed had a certain amount of feeling in his legs. It took him ten minutes just to get to the wheelchair. Then another ten to fumble around with the crutches and get his useless legs underneath his body. During the process, he felt a tickle in his throat and coughed into his fist. The blood that splattered on his hand was bright and terrifying.

It took a half an hour to get the pee jugs into the bathroom and flush them down the toilet.

He took a break and went to the fridge for the beer. Half of the case of Miller High Life was gone, and he didn't remember drinking it. There were cans in the sink and on the kitchen counter. He had left food out, and the kitchen was rank.

He kept seeing flashes of the porn videos. It was as if they had hijacked his cerebral cortex. He thought about habits. He wondered if doing porn was a habit, like anything else. Cue, routine, reward. He wondered what Rebecca's first cue had been. He wanted so badly to talk to her father, Alexander Heilshorn, Mr. Big Deal New York City Doctor.

An idea flickered in the back of his mind. A connection. But it was tough to bring to the surface. The meds and the booze and the lack of nutrition were conspiring to cloud his brain. Blood from his mouth was drying on his hand. He cracked a beer and guzzled it down. Nothing had ever tasted better. Not even ice chips.

\* \* \*

He forgot, temporarily, about going out for the vodka and went to check his email. He saw he had finally gotten a response from XList, which turned out to be the only porn site which offered an email address. All the rest had been download-only, and no customer service.

He drank from his second can of beer and eagerly clicked to open the reply.

> Dear Valued Customer,
> Thank you for your interest in The XList Company! We're proud to offer the highest

quality in erotic entertainment. Our "Danice"
excerpt can be found at the following link:

A complicated URL was provided.

For the full feature DVD to be shipped to
your door for only 19.95, click here:

And a credit card button had been embedded in the
email.

Thank you and happy viewing.
The XList Company

Brendan shuddered when he thought of the XList
"Company." He also thought of the people who genuinely
considered erotic entertainment to be a service. Some
would say it helped married couples keep their sex lives
spicy. Others would point to the lonely men who needed
release – they might even go so far as to say it helped to
prevent sex crimes. Brendan had heard it all.

He considered the videos featuring Rebecca, aka
Danice. They were all professionally done. She was not in
the "amateur" section of Red Light. If she had started out
doing tricks for senators and congressmen in Albany,
someone in the escort service had introduced her to
pornographers. She had then done the "casting interview,"
and went on to perform in a handful of videos, but only a
couple of years later. Had it taken that long for her to
break into the business? Or had she hesitated, after doing
the "interview," and had second thoughts? Was there
some motive, other than a zeal for exhibitionism, or a need
for money, that had made her return to the trade after a
hiatus?

In a flash of clarity, Brendan realized there was no need
to transcribe his descriptions of the three men in the
videos. He wasn't a computer-whiz by any means, but he

knew how to take a screen shot. He cued up each video to the best image of the man involved, paused it, and instructed his computer to take a "snapshot" of the entire screen. He cropped the images to get a headshot of each man, even the interview video where the man's head was mostly blotted out. Then he got back to looking into the names of the websites who proffered the videos to Red Light. There was only the one other which declared itself: Adult Royale dot com. He visited the site.

Again he looked for the Danice video by using the in-site search tool. He found the video and used the buttons to act as if he were ordering it. They were download only – no shipping. There was no address for Adult Royale productions listed anywhere on the site. No customer service.

He did a separate Google search for Adult Royale. There were a number of hits, including one for the Adult Video Awards, or "AVAs." At last he found a home page different from the one which offered the downloads. This listed an address in Culver City, California, but no phone number or email.

Brendan sat back from the laptop and rubbed his eyes. Was he barking up the wrong tree? What if the videos had nothing to do with Rebecca's death? They could just be a part of her life that she had tried to leave behind, by moving to the country and starting again. She had full custody of her daughter, but her parents had kept the girl most of the time, at least while she was setting up house.

He imagined her: She has shunned the life of the erotic entertainer, a road she embarked on due to some as yet unknown catalyst while she was in college. Perhaps this was to spite her parents, but maybe for some other reason. She turns away from the industry and gets married to Eddie Stemp. They attempt to carve out a life together.

Did she meet Stemp after she'd already left the business?

Brendan's eyes widened and he sat up on the couch.

Or did she meet Stemp *while* she was in the business?

Maybe Stemp and Rebecca got out together; he from politics, she from escorting. But he found God and she didn't. And the daughter was not his blood. Was she the illegitimate child of someone she'd had relations with in the videos?

Or one of the men she'd slept with during her time as a high-end call girl?

He'd said he was a bodyguard after the military. A bodyguard for whom? Who had bodyguards? Rock stars and politicians.

There were no rock stars in Albany.

Brendan started to get himself off of the couch. He wrenched his body towards the crutches, ignoring the various alarms of pain going off in his hip, groin, and chest. He fumbled around until he got a crutch beneath himself.

Dear God – was Leah the daughter of some government official?

Well, that wouldn't make sense if certain assumptions were correct, and that the timeline reflected her history accurately. If she had left the escort service and then joined up with the video-production, Leah would have to be almost ten years old. The child was too young to fit that scenario.

Unless Brendan was thinking too rigidly, too linearly. Life didn't always happen that way, did it? People thought they quit something, but then they were back at it. Look at him, eight years of sobriety, and he was right back where he'd left off. Life moved in cycles, not timelines.

As if to echo this thinking, he bent at a painful angle and picked up the Miller can and drained its contents. He leaned on his crutch until he nearly toppled over. He dropped the empty can on the carpet. So much for cleaning up.

Rebecca might have never completely left the escort life. She could have kept up with it all along. Maybe she had moved to the west coast for a while – they had found no residences listed for her there, but that didn't mean she hadn't just stayed with someone for a while – but maybe she had never quit the escort game. Then again, maybe she had never gone to the West Coast. So what if one of the video "production companies" had a Culver City address. People could make the videos and send them in from all over. It was the age of outsourcing.

The "Company," so to speak, out there making movies worldwide and sending them back to California where, for all Brendan knew, one guy sat with a credit card machine and the servers running. Brendan didn't know much about filmmaking, but he knew that the technology had evolved dramatically over the past decade. A person could make a high-definition video with a Canon camera and a microphone.

Halfway to the kitchen for another beer, Brendan had a sobering thought: all of this stuff running through his head was built on unsubstantiated material. What were the facts? That a woman who looked just like the deceased Rebecca Heilshorn was in half a dozen porn videos under the name Danice. And that an ex-husband-turned-religious-zealot had hinted that she had been involved in some sort of organized prostitution in Albany, or thereabouts. These connections were pure conjecture.

But the little girl, Leah, she wasn't conjecture. Neither was the lack of evidence for her biological father. For all intents and purposes, he was just a ghost.

And the man who had nearly run him over with a truck wasn't a fantasy, either.

Who was he? That was, of course, what the whole thing boiled down to. Whatever Rebecca had gotten herself caught up in was incidental. Important, but incidental. The killer was the objective.

Brendan found himself putting on his coat. He had no idea how he was going to drive with his leg and hip in so much discomfort, but if he was going to make it through this, there was no stopping the drinking now.

He did one last thing first. He went back and opened up his fake John Porter email. He bent and gritted his teeth against the pain and typed on the laptop.

Five minutes later, and he had sent two emails. One was to Colinas, with attachments of the head shots he had created for each of the men in the videos.

The second was to XList. He didn't expect a response, but he'd sent it anyway. It read:

> Dear XList,
> What happens if one of your actresses gets pregnant?

* * *

Somehow, Brendan survived the trip to the liquor store, and then one to a Walgreens where he bought another case of beer, some milk and some bread. He drew a few looks, and was not surprised. Dressed in sweat pants, unlaced sneakers, and a beige trench-coat, his hair unkempt and undoubtedly reeking of booze, he was the picture of a man off the rails. He didn't care, though. He smiled at the checkout boy, who reminded him of the kid with the acne who'd worked for Kettering and who'd been in Rebecca's house not long before she was killed, picking up Kettering's tools and supplies. Jason Pert.

And she had called him to ask about hooking up a diaper sprayer.

The checkout kid was giving Brendan a wary eye, and Brendan realized the transaction was complete. He hobbled out of the store hanging on to the case of beer, bag of milk, and bread, with one arm. His grunting struggle elicited more looks, a mix of concern and thinly veiled disapproval.

Back at his Camry in the parking lot, he loaded the groceries next to the case of vodka. He looked glibly at the case of grain alcohol for a moment, blinking. He wondered if it would kill him. Then he shut the trunk on it.

He tried not to think of his wife and daughter as he drove back home. He needed to just focus on the road. Still, their memories seemed to come over him at the worst times. Their faces had faded some, too, and this made him angry.

Before he got home he pulled off the road, limped to the trunk of the car and removed a beer from the case. He returned to the driver's seat and then drank as he drove.

His jaw was clenched so hard it was starting to hurt. Blood sat beneath his tongue.

\* \* \*

Colinas had responded to Brendan's email with the headshots.

"Thanks for these. I will run them. I will say they were an anonymous tip. You know I can't share the results with you. Sorry. – R.C."

Brendan was smiling when he started to read the email, and frowning by the end. He responded to Colinas. As he typed, a runnel of beer trickled down his stubbled jaw.

"Hey Colinas, how does it feel to have my job?"

He hit send before he had a chance to re-think. Brendan wanted to hurt him, this guy that had come in and taken over his role in the investigation. It wasn't Brendan's fault that Kevin Heilshorn had gone on a shooting spree which cost him his life. And the man in the truck had tried to run him over because Brendan was close. And everyone knew it. Colinas knew it. The Sheriff knew it. Delaney did. Even Olivia, she knew it. But they were all holding out on him. They had turned their backs.

Brendan flipped to the Red Lights site again. He started going through the videos. He began to cry at some point, and got himself back into the vodka. He hadn't eaten anything for so long he couldn't remember.

They were all on the inside, and he was out.

Even his wife and daughter. If only they had listened to him. If only his wife hadn't had to have been such a *bitch* and so pig-headed and gone off on her own. So he had been a little tipsy? So what? He had driven hundreds of times under the influence. Maybe thousands. He would have gotten them home safe. He would have.

She just hadn't trusted him.

No one trusted him.

Not the Department, not Delaney, not Olivia.

Goddamn that Olivia. Fucking therapist-client confidentiality. Extending beyond death? Ludicrous. People worried too much about what everyone else thought.

Not Rebecca, though. Rebecca hadn't cared. She'd done her thing. She'd said to hell with them all.

He liked her. Brendan liked Rebecca. He would find her in this mess. He would find her killer.

He would bring her spirit peace.

Sitting half on the couch, his leg stuck out at an awkward angle, Brendan passed out.

## CHAPTER THIRTY-THREE / FRIDAY, 2:02 PM

Someone was pounding on the door. Brendan woke to find himself in between the couch and the coffee table, lying on the floor. As though in a crypt.

He tried to get up, but it was tough going. His head felt like it was encased in stone. His whole body ached. His guts had been swabbed out by wire wool. He was afraid he might have wet himself.

He heard the door open. He was sure he had locked it. He called out.

"Hello?" His voice was a croak.

"Shut up," he heard. "I'm gonna do the talking, I'll tell you that right now."

There was no mistaking the voice. Brendan managed to raise himself up enough to look over the coffee table as the man walked through the doorway into the living room.

Seamus Argon had auburn hair with swaths of gray around the ears. His beard was curly and mostly gray. His eyes were hard and alive. He scanned the room, and then his gaze fell on Brendan.

"Jesus," he said. "This is worse than I thought."

* * *

"You haven't been going to meetings."

"I've been on a case," Brendan said.

"I don't care if it's your own murder case and you're the victim, you got to do the meetings."

"I've never . . . I don't know how to handle this case. It's a mess."

"Shut up," said Argon softly but firmly. "Like I said, I'll do the talking."

He had one bag with him. It was a grey and maroon gym bag that looked like it had been around since the seventies, with a faded "Nike" emblem on one side. He set this down beside him.

"What good are you to anyone like this?"

"Why are you here?"

Brendan was helping himself onto the couch. He grimaced with the effort; his body was sore and his hip had stiffened up something wicked. He looked around for the vodka.

"You know why I'm here."

"I mean, who called you?"

"Your Sheriff called me."

Brendan nodded. He found the vodka at the far end of the coffee table and stretched for it. There were a few ounces left in the bottle. Nearby was an overturned glass. Brendan righted it. It was smoky with smeared fingerprints and lip-prints. He unscrewed the cap on the vodka bottle and poured.

Seamus Argon watched the ritual wordlessly.

Brendan drank the liquor and sat back. His eyes met Argon's with a defiant look in them.

"So?"

"For the third and final time, Healy, shut your mouth. Sit there, and don't say a fucking word. Nod if you understand me."

Brendan nodded. His head was splitting. He poured the rest of the vodka into the glass and drank it. He would need to go into the kitchen and get more.

Argon found a chair in the dining nook and brought it over. He set it in front of the couch and coffee table and sat down. Argon was lithe for a man in his sixties. He was heavy, but it was solid weight. He leaned forward and rested his elbows on his knees.

Brendan chanced saying one more thing. He looked at the empty vodka bottle.

"I'll quit."

" 'I'll quit,' said the drunk." Argon looked less than amused. Now he sat back and lifted one leg across the other.

"This is how we met. You, a wreck. Hammered out of your gourd. For weeks. Not doing anybody any good, dishonoring the memory of your wife and child. Car in the garage, engine running . . ."

Brendan shot Argon a look as sharp as knives. Argon dismissed it.

"Oh, that pisses you off? That's all you got, Healy, is your anger. Your guilt. So what, get pissed off. Is that what happened with Kevin Heilshorn? Did he piss you off?"

"No," said Brendan firmly.

The men glared at each other. Then Argon softened a little. "You know, someone once told me a story. About human habits. Do you remember? It was interesting – I had never really thought about it. But I was told that humans, because we've only been out of the jungle just so long – still have a lot of old tapes playing, like they say in the program. And while we may have started weaving baskets 30,000 years ago in our hunter-gatherer shit, civilization as we know it has only been the past five grand. So we're still mostly these little nomadic groups, with these instincts to hunt, to store up goods. Look at what we've done with that. Americans have so much stored up that we have to rent space to keep the shit we got. We also carry with us this negativistic thinking. A necessary survival mechanism from when we were running from the tigers and bears. Keeping a lookout for the next potential threat.

Now we've killed most those lions and bears and put the rest in zoos. But we still have that wariness. That's what you told me the night I became your sponsor, and we stood outside the church on Broad Street. Smoking cigarettes. You remember?"

Brendan stared back impassively.

"Negative thinking was one of the oldest human habits, that's what you said. And I believed you."

Argon fell silent. Outside the light was already fading. The cold snap over the past few days was gone and warm weather was returning; things were expected to return to the eighties, even the nineties, by the weekend.

"So, I had a long talk with Taber. He likes you. Likes you a lot. Acts like he hit the Irish Sweepstakes with you, in fact. Delaney is a good investigator, but that's all he's ever been. Good. Adequate. And he's a little shady. Taber's never been able to catch him red-handed, but he suspects Ambrose may have pocketed a seizure or two, in his time. He's one of these guys who is cliquey, you know. Dyed-in-the-wool Central New Yorker; traces his lineage back to the Dutch settlers, that kind of shit. But Taber likes you. Thinks you're sharp. He hated what happened but he handled it the best he could, with the shooting, with this girl's father poking his narrow, well-heeled ass into things."

"He's covering."

Seamus raised his eyebrows. "Is he? Heilshorn, you mean?"

Brendan nodded.

"For who? Himself? His daughter? Or these politicos in Albany who like XList escorts?"

Brendan sat up straight.

"What did you just say?"

Argon narrowed his eyes. "I know about them. Taber knows about it, too. But they're not what you're tracking. You're tracking Rebecca's killer. And you have to stay focused on that."

Brendan nodded absently. He wiped his mouth with the back of one hand. He temporarily forgot about getting more to drink.

"But the name – XList. I know that name."

"Yes, I'm sure you do. But, like I said, that's not what you're tracking."

"Then what am I tracking? I don't understand."

Argon leaned forward again.

"You need to get better. You need to physically and mentally restore yourself. Then you can restore your spirit. Do you understand? First the spirit gets sick. Then the body. Then the mind."

"What do you know, Argon? What aren't you telling me?"

"Nothing."

"Goddammit, you just said the name of a company that has Rebecca Heilshorn in a pornographic video, and that same company is the escort service. That's something."

"XList is an underground thing. I've heard it also just called 'the Company.' There are rumors about politicians – all types – with a taste for porn stars, models, what have you. It's come up here or there, but that's it. It's an expression. That's all you need to know. And I'm not a detective. I'm a beat cop, Healy. That's all God ever meant for me. I know where I stand. But, I found you, didn't I? I was put in your path. I've picked you up and dusted you off before, now here I am again. There won't be a third time. And I've been in the game long enough, I've seen enough to know where to look in a situation like this. The victim, Rebecca, she has a daughter. Right?"

"Yes."

"I want you to think about something, because it was a long drive over here, and I had a lot of time to ponder, myself. I wonder about something. I wonder about these women who get into this kind of business, what happens when they get pregnant. I wonder if they decide, for whatever reason, that they don't want to have an abortion.

But, let's say they have a contract. The kind of contract that, well, you can't exactly hire a lawyer to get you out of."

Brendan's addled mind started to focus. He recalled the idea he'd had that Rebecca had been protecting something. The possible reason why she hadn't identified the man who came to her door the morning she called 911.

Things started to line up, then.

The diaper sprayer she'd mentioned to Jason Pert, the kid from Kettering's hardware store.

The fact that no paternity record was on file for Eddie Stemp as Leah's father.

The thought recurred that Leah's father might have really been some judge or congressman in Albany.

And what about Kevin Heilshorn?

Some new idea, exciting, horrifying, seemed to bite at the back of Brendan's sodden mind.

"Jesus," he breathed.

"Getting something?"

"What if . . .?" Brendan began. He shook his head for a moment. Was it too reaching? Too absurd?

"Tell me."

"What if her brother, Kevin, what if he had been trying to protect someone, too. And what if he was so protective of that something that he was willing to kill the people who might expose the secret?"

Argon cocked his head, waiting for more.

"A baby," said Brendan. "A child. Maybe more than one child. Like what you're talking about. Illegitimate children born of these relationships. Held as collateral, blackmail, until certain . . . obligations are fulfilled. Certain contracts honored."

Brendan shook his head. "It's crazy. Is it possible?"

Argon did not share the skepticism. "Remember the woman who called us, oh, I don't know, maybe twenty times that one month? That DD we kept coming back to?"

Healy looked up at his old partner. He did remember. A woman in her mid-forties had called repeatedly about her husband, who she claimed was beating himself up. She had been a Wall Street broker, one of few women in a man's world, and he had been the Dean of Students at a preppy private school. Not the type of people who were stereotypically calling the cops about domestic violence, missing teeth, and wearing dirty white t-shirts.

It turned out that the couple had lost a child. Their two-year-old had gotten away from them at a theme park some years before and had never turned up again.

"Situations involving children, involving blood, they can be a whole different ball game." Argon gave Brendan a grave look.

Brendan barely nodded. He was recalling pulling up at the door of the nice home in Hawthorne where the couple lived. She had quit her job, and he had been fired from his, following the disappearance of their child.

"She had made him promise," Argon said quietly. "She made him promise to find their child, and that until he did, there would never be peace in their home. That hell would stay with them. The husband had hired every notable private investigator, and worked personally with the FBI every day since the child had disappeared. You know the saying: to a worm in the horseradish, the world is horseradish. And in the meantime, he had been smashing himself with a hammer in various places. He said it kept him vigilant."

"That's right," said Brendan, now remembering it all.

The first few times they'd gone to the house, they'd been understandably cynical about the situation. The man had been careful to hide his injuries. Finally, Argon had noticed that two of his fingers were smashed and called for him to be hospitalized, since he was clearly a danger to himself. In the hospital, he tried to bite his own tongue off. He blamed himself for their missing child.

"And you saw it," said Argon. "You saw that blame, that guilt, and what it did to him. And I remember thinking that there was hope for you, that you would see your way to forgive yourself for your own wife and child. For not getting in the car with them that night. For doing what you thought you should do in that situation. You wanted to protect them, Brendan. That's what you were doing."

Brendan felt the hot sting of tears in his eyes. He had been protecting them, yes. From himself. And in doing so, he had gotten them killed.

As if reading his thoughts, Argon said, "You did not get them killed. The driver of that truck did. He had been up for three days straight. The Saw Mill is a fast highway, fast as I-95. Accidents all the time. You can feel the movement of the earth there, you know that. And that night, the earth swallowed them up. It spared you, Brendan, because you were meant to continue on. You were meant to find this girl's killer."

The tears were running down his face now. Mucus dripped from his nose.

"And if by finding her killer I compromise the protection of the innocent? What then? These people were willing to die to keep this child – or these children – safe. What am I doing, coming into the middle of it?"

"But they're not safe. Wherever they are, whoever has got them, they're not safe."

And a silence fell over the men, and the room, as the afternoon shadows stretched longer.

Brendan knew his recovery now would be painful. He would suffer every terrible notion his mind could render. His thoughts would be nightmares. His body would be sick and crave the alcohol it needed to keep going. He would fight to keep drinking, and he would fight to stay sober. His mind would be a battleground for the coming days.

He looked across the room at Argon, who gave him a cool, steely gaze.

Argon would stand between Brendan and oblivion. "All that shit that happened – you called it your reckoning. But this is your reckoning, now. It never ends."

Brendan got to his feet. Argon stood, too, and helped the limping detective into the kitchen. The two men then went about pouring the poison down the drain.

## CHAPTER THIRTY-FOUR / MONDAY, 7:18 AM

He had woken up and dressed very early that morning, but it wasn't early enough to catch Argon, who was gone.

Brendan stood in the living room, holding his fresh mug of coffee and looking at the couch where Argon had slept for three nights. It was now empty. The old cop had even folded up the blanket he'd drawn across his large frame each night. He had placed a small object on top of the blanket, a gift to Brendan.

Brendan sipped his coffee. He felt good. He knew from previous experience that post-acute withdrawal from alcohol had effects which could last for a long time. Aversion to people and crowds, claustrophobia, depression; it all came with the territory. But the last time he had gotten clean had followed a twenty-year drinking period, and those final days had been round the clock abuse. This time, he'd only been inside the bottle for a week. It had taken everything he had to crawl back out again.

He leaned on his crutches. He had a doctor's appointment later in the day, but first he was going to go in and make the IACP meeting, as Argon had instructed.

Brendan had called them just a few minutes ago to set it up. They had been happy to hear from him, and he would meet them at eight that morning.

He had dressed in his navy tie and a powder blue shirt. He slid his dark gray blazer over this. As he looked at himself in the mirror he thought his hair had grown too long, but for now he brushed it back. He trimmed his finger nails and, of course, shaved, leaving a mustache and bit of beard framing his mouth. He had been shaving every day since he'd started the job, but change was good.

He would miss Argon. He could imagine no one else seeing him through the darkness of the last 72 hours. Getting off a serious binge was hell. But it was over now, the last fumes dissipated from his pores and evacuated from his intestines. His mind felt clear.

He got into the Camry ten minutes later. He opened the back door first and fed in the crutches, turning them at an angle so they would fit. Then he carefully got himself into the driver's seat.

He adjusted the rear view mirror and took Argon's gift, a small crucifix, and fastened it around his neck. Seamus Argon was not an overtly religious-type. He had found his faith years before – or rediscovered it, to use the man's own term – and claimed that it had seen him through. He didn't expect others to follow in the same path, but like most AA members, he believed that acknowledgment of a higher power was a key element in the healing process. It had been something Brendan had struggled with in the past, but he found the crucifix hung round his neck more easily that morning.

He paused before backing out of the driveway. He wondered at the nature of addiction, and habit. He was a man of science. Investigation and evidence were the hallmarks of his process of understanding the world, not faith and superstition. Yet as he grew older, where one ended and the other began, became less distinct. He thought of Eddie Stemp talking about possession. About demons and spiritual access points. When a man like Seamus Argon came into your home and helped you rid yourself of a horrible toxic affliction, it was, on the one hand, a simple biochemical scenario. The neurotransmitters in the brain became hijacked with the extra dopamine that the alcohol amped up. The cellular receptors in the body became literally addicted to the peptides spilled by the affected glands of the body. In order to pull out of it, they needed to be denied the substance which had laid siege and be given time to readjust. There were no slippery, scaly demons lurking somewhere within the body, but, on the other hand, through all the research Brendan had done in school and then at the university laboratory in his earlier career as a neuroscientist, the discipline was unable to provide answers to some very basic questions.

It was unimportant whether or not Argon had merely helped Brendan slip the chemical noose and withstand the crippling period of his body's regrouping, or whether the grizzled older cop had performed some sort of exorcism. Argon drew strength from somewhere, and he had offered Brendan the chance to do the same.

Brendan figured he could use all the help he could get.

He cleared his mind of these thoughts, realizing that showing up to a meeting with the IACP thinking about demons and possession was not necessarily the best tack. At the same time though, he felt he had nothing to hide. Let them see what they wanted to see – he had no control over that.

The bits of dread and guilt that were accumulating while he sat in the Camry dwindled away as he at last found this sense of personal freedom.

As he pulled away from his house and headed towards the Department, he was absently aware that he hadn't even smoked a cigarette for three days.

\* \* \*

Agents Roman Scalia and Cindy Barrister greeted Healy warmly. Taber was there for a time, offering a serious countenance, though his eyes glinted with hope. When Taber left, he requested that Healy come to his office after the session was over. The agents set a digital audio recorder down on the table, and the three of them began to talk.

"We were pleased to get your call this morning," Barrister began. She was a pretty woman in her forties, wearing a dark suit. Her blond hair was pulled back in an immaculate bun. "It's our policy for the officer involved in a use-of-force situation to have time to recover, but of course you don't want too much time to pass. Things can become sanitized, or worse, any negative effects the incident may have on the officer can go unchecked."

Brendan smiled and nodded once. "Understood. I felt ready, so I called."

"Excellent," Barrister said. "So. Let's get going. How have you been?"

Brendan glanced at the set of crutches leaning on the table next to him. "All things considered," he said.

The agent looked at the crutches, too. "And how are things with that? Any leads?"

"They're looking into a late-model Ford, either black, dark red, or maybe even purple. Not much to go on, nothing found at the scene." He looked at both agents. "When the truck hit me, it didn't leave any part of itself behind."

The agents looked grim.

Brendan shifted his weight and smiled politely.

They proceeded.

"Mr. Healy," said Agent Barrister, "the IACP guidelines we work from were established to constructively support officers involved in shootings and other use-of-force incidents. Shootings and other use-of-force incidents can result in heightened physical and emotional reactions from the participants. So I want to ask you again. How have you been these past few days?"

Brendan sighed. Typically he was very uncomfortable with seeking approval. They wanted honesty and acted like they were on his side, but the two agents regarding him had the power to close the door on his law enforcement career. At the same time, he realized he had nothing to lose.

"I was given morphine following the incident with the pick-up truck. My injuries were extensive. The morphine – and the incident, too, I have to admit – triggered an emotional response I hadn't really seen coming."

"And what was that?"

"I started drinking again. I had eight years of sobriety."

"And are you drinking now?"

"Not for the past 72 hours."

"Are you a part of any support group?"

"I'll be attending AA meetings this week. A friend of mine found me a local chapter. It's in the basement of the Resurrection Life Church."

"That's good."

Barrister had been doing all of the talking, and her face indicated genuine sympathy. She seemed to shake something off now, and reverted back to her more monotonous recital of IACP protocol.

"Mr. Healy, given the extreme nature of both of your recent incidents, we feel that an intervention is necessary."

"Intervention?" Healy thought of Argon. Hadn't the old Scottish cop already provided what the health people called an intervention?

"Post-shooting interventions are conducted only by licensed mental health care professionals trained and experienced in working with law enforcement personnel. You may not feel it is necessary to participate – most cops don't – but we think you will get a lot out of it. That's why we're requiring you to attend."

Brendan shifted his weight again. They didn't leave him much choice. A trill of electricity zipped up his spine when he thought about who the so-called mental health professional might be. Wouldn't it be an ironic twist of fate if Miss Olivia Jane were to sit down across from him? The chances were slim, and even if it were to come to pass, she'd be sure to pull out of it and reassign Brendan to someone else.

This thought left a bitter taste in Brendan's mouth and he realized the agents were looking at him curiously. He smoothed the scowl in his forehead with his fingertips. "Okay," he said.

"Good. We can reconvene with this investigation after you've had a chance to have at least two appointments with your care provider."

"Reconvene?"

They both looked at him blankly, some of their humanity displaced for the moment, as they each undoubtedly wondered if Healy was going to be a problem. Agent Roman Scalia spoke up.

"Yes, Mr. Healy. After a life-threatening incident – two, in your case – most officers are concerned if their physiological and emotional reactions are 'normal.'" He hooked his fingers in the air to hang the quotations around the word. "A post-shooting intervention is not a head-shrinking, despite what you may think. It's intended to be educative, to reassure you and reduce any anxiety."

"I'm not anxious."

"Mr. Healy, you just told us that . . ."

"I know what I just told you. I had a relapse. I've taken care of it. I called you to set this meeting so that I can move on with my life. Please. I'm in the middle of a murder investigation."

"We understand," said Barrister. "But you understand that we deal with these types of situations on a regular basis, working all over the state of New York. Helping officers with coping mechanisms, maintaining their sleep functions, accessing social support, and abstaining from alcohol abuse – these are our priorities."

Healy was silent. They weren't going to budge. And then Scalia added, "Given your past, we're especially concerned here."

Brendan felt a twinge of anger. "My past?"

Barrister shot Scalia a look, seeming to warn him about proceeding, but Scalia ignored her and cocked his head. "You don't think that's material?"

Healy stared back at Scalia.

"If you feel you're ready to move on with your life, as you say, maybe you'd be willing to furnish us, in your own words, with the information about what happened to your wife and your daughter."

Healy glanced at Barrister, who suddenly looked sorry to be in the room. Then he leveled his gaze at Scalia.

Brendan took a breath.

"I started drinking in my teens, like a lot of people. Only my drinking carried through into my twenties. It interfered with school, but I still graduated with my masters in neuroscience. I met my wife while in school. Shortly after graduating, we had our daughter. I went to work for the university in the research department, working towards my PhD. On the surface, we had a very successful life. But I was drinking every day. It was a real problem in our marriage. Of course, I didn't know that at first. I found every other thing to blame. But, my wife knew it. And she loved me, and so endured it for as long as she could.

"One night, we went out to eat. We went to our favorite place, called Tramanto. It's a lot like the Savoy, in Rome. You know that place? It's a family place. But they have huge drinks. Not the kind I usually go for, but then again, I went for every kind. So I had two piña coladas and two margaritas. The waitress gave me a look when I finished up with a stout beer. Not even much for me, five big drinks, I was fine. But my wife . . . she was trying so hard to get out from under it. She said it was like living with a time bomb. She tried to put her foot down. She snuck the car keys from my jacket when I went to the bathroom for my third or fourth trip. She got our little girl ready to go and said she was driving. I figured, *let her.* I thought, *even on my worst drunks I'm a better driver.* Those were my last thoughts about my life partner of seven years, wife for four of those years. But, I told her I wasn't going to go. If she wanted to drive, then fine. I told her I would get a cab home later."

Brendan looked at the two agents and realized that he had their complete attention. He felt the prickly heat of tears, but that was all. His heart beat a steady rhythm.

"I stayed at the bar and drank more. I flirted with the waitress who had given me the look – or, well, I tried to flirt with her. Meanwhile my wife and daughter got into our car. Less than a mile from the restaurant on the Saw Mill parkway they were slammed into by a truck. They both died in transit to the hospital. While I was sitting there watching the bar TV, drinking, my wife and baby girl died."

## CHAPTER THIRTY-FIVE / MONDAY, 9:54 AM

Taber let Brendan into his office. He pulled out a chair and offered to help Brendan sit.

"I got it," said Brendan. He put on a smile.

"You're not looking too bad," Taber said. He took his seat on the other side of his desk.

"Thanks, I think. And thank you for calling Argon."

The Sheriff looked embarrassed and bypassed the situation. "Considering what you've been through, I'm surprised you're even up and walking about. Which makes it very hard, what I'm about to ask you."

Brendan raised his eyebrows. *What fresh hell is this?*

"Alexander Heilshorn wants to meet with you, that's one."

"He does?"

"Have you been watching the news?"

"Not really. I don't have TV."

"Good for you. So far, we're lucky. Nothing has leaked about Rebecca Heilshorn's involvement in . . . erotic entertainment."

"That's good." Brendan paused. "Is it good?"

"It's good. It's . . . well, it is what it is. Sometimes the media can help. They got contacts for us at Cornell before we even knew she was a student there. But other times, well, there can be pressure. Undue pressure that doesn't help anyone, and can scare off people who might otherwise come forward, assured of their anonymity."

"I understand."

The Sheriff paused and considered what he was going to say next with a grave air. Brendan looked around the office. There were two large sets of bookshelves behind Taber. There were file cabinets in the corner with a coffee maker on top. Two windows overlooked the street below. The room smelled of coffee and aftershave.

"This is pretty wild for your first case here," Taber said. Brendan felt like the Sheriff was stalling.

"It is."

"Normally, I would never ask this of you, to meet with Heilshorn. We don't cow to civilians, even when they are related to the deceased. It never does any good. But Heilshorn, to my surprise, indicated very strongly that he wanted to speak to you."

"I thought he didn't want anything to do with me, considering."

The Sheriff looked uncomfortable. "That was Delaney's call."

"Delaney made it up?"

"No, no. He had every reason, every reasonable reason to think that Heilshorn would have a chip on his shoulder about you, to say the least."

Brendan suppressed the urge to comment on Delaney's judgment. "What has Heilshorn said? Relating to the case?"

"Not much. We get the impression he's been estranged from his daughter for some time. They only communicate through the mother. You know how that goes. And the family accountant handles affairs that affect them both, financially."

"Is the accountant anyone interesting?"

Taber lifted his eyebrows and looked at Brendan, then dropped his eyes to the desk, he rubbed at some stain only he could see. "No, not at all. But Heilshorn is. I believe that he's not telling us things. I'm not sure exactly what, but we need to know."

"And you think he'll speak to me."

"He seems to want to."

Both men took a breath and settled back. The air in the room seemed to become cloying, and now the coffee smelled a touch burnt.

"Okay," said Brendan.

"It's not that easy. You've been involved in two major incidents. IACP wants to run full diagnostics on you. I'm sure they've indicated that."

"They've been forthcoming, yeah."

Taber looked serious, and held his gaze. "I made the right call, putting you on a short leave."

"I know you did, sir."

"And it seemed appropriate, given my instincts about Heilshorn, that you be the one to look into the erotic entertainment."

"Yes, it did." Brendan realized that a moment ago, the Sheriff had indicated that Delaney had made the call about Heilshorn wanting Brendan booted from the case, but now the Sheriff was taking responsibility for that prejudgment. He knew Taber wasn't the type to scapegoat, and wondered if the admission about Delaney had been a slip.

"And now I think – I hope – it's the right call to have you fully reinstated on this case. That is, if you want it."

Taber searched Brendan with his hazel eyes.

"I want it," said Brendan.

"Okay. We're going to see this thing through to the end. Together."

"And Delaney?" Brendan couldn't help but ask. He saw something like a twitch under the Sheriff's eye.

"Delaney has turned up bupkiss, frankly. I've worked with Ambrose for over twenty years, and I trust him, but on this one . . . I've got to go with my gut."

"And your gut is telling you to put the rookie, who has shot someone, been shot at, almost run over, is in need of psychological treatment, and is on crutches, back on the case."

Taber looked across the desk at Brendan, gauging him. Brendan reminded himself that levity usually didn't go down well, because of how matter-of-fact Sheriff Taber was. But the Sheriff surprised him.

"We're short-handed," he said, and offered a grim smile.

\* \* \*

Alexander Heilshorn was not what Brendan had expected. For some reason, maybe it was pop culture stereotypes, Brendan had for all this time envisioned a tall man who was tow-headed and hawkish. Heilshorn was short, dark-haired, and if anything, looked a bit like Adolf Hitler, though his mustache was gray and made the full bridge above his lips.

He was spry and quick for his age – Brendan guessed that he was almost seventy. He looked in good shape. He stepped down from the front door of the house he apparently owned, just outside of Rome. He crossed the yard to greet Brendan, who stepped out of the passenger side of a Sheriff's Department vehicle. Deputy Bostrom was at the wheel. He watched Heilshorn approach, looking like the cat that had swallowed the canary. Brendan waggled his eyebrows at the deputy and pulled his crutches out of the back seat.

The Sheriff had commissioned Bostrom to stay with Brendan until otherwise instructed. Brendan hadn't argued, but Bostrom had looked less than pleased to play chaperone. Brendan closed the car door and turned his attention back to Heilshorn.

The man was smartly dressed, with the aesthetic of a rich guy doing a stint in the countryside. His slacks were crisp and flat, and a fresh flannel shirt sprung from an LL Bean catalogue showed beneath a grey wool sweater. He wore pristine hiking boots and stepped onto the driveway with his hand out in salutation.

Brendan took it. The man's grip was dry and warm.

"Please, come inside," said Heilshorn. "Can I help you?"

"No, thanks, I can make it okay," said Brendan. He caught Heilshorn looking in through the windshield at Deputy Bostrom.

"Is he coming in?"

"No, he'll be fine there." Brendan got his crutches hooked into his armpits and started towards the house before stopping a moment. "Is that alright with you?"

"That's fine," said Heilshorn.

Brendan nodded and let Heilshorn lead the way. He realized he could scarcely believe the man's conviviality. Less than two weeks ago Brendan had gunned down this guy's only son. And now here he was acting as if Healy was the gentleman suitor for his daughter instead of the lead investigator on her murder.

It couldn't be real. He wondered what awaited him inside the house. In a moment of weakness, he felt glad that Bostrom was with him.

\* \* \*

Inside, the genial host continued with the pleasantries, offering Brendan tea. Brendan accepted. It reminded him of Olivia, and he found himself wondering where she was, how she was doing. He realized he hadn't left things very well with her, and felt a sting of guilt.

With the tea made, Heilshorn inquired as to where Brendan would be most comfortable.

"Hardback chairs actually seem to be better," he said.

Heilshorn nodded as if he understood perfectly, and showed Brendan to a small table in the kitchen. He put down the tea, and the two men arranged themselves across from one another.

Brendan suddenly felt aware that life was just a series of meetings. A string of encounters with another person. It was barely eleven o'clock and he'd already had three appointments; three times he'd sat across from someone to share information.

He may have fancied himself a tracker, but mainly he accumulated data. With that same sudden assurance, he felt that this would be one of the last meetings of its kind on this case. There might be only one left.

Heilshorn looked wistful. "Ma'am is with our granddaughter today."

"Greta, your wife."

"That's right. They're going apple-picking in Westchester. That's where you're from, isn't it? New Rochelle? Hawthorne? I'm sure you know I have a private investigator in my employ."

Brendan was taken aback. The man had gone from conversational right down to business in almost the span of one breath. He also realized he'd forgotten about Heilshorn's P.I. He felt heat start to creep up his neck as he thought about someone peeking in his window at any point over the past few days. They would have gotten an eyeful to report back to Heilshorn.

"That's right; I lived in Hawthorne before I moved here. Mr. Heilshorn, let me say something right away. I want you to know how deeply sorry I am for your loss. Both of your losses."

Heilshorn's lower lip quivered, and he looked away for a moment. Another surprise. Brendan had imagined him as unemotional, made of stone. Unless it was an act, after all. But Brendan didn't think so.

"A parent should never have to outlive his children. I know that sounds like a platitude. People just have no idea.

I wouldn't wish it on my worst enemy. To know it, is to live with the worst suffering I think imaginable."

He turned to face Brendan again.

"But you know it, Detective."

Heilshorn was referring to Brendan's daughter. Unexpectedly, Brendan felt emotion rise up in him, too. "I know it," he said in a quiet voice.

He wondered, as they sat there in their shared grief, where the conversation could possibly go from here.

"I understand you've had a very rough time on this case," Heilshorn said. "My purpose here has not been to make things any harder on you, or on your department. I know you work with good men who have pursued my daughter's killer very diligently, and I thank you for your service."

Again, Heilshorn's cordiality was unexpected. Brendan offered a wan smile. "That's very kind of you."

"I'm sure you still have a lot of questions."

"I do."

"One of the things you're likely to have hanging is about my granddaughter Leah. Rebecca's little girl."

"I've wondered about her, yes. You say she's apple-picking today. That sounds nice."

Heilshorn gave a brief nod. "You have been unable to uncover her birth records."

"That's correct."

"That's because I've hidden them. Sealed them away."

Brendan opened his mouth, perhaps to ask why, but thought better of it and resumed listening.

"This whole situation . . . I have to take my responsibility. That's what a man needs to do, yes? Be accountable for the things in his life, just like you have done. I never wanted to push Rebecca away. She was just so much like me, we often butted heads. You understand. I couldn't have imagined what she would turn to, what she would have gotten herself into."

So, Brendan thought, Heilshorn already knew. Unless he was referring to something else, but Brendan doubted it.

"One day she came to the city to collect some of her belongings – one of the last times I saw her before things became . . . more complicated. Normally I wouldn't have seen her until she came up to our floor. But this day I was on my way back from the hospital – I live only four blocks away – and I saw her getting out of a car, a blue sedan. There was a bumper sticker on the back that said 'Four Doors for More Whores.' I couldn't believe Rebecca would be with someone like that, but I chalked it up to the times. You lose touch as you get older. We're not stodgy in our family. I guess we're liberal."

He offered a short, humorless laugh. Then he diverted from the subject.

"I knew your father, Doctor Gerard Healy."

Brendan was shocked. "You knew my father?"

"Yes. I recognized your name right away after . . . Rebecca's death. I looked into you right away. Your father was a cardiac surgeon. Very good, too. And you – you went to school for neurobiology at New York University. You wound up in the Vesalius Program. But you never obtained your doctorate."

Brendan was unsure which part to respond to. "I did research at Langone, and I also taught two classes."

"It was a struggle for you."

"I was trying to follow in my father's footsteps, in a way."

"But then you found a new father of a sort. A policeman named Seamus Argon."

The man knew everything. "Yes."

Heilshorn nodded. "I only knew your father by name. We never met. It's a small world, but perhaps not that small." He drew himself closer to the table, and lowered his voice. "I've lived a very compromised life."

"How so?"

"Do you know what I do as a doctor?"

"No." Brendan recalled Donald Kettering saying that Alexander Heilshorn had invested in some medical company, a patent or other, and that's where the family's big money came from. He hadn't considered Heilshorn as a practitioner. Then he suddenly remembered the story about Heilshorn injecting a baby with oxygen to keep it alive.

"I'm an OB GYN," said Heilshorn.

"Really."

"Yes, really. It's a surprise to me, too, considering that I don't favor abortion. And that I spend a good deal of money angel-investing in lifesaving, cutting-edge medical technology."

Brendan's mind looped back to his meeting with Eddie Stemp, who had talked about the subject. He felt a chill. And he thought again of the oxygen-deprived baby. Heilshorn had perhaps used the very technology he invested in. Quite an endorsement.

"But, life is not black and white. I think at one time or another, every one of us wishes it was. But, it isn't. You were involved in an incident that saw the death of my son. But I can't blame you. Things aren't that black and white. You see? My son died because of what he believed in."

Brendan's voice was small. They were dancing around the heart of what he'd been pursuing for two weeks. "And what did he believe in?"

"He believed in the preciousness of all life." Heilshorn then sat back a little. He took a sip of his tea. "We're not crusaders. We're not pro-lifers. I don't know. Maybe we should be. Maybe this is my penance. As a doctor, we're trained to see tissue as tissue. The organization of life is something which happens of its own accord, part of a mystery we cannot fathom. Systems characterized by a two-way exchange of information. Yet, we inject it with meaning. We try to think in terms of black and white, right and wrong. But when you've lost your children, that meaning becomes more apparent than ever, and doesn't feel like some arbitrary construct. You feel it in your bones. You ache for your children. I know it's a physiological response, it's the chemical version of what we call love – but what of that? I've spent my life studying the names, the charts, the functions of the body. Everything neatly labeled and categorized. But I don't know what any of it is. I'm seventy-two, and I'm no closer to understanding the world than I was at twenty-two."

He took another sip of his tea. Then he nodded towards Brendan's cup. "Is it hot enough? Would you like more?"

Brendan didn't want more, but he smiled and nodded just the same. Heilshorn seemed to need to get up, to busy himself. He watched the diminutive man rise and retrieve the teapot. Heilshorn filled both cups again with steaming liquid and then returned the pot to the stove. He remained there for a moment.

"Rebecca got involved in something that threatens life. When she was in that . . . business, she became pregnant. I knew, because I had my private investigator following her."

Now he came and sat back at the table once more.

"I was afraid of what her intentions were. So, I went and got her. She didn't like it, but I did. Only, it wasn't just her I had to contend with."

Brendan interjected, "At this time, she was in Albany?"

Heilshorn's eyes flickered. "Yes. Affiliated with some very unsavory people. People that didn't like it when I decided to take my daughter home. People that didn't want her to take her baby to term."

"Why?"

"Why? Because once a woman has a baby, she's not going to be an escort to a cabinet-level officer, or a senator, that's why. Once in circulation, as the bastards call it, an escort is a huge commodity. Some of the clients like variation. Others prefer the same girl. It's horrible to know these kinds of things. There's no purpose to any of it . . ."

He was trailing off. For the first time since he had invited Brendan into the house, Heilshorn seemed to be losing his composure.

"And they are apt to use the child as leverage to keep the escort in service," Brendan said. It was more than a guess. He felt sure. And Argon had already helped lead him to the same idea.

Heilshorn fixed Brendan with a look. His eyes conveyed appreciation that Healy already understood, but also evoked the gravity of the issue. "Yes. They have ways of handling the situation that are absolutely nightmarish. To either force a woman to abort her child, or use the child against her. It's the work of the devil."

"Why not go to the police? Why not seek help? Expose the situation?"

"By the time Rebecca knew what she was in for, it was too late. These operations have trap doors like you wouldn't believe. They are escape artists. They have a dozen fake fronts. They are portable. They cover city upon city. This is the oldest profession known to man – they've figured it out by now. She could have gone to the authorities, but they would have found nothing, no one, smoke."

The last word sent a chill through Brendan. *I was born under the black smoke of September.*

"But she would have gotten out."

"And done what? Gone into police protection for the rest of her life? Just because they're elusive doesn't mean they leave anyone out there in the open to continue the whistleblowing. These clients – these Eliot Spitzers, these Philip Giordanos – they are presidential hopefuls, some of them. Judges, congressmen, cabinet members, the U.N., for God's sake. It's just people. Underneath it all, it's just people. It's these basic drives. Avoid pain. Pursue pleasure."

Heilshorn seemed flustered again. Brendan relented. "I understand. So, you were able to get her, to get her away from them."

"Yes. Seven months pregnant."

"And she stayed with you until she had the baby."

"Yes. And she was delivered the only way to keep Leah safe. I performed the delivery myself."

Brendan was shocked. He inadvertently leaned back from the table. This was why he was never able to find any record of paternity, any birth records for the child. Her own grandfather had brought her into this world. Brendan could scarcely imagine what a position that had put both father and daughter in. No wonder they had been estranged since.

"My God," Brendan said. It slipped out.

Heilshorn was unoffended. "It kept that little girl safe. And she remains safe. Her name is unknown to them, her whereabouts a secret. They will never find her. And with Rebecca departed, I suppose they will never need to."

The pieces were coming together at last. Some of them. "And Kevin knew this. He knew that Leah was safe as long as she remained anonymous. That anything we might uncover could lead to her exposure. But . . . like you just said, with Rebecca departed, there would be no need to. Why would Kevin come after me? Why risk his life – or give his life – to protect Leah if she was no longer threatened?"

But before Heilshorn could respond, Brendan felt he already knew the answer.

He breathed: "Because he believed there are others."

Heilshorn just looked at him. The man had cobalt blue eyes, and they were now hard like stone.

"Yes," he said after a moment. "There are others."

Brendan felt hot and cold waves passing through him. His hip flared with pain and he realized he had been sitting too long. He needed to get to the doctor and get some of the non-addictive pain medication he could handle. But his mind was spinning with more questions.

"But why would she relocate so close to Albany? If she wanted to stay hidden . . . I don't understand. You have money. With all due respect, you are practically the Trumps, from what I've seen. Why not send her away to her own personal island somewhere?"

And once more, the answer to his own question tugged at the back of his mind. But this time, he let Heilshorn articulate it.

"Because she was helping the others. She was helping the women get out, and she was helping to keep their children out of harm."

Brendan shook his head with exasperation. It made sense in some cloak-and-dagger way, but he remained dubious. There were law enforcement agencies for this type of thing. The FBI. Even the Department of Justice. They could operate free of jurisdictional restraints and the limitations of pay grades and elections. There were tasks forces, sting operations, and Grand Juries to handle crimes of this magnitude and sensitivity. One woman – one family acting as vigilantes for prostitutes seeking escape? And with their children in danger of being used as leverage, it just didn't seem realistic. It was like the Underground Railroad, but for escorts. Approaching absurd.

But she had installed a diaper sprayer in her remodeled bathroom. That detail was in line with what the old man was saying.

Brendan looked at Heilshorn, but there was no guile in the man's face, no duplicity to speak of. What Heilshorn was saying was true – Brendan was sure, at least, that the older man believed it, through and through. Brendan just wasn't sure *how* it was true yet.

"So, what do you want me to do?"

"Nothing." The word came fast and sudden, as if Heilshorn had been preparing for the question all along. "I want you to leave it alone. Let us continue our work."

Brendan pushed back from the table a little. His hip was a constant siren now. "You know I can't do that. I understand you feel a sense of obligation . . ."

"You don't understand. You may never understand."

"What I understand is that this is the reason the law exists. I need names, I need dates; I need people. This needs to be exposed, taken down, and dismantled. That is not a civilian's duty."

Heilshorn was shaking his head. "You're wrong, detective, I'm sorry. I thought you, of all people, would understand my sense of personal responsibility. It's more than just a calling. This is the way it has to be done. You'll never get any names, dates, or people. You'll only chase your tail, and in the process, you'll get innocent women and children killed."

Brendan stood, wincing with the effort. Heilshorn stood too, instantly concerned. "Are you okay? Can I help you?"

"I'm okay. I just stiffened up. I can't sit too long."

The men were now facing each other, standing by the table. They were almost eye-to-eye, with Brendan just a few inches taller. The clock on the wall was closing in on noon.

"You're a good man," said Heilshorn. "I don't want to have to threaten you, Detective."

"Threaten me? With what? More bad tea?" He regretted the silly little remark as soon as he'd made it, but he could feel Heilshorn starting to put the bite on him, and he didn't like it.

"With peeing in jugs beside your bed. Throwing up on yourself. Masturbating to the porn on your computer."

Brendan's blood ran icy cold. He knew he had likely been spied on, but to hear it put this way was still totally disconcerting. He steeled himself and said what he knew was in his heart, what he knew was true.

"Go ahead. I've got nothing to hide. Tell anyone, tell everyone. Make pictures of me and send them as

Christmas cards; I don't care. I've listened to you, now I want you to listen to me. I'm too aware of what doing nothing can lead to. Of what can happen when you look the other way.

"I am going to do my job. I am going to find the man who killed your daughter, which led to the death of your son and nearly cost me my own life, and I am going to bring him to justice. And I can either do it with your help, or without it. I'll leave you the afternoon to decide. Please excuse me; I have to go to the doctor. My hip feels like it's being sliced apart by saw blades."

Brendan gathered his crutches and hobbled away, Heilshorn watching after him, but not following him to the door.

Outside, Bostrom waited dutifully in the driveway.

## CHAPTER THIRTY-SIX / MONDAY, 1:24 PM

"We need to go back to the beginning," said Brendan. "Keep it simple."

Bostrom drove as Brendan spoke. They had left the doctor's office a few minutes before and were en route to pick up the prescription painkillers at a nearby pharmacy. Brendan could feel Bostrom's resentment – the deputy was like a nanny, driving the detective around and tending to him like this. So Brendan started sharing his thoughts.

"The killer entered Rebecca Heilshorn's home with no sign of forced entry, right? You were the first officer on scene. What did you see?"

Bostrom sat up a little straighter as he drove. "Door was closed, but not locked."

"And the back door to the house was locked."

"Correct."

"The victim was stabbed with a knife. We were unable to ascertain whether or not he pulled the knife from Rebecca's kitchen, or had come with it himself."

"Right."

"Boot print on the door to the bedroom, which he kicked open, showed someone in a size eleven work boot.

No particular brand of boot we could discern, but forensics determined his height about six foot, maybe a hundred and ninety pounds. Sounds like the same guy who tried to run me over with his truck."

Bostrom glanced over.

Brendan continued, "And he was in the kitchen for a little while before going upstairs. I went back to the house to try and figure out why, and I was compelled to look at the collection of photos again. You realize none of this can be discussed with anyone. Not even your wife."

"I'm not married."

"No? Ever been?"

"Once. Lasted about six months. I was young."

Brendan regarded the deputy. Bostrom had bright blonde hair and a strong jaw and hatchet nose. He was famous for his temper, but Brendan had always thought it a mistake to write off the deputy as a brute, as others in the department seemed to. Brendan sensed intelligence in the man, and the propensity for fierce loyalty. On the other hand, if he didn't like you, he was a prick.

"I found writing on the back of each of the photos. A sort of poem. And at first, I thought that this was what the killer was doing while taking time in the kitchen. But it doesn't make any sense, actually, I was wrong. Forty seconds is not enough time to take the backs off several framed photos and write on each of them. He must've written it at an earlier time."

Bostrom made a turn into a Rite Aid parking lot. "So he must've been in the house before."

"That's what I'm thinking."

"Makes sense," said Bostrom, parking. "Nine times out of ten, the killer is someone the victim knows, or has at least met before."

Brendan considered this silently. He got out, gathered his crutches, and went inside for his prescription.

\* \* \*

"I got something," said Colinas. The State detective sounded excited on the other end of the line.

"Can you meet me at my house?"

"Sure. Be there in fifteen."

Brendan told Bostrom to gun it. The deputy seemed happy to oblige. He lit up the light bar and tramped on the accelerator.

* * *

At Brendan's house, the three men crowded around Colinas's computer.

"I took this from the database. It took a couple of days, but this is who we got. Reginald Forrester, the name of the guy who owns the rental house in Boonville."

Brendan instantly remembered. This was the house where Rebecca Heilshorn had stayed while she was ostensibly closing on the Bloomingdale farm. Brendan had called the property manager who had seemed more huffy than helpful. But she had provided the owner's name, in what may have been an ethical breech, but was certainly a stroke of luck.

They looked at the picture. A man, in his late forties, smiled humorlessly for a headshot. Even just looking at him from the shoulders up, Brendan could tell he was well-built. Athletic. His hair was salt and pepper. He wore a black moustache with dashes of grey in it.

"Who is he?"

Brendan's eyes were scanning the page for information, his heart beating. He couldn't digest it all quickly enough.

"Was a professor of English Lit at Cornell. Also, ah, taught Creative Writing. Resigned in 2003."

"He could have known the victim," Bostrom said.

Brendan almost forgot the deputy was still there. Technically, he shouldn't be seeing any of this. But Brendan let it slide. Bostrom was in it now.

"Oh I'm betting he did," said Brendan.

"I did a pretty extensive background check on this guy. He's got quite a history. Nothing overtly illicit, but his past is full of head scratchers. Apparently he was in New York City attending a conference during the 9/11 attacks. Then he comes back to Cornell and he seems to go off the rails a little bit. He takes to writing some twisted shit and publishing it, and then he's asked to take a leave. A sabbath, or whatever they call it."

"Sabbatical." Brendan was hanging on every word from Colinas.

"Yeah, sabbatical. Supposedly he starts a blog talking about how Osama Bin Laden wanted to bankrupt America, and he figured provoking a war was the best way to do it. How we're all oblivious to, in denial of, or reacting the wrong way – stockpiling munitions and whatnot – to the impending economic collapse. He claimed he was working on a way to reboot the American economy. Blog was called 'Nero Fiddled While Rome Burned.' Talk about a fruitcake."

Brendan's mouth felt dry. Where had he heard that phrase? He thought to check his notes. But first, he wanted to see more on Forrester.

"Let's take a look at the blog," Brendan said.

"Can't." Colinas raised his dark eyebrows. "It's gone. I got this info from a newspaper article talking about Forrester resigning from his professorial duties at Cornell. With 'resigning' in big old scare quotes. Apparently the administration didn't like his anti-American, anti-human diatribe." Colinas looked at Brendan and Bostrom. "Anyway, this is what I got. And you know . . ."

Brendan waited.

"This may be a stretch, but he looks to me like the same guy as in the 'interview' video. Even though the face is censored out, you still get bits of the hair, the body type. You know which one I mean? The one where she comes in and is on the couch answering questions before she . . ."

"You watched the videos," Brendan said.

"Oh yeah." Colinas's voice grew tight. "Never really want to see a porn film again."

"I hear you."

Deputy Bostrom looked at the two men like he had no idea what they were talking about.

"This is incredible." Brendan rubbed a hand over his jaw.

It was turning into a long day.

# CHAPTER THIRTY-SEVEN / MONDAY, 3:30PM

The phone rang. It was Alexander Heilshorn.

"Okay. I'll help you."

"That's good. Because I think I found the man who killed your daughter."

Brendan waited for the reaction. It was not what he expected. "You're thinking of Reginald Forrester."

"That's right. Jesus, you knew?"

"I know who he is, yes. He taught at Cornell for ten years before being persuaded to leave. For his extracurricular activities and for misconduct."

"What are you saying?"

"My P.I. looked into him long ago, the first time Rebecca went missing and I wanted to get her back. Forrester was an alcoholic, and a never-was writer. He published some poetry and prose at various times, with minimal success. After 2001, his writing described a loss of God, and people's unwillingness to face and consider the real cause of their own destruction. He assembled it all into an ambitious manifesto. A horrible mass of darkness and dread reflecting his changed view of the world. It scared his students, the faculty, and administration. He was even put on a modern-day black list. Read *The Professors: The 101 Most Dangerous Academics in America,* by David Horowitz." Heilshorn took a breath. "He performed very well academically, even after he became a drunk. Just like you, Detective Healy, he was high-functioning. Until he wasn't."

"And what happened?"

"He disappeared. My P.I. lost him completely. But then he resurfaced. He became involved with XList."

"The escort service."

"In its current incarnation, yes. XList probably doesn't even exist now, not on paper, not on the web, not anywhere. Not with this very investigation ongoing. Not for the moment, anyway. It is a chimera, Detective – XList, Silk Road, Sheep Marketplace – they can be taken down, but then they spring up somewhere else. My sources have linked Forrester's name with *Titan*, which protects the interests of the black markets."

Brendan had never heard of Titan. "I sent an email to XList, to see about ordering one of their videos."

There was silence on the other end.

"Hello?"

Heilshorn's voice sounded strained. "You *wrote* to them?"

"Yes. I was trying to ferret out some more information about the videos your daughter was in; who the producers were, other actors, that sort of thing."

"And you got a response?"

"I did. Why?"

"Detective . . . I'm sorry."

"For what? Mr. Heilshorn?"

"You're in a lot of danger."

Brendan looked around his house. Colinas and Bostrom had been gone for about an hour. He was going to meet with Colinas later, and Bostrom's shift was ending at four. The Sheriff was likely to assign another detail to watch his back, Watts or Lawless maybe, but until they showed up, Brendan was on his own.

"Why? Why am I in danger? Mr. Heilshorn, you said you would help me with this. So, help me. Tell me where I can find Reginald Forrester. Is he Leah's father?"

"You can't find him."

"What do you mean I can't?"

"He's not . . . He won't let you."

"What? Mr. Heilshorn, he's just an English teacher, not a superhero. I can find him."

"He's a . . . different sort of man."

"I get that. Has relationships with his students. Writes Marxist manifestos. Runs a branch of an escort service. How have you . . . why have you kept this from me? From the police? Alexander? This is just nuts."

"I've already told you," said the older man, sounding weary.

"To protect the innocent, I understand. The other women who are like your daughter was. And their children. But how does finding Reginald Forrester endanger them? You know, I hear this all the time. The woman too afraid to turn in her abusive husband. The people afraid to blow the whistle on the corrupt company they work for. It's paranoia, for the most part, let me tell you. If Reginald gets arrested, what – XList, or Titan, or whoever is behind them – they just turn around and behead a couple dozen women and their illegitimate children? No. I'll tell you what will happen. I'll get Reginald, I'll bring him in. He'll either do life in prison without the possibility of parole, or he'll cooperate with the prosecutors and deliver names of the people who organize the Company, who coerce these girls out of college, or pluck them off the streets, or wherever, and get them turning tricks for senators, and get them into making these videos. We'll get the names of the recruiters, the investors, the johns, all of it. And a task force will take it down."

Brendan realized he was sweating. The pain pills he had swallowed and hour ago were just starting to kick in, and the shooting pain in his hip was beginning to abate. But he was gritting his teeth, and gripping one of his crutches so hard his knuckles were white. He realized he was slipping into that anger-mode which frequently landed him in trouble, and he thought he even tasted blood again. He was surprised Heilshorn was still on the line when the man spoke.

"I'm very sorry you see things this way, Detective. But I understand it. It's what makes you the man you are, this faith in the system."

"It's not just faith in the system."

"You're awfully sure of yourself for a man who just spent nearly a week in his own filth and misery," said Heilshorn with a flash of his own anger.

Brendan sighed. He took a breath and rubbed his face. He realized he couldn't remember the last time he had eaten. When he was hungry he could get rambunctious.

"I'm sorry," he said. "I need your help. Look, tell me how you can help me and be assured that no one will get hurt."

"I can't."

"But you said you would help. That's why you called."

There was a long pause. Brendan was opening his mouth to ask if Heilshorn was still there when the man spoke at last.

"I do want to help. You have to know, despite everything, part of me wants to believe you. That after your critical move, the cavalry will ride in and this will all be over. I want to have faith in you, too, Mr. Healy. And I want justice for my daughter, and for my son. That's why I'm going to tell you this, and I'm going to hope to God that I'm making the right decision."

Brendan waited. He could feel the pulse of the artery in his neck. He saw a flash of Rebecca's face, her dead eyes staring at him in the mirror.

Heilshorn sounded weary, "Rebecca was working out a deal with Forrester. She was going to continue . . . working for him. But there was to be an exchange. This is what she told me."

Again Heilshorn paused. Brendan fought the urge to implore the man to continue. He tried to remain patient.

"You're right; if Reginald goes, it does not necessarily mean a beheading of all the others, as you put it. But, he has a child with him."

"Oh Jesus," Brendan said under his breath.

He thought of the master bedroom being fixed up in the house. He thought of the question Rebecca had asked Marcus Burnell about hooking up a diaper sprayer. He thought of Rebecca returning to the business, and somehow Eddie Stemp, her ex-husband, finding out, and not knowing the details. So Stemp had tried to get her to quit by offering her that passage in *The Screwtape Letters.*

"She's just a child," said Heilshorn in a voice so small Brendan could barely hear. "And Forrester is a monster. Make no mistake. If he gets even the slightest hint that the police are narrowing in, if the cavalry does in fact ride up to save the day, he'll kill that baby, and he'll run."

The silence in the house was like a weight. Brendan had never felt so alone as he sat at his table and looked out into the grey afternoon.

"The fact that you wrote in to the Company – they'll know it was you – has likely alerted them. Forrester tried to take care of you already. But you're still alive. You . . . that must mean something."

Brendan tried to breathe, but it felt like his clothes were constricting him. What did it mean, that he was still alive? Did Heilshorn mean in the sense of fate, or the divine? Or did he mean that Forrester had been toying with him, letting him live for some other unknown reason? He loosened his collar, and at last he spoke.

"I'll go alone. Tell me where I can find Forrester."

# CHAPTER THIRTY-EIGHT / MONDAY, 6:06 PM

Brendan stood in the kitchen of his rented house. The lights were off – he hadn't bothered to turn anything on as the sun dropped and the dark encroached. He stood next to the front door, where the streetlight filtered in, and checked his weapon. He opened the cylinder, examined the chambers for any debris or obstructions, and then loaded in fresh .38 caliber rounds. He snapped the cylinder home and replaced the firearm in the shoulder holster under his arm.

He left the house unlocked and stepped outside. The evening was cool but the low clouds kept things humid. Brendan wore a light windbreaker over a sweater and jeans. He zipped up his coat and walked slowly towards the Camry.

His hip was a dull ache, but he was surefooted on the driveway. He got into the Camry and called Colinas. His eyes flicked to the rear view mirror. He kept expecting a deputy detail to show up, but so far, none had.

"This is nuts," he said to himself.

He realized that his hands were shaking. He took a moment to calm himself, and then he dialed Colinas. As the line rang, he realized that everything he had planned to say had suddenly left his mind. Colinas didn't answer. Instead, his voicemail picked up.

Brendan searched for the words. "Colinas. Healy. I . . . I ah, I got a tip on Forrester. I'm proceeding alone. That's the only way I . . . This is just the way it's gotta be, I guess. My GPS is on. If you don't hear from me in two hours . . ."

He didn't know. Heilshorn's words haunted him. The idea, no matter how far-fetched it may sound, that women and children could be harmed if the police got too close, was chilling. If something happened to him and a whole group of cops were dispatched, what then? What would be the point? Going it alone was only going to work if he succeeded. If he failed, and more police responded, it could be catastrophic. There was nothing to tell Colinas.

This was all based on Heilshorn's statements, though. Brendan searched his intuition and tried to determine whether or not the man could be trusted. He was obviously emotionally impacted by the loss of his children, and people in such situations often behaved irrationally. On the other hand, he had knowledge of things that supported his claims to have been investigating the situation on his own for a significant period of time. Heilshorn seemed to know his enemy in this case, and Brendan's gut told him that the old doctor wasn't trying to be misleading.

While he sat thinking about this, the voicemail clicked over with an automated voice: "If you're satisfied with your message, press one. If you'd like to rerecord your message, press two."

Albany was a two hour drive. Heilshorn had given Brendan a specific location, and Brendan knew that it was one turn off 90 onto Western Ave. The whole thing would take two hours ten minutes, tops. He could call back when he got to Albany, in which case anyone coming for him would be far enough behind that Forrester might not get wind of anything. At the same time, his gut feeling told him he needed some sort of back-up.

Brendan pressed two.

"Colinas. It's Healy. I got a tip on Forrester. But it's got to be kept totally off the radar. I'm headed to Albany. Call me back and I can tell you more."

He hung up.

A second later, a peculiar sense filled him like a cold liquid. Maybe calling Colinas had set it off – he didn't know. But suddenly Brendan saw a complex scenario form in his mind's eye, connecting it all together, each player bound in an intricate web.

Rebecca Heilshorn in trouble. Kim "Eddie" Stemp informs on her to her father, Alexander. Mr. Heilshorn then contacts the local Sheriff. He explains the sensitivity of the situation and asks the Sheriff to look into it with the utmost discretion. Was that plausible? Did Taber already know?

Brendan even imagined Argon being involved. He'd displayed knowledge about XList. So Taber called his old pal Argon for advice. For some reason, the Sheriff felt like the killer was about to strike. Why? How? Some inside information. The P.I. maybe. Or, Brendan suspected, even Delaney. Delaney had been acting, from the beginning, like he had some kind of inside information, behaving in a laissez-faire way unbecoming of a lead investigator. But Taber needed someone with no prior knowledge. A fresh player, untainted. So Argon served up the broken man – Brendan Healy. And then the killer strikes, and Brendan hunts the murderer of Rebecca Heilshorn.

But then, just as it had all formed so quickly in his mind, this conspiracy theory evaporated like dew. The web disappeared.

His heart was thumping in his chest. He keyed the ignition and then backed out of the driveway.

\* \* \*

Interstate 90 was clogged with traffic by the time he neared Albany an hour and a half later. It was after seven, but apparently there were still plenty of commuters on the way home. Then, at seven-fifteen, they all seemed to magically disappear, and he had the road almost to himself. In fifteen more minutes, he was making the exit onto Western Ave. Within another minute and Brendan was turning into the University of Albany campus.

He followed Heilshorn's verbal instructions, and drove around the campus to the other side. There sat the building under construction; Albany's new School of Business.

He had asked Heilshorn why in the hell Forrester would be holed up in a building being built for a state university. Heilshorn told him he would understand when he saw the signs out in front.

Brendan swung the Camry down an access road a few moments later. A giant crane sat next to the incomplete three-story building. Next to the crane was a sign declaring the building contractor. Brendan's breath caught in his throat. The company that had been awarded the thirty-five million dollar contract to erect the school's new building was called "Titan Construction Management, LLC." The emblem beneath the name was a heraldic lion with a long, snaking tongue.

It's like they are boasting about who they are, Brendan thought.

But who would ever link a general contracting business to a porn business? Still, it was audacious. Brendan imagined that the organizers behind the escort service had to have a front to funnel their money and clean it for the IRS. He had previously thought that the erotic videos would have taken care of that. The IRS didn't judge the morality of one business or another, it just wanted accurate bookkeeping. So maybe the escort service was taking in so much money that even porn video sales through the roof weren't enough to be convincing. Brendan had believed that the situation with the escort service had been significant, but now he was sure that it was even bigger than he'd first suspected.

He remembered what Heilshorn had said. *My sources have linked Forrester's name with Titan, which protects the interests of black markets.* One of Titan's jobs could have been to launder the money made by XList.

And the fact that they were flaunting it, right here, in the middle of a state university, in plain public view, that was just incredible.

This company that serviced government officials with prostitutes was a chameleon, with a dozen different identities that continually shifted. XList was just a face, a mask. *XList probably doesn't even exist now, not on paper, not on the web, not anywhere. Not with this very investigation ongoing.*

He also thought of Heilshorn saying that Brendan must still be alive for a reason. Brendan didn't believe in a god that manipulated the world, and he didn't think Alexander Heilshorn did either. While he had reached the limit of his scientific patience and adopted a faith in a higher power, he was still sure that people were the manipulators, not God Almighty.

If he was alive, it was because he had survived.

And if anything, God was passive-aggressive.

Brendan smiled. At the same time, he killed his headlights as he drifted past the construction sign, towards the hulking crane and the dark, unfinished building looming ahead. The crucifix Argon had given him hung around his neck.

\* \* \*

He parked near some other vehicles which looked like typical construction-worker trucks and cars. A tool bin was in the back of one pick-up truck, which was next to a beat-up looking Honda Accord. Another truck sat in the distance, out of the throw of lamplight. He wondered if there were workers inside, now. He scanned the four-story building and found that there were no discernibly lit rooms, only a glow in most windows from what were likely the hall lights. It was slightly brighter in some windows than others, but they were definitely not individually lit rooms.

Then a thought struck him: Forrester was working for the company. This was his day job. By night he robbed prostitutes of their babies, in order to keep them in the game or to keep their mouths shut about the congressmen and senators they serviced. By day he wore a tool belt and swung a hammer, listening to CCR on a battered radio.

And somewhere in there was he keeping a child? How exactly would that work out? A man like Forrester wasn't capable of keeping a small child healthy and cared for, let alone concealed, especially if he was working a day job and moonlighting as an enforcer for a black market organization. There had to be an accomplice. He had to be working with somebody.

Brendan glanced at his phone. There had been two missed calls. One was from a half an hour before, the other thirty-one minutes ago. He realized that, in his nervousness and haste, he hadn't activated the ringer on his phone. He usually kept it on silent – nothing was more disturbing to an interview with a witness or in the middle of a forensic investigation than a ringing phone.

Both calls were from Colinas.

Still sitting in his car and looking up at the building, he listened to his voice messages.

"Healy? Where the hell are you? Boy, you know how to ruin a surprise. We've been at your house for ten minutes now, dude. Oh, I see I got a call from you. Alright, let me check it."

Brendan scowled in the dark. Ruin a surprise? What in the hell was Colinas talking about? He said "we've been at your house." Who was "we?" Why were they . . . ?

And then Brendan realized. Today was his birthday. He was thirty-five. It had been his goal to quit smoking by today, he also remembered.

He hadn't had a cigarette in more than forty-eight hours.

He closed his eyes and breathed through his nose. He couldn't help but smile and shake his head. The next message wiped the humor from his face.

"Healy, are you fucking nuts? Listen, I'm here with Taber and Bostrom and Lawless, man. We came by to give you a fucking box of donuts, dude. I . . . you've put me in a tough spot, here, Healy. You've got to be fucking kidding me. Call me back. I don't know what I'm going to tell these guys."

Colinas had hung up.

Brendan pulled the phone away from his ear. He suddenly felt cold and nauseous. Every instinct that had told him he ought to be here, was now gone. He looked at the flat, characterless Business School building and felt a shudder. Colinas was right. He was fucking nuts. He needed to back out of the parking lot right now, turn around, and get the hell out of there. This was a job for a SWAT team. At least, it was a job to be commanded by men with far more field experience than he had.

The Camry was still running. He reached the shifter and was preparing to put it in reverse when one of the lights in the building winked on.

Brendan froze. He leaned forward and peered through the windshield. At the far end of the building, on the third floor, a light had indeed come on in one of the rooms.

## CHAPTER THIRTY-NINE / MONDAY, 8:19 PM

Brendan was walking towards the building when his phone rang. This time, he felt the vibration in his pocket and pulled it out. The incoming call was a number he didn't recognize.

"Hello?"

"Mr. Porter?"

"Who is this?"

"This is Jerry with Titan Inc. We're the parent company to XList. Is this a bad time?"

John Porter was the name he had used to email XList.

Brendan froze. Instinctively, he looked around the parking lot. A dozen light towers with buzzing arc-sodium lamps glowed over a vast and mostly empty tarmac the size of a football field. The air smelled like construction – sawdust and burnt metal. In the distance, a single car was tracking along the service road off of Western Ave. It was headed his way.

"I'm sorry for taking the liberty of calling, sir. I just wanted to follow-up and see if you were still having any trouble with your XList order."

Brendan's lips were pressed together. He watched the car approaching. Suddenly, its lights winked off.

Though the evening was humid and only in the fifties, Brendan felt cold. He licked his lips.

"No, I think I was able to find what I've been looking for."

"That's good to hear, sir. We can take the order over the phone, if it's convenient."

Brendan glanced at the phone. The incoming call on his display read BLOCKED. That didn't help. But he could swear he heard an engine in the background – hard to tell if it was coming through the phone or from Western Ave, though.

"No, actually it's not convenient. I'm not . . . I can't get to my credit card right now."

"Very good, sir. Again, I apologize for calling you like this. We just like to reach out to our very special customers."

"What makes me so special?"

"Well, you're interested in Danice. Anyone who's interested in Danice arouses our interest, if you'll excuse the phrase."

This was no punk getting paid seven bucks and hour to cold call potential porn customers, Brendan was sure now. The person calling himself "Jerry" was clearly involved in all of the rest of it. Brendan looked for the approaching vehicle. He glimpsed it beneath a streetlight on the service road, and then lost sight of it again. It was almost at the parking lot.

He thought he'd even heard the name Jerry before, and racked his brain.

"I'm going to find you," said Brendan. "I'm going to shut you down."

Jerry laughed. "You really got your bell rung, didn't you? I don't believe you're thinking straight, Detective."

"Meet me. Name a place and meet me. I'll show you how I'm thinking." Brendan felt the hairs rising on the back of his neck. He now stared at the lighted window on the third floor as he spoke. Was "Jerry" waiting for him up there? The voice on the phone was gravelly, sadistic. Who were these people?

In a burst of adrenaline, Brendan started heading for the front doors of the Business School.

"Come open up. Let me in."

"Little pig, little pig, let me in," said Jerry.

"You guys think you're so smart with your Titan Construction company. Your big sign right here, right under everyone's nose."

"The thing under everyone's nose is you, Detective Healy."

"You weren't on to me until I got in touch with *you*, Jerry."

"Yes. From your sick bed, after we ran you over, if memory serves."

Brendan reached the door. He had built up a good stride by the time he got there, the pain in his hip either forgotten or suppressed by the meds. He was using only one crutch, and now he tossed it aside and grabbed the handle of one of the glass front doors. He pulled, and the door swung open.

For a moment, his heart seemed to stop. He realized he'd been expecting the place to be locked up. He'd thought his mind was playing tricks on him; that the person in the far window was just a carpenter working late, and that the rest of the crew had locked up hours ago.

The door was open in front of him, leading in to a glass vestibule. There were another set of double doors just beyond.

"What do you want, Detective? What do you think you're going to achieve with this? You couldn't get to the bottom of a pool with a concrete block wrapped around your ankle. You've got nothing on us. Better men than you have tried and failed."

"I won't fail."

"Yes you will. Ultimately, you will. Men like you always do. And we will continue to be here, just like we've always been here."

Jerry hung up.

Brendan paused and glanced at his phone. He was sure that even if he was able to uncover the blocked number, it wouldn't connect him anywhere. Or, to a pay-as-you-go phone. Still, he would try it later. For now, he slid the phone into the pocket of his windbreaker and opened the next set of doors.

* * *

Once through the entrance, Brendan was in a short, wide corridor. Within a few paces, he came into a lobby. It was an impressive room, with the ceiling three stories above a marble floor. A large mahogany desk sat in the center. There were two tremendous potted plants flanking the front desk – they were ficcas, perhaps. To the right, a set of scaffolding was stacked four-high almost to the ceiling. There was plastic around its feet. The room was lit with tungsten sconces along the wall – two behind the front desk, one on either side, beneath what became an overhang for the second floor. He spied two emergency lights boxes beneath these cantilevers as well.

He walked up to the front desk and looked around. The wood was coated with a patina of sheetrock dust. Seeing nothing of use, he walked around the desk to the back wall where there were two elevator bays. Between the bays was a plaque showing a map of the building. The layout was pretty simple: Four floors, a north wing and a south wing, mostly classrooms, but with three lecture halls, a conference center, cafeteria, and a full gymnasium on a sub floor, including racquet ball courts. A student would never have to leave.

After absorbing this, Brendan turned and limped hurriedly back to the front doors. As he neared them, he put his back to the wall and he slid more slowly towards the glass. He peered out into the dark parking lot. He reached in his jacket and felt the butt of his gun.

He waited for what felt like an eternity, but was, according to his phone clock, only five minutes. No one was coming from the parking lot to the front doors. If they were from Titan, likely they knew a more discreet way into the building anyway.

He decided it was time to go and see who was on the third floor. His phone buzzed in his pocket. He glanced at the screen and saw that it was Colinas. He answered it in a low voice.

"Yeah."

"Where are you?"

"UAlbany. New Business School building."

"What the hell are you doing there?"

"You can't tell anyone I'm here."

"What?"

"I'm going after Forrester. But there's a chance that people could get hurt if Forrester knows we're onto him."

"You're nuts. Get out of there."

"I can't." Brendan thought to say more, but he stopped himself. "I'll call you back in one hour."

Brendan hung up. He turned his phone off. *If I'm alive in an hour*, he thought.

He was terrified by the notion, but at the same time, felt a kind of peace with it; it was a paradoxical emotion that resided within him.

He continued to the stairs and opened the door quietly and began to ascend.

Once on the third floor, he drew his weapon and entered the corridor cautiously. He had a flashlight in his pocket which he pulled out and brought into a grip beneath the weapon. He kept the light off for now. The same soft, ambient sconces lit the hallway. Overhead were fluorescent light panels, dark.

He looked down the corridor one way – towards the north wing. He was closer to the south wing, and he started that way. He passed by three rooms with the doors closed before reaching a set of double glass doors which marked the entrance to the south wing. He found the doors unlocked and went through silently.

He started down the corridor again. This time the rooms were open – no doors had yet been hung at their entrances. He looked in the first room, his gun in front of him. He clicked his flashlight on to reveal construction items on the floor – plastic, tools, scaffold. A quick inventory indicated that the construction crew was in the process of mudding the walls – covering over the sheetrock to make it smooth and ready for paint. It didn't look like anyone had been at it today, however. There was a sense that the dust coating everything was old. The air was stale. No smell of drying caulk, mudding, or sawdust.

He exited and turned down the corridor in the direction he'd been going.

When he emerged, he saw a man standing in the hallway further down, pointing a gun at him.

The man fired.

Brendan cried out and dove back into the room as a bullet punched through the air inches from his ear. He crashed into some scaffold, and his gun and flashlight clattered to the ground.

He found his footing quickly and bent and scrabbled for the lost items. He found his gun. He couldn't locate the flashlight right away. His heartbeat thudded in his temples as he dragged his fingers over the gritty bare floor, looking for it. The man who'd fired could be coming down the corridor right now, ready to jump into the room behind Brendan and finish what he'd started. There was no time to keep searching for the flashlight.

Brendan turned and aimed at the door to the hallway. He started towards it in a crouch. His blood roared in his ears. He took huge, gulping breaths. He needed to steady himself. It was no use – his body shook terribly. He reached the door and quickly left the room and swung into the corridor, prepared to drop prone to the floor and fire.

There was no one there.

The corridor hooked right further down, past four or five more rooms like the one he had just come out of. The man who had fired at him was either in one of those rooms or had turned out of sight down the hallway.

Brendan started after him, slowly, limping, trembling, biting his lip, willing himself to calm.

Then the lights went out.

\* \* \*

His first thought was to get out. To finally come to grips with reality – that he was in way over his head, well outside of the boundaries of proper police procedure, and in no physical shape to continue on. The place was nearly pitch black, with only scant light filtering through the windows in the classrooms from the parking lot outside, and some meager illumination from the city beyond. It was barely bright enough to see the edges of the hallway, and his hands in front of his face. Time to go.

He started backing down the corridor the way he'd come, and then stopped. He cocked his head, listening.

Brendan thought he could hear a child crying. Just a baby, by the sound of it. It was faint and muffled, but it was there.

He rallied himself. His mind raced ahead, considering the possibilities. If what Heilshorn had said was in fact true, then Reginald Forrester had a child with him. It made no sense at all, to be hiding out in a half-built academic building with a hostage child, but it was possible.

It was also possible that Forrester was toying with Brendan. The killer could be playing a recording, something to lure the detective on with. If that were the case, then Forrester knew about Alexander Heilshorn, or at least had a reason to suspect that the police knew about the captive children.

Brendan searched his memory, trying to dig up anything that would have inadvertently passed an unequivocal sign to Forrester, or anyone at Titan, that the police knew about the element of the case involving children. He came up empty; despite the conspiracy theory Brendan had briefly conjured while sitting in his driveway, Taber knew nothing, and as far as Brendan knew, neither Delaney nor Colinas had uncovered anything about kids relating to the Rebecca Heilshorn killing either. Nothing more than knowing that she had a daughter, anyway.

No, the only time in the investigation that the subject of children had come up was when Alexander Heilshorn had presented it. Heilshorn had even seemed to know the child's gender.

Still, Forrester and Titan could be just assuming that the police knew. There was the situation with the young guy, Jason Pert. They might know about him, and know that Rebecca was preparing a room to take in a sort-of foster child.

If, in fact, she had been.

The whole thing was sordid, and still unclear. The only thing Brendan knew for certain was, at that moment, he could hear the sound of a distressed child somewhere on the floor of this building. He couldn't take the chance that it was a recording. If he was wrong . . .

He couldn't be wrong.

Brendan started moving forward again. As he drew near the turn in the corridor, he favored his bad leg and braced himself along the wall. He tried to make himself as small a target as possible. The only advantage to being in darkness was that the killer would have a hard time seeing him, too.

Unless the killer had a light.

Brendan thought about going back to look for his own flashlight again. He paused and turned to look behind him. Now that the killer seemed to have retreated, Brendan might have some time to find the light. He realized with a sinking feeling that he couldn't recall which doorway he had jumped into. There were four classrooms on the right, between himself and the doors in the hallway to the south wing. Had he jumped in the first one? He didn't think so. But the second or the third? He didn't know. He was losing his bearings in the dark.

Once more, he decided to press on without the flashlight. His heart pounded in his chest, and sweat ran from his temples. It was warm in the building, almost balmy. He took pains not to touch the sweat with his hands, lest he wind up with a slippery grip on his gun. He held it with one hand and braced the wall with the other, moving towards the corner ahead.

As he went, the sound of the baby's cries grew louder. At least he was headed in the right direction, he thought.

As he reached the turn in the hallway, he suddenly had the idea that the killer could have gone a flight down, or taken the stairs up, and gotten around behind Brendan. He could be coming up the hallway behind Brendan now, ready to pounce.

Brendan swung around. His eyes were adjusting to the dark. He thought he saw the glimmer of the glass doors further down. There appeared to be no one on his tail.

He faced forward again, and took the right turn in the hallway with a fast swing around the inside wall, both hands now on his gun.

Before him was another stretch of corridor. Straight ahead was a window to the outside. The hallway then banked left. There were half a dozen classroom doorways, two on the left, four on the right. Brendan proceeded to check them all, occasionally flipping the light switches, just to see if they would work. None did, and he continued in near-darkness. Even the emergency lights were dark; perhaps the construction company hadn't rigged them with batteries yet, or wired them to turn on in a power failure.

He realized that the killer must have gotten somewhere where there was access to the building's power. A room with all of the breakers. Would such a room be up on the third floor? Maybe there was one for each floor. It was possible that the floors below and the one above still had power.

But the cries of the baby had intensified. He decided that it sounded like a girl after all, though he couldn't be a hundred percent certain. Her cries seemed to resonate through the building, as if each room portended the appearance of the captive child.

The sweat continued to pour down the sides of the detective's head. He went into the last room in this section of hallway and did a quick sweep.

When he'd finished and was about to leave, he saw there was a man standing in the doorway.

## CHAPTER FORTY / MONDAY, 8:44 PM

"Little pig, little pig, let me in," said the shadow standing in the doorway. It was the voice from the phone.

"Don't move."

Brendan aimed his gun at what he thought was the center of the killer's body, his chest. He was distantly aware that his nerves had settled. His heart had eased into a steady rhythm. His mind felt clear, as if the sun had momentarily appeared in an otherwise overcast day.

"I was born under the black smoke of September."

A chill ran through Brendan, rippling his calm. He focused.

"I want you to take out your weapon and toss it into the room."

"You like that? I wrote it years ago. Years, I mean, God, how time flies."

"Take your gun by the very end of the handle and toss it into the room. Do it now."

"You hear that baby? I have to feed her. We'll have to postpone this for now, Detective Healy. The needs of the child come first. You ought to know that. You're a parent.

Or, woops, sorry, *were* a parent. Didn't put the needs of your child first, though."

"I'm going to tell you this one last time, and then I'm going to shoot you. Take your gun and toss it into the room. After that, you're going to get on your knees. Do it now. The place will be surrounded in minutes. You don't want to go the other way, unless you're into suicide by cop."

The words just came out, as if by some other force. Brendan had been in tense situations during his time on the beat, but he'd always had Argon to back him up. And nothing, really, had ever been quite like this. He'd only ever had to draw his piece once in Hawthorne, and it had turned out to be nothing. Yet he felt like he'd been here before. He felt like he'd been doing this his whole life.

Tracking. He was a tracker. And now he had his quarry.

"No," the killer drawled. "There's no police squad en route, no SWAT team about to come ramming through. It's just you, Detective. It's just you and I."

"Don't count on it."

"I don't have to count on it. I know it's true. Now, it's been fun playing cat and mouse with you. Of course, you probably think you've been the cat, just like you probably believe someone is coming to help you. But I really do have to go see to that baby."

Brendan opened his mouth, and the shadow slipped out of the doorway.

"Hey!"

Brendan jabbed the gun towards the hallway in a helpless gesture. His finger pressed against the trigger, but not hard enough to release a round. Instead, he snapped into action and followed.

As soon as he reached the doorway he stopped. His pulse had quickened again, his preternatural calm had left him. He breathed and his heart thudded and he imagined the killer just a few feet away against the corridor wall, taking aim.

*Shit. Shit shit shit shit*

Brendan jumped out of the doorway. He managed to clear such a distance that when he landed, his hip flared with bright pain, as if he'd ripped open the stitches, or aggravated the damaged cartilage.

His arm and gun was out in front of him like a spear. He was squeezing the trigger so hard that he inadvertently fired.

There was no one in the hallway, and the bullet punctured the glass and flew out into the night.

He stood, stunned, motionless, breathing hard. Then he forced himself to move again. He was limping worse than ever. Every step sent a bolt of pain up his side, and tentacles of pain around his midsection, knotting in his lower back. His ears rang from the explosion of the gunshot.

He reached the left turn and continued on with his weapon in front of him.

This hall was different. The wall to the right was an exterior wall, and there was more light coming in from the windows lining it. There was only one doorway on the left that he could see. Another set of double doors.

The crying was coming from there – as the ringing in his ears faded, Brendan was sure of it.

He headed towards the doors as quickly as he could, his whole body rigid with flashing pains.

The doors opened outwards and Brendan yanked on one and stabbed the gun in. To his surprise, the room was lit up.

It was one of the lecture halls he'd seen on the building map down in the lobby. The room was large, arranged theater-style with a raised platform featuring a lectern and a retractable screen at the front. The chairs were bolted into the floor – maybe two hundred seats in all. With the downward slope, Brendan figured the room cut into the second story, below. And it was a clerestory space, so it took up the floor above it as well.

There was a door on the left of the platform with the screen and lectern. Everything was still, and Brendan scanned the room. The baby was still crying – and it was coming from beyond that closed door.

Then, a second after Brendan decided this, her cries fell silent.

What in the hell was going on?

An icy pit formed in his stomach. Had the killer just done something to silence the child?

Brendan started running. It was a painful, hobbled run through the dimly lit auditorium, his .38 caliber out in front of him. He felt nothing but cold, nothing but terrified as he imagined what lay beyond that door, and summoned the courage to go through it.

\* \* \*

A moment later, he reached the door and flung it open.

Reginald Forrester was standing there with a baby in his arms. The child had a bottle in its mouth, and was sucking greedily. This room was well-lit, with the fluorescents shining down from above. It was a private quarters, a place where perhaps the teacher would retreat to grade papers or favor a nip of brandy, while the bright young business minds of tomorrow took their tests on economic models and S-corp fundamentals in the lecture hall outside.

The killer was leaning on a heavy oak desk, holding the baby. Behind them, handsome shelves were filled with colorful books. An Apple MacBook sat on the desk. An antique chair was in one corner; a flat screen TV in another, on a stand with DVDs and Blu-rays arranged beneath. There was a hutch next to this with expensive looking liquors on display. It reminded Brendan a bit of Donald Kettering's office in Boonville, only with a million dollars thrown at it. And on the floor was a bassinet, a pile of blankets, baby toys, and what looked like a diaper bag.

Brendan stood, out of breath, gritting his teeth through the nearly blinding pain his leg and hip were pumping out through his body like hot, electric shocks. He kept his gun level and carefully observed the baby.

He'd been right; it was a girl. She was wearing pink pajamas. He put her at about ten months old, give or take. There was a tear that had tracked down the side of her face, but otherwise she appeared content for the moment. Yet she wasn't exactly plump, with a radiant glow. Brendan was no pediatrician, but he'd done three solid years of basic medicine. This baby was not in very good health. She looked tired and malnourished.

His eyes flicked up to Reginald Forrester's face.

The man looked older than in his Cornell picture. His hair had gone almost completely gray.

Brendan didn't know what to say or do first. Nothing could have prepared him for this, whether he had believed Heilshorn or not. It was tough, for one thing, to threaten a man with a helpless baby in his arms. None of it made any sense. The room – the office, or study, whatever one wanted to call it – was clearly used, and used a lot. It appeared to be Forrester's hideaway, or something like it. It had "English professor" written all over it. The books, the liquor, the thick oak desk. Yet it was in the middle of a construction site. There was no way that Forrester had been here with a tiny baby for any extended period of time, not without being noticed. And if he was, that meant every carpenter and electrician who'd seen him would have to be in on Titan's other businesses, or at least have had to sign some form of gag order before being hired.

"You're having a hard time working it out," said Forrester. His voice was almost a whisper. The child looked up at him as she drank. She was clearly used to the man. That, or grateful for a merciful feeding.

"There's nothing to work out. You're going to hand me that baby. Then I'm going to leave with her."

Brendan realized that he had no handcuffs with him. He was regretting more and more the hasty manner in which he'd left Rome. He felt more like a civilian who had taken the law into his own hands than a police detective.

He thrust the gun forward.

"Now."

Forrester looked back at him and didn't move. The man had crow's feet around his eyes that made him appear happy, or smiling, but his mouth was set in a grim straight-line. He was broad in the shoulders and chest. He probably outweighed Brendan by thirty or forty pounds. Brendan took aim at his shoulder. The baby girl in his arms was just out of the line of fire.

Brendan's eyes dropped as he caught sight of the killer's own weapon, tucked into the waistband of his pants, near the small of his back.

Why was Forrester being so cavalier? What cards did he think he was holding?

Of course, the child in his arms made him a less than optimal target, even at close range. He could place her in the line of fire the second he saw Brendan's trigger finger twitch. Still, Brendan held his weapon steady. He considered aiming higher. For the head.

Then, of course, he would know nothing about the others Heilshorn spoke of.

Brendan was not getting a response from Forrester, who continued to hold and feed the baby, bouncing her faintly, absently. He may have had some experience with children, Brendan thought, but if he was enjoying himself, it was an act.

"Who else is here in this building?"

Forrester looked at him. Inside the thatches of crow's feet, his eyes were dark and blank.

"Little pig, little pig, let me in."

"I get it. That was you on the phone. Amazing."

After this sarcastic comment, Brendan felt a sudden thrill – a sense of possible enlightenment. It was as if Forrester had a secret, and he was dying to reveal it.

"You wrote the poem on the back of Rebecca's pictures?"

"Not really a poem," the killer said right away. "More like flash fiction with a poetic bent."

"You wrote it all, the night you met her?"

"No, no." Forrester shook his head, irritably. "You know better than that. I wrote that during my visits. I was at that old farm . . ." He glanced up to the ceiling. "Oh, four or five times, I guess."

"Why did you write it?"

He shrugged.

Brendan cocked his head. He affected an amused face. "Are you the clichéd writer-that-never-was? A teacher who lost his tenure for feeling up the co-eds, a failed author with nothing more than a swollen liver to show for his talent?"

Forrester didn't flinch. "I suppose so. Just like you are a failed husband, a failed father, a murderer of his wife and child."

He continued to gently bounce the baby. Now he looked down at her. His face pulled back in a death mask smile. "There we are," he said in a sing-song voice. "There we are."

The child had almost finished the bottle. Brendan saw the door behind Forrester and figured it led to a private bathroom. He bet if he entered the room he would find baby bottles and formula. He hoped there would be nothing else.

"How long have you been keeping her here, Forrester?"

The man looked up from the baby, as if he'd forgotten Brendan was there. "How long? Oh, not quite two weeks now."

*Just since he killed Rebecca*, Brendan thought.

"And you go unnoticed by the construction crew? How is that possible?"

Forrester scowled. "You're not very good at detecting, are you, detective? The job has been shut down for almost a month, caught up in bureaucratic bullshit. Same shit, different day. That's higher education for you."

"So no one knows you're here?"

"Well, someone does," Forrester said with a sly look.

*He's crazy.* Brendan felt that inner glow of illumination again. He was growing more and more assured of something with every second he stood in the room with this man: Forrester was deranged.

Brendan's mind raced. He constructed the scenario in seconds: Forrester meets Rebecca, an undergrad. The two have an affair, which leaks out. Between that and publishing his manifesto online, Forrester gets fired. Afterwards, she turns to prostitution. Or, it was more likely that Forrester recruited her, getting her involved in XList, which is his new business. Rebecca repeatedly tries to leave, but Forrester has the videos to blackmail her. Maybe he threatens to blackmail Heilshorn, too. It made sense – Stemp may not have been a whistleblower; he could have called in what Heilshorn already knew. In the meantime, Rebecca gets pregnant. Maybe it's the baby of one of her clients – or maybe it's Forrester's own. She has the child in secret but Forrester finds out. He comes after her and kills her.

The baby was near the very end of her bottle.

Forrester was staring at Brendan, as if watching him think. A question hung suspended in the room, and Forrester answered it.

"You're going to wish you never came here."

## CHAPTER FORTY-ONE / MONDAY, 9:02 PM

There was a knock on the door.

It was so surprising that a breath escaped Brendan in a rush. He reacted instinctively by stepping away and doing a half-turn. He wanted to keep Forrester in his sights but be clear of the door. Who the hell was knocking?

"Come in," said Forrester.

The door opened. Brendan took another step back and renewed his grip on his gun. He swung the barrel towards the door.

A man Brendan had never seen before stepped through. Brendan instantly associated the man with law enforcement, but not quite a cop. The man was older, about Forrester's age, with trim gray hair, buzzed around the neck. There were pouches of skin beneath his rheumy eyes. He wore a zip-up jacket that looked like a *Member's Only*. Jeans and plain black shoes beneath. He was carrying a small gym bag.

He turned his head and looked at Brendan.

"Relax," said the new guy. His eyes fell on the gun Brendan wielded. "Put that thing down before you get somebody hurt."

"Who are you?"

"I'm a private investigator. Let's all settle down here, there's a baby in the room, for chrissakes."

Brendan kept his weapon up. A private investigator? He'd seen someone entering the parking lot in a vehicle some forty minutes ago. They had shut off their headlights, and then Brendan had waited by the front doors for a little while. Was he one of Heilshorn's guys? That was the only reasonable explanation. Who else would know that Brendan was here?

"Come on," said the P.I. "Lower that weapon before this gets any worse. Take a pill, kid. Relax."

His eyes were dark brown and he stared at Brendan. He seemed unwilling to do anything besides stand in the doorway and glare until Brendan complied.

Brendan cut his eyes over to Forrester. The man was expressionless, watching the P.I. In his arms, the baby had fallen asleep at last.

"I asked you who you were," said Brendan, keeping his voice low. "I'm Investigator Healy, with the Oneida County Sheriff's Department. I'll put down my weapon when I'm ready. Tell me who you are."

"My name is Brown. That's all you need to know, detective."

"Do you work for Alexander Heilshorn?"

He seemed to consider this. His mouth curled down at the corners, and he shrugged.

Brendan looked at Forrester. The killer widened his eyes slightly. "These private eyes are a biddable bunch. Sorry, Brown, but it's true."

"You pay, I play."

Brendan blinked. "You're telling me that you were one of Heilshorn's P.I.s, and you changed clients to this man because he pays better?"

"I was born rich to a poor family," Brown said. "Ya know?"

A second later, Forrester made a move towards the other side of the room where the bassinet was. Brendan stiffened and brought the gun back around to aim at the killer. His neck and ears felt like they were filling with blood.

He heard a click, and saw that Brown had his own gun out, a Colt .45. He leveled it at Brendan's head.

"I said to relax."

Brendan swallowed. The situation was becoming unmanageable. He had no idea what to do.

Forrester placed the baby in the bassinet with a kind of practiced ease. He stood up and looked down, as if admiring his handiwork. Then he turned to the other two men in the room. "Let's have that piece," he said to Brendan. His own gun was still stuck into the backside of his pants.

Brendan felt a stitch of pain in his stomach as Brown took his .45 and aimed it at the infant in the bassinet.

Brendan cycled through the options. He could wage a shootout with two armed men here in the confined quarters of the lecture hall office, or he could play along. There was always hope that Colinas and other reinforcements would arrive in time. That was, of course, if Colinas ignored Brendan's warnings to stay away.

*That's what I did*, thought Brendan. He had pressed on despite Heilshorn's ardent entreaties to the contrary.

He had no choice. Brendan flipped his gun around and handed it to Brown, handle first.

As Brown took it, Brendan said, "That was you on the phone before. Not him. Your first name is Jerry." Brendan had full recall now – Taber had talked about Heilshorn's P.I. at the diner, the morning Brendan had first been asked to walk off the case. The P.I. described by Taber had been named Jerry Brown.

"Good for you," the P.I. said.

"Why would you quit working for Doctor Heilshorn to work for this murderer?"

"Who says I quit working for Heilshorn?"

"You work for both of them?"

"Bingo. Did you graduate top of your academy, or what?"

"Healy here, is a scientist," Forrester said.

"That's right, that's right. A brain doctor. Awfully slow for a brain doctor, wouldn't you say?"

Brown set the bag on the oak desk. He unzipped it and then shoved Brendan's firearm inside.

Simultaneously, Brendan slipped a hand into his pocket and felt around for his phone. Once he had it in his grasp, he thumbed on the power button. Then he eased his hand back out.

After Brown had secured the detective's piece inside the bag, he pulled out a small shiny object. It was a small, compact camera. Brown handed it over to Forrester.

Forrester took the camera and looked down at it, turning it over in his hands as if it were some extraterrestrial object. Then he lifted it up and held it out towards Brendan. "From Rebecca's dresser drawers," he said.

Brendan instantly remembered. The drawers which had been pulled out haphazardly. The killer had grabbed this camera before he left.

Brendan swallowed.

He watched Forrester reach into the bag and take out a small cable. Then the large, mostly silver-haired man walked to the corner of the room where the flat screen TV was.

He fumbled for a few moments, muttering and cursing under his breath, and then stuck the USB end into the TV. He stepped back then, and glanced at Brendan. He pressed a button on the remote control and selected the input. A moment later, a large icon appeared on screen. The icon was titled "116.mov."

"Technology just amazes me," Forrester said. Then he cut a look over to Brown. "Move him closer."

Brown shoved Brendan forward, forcing him to take steps towards the screen. After a few paces, Brown rammed a chair against the back of Brendan's legs, making him sit down, hard. He was now only a few feet from the TV. Brown clamped his hand down on Brendan's shoulder. He pressed the barrel of the .45 against Brendan's right temple. At least it was no longer pointed at the baby.

Brendan's stomach was on fire now, with lightning pains tearing through his guts. *Ulcer*, he thought. Of all things.

"This is for you, Detective," Forrester said. His voice had taken on a dead quality, like someone speaking from beyond the grave, if such a thing were possible.

A moment later, Forrester was at Brendan's side. He leaned down and whispered in the detective's ear. The killer's breath was hot, and smelled sour.

"I know how you love these videos."

Brendan felt cold chills – his skin was crawling. The icon on the screen disappeared, and an image flashed on in its place.

* * *

Brendan was instantly familiar with what he was looking at. It was the Bloomingdale farm, and the sun was just coming up. Whoever was holding the camera was facing the front door, standing in the dirt patch where Kevin Heilshorn had fallen to his knees, weeping for his sister.

Brendan had looked at that door many times. Now he was looking at it through the eyes of a killer. Of that he was instantly sure.

Forrester stood behind him, watching along. Forrester had replaced Brown and was now holding onto both of Brendan's shoulders, crouched close. On screen, the camera turned to look into the tractor shed for a moment. As it did, with the image darker, Brendan could see the reflection of the people in the room behind him. Forrester was a pale moon face looming over his shoulder. Brown stood just beyond, near the baby.

Then the image changed to the brighter colored house and the reflections disappeared. Brendan watched as the killer advanced towards the door. With a gloved hand, the killer reached out and opened it. He entered the house.

Brendan was now inside the Bloomingdale farmhouse, standing in the killer's shoes. The camera turned to the right, looking into the kitchen, and then to the left, looking into the dark living room there. Finally, the camera faced straight ahead, and then tilted to look up the stairs at the walkway crossing the open story room.

Brendan knew the layout well. That was where Rebecca Heilshorn would walk from the shower to her bedroom, spotting the killer down below as she made the short trip.

But as the camera lingered on the upstairs hallway for a moment, Brendan did not see Rebecca Heilshorn yet.

By the timeline of the 911 distress call, it should be any moment. Brendan braced himself, his stomach in rolling painful knots as he prepared to see the murder victim alive and in her house moments before her death.

There was no date and time in the lower corner of the screen to indicate when the video had been taken, like there had been in the old camcorder days. Brendan realized that this didn't have to be the morning of the murder. And a split second after he had this thought, Rebecca appeared in the hallway after all.

She took a few steps, coming from the direction of the bathroom and the unfinished master bedroom.

Brendan's stomach clenched, exciting fresh bolts of pain. He held his breath as his eyes appraised her.

She was not in a bath towel. She was in a casual outfit – a pair of body-fitting pants, like yoga pants, and a loose hoodie.

She looked down the stairs, at the person holding the camera, right through the television screen and into Brendan's eyes.

"Jesus, you scared me. What are you doing?"

Her voice was loud. The TV volume must have been cranked up. It was like she was in the room with them. Brendan began to squirm. Forrester's grip tightened. His lips were close to Brendan's ear. "Shh. Watch."

"Did you find my poem?" This was the cameraman's voice. It was unmistakably the voice of Reginald Forrester. He pinched Brendan's shoulders as the TV version of him began to climb the stairs.

"No," said Rebecca.

"You always liked it when I wrote to you."

The young woman on the landing offered a grim smile, which faded quickly. The camera work was a little shaky as TV-Forrester ascended, but the image stayed mostly centered on Rebecca. Brendan could see that she looked wary, and tired. He'd always thought she was a pretty girl. Here she appeared older than she actually was, fatigued and worn. Brendan thought the killer was talking about the words he'd written across the back of the framed photos in the dining room. In particular, one photograph that showed Rebecca and Leah and Donald Kettering posing as a happy family. Probably Forrester hadn't liked Kettering very much.

From Rebecca's right came a baby's cry. For a split second, Brendan thought it was the baby girl in the room with them. He started to look around, to see if she was alright, but Forrester gripped his shoulders. Between his injured leg, the churning rat teeth in his stomach and a blistering headache forming, Brendan was not in good shape. But that baby's cries – on the video, yes, as he listened he was sure now – somehow made everything else muffled in comparison. He felt far away from himself, in limbo between the video playing in front of him and the room he was actually in.

Rebecca turned as the killer neared the top of the stairs. She looked behind her, and then wordlessly disappeared that way.

The cameraman-killer, Forrester, finished the climb and then turned after her. Brendan watched the image float down the hallway and into the master bedroom.

The baby girl was on the bed. He was sure that it was the same infant who was in the room with them now, maybe about a month younger. This put the time of the video at about two weeks before the murder, maybe less.

The child was too young to be able to move much on her own, even more helpless than now. Her legs kicked frantically and uselessly in the air. Rebecca was at her side an instant later, leaning down and scooping her up. She held the child close to her breast and shushed her. Then her eyes lifted to the cameraman and Brendan saw fear in them, and pain, and resignation.

Behind the camera, Forrester was cooing at the baby, too, as he neared. "Little piggy," he called softly.

"Don't call her that."

"Oh, she doesn't know. She doesn't know." His voice was sing-song, lilting, like a cartoon character. "Does she? Does she know anything about anything? Nooo."

The unseen Forrester neared Rebecca and the child.

Seeing them together for the first time, Brendan was struck by the resemblance. The baby had Rebecca's large, dark eyes. Her nose and lips reminded Brendan of someone else – Kevin Heilshorn. Her uncle. And there was another familiar quality about her, too, one which escaped him for the moment.

"Put her back down," said Forrester. His voice had lost the playful quality and was firm and commanding.

"No. She needs to eat."

"She'll be fine. Set her back down on the bed."

Rebecca did as she was told. Her face told a story of internal horrors.

A second later, the camera whipped away. The unseen Forrester started moving in the other direction. He headed to the bathroom. "Be right back," said his disembodied voice.

The bathroom door was opened by a hand which appeared in the video. Then Forrester closed himself in.

Brendan's heart pounded. The bathroom on screen was the same recently refurbished room he had stood in just weeks ago. The fixtures were new. The mirror over the sink was unblemished, without those toothpaste spittle spots that collected on the rest of the world's bathroom mirrors. If only Forrester would . . .

And a second later, he did. The camera tilted up and Forrester, holding it with one hand, looked at his reflection in the mirror. Or, more accurately, he looked into the camera at his reflection in the mirror.

He didn't grin. He didn't say a word.

Brendan looked into the face of the killer on screen. Then the churning thoughts in his mind settled abruptly. He was struck with a truth that resonated in the deep recesses of his being.

Forrester was drunk.

From his chair, with the real Reginald Forrester standing behind him, holding his shoulders, Brendan looked at the screen as the inebriated Forrester documented his presence in Rebecca Heilshorn's home, his eyes glassy and emotionless. Then the camera tilted down and away from the mirror and the sink and continued recording as the killer undid his belt and pants with his free hand.

"I don't want to see this anymore," Brendan said. He was surprised to hear his own voice. He thought he was going to be sick. If he vomited, it would be blood that came up. He could taste the bitter copper of it in the back of his throat.

"Shhh," Forrester soothed.

On the flat screen, Forrester took out his flaccid penis and began to fondle it. He was breathing heavily. The sound of his exhalations filled the small room. Brendan hoped the baby, the one here, now, was asleep. He also wondered what was going through Brown's mind. If he was as demented as the killer. To serve someone so mentally sick – what was Brown's game? Was it really just double-dipping for the money? If he had betrayed Heilshorn, how much false information was he feeding him? Heilshorn had provided the intel which had led Brendan here, so disinformation didn't seem to be part of Brown's M.O.

And that idea tripped something in the back of Brendan's mind. Some connection tethering Brown to Reginald Forrester, but then that too was gone. What was filling his vision was too much to keep many other thoughts intact. The cameraman was masturbating himself. And just when Brendan thought the vomit was sure to come, the video changed focus. The camera flicked to the right, showing the toilet. Next to it was a chrome device, set in a holder on the wall, connected to the toilet basin by a tube. It was the diaper sprayer.

The image held there for a moment, with Forrester panting as he held the camera in one hand, his penis in the other.

Then he quickly banged out the bathroom door and back into the bedroom.

The baby was still on the bed. Not crying now, but fussy, whimpering. Rebecca lay beside her.

*Why are you still there?* Brendan screamed at her in his mind. Why hadn't she run?

And as Forrester crossed the room to the bed, Brendan thought he had an answer. He glimpsed someone else standing in the doorway to the bedroom. For less than a second, as Forrester moved quickly towards Rebecca, Brendan had seen someone. Was it Brown? That brief sight of the second person looked nothing like the grizzled P.I. That flash had suggested a more slender, perhaps younger, person.

A flag waved far back in his mind, planted there during a time when he had briefly considered the possibility of two aggressors in the Rebecca Heilshorn case.

But there was no time to speculate further on that now. The killer had given the camera to the other person and was now undressing Rebecca. She was like a doll, passive and unresponsive, but it didn't seem to deter Forrester. He took her pants off as she lay next to the whimpering child. She turned her head away from the camera, now held by this unknown second person.

"When did you put that new bathroom fixture in?"

"Yesterday," came a muffled voice.

"You put it in yourself?"

"Yes."

"You can barely pump gas, and now you're a plumber?"

Forrester was stroking himself as he spoke. Now he threw Rebecca's legs open and moved closer.

"I said I don't want to see anymore." Brendan's voice was close to a shout. "Turn it off."

On screen, the man mounted Rebecca and began crude intercourse with her, with the child on the bed next to her. Brendan's words caught in his throat as Forrester spoke into his ear, hot and breathy. Meanwhile, the Forrester on-screen drove himself into the rag doll Rebecca Heilshorn had become.

"'I was born under the black smoke of September,'" Forrester declaimed. "I was trapped beneath all of that weight. I was reborn in that darkness."

The version on screen thrust and penetrated. Brendan's stomach wrenched with jagged anguish. His head and heart pounded in tympanic unison.

"'I was born to you, and your infinite forms.' I was reborn to you, detective, in you, and everyone like you."

Brendan looked at the helpless child on the bed next to them. The person holding the camera was unsteady, as if shaking a little. He was reminded of the girl on the couch in the fake interview on XList, but other than that, the comparison faltered. This was not pornography. This was sadism, rape, humiliation, the corruption of a child. And, Brendan was sure, a prelude to Rebecca's murder.

"And so now I have come for you." The breathy words hissed right next to Brendan's head as the demon on screen huffed and gyrated. It was as if the voice was in stereo inside of his head.

"I've come to steal your children."

"Stop," Brendan said weakly. The authority in his voice had crumbled. The word was an impotent plea.

The video-version of Forrester pulled away a moment later. It was tough to be exactly sure, but he appeared to ejaculate on the bed off to the side. The bed, Brendan recalled, that was sometime later covered with plastic, as if brand new, fooling investigators into not checking the mattress below for forensic evidence.

Forrester retreated from the lifeless, prone Rebecca quickly. The baby was once again crying next to her. Forrester snapped and zipped himself back up and then turned to the camera. "Shut it off," he barked.

A second later, and the screen went dark.

"Now let's take a walk."

## CHAPTER FORTY-TWO / MONDAY, 9:36 PM

Brendan was marched out into the hallway beyond the lecture hall. Brown had the barrel of his .45 pressed between Brendan's shoulder blades. They headed to the end of the hallway where the stairwell was. They passed by two window casings which contained no glass, and were only covered with clear tarpaulins which flapped gently in the breeze. Brendan felt the air. Outside, the night was damp.

The campus out there was quiet. For one, it was Columbus weekend. For another, this entire side seemed to be shut down for the construction of the new Business building. The nearest building was over a hundred yards away, dark and still.

They passed out of the hallway, entered the stairwell, and began their way down. Forrester carried the child in the bassinet. From a faraway part of his mind, Brendan remembered that people called them Moses baskets. It had been so long since his little girl had lain in one herself.

So long since she had been inside that tiny casket, in the end.

Brendan's pains seemed to vanish at the thought of his own little girl. Another little girl's life was at stake here. His mind grew still. Their footfalls echoed in the stairwell as they descended, turning with each flight. Forrester's head bobbed below. He had taken a flashlight from his office and was lighting the way for them.

At first Brendan had wondered why the killer would show him such damning evidence. The video didn't depict a murder, but it was enough for any D.A. to build a solid case around. There was Forrester's ownership of the house in Boonville to consider as well. And chances were that his shoe size would match the boot print on Rebecca's door. There were a half a dozen other puzzle pieces which would form a picture of this man's guilt, but the video of Rebecca's rape – right in front of the child – that was enough to send Forrester away for life. Maybe even to kill him.

As they came to the bottom floor, Brendan figured that he would never leave this building again. It was the only way he could explain being shown the video. Forrester and Brown meant to kill him down here.

* * *

The basement floor was where the gymnasium was located. Brendan remembered the map from the lobby, and thinking that the building contained enough amenities for a person to hardly ever need to leave. They passed two sets of double doors looking in on a brand new gymnasium lit by emergency lights, reflecting in the shiny floor. So there were lights down here, Brendan thought. Forrester had the place wired, for sure – this was where he wanted to be able to see. Why?

Brendan's stomach flipped as he thought of the answer. A moment later and they reached the racquet ball courts. Forrester paused in front of one of the solid white doors. He set the bassinet down and then pulled keys from his pocket.

Brendan felt numb. His blood moved sluggishly through his body. His guts slowly churned with bile.

Forrester glanced over his shoulder at Brendan.

*You're going to wish you never came here*, he'd said.

The killer pushed the door open. Brendan looked over Forrester's shoulder at what was in the room. The court had shiny floors like the gym. The walls were smooth and white. The emergency bulbs in the corner cast a sterile glow.

Brendan suddenly imagined a dozen children huddled together in the center of the room, shivering in the cold light.

Then he blinked, and the children disappeared. A sober question passed through him simultaneously – where do you hide illegitimate children? Where do you put babies born of illicit relations between prostitutes and government officials, or God knew who else?

Sitting there in the room was the answer. Alexander Heilshorn sat in a solitary chair, his hands tied behind his back, his mouth gagged.

"You two have met," said Forrester in an unemotional tone.

A second later, Brown urged Brendan into the room by pressing the barrel hard into his back. Brendan winced and stumbled forward.

"Get over there," said Brown.

Brendan walked over to Alexander Heilshorn, who looked up at the detective with sad eyes. And Brendan saw in those eyes the answers to so many questions.

Years before, when his daughter had first come to the old doctor with an illegitimate child in her belly, Heilshorn had performed the delivery. But it wouldn't be the last child he brought into the world under those circumstances, Brendan concluded. Rebecca must have confessed everything to her father. And she had Stemp's phone call to the wealthy doctor to corroborate everything she'd said – Stemp had very likely been a bodyguard to some high-ranking official, some politico with a taste for brunettes on Thursday nights. He'd probably met Rebecca while driving her to the brownstone building which housed a greedy congressman or businessman. Heilshorn, a man who had already disclosed to Brendan his disapproval of abortion, had then taken it upon himself to assist these other, distressed young women. Chances were he even used his money and influence to secretly shepherd the women to safety. Maybe even help get their babies adopted. And perhaps somewhere, Alexander Heilshorn was even stowing escaped escorts and their incriminating children.

It was circumstantial, mere conjecture, really, but it felt right. Looking into Heilshorn's haunted eyes, it felt terribly right. Heilshorn had played a highly dangerous game with these people.

But now Titan sought to close this loophole. Rebecca's murder had set into motion a chain of events which had led here. Brendan was the investigator who was in-the-know. And Heilshorn knew everything, too. Perhaps Titan had let things go for a time – or maybe for a time they hadn't known the identity of Alexander Heilshorn. Now, though, they had him – his own private investigator had betrayed him and handed him over to Forrester, the raving enforcer in the lurid affair. The ex-professor turned pimp, drawn into darkness after the worst attack on America had left him pinned beneath its immense weight, forging him into this inhuman creature. One who raped a woman in front of her own child. Who kept the fathers of his murder victims locked in the bowels of a dark building.

Brendan stood next to the old man in the chair and looked back at Forrester. The killer stood just inside the doorway, Brown on his one side, the baby in the bassinet set down on his other side.

Then Forrester closed the door behind them.

He looked both men over, and then with macabre show, he recited the last lines of his dark, obscure poem.

"'There I once was cradled in that autumn wind, a human as unsympathetic as the winter which follows, with its starving creatures, coming in low through the howling cold.'"

Brown cocked the .45 and aimed it at Brendan's head. Brendan closed his eyes. In the distance, he heard the sound of thunder. The humidity had portended a storm, and now the skies were about to open up.

* * *

But the rolling thunder continued. It did not let up.

Brendan heard a door slam out in the hallway beyond the racquetball room. They all did. Forrester jerked and looked around. The noise was followed by swiftly approaching footfalls.

Both Forrester and Brown reacted in a similar fashion. Each man tensed and turned towards the door, backing away. Heilshorn's haunted expression tightened into a mask of fear.

Then all of them looked at Brendan.

Forrester suddenly lunged across the room, his arms out, his hands hooked into claws. His face was contorted with hate and anger. He tackled Brendan and the two men fell to the floor with a tremendous thump.

Forrester wrapped his hands around Brendan's throat and started to squeeze. Brendan's windpipe was choked by the killer's iron grip. The world began to show spots. Brendan gagged and his tongue flopped.

The footsteps thudding down the hallway subsided and were replaced by murmuring voices. Men were gathering just on the other side of the office door. Brendan flailed and struck Forrester about the body and head. He was getting in some good shots, but Forrester was like some kind of beast who could feel no pain. The killer's face snarled with rage. Spit flew from his lips as he hissed. He squeezed, and squeezed. Brendan began to black out.

"New York State Police. We know you're in there. Open up or we will break down this door."

Brendan struggled and twisted futilely beneath the killer's weight. He lost sight of anything for a moment, his vision filled with black ink, and then the nightmare reeled back into view.

Suddenly Heilshorn was leaning over Forrester and Brendan. His hands were still tied behind his back, but he had gotten free of the chair. The old man grunted and kicked out with his foot, catching Forrester in the ribs. The killer may have been invulnerable to Brendan's blows, but the kick caught him right, and he rolled off to the side, wheezing and grabbing at his chest.

Brendan took an explosive breath. He tried to cry out, but his voice was sandpaper, and all that he could issue was a worthless rasp. He took a whooping breath, looking over at Brown. He saw that Brown's weapon was trained on the door. The baby was only a few feet away, crying now from the bassinet. If there was a shootout, it would be gruesome.

Finally, Brendan found his voice. His throat was ragged, but Brendan summoned everything he had and shouted at last.

"This is Investigator Healy from Oneida County." This caused him to cough and gag. He rolled over and spat. Blood splattered onto hard, shining floor.

The men paused outside as Brendan drew another painful breath. His entire torso felt as though it were wrapped in barbed wire. He strained his hoarse voice to be as loud as he could manage. "There is a baby in here with us. Stand down. Repeat, stand down."

There was silence from the other side of the door, and perhaps some shuffling of feet, followed by murmuring voices. Then, "Okay, Healy. Can you get them to come out?"

There was no time. Forrester was already recovering, and getting to his feet.

*Get up, NOW.*

Brendan pushed off with his palms and managed to stand up. His legs were rubbery and weak – his hip injury pulsating, his neck lashed with a pain that seemed to burrow into his skin. Forrester turned, and the two men locked eyes.

Everything hung suspended for a moment in time. Heilshorn stood, his face wearing the same fearful, resigned look as his daughter Rebecca had shown in the video. Brown took a step towards the door. Forrester reached into the black bag which Brown had brought down and took out Brendan's own service weapon.

At last it was clear. Forrester had planned this. He had allowed Heilshorn to provide the information which had led Brendan here. He meant for the two men to meet like this, and to stage a murder that would place Heilshorn as the man responsible for his daughter's own death. It would look like Brendan had tracked the old man here, they had fought, and Brendan had killed Heilshorn before succumbing to his own massive trauma.

But now Forrester reached down and picked up the wailing child. The twisted plan had come unraveled, and he was improvising with devilish intent. He held her tiny body against his chest with one arm, and aimed the .38 at the door with the other. Now both men were standing, one with an innocent child in his arms, ready to open fire on the first cop who came through that door.

"Come and get me," Forrester said.

To him, Brendan thought as he took a struggling, tearing breath, the world was full of Neros. They idled away the time, oblivious as Rome burned around them. No life was sacred; nothing mattered in this world of utter nihilism. Not even an infant child.

Detective Healy's world dipped and yawed. He was falling into unconsciousness. He was about to topple over.

He reached out. It was a blind gesture. He just reached out, lurching toward Forrester and the baby.

Brown fired. The sound was deafening in the room. It sounded like war, echoing and rebounding in the court with shattering force. There came one ear-splitting report after another as Brown unleashed on the door, the powerful slugs from the .45 tearing through and leaving huge holes.

Brown emptied the clip. The world was muted and rank with the smell of cordite. The baby's cries were like a mosquito in the distance. They transported Brendan back to Eddie Stemp's yard, where he had sat talking with the man and slapping at bugs. Time became jumbled. Where was he? Then things came to a halt for a moment, and the world was suspended.

A second later and the door flew open, breaking the spell of timelessness and throwing everything into high speed chaos. From behind Brown, Forrester started firing into the hallway.

There were shouts then, and a male screaming. Brendan watched as one side of Brown's face was sheared away as a round of return fire tore into his flesh. Brendan felt the splattering of Brown's hot blood across his own face and neck. A second later, Brown started to collapse, and Forrester jumped away.

Brendan continued to move, on automatic. He crossed the room with three paces so that he was now behind where Brown had been standing, directly in the line of fire.

He was between the cops in the hallway and the baby in Forrester's arms.

His hands were up, but it didn't matter. Having been fired upon, the half dozen or so Troopers standing in the hallway were like an angry swarm of wasps. They stung back, firing into the room as soon as Brendan appeared in the doorway. He realized that none of them had any clue what he looked like anyway.

He was hit in the chest and in the shoulder. He felt one of his fingers taken by a bullet – the appendage literally exploded beside his head.

In that moment, a strange thing happened. As he registered the injuries to his body, and as the State Troopers coming into the room glowered behind their smoking service weapons, he found himself thinking of a professor of his own, from years ago as an undergraduate student. He couldn't recall which course it had been, but the teacher had once said that the answer to ninety-nine out of a hundred questions could be found by "following the dollar." Everything came down to money, the professor had warned. The market system drove all inequality, which led to nearly every crime there was a name for. Money, it seemed, was the mother of all habits. No matter the pain it caused – war, poverty, greed – it remained fixed in civilization; the great and unconquerable addiction.

His legs were giving out beneath him. He saw his wife and daughter getting into the car, and he saw himself retreating into the restaurant bar, disappearing into the gloom.

The troopers were shouting about the baby. But while that was happening, Reginald Forrester was trying to get away. He was still firing into the oncoming policemen. Brendan had time to see one of them take a bullet in the stomach before Forrester was taken down by two other troopers, who tackled the killer to the ground. Another scooped up the baby a second later. She appeared unharmed.

Brendan swayed on his feet. His arms were stretched out either side of him, still forming a sort of human barricade, or shield. His left hand was a bloody mess, dripping quarter-sized drops on the smooth court floor.

His knees finally buckled. The wounds in his chest and shoulder were coming to life. That was how it felt. For a few seconds there had been nothing, and now they seemed to grow, like mouths. Howling, burning mouths in his body, releasing their liquid. His vision swam once more as he dropped.

He felt an arm around him and for a moment thought a State Trooper had him. But then he realized that no one did. One Trooper was slumped in the doorway. Another had gone around the detective and was pulling Alexander Heilshorn away from the scene. Two others were subduing Forrester, yanking his gun from his waistband, prying the other from his grip, and handcuffing him. A fifth Trooper was tending to the child.

The baby was squalling. Its cries filled the room.

Brendan turned to look up in time to see Heilshorn being led away. The old man looked back at Brendan, and Brendan thought he saw pain in his eyes. And fear.

Then a silken blanket of unconsciousness slipped over the detective, and all was dark.

# CHAPTER FORTY-THREE / MONDAY, Time Unknown

He was in an ambulance. A moment later, he was in a hospital. He was being rushed down a hallway. He lost consciousness again.

\* \* \*

Rudy Colinas was there. Colinas was explaining that he had given the troopers and Albany City Police a description of the red pick-up truck used in the attempt to murder Brendan, and Healy's last known location. Since he had turned his phone on, they were also able to locate the detective, but the truck had been spotted before they'd even needed to use GPS to triangulate his position. It was registered to Jerry Brown.

Brendan tried to talk. His lips felt gummy and numb. The expression on Colinas's face was not good. He said a doctor described one bullet wound as having severed the subclavian artery. Brendan needed a blood transfusion. Colinas was already removing his jacket and rolling up his sleeve.

\* \* \*

The transfusion worked, but there were other complications. Brendan swam back into consciousness again. He had been with his wife and baby girl. It was hard to leave them behind. He wanted to go back.

A woman stood over him with AED paddles in her hand, having just shocked Brendan back to life.

He didn't see himself, not like in those pulp stories and quasi-documentaries about out-of-body experiences in times of mortal trauma. He knew what the brain did in situations like this. He understood how the synapses were firing like a wild west shoot-out in his grey matter, and that random thoughts and memories were stimulated. Like things he'd seen over the past few days. A stretch of road. The woman at the vegetable stand. The glimpse of someone in the room on Forrester's video – the one who then held the camera. The open dresser drawers at Rebecca Heilshorn's murder scene. Olivia Jane's locked office door.

For a brief moment, Brendan thought that Delaney was standing over him. The vision – if it was that – triggered another gush of recall. Brendan found himself remembering back as far as the first morning at the Bloomingdale house. He saw Kevin Heilshorn spilling his bike in the dirt driveway. He saw Kevin wrestling with the deputies, trying to get inside to see his dead sister.

And he saw Kevin lying in the garden behind Olivia Jane's house. The blood spatter around his head; the crimson dapples on the summer squash.

Hadn't it been Delaney who had suggested Olivia Jane as the grief counselor? Certainly it was Delaney who had been hot to pin Rebecca's murder on her brother, Kevin. Delaney who assumed, as did much of the department, that Kevin had come after Brendan and Olivia because he was afraid the therapist would reveal his guilt.

Yet Olivia was so ethical. She wouldn't speak about what had transpired between her and Kevin. She was a vault, locked up like her home office. She wouldn't treat

Brendan either, though she clearly wanted to know what he was thinking, what he was feeling. As a friend, she'd said. She was highly ethical.

Except, perhaps, for her duplicity regarding her treatment of Rebecca Heilshorn.

These things spun through the detective's mind like celestial events, gliding in and out of his semi-conscious mind. Thoughts and faces.

Seeing light was common in such circumstances, too, some part of him reflected. The light at the end of the tunnel, a frequent trope about coming close to the afterlife. Even his wife and daughter were nothing more than snapshots of his past, animated by his addled, oxygen-deprived mind.

But they were convincing. They stood and beckoned to him, and they were oh so convincing.

It felt warm where they were.

He began making his way toward them, in a world that resembled their neighborhood in Hawthorne, only at night, only on a much larger scale, so that his wife and daughter were tiny. So small, and they kept shrinking. He chased them. His wife waved. It was now hard to know if it was a beckoning wave or a gesture of goodbye.

## CHAPTER FORTY-FOUR / THURSDAY, 12:22 PM

Colinas went to the evidence locker for the Heilshorn case and stood looking at the crumpled lump of burnt laptop. He looked at it for a long time, wondering what secrets it held. Correspondence between Rebecca and her family was evident on the laptop which had not been destroyed, plus emails between her and Kettering, reinforcing his statements about her. This other computer could have contained much more. Maybe threats coming from Forrester, maybe threats from others.

Forrester had enough common sense to know that cops could seize any device like a laptop or a phone or iPad and lift all kinds of information from the drives, and so he'd completely destroyed it. That was one thought. But, Forrester had held onto another device – the camera. It contained incriminating evidence that he was intimately involved with the murder victim. And that was to put it mildly.

Colinas stood looking at the small camera, and tried to imagine Brendan Healy sitting in a room with this psychopath, forced to watch what was on it. Colinas himself didn't have the clearance to access it. Taber was keeping things under tight wraps until he knew which way IA's sword was going to fall. Someone was going to pay, and already it didn't look good for the Department, who had been cooperating with a man who was also deeply involved in the sordid mess.

Alexander Heilshorn was an enigma. He was currently being held in the County Jail on suspicion of kidnapping and obstruction of justice. Colinas believed that the victim's father had had good intentions if it were true that he'd harbored prostitutes. But the State Detective also sensed a sinister undercurrent at work. The old man had withheld information to protect children, or so he claimed. It was hard to envision the charges sticking. But Heilshorn was afraid of something. With his daughter's murderer captured, Heilshorn should have been enjoying some measure of relief. Only the wealthy doctor, robust and affable just five days ago, had seemed to wither and shrink.

Colinas felt a chill and left the evidence locker.

## CHAPTER FORTY-FIVE / THURSDAY, 3:33 PM

Taber, Colinas, Senior Prosecutor Skene, and several consulting detectives stitched together the events they now believed had led up to the murder of the young Heilshorn woman.

The 911 transcript clearly indicated that the killer was male. The victim had referred to the killer as "he" several times. Plus, there were the boot prints in the dooryard and the mark found on the door to the victim's bedroom – size eleven work boots, the kind a man wore on a construction site, typically. Hai Takai, the footprint analyst, matched the prints to the footwear of a recent arrestee.

They were Forrester's.

Reginald Forrester had tried to set up an alibi for himself that he was at work when Rebecca Heilshorn was killed. But the contract to build the new Business School building had been stalled the day before her death. His alibi was not corroborated. It was so transparent that it felt to many of the men that it wasn't even a serious attempt at a lie. It was as if Forrester didn't care, or was toying with them.

He had been in the Oneida County Jail that morning, awaiting arraignment when he was found dead in his cell. The men's pod at the jail had one isolation area, with suicide-watch and round the clock guards, and Forrester had been in it. A full blown investigation had been launched immediately.

Forrester was dead. An autopsy was scheduled for the afternoon, Stanley Clark to perform. The Deputy Corrections Officers on duty were being questioned.

"How did Healy get onto this Forrester guy?" Skene folded his arms and looked at Taber and the rest. "Because that's going to come up, and you know it."

Rudy Colinas stood in front of Prosecutor Skene and Sheriff Taber. "Because Healy is smart."

Skene shot Colinas a look, and Rudy lowered his eyes in a humble gesture. Best not to get Skene all agitated. Their whole Sheriff's Department was looking bad right now. Chaos was descending. Best to play the dutiful servant, just the messenger. The Sheriff listened silently, his arms folded.

"Healy met with Heilshorn, as you and Sheriff Taber know. Heilshorn is the one who told Healy about Forrester's whereabouts. He actually warned him to stay away. Healy went anyway, as we all know. It looks like Forrester was luring Brendan into a trap."

"Let me see if this holds up," Skene said. "After disappearing for a while into her stint with the escort service, erotic entertainment, if that in fact happened, Rebecca Heilshorn gets pregnant. It's her second time. She's scared; she's too afraid to get another abortion, too afraid that having the child will ruin her so-called career? Or what? We need testing on that girl – Leah, right away. The other one, too. What's the other one's name?"

"Aldona," said Colinas.

"And she's with social services now. Okay, so Rebecca Heilshorn goes home to her parents. After she has her child delivered by her father, she tells him everything.

There are other women, too, who have gone to term with babies born of escort relationships with politicos – women unwilling to abort, who want to use the pregnancy as a way out. So Heilshorn starts delivering them in secret, using his money and influence to then shepherd them to good homes."

Skene leveled them all with a look that could kill.

"If any of this is true, you realize we're into the very deep end of the pool, here. Where this goes could be unbelievably huge.

"But back to the case at hand. Our prime suspect is dead. We can still prosecute, but it's going to be a clusterfuck, I can tell you that right now. We need simplification. Juries don't like complex denouements, if you catch my drift. This thing with the escort service, I think we're just seeing the tip of the iceberg here. Whether or not Heilshorn was lying about this thing with the kids . . . being held as leverage or not, we've got some serious implications floating around here."

Colinas regarded Skene. Despite the prosecutor's efforts to steer things back on course, he seemed hot to get those hands on a government conspiracy. Elections were closer than ever, Colinas figured. Now only a month away.

"But anyway, for Forrester, we have motive, we have opportunity," Skene said, sounding pleased. "And we have that video."

"We have motive?" This was the first thing Sheriff Taber had said for a few minutes. Skene looked surprised. "I don't think we've established that. Forrester makes this video, for what?"

"He's a sicko," said the prosecutor. "Who cares why?"

"The defense might."

Now Skene truly did look wounded. He clearly wanted this wrapped up neat with a bow, and it wasn't quite going down that way. "You're not trying to do my job, are you, Sheriff?"

"He's in the video, clearly. But why kill her? Forrester has Heilshorn in his pocket already – this well-to-do doctor has a prostitute daughter. But Heilshorn has Forrester pinned, too – he can blow the whistle any time. But he doesn't because of these other children. It's a mutually beneficial relationship in a sad, twisted way. Everything is working. Why kill the girl?"

Skene had no response. Taber walked around his desk and sat down, immediately picking up the phone. Colinas had to stifle a smile.

"Get me Robertson," Taber said into the phone. Robertson was Taber's head of the C.O.s at the County Jail. Robertson was probably a nervous wreck, Colinas figured, given what had just happened on his watch.

Sheriff Taber then looked up at Skene and Colinas.

"Maybe it wasn't Forrester who committed the actual murder. We could have a Charles Manson-type here. Forrester may not have acted alone."

## CHAPTER FORTY-SIX / FRIDAY, 8:18 AM

The clouds had gathered but the birds were still chirping in the tamarack trees as a nurse wheeled Brendan out of the hospital.

Once clear of the entrance, Brendan took his legs out of the stirrups and stood up. The nurse folded up the chair and wished him well. Colinas pulled up in Brendan's Camry a moment later. He insisted that he drive, and Brendan acquiesced.

They cruised along for a while in silence. Colinas kept stealing looks at Brendan.

"It's worse than it looks," Brendan said.

He was covered in bruises, one in particular around his neck – thumb and finger marks were visible as yellow-purple hematomas. There was a gash along one side of his head. His hand was in a bandage and his arm rested on a support. This was both to elevate the hand, but also to reduce pressure on his ribs and clavicle, which were bruised from the bullet wounds. These wounds were on the opposite side from his damaged hip which he favored while he sat, leaning a little to the right.

"You're a fucking train wreck," Colinas said.

The men laughed. It was short lived – the rapid breathing was painful. Brendan took a shallow breath, held it, and looked out the window.

"I had a lot of time to think in there."

"I bet. Nice little paid vacation. What were you thinking about?"

"I was thinking that you gave me your blood."

"Think nothing of it."

"Thank you."

Colinas smiled and looked embarrassed.

Brendan shifted, wincing, and then continued. "We still don't know why Rebecca was murdered. Not exactly. So, I was also thinking about Kevin Heilshorn."

"Let me hear it."

"If Alexander Heilshorn was truly running this sort of underground railroad for these illegitimate children, that's a little bit different than the idea that the Company – Titan – was holding the children and using them to leverage the women into continued work, a kind of indentured servitude."

"Maybe it's both."

"Maybe. Probably. The depravity here knows no bounds, I'll give you that. But either way, the idea that Kevin Heilshorn came after me to stop the investigation from potentially putting these children in harm's way – I just can't swallow that. Not any more than I thought he was afraid of having his own guilt revealed."

"With your extensive injuries, you shouldn't be swallowing anything that big." Colinas winked.

Brendan gave a wan smile. He really liked Colinas.

The State Detective continued by asking, "So what do you think motivated him?"

"Not what, but who. I think he was after Olivia Jane."

"Interesting."

"Here's what we know. Olivia Jane meets Rebecca at Cornell when she answers an ad to be her roommate. They have several classes together. Olivia Jane is two years her senior. She graduates, and she doesn't go far. She settles here, and sets up practice. Rebecca's senior capstone project is under the guidance of our late psychotic professor Reggie Forrester. But – she doesn't finish."

Brendan thought about how near he'd come to completing his PhD himself. It was a lot to walk away that close to the end. But it was also easy, like sabotage.

"Rebecca spirals down from there. She gets mixed up in the wrong crowd – I just don't think it's by accident. We know Forrester was involved with XList. I bet he recruited her. She tries to scramble away several times. She marries a driver she meets while working. He tries to turn her to the Lord, and it's her way out. She even starts seeing a therapist. Her old college roommate."

Colinas glanced over. He didn't question it. He turned in the direction of the Sheriff's Department.

## CHAPTER FORTY-SEVEN / FRIDAY, 4:12 PM

It took most of the day to convince the judge and obtain the warrant.

In the late afternoon light, Colinas and two deputies from Oneida County entered the home of Olivia Jane. She was nowhere to be found. Deputies were dispatched to find her and bring her in for questioning.

Delaney followed the State Detective and attending deputies into her house, and observed.

The men went through the therapist's kitchen drawers with rubber gloves on. They found, in all, fourteen different kitchen knives. Of these, Colinas selected four to be checked first, for the DNA of the victim, Rebecca Heilshorn. The full work-up of the victim's DNA had been prepared by Clark and his team and they were ready to compare anything with it.

Delaney stood with his arms folded, watching the search. He felt a distant, uninvited tug of fear. He had known Olivia for many years. He knew that she'd had trouble with the Heilshorn girl. He speculated that the Heilshorn girl had made some vague threats toward Olivia. He'd sensed that there was some rivalry over a boyfriend the therapist kept in secret. Delaney had never pried into the matter, and Jane was totally tight-lipped as it was. She'd done a little pillow talking, that was all. She'd asked that Delaney look into the Heilshorn girl, said that Olivia thought she could be a danger to herself or others. But it needed to be kept off the record.

The Heilshorn girl was hardly ever home, and after Delaney had dispatched deputies for a week to drive by and check on things, nothing had come of it. Still, if Olivia was involved in the murder of Rebecca Heilshorn, he would be in deep shit. And it would even mean more trouble for the department.

This one was a mess. The whole thing could come down.

He had liked Colinas at first, but the young State Detective had shown a foolish loyalty to the rookie CI, Healy. Healy was OK in Delaney's book at first, too, and had asserted himself, which Delaney generally approved of. But when his cocky downstate attitude had rubbed the senior investigator the wrong way, Delaney had revised his tacit endorsement of Healy. If Colinas was right, that Healy had at last found Rebecca's killer, then that too would reflect poorly on Delaney.

Very poorly.

"I've got to find one other thing," said Colinas, and disappeared into Olivia's office in the back. Colinas spent some time looking through a file cabinet. Then he started fumbling around with a rolltop desk. He broke it open.

Delaney sighed. He chewed on his sunflower seeds and watched Colinas bag the evidentiary properties from the therapist's office and kitchen. Delaney looked down at the seed casings stuck to his fingertips. They were messy, and not a good thing to bring along to a crime scene. He cut a glance at Colinas and considered if it would be worth just taking the guy out back and shooting him. Then he wiped the seed casings into the bag and wondered if it was time to retire instead.

* * *

Clark performed the DNA tests on the knives. Inanimate objects were easier to work with than tissues, which were a hodgepodge of other oils and chemicals. The results came back rather quickly. Rebecca Heilshorn's DNA was on one of the knives in Olivia Jane's kitchen.

Clark had heard about the video which showed Reginald Forrester having nonconsensual sex with the murder victim, and he felt, for a moment, professionally inadequate. There had been no physical evidence of rape, or serology to confirm a suspect. And a person with numerous sexual partners had traces of many of them, so DNA profiling was almost always a wash. Still, he felt like he had let the department down when he had examined Rebecca Heilshorn.

Now, though, he had another body on the slab to contend with. The rapist himself.

Reginald Forrester had been taken into custody nearly a week before. He had been thoroughly searched at that time, including all body cavities. If he had smuggled something in, some sort of weapon to inflict harm on himself, he'd hidden it in a place that only God had known about. But there was no forensic evidence of any kind to show he had punctured, stabbed, or slit himself in any way.

There were no other signs of trauma either. He had a fading bruise on his hip, from when he'd been kicked in the skirmish leading to his arrest, some contusions around his wrists from the troopers who had put the clamps on him and then jockeyed him into custody in a way that couldn't quite be described as gentle. But there were no ligature marks around his neck, however. He would have had nothing to hang himself with as it was. He'd been in buttoned fatigues with Velcro shoes on his feet.

The peculiarities of Forrester's condition, however, turned Clark towards other scenarios.

Forrester had lost some of his hair. He had begun to go bald during his week-long stint in the jail. He also appeared to have lost weight. An examination of his bowels showed that he'd eaten next to nothing in the days leading up to his death. Clark had also learned that the Deputy Corrections Officers had noted Forrester's lack of appetite and generally distressed condition.

When Clark completed the toxicology report, it confirmed his mounting suspicions. Forrester had died of a slow poisoning. He would need to run a couple more tests for it to be conclusive, but it was looking like something called Thallium, which was a highly toxic compound that was odorless, colorless, and could be absorbed through the skin.

Usually, significant contact with Thallium, unless treated by Prussian blue, the antidote, would render its victim dead within three to five days. Absorption into the body, typically through potassium uptakes, wrought havoc on the cells. The drug laid siege to proteins like cysteine residue, and the body basically broke down. The peripheral nervous system was disarrayed and became unruly.

Clark had heard of victims of Thallium poisoning experiencing horrific hallucinations. The nerves in the feet making a person feel like they were walking over burning coals. The hands and arms might signal alarms as though they were being mangled by a machine. There were many possibilities.

If Reginald Forrester had committed suicide, Clark wondered if the man had known this road through hell. Maybe he hadn't cared. Or maybe someone had killed him. Usually, Clark effectively divorced himself from feeling anything about the bodies he examined – be they victims or suspects, and there were a lot of both. But he thought about this man, who the police were saying killed women, who kept children from their mothers, who reveled in perversion and torture, and wondered how he had experienced the effects of the Thallium, hoping it had been most unpleasant. Clark imagined Forrester had met his end while feeling that his lips, tongue, and the muscles of his face were being eaten alive by a swarm of insects.

* * *

Olivia Jane was picked up at the house in Boonville, the one owned by Reginald Forrester. Brendan had suggested she might be found there. He didn't expect her to flee entirely, not yet, but he'd suspected she would put some distance between herself and the Sheriff's Department. She had no idea that Brendan had learned about the house in Boonville, a place probably used as a halfway house for many of the girls on the circuit. She immediately requested legal counsel.

Healy leaned on a crutch and offered a debriefing to Taber and Skene. Delaney was not present. Colinas was allowed to observe.

They sat in the Sheriff's office as the sun waned outside.

"She claims she is innocent, that she had no knowledge of Rebecca's involvement with Forrester, or that Forrester had any kind of relationship with her."

Skene was brusque. "We have the murder weapon in her house, but the defense is going to claim that it was planted there. Probably by Kevin Heilshorn on his way through the kitchen during the shooting incident. We need a confession out of her."

"I think she'll talk to me," Brendan said.

Skene looked doubtful. The Sheriff seemed more hopeful. "Take Colinas with you," he said.

# CHAPTER FORTY-EIGHT / FRIDAY, 7:37 PM

Olivia was being held in the smaller pod where women were housed. She was wearing orange inmate fatigues with "ONEIDA" on the back. A corrections officer was in the room with them, and her lawyer, a pugnacious-looking man named Carl Guth. They sat at a table with two empty chairs opposite them.

Colinas held the door open for Brendan. He walked through on his crutches. Colinas pulled the chairs out and helped him to sit down.

"Hi, Olivia."

"Hello, Brendan."

He tried to arrange himself comfortably in the chair, but it was a challenge.

"Look where this friendship has got us." He smiled, but she didn't appreciate his attempt at humor. "This was my first case," he continued. And look at me. Should've stayed where I belong."

She was impassive.

Brendan studied her face. Her mouth was set in a grim, determined line. Her eyes were gelid.

"I just wanted you to know that I think you killed Rebecca Heilshorn. I think that you came in the room after Forrester and put her to death. And I think that I saw you in the video."

Olivia blinked. She seemed incredulous that Brendan was making these statements. Her lawyer, Guth, leaned over and spoke quietly in her ear.

Olivia said, "Aren't you supposed to have an observer present when you question someone like this? I could have you written up."

"This is not an interrogation. This is just a visit. I'm just sharing what I think. And I also think that Reginald Forrester's relationship with Rebecca made you jealous."

"This is absurd. I haven't seen or heard from Reginald Forrester since he was my professor in college."

"I still think you're the killer."

The lawyer leaned over again, but Olivia Jane pushed him away. She smiled, though her face was ashen and weary. "You're trying to play a little psychological poker with me, Detective Healy. I'm a psychotherapist. You think I'm going to reveal something?"

"Have you got anything to reveal?"

"You're a depressed alcoholic who is obsessive and anxiety-prone. Your neglect as a husband and parent led to the death of your spouse and child. Since then you have become delusional. You're what we call in lay terms 'a wreck.' I'm a respected psychotherapist with an Ivy League background who has worked within this community for eight years. And I have worked with the police for three of those years. But you have the audacity to come in here with your unfounded ideas, and treat me like a piece of shit, questioning me."

"I'm not questioning you. Just telling you what I think. The system protects that. Just like it protected your withholding, so it protects my espousing. So, listen. You said before that you wanted to help me. If I'm wrong about you, then show me why."

She scowled.

Brendan held her gaze as he shifted in his seat, crossing his legs. Beside them, Colinas watched with rapt attention. Normally Colinas sat like a linebacker squatted – that was how his wife put it. But here he was in the presence of well-educated individuals and he was trying to affect an air of decorum.

"I think that Reginald Forrester used you," said Brendan. "He exploited a deep psychological connection – something which formed when you were just a young woman."

She looked at him flatly. But Colinas thought he saw some small crack of light in her mortar.

"He's a monster, you know," Brendan continued. "He's not human." Brendan could remember everything, with gruesome clarity, that had transpired when he had been in that building with Forrester. He was sure he'd carry it to his grave. "We've got him on video having sex with the victim. But, you knew that. Maybe you didn't know that we've got his boot print. And with the CSI team back at the Bloomingdale house for another pass, I'm sure we're going to turn up more. Maybe something under the plastic-wrapped mattress?"

Olivia looked away.

"You're going to post bail. I'm sure your counsel has informed you of the charges of aiding and abetting. Very flimsy charges. But I'm about to open a new case on you, alleging that you're the actual perpetrator of Rebecca's murder, that it was you who stabbed her to death with your own knife. And I'm going to further allege that Kevin Heilshorn knew it was you – that when you met with him the morning of his sister's murder, he knew who you were, and he discovered the truth for himself. He came to your house and opened fire on you, not me. So, if you have something else to tell me, something that would explain you had nothing to do with Rebecca's death, no knowledge of Forrester's intentions, you need to tell me now."

He looked across the table at her. It was hard to imagine that it was the same woman he had sat with in her house – twice. The first time had erupted in the tragedy with Kevin Heilshorn, but their second encounter had actually been pleasant. Almost as if they were starting something together. As if, after eight long years, he was going to be truly able to start a new life. A new town, a new job; maybe even a new relationship.

He'd always had a problem being presumptuous.

The lawyer spoke up. "Okay, this is coming to an end." He stood, expecting Olivia Jane to do the same.

But she remained seated. "Why don't you ask Forrester about this yourself?"

"I can't. He's dead. There's an internal investigation going on in my department. Alexander Heilshorn is being watched around the clock, with extra security. Everything is upside down. They found poison in Forrester's body – that's what killed him. Your life is in danger, too, and you know it, don't you? Let me help you."

Her face was drawn, growing paler by the second. She hadn't known about Forrester's death. He watched her absorb it, and then he continued.

"This is the story the prosecutor is going to spin: You came in after Forrester and you put a knife in Rebecca's body. You stabbed her multiple times. The motive that will stick is that you were recruiting girls for the escort service, along with Forrester, and Rebecca was one of them. She had grown unruly. Too many children lost; too much pain. No matter how you threatened her, she was going to blow the lid eventually. Her father was involved, but compromised, not going to talk. But when she started meeting with her brother you began to worry. So you had Forrester show her who was boss, by making that video. Only when she didn't respond the way you wanted, you killed her."

"Enough," said Guth. "Olivia, don't say another word."

Brendan leaned forward again, oblivious to the searing pain in his upper body. He was not on the full-strength painkillers, because they were addictive. Brendan had spent the last two weeks building up a tolerance for the piercing bolts of pain that coursed through him like jags of barbed wire tearing his flesh from the inside.

"Damaged women, coming to you from abusive families, violent husbands. Or maybe just foolish young girls wrapped up in the sexual hedonism of today. Maybe they've been captured by the rampant libido at work here in the existential vacuum."

She opened her mouth, maybe to respond to his attempt at philosophizing, but Brendan barreled forward.

"The D.A. is going to put you at the scene. They're going to put a murder weapon in your hands. I remember fretting over those forty seconds of silence on the 911 call. The forty seconds the killer lingered downstairs. Doesn't take that long to come up the stairs, but it's not enough time to do anything significant, like write poems on photographs. It's just enough time, though, to let *you* in, to have a little conversation with you before going upstairs."

He was close to her. He could smell the stale linen of the fatigues she was wearing. He could smell her fear beneath. Or maybe it wasn't fear. Maybe it was something else.

"You know," he said, "I marvel at you a little bit. You're good. So by-the-book. Never willing to bend. Except in treating your former college roommate. That type of dual relationship is unethical. Which is how I explained to myself why you hid it. Maybe your heart got the better of you. But it just didn't stay put in my mind, and I came to see how you were using the veneer of ethics to keep your real relationship with her concealed. You also used it to conceal your real connection to Kevin. I don't think he knew who you were – not when he first saw you, but I think Rebecca had been telling him things. But you, I bet you came right out and told him exactly who you were. And that you would kill women and children if he said anything."

Brendan took a deep breath. His ribs hurt, but he paid them no mind.

"And as your attorney here full well knows, all your confidentiality with Rebecca and Kevin is going to be countermanded by this investigation. There's nowhere to hide any longer; we have an ironclad case."

"Guard," said the lawyer, Guth. "Let us out of here, now."

The Deputy Corrections Officer, Robertson, glanced at Colinas and then at Healy. Taber had already called and spoken with him to insure full cooperation. No one was going anywhere without his say so. Carl Guth could sue the entire Department – it didn't matter. They were going down, anyway.

Brendan remained leaning forward, very close to Olivia. His eyes searched her. "Who is Titan, Olivia?"

Her face had taken on an ashen cast. Her eyes were vapid. Her lower lip seemed to quiver, just a little.

"Alright," said Guth. "Then let me out."

Robertson promptly escorted the lawyer out of the room.

Finally, Brendan sat back. He tried to give her space. He was patient. After nearly a minute passed with her looking down at the table between them, Brendan grabbed the crutch propped beside him and Colinas rose and stood at the ready.

Then she spoke. She leaned forward, and she whispered in Brendan's ear.

Then she sat back. Her face was an inscrutable mask.

Brendan suddenly felt hot. The room seemed too small. He needed air.

And then he got out of there

\* \* \*

Colinas was driving, but his mind seemed to be anywhere but on the road. They turned a corner and an angry driver shook his fist at Colinas for coming too close.

"Watch the road, Rudy."

"What did she say?"

Colinas looked over at Brendan.

"Healy, Jesus. There's something huge going on here. Something we can't even touch. What did she say?"

Brendan continued to look out the window. He shook his head, as if trying to come to terms with something.

"She said, 'Titan is the government.'"

Colinas turned his head. The car swerved. "What?"

Brendan glanced at him. Colinas resumed watching the road, and righted their course.

"She said," Brendan amended, "'Titan is so entwined with the government that you'll never get it free.' I distilled it."

The men fell silent as Colinas absorbed what Brendan had told him. Then Colinas said, "It's amazing you're still alive."

Brendan found himself remembering that Heilshorn had said the same thing.

He hoped Heilshorn was doing okay. Men his age didn't fare well in lock-up. Brendan told himself he would do whatever he could to help Alexander get back on the right side of things again. He believed that whatever the man had done, he'd done for the best of reasons.

It was disconcerting, though, what had turned up from the little bit of digging Colinas had done while Brendan was recovering. Heilshorn's accountant turned out to be an interesting person after all. A subpoena opened up Heilshorn's accounts. Heilshorn had made substantial investments in a company which patented advanced medical technology. It was called Titan Med Tech. The records also showed that Heilshorn, a registered voter, had donated hundreds of thousands to a gubernatorial candidate not of his party. Money was flowing between Alexander Heilshorn and some very influential people.

"What – I mean what exactly does that mean? 'Titan is the government?'"

"It means, for one, that Leah is probably the child of someone who would never want his paternity known. Probably Aldona, too."

"No. We got a match for Kettering on the Aldona baby."

Brendan's eyes widened. "Really?"

"Yeah, I haven't had time to tell you. Aldona is the baby Rebecca had with Kettering."

Brendan took out a cigarette and lit it. It was a challenge with his bandaged hand, but he was going to give himself a little time with this relapse.

"This is huge," Colinas breathed. "Is that why Forrester is dead? Because of Titan? Because they are – what, top brass? I mean, an escort service, prostitution, porn, all of this – and the government is supporting it? Protecting these black markets? Is that possible?"

Brendan looked off in the distance, in the direction of Albany. He thought of how the city had looked from the windows of the darkened Business School building. "I think that's a very dangerous question."

Colinas spun the wheel and they turned down a side street. He grew thoughtful for a moment.

"You know, you hear crazy shit."

"Like what crazy shit?"

"Oh, I don't know. Like Bin Laden. Like the attacks of 9/11 were meant to bankrupt the economy. And look at us."

Out the window, Brendan observed the single-story homes with junk out on the front porches.

"And you hear about how the US is the biggest provider of funds to the World Bank. You know, how we kind of prop up the world economy."

Brendan waved some smoke out the window. "That great divergence is ending. China and India are going to have stronger economies than the U.S. very soon. We won't be number one for long."

## CHAPTER FORTY-NINE / SATURDAY, 9:44 AM

Donald Kettering was sitting in his office. Things looked pretty much the way they had the last time Brendan had seen the place. Like Kettering didn't know if he was coming or going.

The hardware store owner offered his wide, game-show-host smile and greeted the two cops. Brendan was tired and leaning hard on his crutches. Kettering looked him up and down.

"My God," Kettering said. Some of the good humor faded from his expression.

"This is Rudy Colinas, an investigator with the State Police," Brendan said. "He has something for you."

Colinas reached into his pocket and pulled out the paternity test results. He handed it to Kettering while all three men were still standing. Kettering unfolded it. His face registered what was on the paper, and he slowly sat down.

"We had your information from the investigation," Colinas explained. "Blood, DNA sample. We ran it and we ran the child's. Your daughter, Aldona, is currently under state care. She's a little malnourished, but otherwise she's recovering just fine."

Kettering looked up from where he had sat down, crumpled in a heap. His eyes were brimming with tears.

"She's okay?"

"She's fine," said Brendan. He gestured to Colinas that they both sit. Colinas obliged, but not before helping Brendan into a chair. Once they were settled, Brendan continued. He folded his hands in front of him. Every part of his body was protesting with pain, but he ignored it all. He felt surprisingly good despite it all.

"How much were you in communication with Kevin Heilshorn?"

Donald Kettering's eyes snapped up from the paper. He looked between the two detectives. He slowly set the paternity paper on the desk in front of him. Then he took a hand and ran it over his face, using his fingertips to smear away the tears. The other Kettering was with them now, Brendan thought. The hound dog Kettering, no longer the smiling, small business owner. His heart went out to the man.

"Only a couple times," said Kettering.

Colinas looked around, surprised. Brendan wondered if the State Detective had been having thoughts of his own along these lines. He figured he had. Colinas, though something of a surfer without a wave, was sharp. He raised his eyebrows and looked at Brendan.

Kettering continued. "I called her brother because I didn't know what to do. I had met him once, and liked him. Angry kid, but a smart kid. I didn't set him up to do anything, I swear to God. I just wanted to talk to someone, to figure out how we could help Rebecca. Things just got worse from there."

"No question," said Colinas. Then something crossed his features. Colinas sat back. Brendan watched the State Detective process the new information. Then he looked at Kettering.

"Did you think Kevin would go after anyone?"

"I thought maybe. I didn't know who, or what, really. I honestly didn't expect him to go after you."

"He didn't. He was going after Olivia Jane."

"Rebecca's therapist?"

Brendan nodded. "The fact that I was there, that was collateral damage."

Brendan started to get up, using one of his crutches, grunting with the effort. Colinas stood and helped him. "Congratulations on fatherhood," Brendan said.

Kettering rose tentatively. "Are you taking me in?"

Brendan got his feet under him and then looked up. "You're not going anywhere, are you?"

Kettering's eyes glistened with tears again. "No."

"Good. Then, when you're ready, come in and give your revised statement. Then take your daughter home."

His lower lip shivering again, the big man nodded. He stuck out his hand. Brendan took it.

"I have one last question," Brendan said.

"Anything."

Your church, the Resurrection Life Church, you know about any AA meetings there?"

"Every night of the week. You know, they alternate. Some are open to all, some are for members. Others are for family, stuff like that."

Colinas, looking bemused, was watching Brendan.

Brendan offered a nod to Kettering. "Thanks."

The two detectives left the hardware store.

In the bright morning outside, Brendan lit a cigarette.

"You going to a meeting, boss?" asked Colinas.

Brendan shrugged. He smiled.

The sun was climbing as they headed south out of Boonville. It was going to be a warm day, but the scorching late summer heat had passed.

## THE END

389

September 2, 2012 –
December 16, 2013
Elizabethtown, NY TJB

T. J. Brearton

Follow T.J. Brearton on twitter @BreartonTJ
Further novels by Brearton are scheduled for release in
2015 by Joffe Books

Find out what happens to Brendan Healy next in
'Survivors' the sequel to 'Habit.'

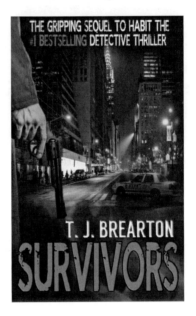

Also available by T. J. Brearton: Highwater

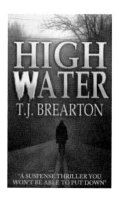

**A riveting suspense thriller with a supernatural touch. Time is running out to save a little boy and stop the waters rising**

"Finely-drawn characters and a striking setting in the mountains add up to a book that you won't be able to put down." Chris Child

"A stunning suspense thriller that will have you gripped from start to finish." Beth Boyd

"Mysterious, beautiful, and wonderfully atmospheric, great for Stephen King/Dean Koontz fans." Sarah Munning

**A suspense mystery that you won't be able to put down**

Detective Tom Milliner is racing against time to save the life of a unique little boy. He needs a blood transfusion and only one person matches. But first Milliner must solve the mystery at the Kingston house, where Liz Goldfine may have committed a heinous crime, and the dark depths of the lake harbor teenage secrets.

If you enjoyed this book please leave feedback on Amazon, and if there is anything we missed or you have a question about then please get in touch. Thanks for taking the time to read this book.
Our email is jasper@joffebooks.com

www.joffebooks.com

# ABOUT THE AUTHOR

T.J. Brearton is the Amazon best-selling author of 'Habit,' a crime thriller set in Upstate New York, and 'Survivors,' the second book in the Titan Trilogy. The final book is set to arrive early 2015.

He is the author of 'Highwater,' a supernatural crime thriller set in the Adirondacks.

Short fiction publications include The Rusty Nail Magazine, Orange Quarterly, Enhance Magazine, Third Rail, Atticus Review, and Nonsense Society.

He lives in the Adirondacks with his wife and three children and can be found at tjbrearton.com.

Made in United States
North Haven, CT
16 October 2022

25530317R00240